T

W9-CEG-170

Havoc

This Large Print Book carries the
Seal of Approval of N.A.V.H.

HAVOC

JACK DU BRUL

WHEELER PUBLISHING
An imprint of Thomson Gale, a part of The Thomson Corporation

Detroit • New York • San Francisco • New Haven, Conn. • Waterville, Maine • London

LIBRARY OF CONGRESS CATALOGING-IN-PUBLICATION DATA

Du Brul, Jack B.
   Havoc / by Jack Du Brul.
     p. cm.
   ISBN-13: 978-1-59722-405-5 (alk. paper)
   ISBN-10: 1-59722-405-7 (alk. paper)
    1. Geologists — Fiction. 2. Terrorists — Fiction. 3. Large type books.
I. Title.
PS3554.U223H38 2007
813'.54—dc22   2006030900

Published in 2007 by arrangement with Dutton,
a member of Penguin Group (USA) Inc.

Printed in the United States of America on permanent paper
10 9 8 7 6 5 4 3 2 1

To the miners:
upon whose backs
civilization was built

MAY 1937

Alone in his cabin for the past three days, the madman rocked gently on his narrow bunk, his eyes fixed on the dull sheen of his personal safe while fever sent alternating currents of heat and cold through his body. He was unaware of the great ship's passage across the Atlantic, the rhythm of her four engines turning the large propellers, the spectacular service offered by the crew, or even the cycles of day and night. It took all his mental ability just to keep his focus on the small safe.

Since leaving Europe, he'd ventured from his cabin only late at night to use one of the communal washrooms. Even on these furtive forays he'd hurry back to his room if he heard other passengers stirring or crew-members attending their duties. On the first night of the trip and during the following day, a steward would knock on his door, inquiring about his needs, asking if he wanted tea, a cocktail, or perhaps some soda crackers to settle his stomach if the ship's motion was making him ill. The passenger had refused everything, struggling to maintain a patina of civility. But when the waiter returned to ask if the passenger wanted dinner brought to him on the second night, the man in cabin 8a flew into a rage, cursing the hapless steward in a mix of English, Greek, and an African dialect he'd picked up in the preceding months.

As the third day slid toward an overcast evening, what little control he'd had over his mind slipped further. He didn't care. He was almost home. Hours now, not days or weeks. He'd beat them all. Him. Alone.

His was an inside cabin and lacked a window. A lamp was bolted above the tiny desk, and lights in decorative sconces shown down on the bunk beds. Everything was made of polished aluminum, with holes punched through the metal to give the space a futuristic appearance, as if he were on a rocket ship out of Verne or Wells. The safe had been manhandled into the cabin's only empty corner by a steward who'd waited a beat too long for a tip the passenger couldn't afford. While the ship was at only half capacity on its seasonal maiden trip, the tickets were some of the most expensive ever for a transatlantic voyage.

Had he not felt the press of time or been certain that those chasing him were closing in, he would have found a cheaper way back to the United States. But then maybe taking this ship had been the most brilliant coup of all. The people trying to catch him would never suspect he would use their own flagship on the last leg of his journey home.

He reached across to touch the safe, feel its cool outline under his shaking fingers, content in the knowledge that a life's ambition was locked within. He shivered, from fever or exhilaration he neither knew nor cared. Bolted to the wall across the cabin was a small mirror. He looked at himself, avoiding his eyes, for he was not ready to face what lurked behind them. His hair was long and unkempt, shot with gray that had not been there two months ago. Clumps of it had fallen out in the past few weeks, and as he ran his hand across his scalp he could feel fine strands pull free and snag in the serrations at the end of his cracked fingernails. The skin on his face hung in folds as though it had been fitted for a larger skull. His beard had once been a thing of pride, a distinctive trademark of well-manicured whiskers. Now it resembled the down of a molting chick.

He bared his teeth at the mirror, more grimace than smile. His gums were raw and red. He assumed they bled because he hadn't eaten a proper meal since leaving his New Jersey home.

His body too had paid a heavy price. While he had never been a robust man, he had lost so much weight he could feel the sharp ends of his bones poke against his skin every time he moved. His hands shook constantly and his head swayed as if it had become a burden to the atrophied muscles of his neck.

The excited voice of a young girl pierced the thin cabin door. "Hurry, Walter. We are approaching New York City. I want a good place on the observation deck."

About time, the man thought. He checked his watch. It was three in the afternoon. They should have arrived nine hours ago.

Against his better judgment, he decided to venture from his cabin. He needed to confirm with his own eyes that he was almost home. Then he would return to his tiny cabin and wait for the ship to dock.

He staggered to the door. In the narrow hallway, a girl of maybe twelve waited for her brother to finish lacing his shoes. She gasped when she saw him, an involuntary gesture that filled her lungs and drained the blood from her face. Without turning her startled eyes from him, she reached for her brother's shoulder and yanked him away. His protests died on his lips when he spotted the deranged passenger. They ran around the corner in the direction of the promenade deck, the girl's skirt flaring above her coltish knees.

The innocent encounter made the passenger's stomach give a wet lurch of protest. Acid scalded the back of his throat. He thrust his nausea aside and closed his cabin door to make his way down the starboard-side staircase. A few idle crewmen and a lone passenger were pressed against the observation window on B deck. Behind them was the crew's toilet, and just as he reached the window a ship's officer stepped from within followed by an unsettling stench. It smelled no worse, or perhaps even a bit better, than the passenger himself. He hadn't washed his clothes or his body since before fleeing Cairo.

Placing his hands on the sill, he could feel the mild trembling of the engines through the metal. He pressed his face close to the glass and watched as Manhattan's impressive skyline emerged from behind dark storm clouds.

The shipping line prided itself on their

perfect safety record, and as he watched the city come into focus, he allowed a ghost of a smile to pull at the corners of his mouth. As promised, the voyage from Germany had been uneventful and soon the flagship of the *Deutsche Zeppelin Reederei* would float gently to her mooring mast in Lakehurst, New Jersey.

A hole in the overcast opened, allowing bright sunlight to form a corona around the giant airship *Hindenburg.* Her shadow spread like a stain across the artificial canyons of midtown, darkening all but the towering Empire State Building. The colossal zeppelin, larger than most ocean liners and four times as fast, had made the crossing in a little over three days, her four Mercedes diesels pushing the 804-foot behemoth through the sky at a surprisingly smooth eighty knots.

The passenger caught a glimpse of people atop the Empire State Building's observation deck waving at the great airship, and for a giddy moment he felt the urge to wave back, an impulse that made him believe that perhaps he could once again connect with humanity after his ordeal.

Instead he turned on his heel and rushed back to his cabin, his breath coming in chopping gulps until he assured himself that the safe was still locked. His body was bathed in an oily sheen of sour sweat. He took his seat on the bunk and began to rock again.

He planned on remaining like that as the airship powered down Long Island Sound, as her captain, Max Pruss, sought a window in the stormy weather to bring his charge to the naval station at Lakehurst. Yet just before five someone knocked on his door. He didn't recognize the knock. The stewards had been timid about interrupting him, respectful, if a little puzzled by his appearance and attitude. This was the knock of authority, a single hard rap that brought a fresh wave of sweat from his pores.

"What do you want?" His voice was hoarse from lack of use.

"Herr Bowie, my name is Gunther Bauer. I am a ship's officer. May I have a word?"

Chester Bowie's eyes darted around his tiny cabin. He knew he was cornered, but he could not help but search for a way out. He'd almost made it. A few more hours and he'd be safely on the ground and away from these Nazis, but somehow they'd learned his identity. Not that they wanted him. He was no longer of consequence. It was what was inside the safe that drove them.

He had come too far to see it end now.

Only one course was open to him and he felt nothing but mild irritation at what he had to do.

"Of course," Chester said. "One moment."

"The officers and crew are worried that you might have a negative impression of our company," Bauer said from the other side of the closed door, his English passable but stiff, his tone mild. Chester wasn't fooled. "I have some gifts," the German continued, "pens and stationery for you as souvenirs of your flight."

"Just leave them," Bowie said as he made ready, knowing the next words and the next few seconds were critical.

"I would prefer to give them to you personal—"

That was all he needed to hear. They wanted into his cabin to steal the safe. Even as the last word hung unfinished in the air, Chester Bowie used what little strength the fever had left him to wrench open the sliding door and grab the German by the lapels of his black uniform jacket. He ignored the flurry of papers that spilled from Bauer's hands, and the sheaf of pens that fell to the deck, and yanked the officer into the cabin.

Bauer's only attempt at defense was a startled grunt. Bowie smashed him into the little ladder that allowed access to the upper bunk bed. And as the officer began to fall Bowie leapt on his back. He jammed his knee into the hollow at the base of Bauer's head. When they hit the deck their combined weight snapped the German's fourth and fifth cervical vertebra hard enough to sever the spinal cord. Bauer went limp and his body settled, expelling his final breath.

Bowie closed the door. They would never let him off the zeppelin. Even though he'd lost them when he fled Africa, he should have known they'd somehow pick up his trail again. He'd been so clever by traveling right into the heart of the beast and taking their own ship home. No one could have foreseen him doing that. But somehow they had. They were unholy. Like all-seeing Gorgons who knew the routes of man.

The body took up nearly the entire floor. Chester had to step over it to grab a notebook he'd left on the writing desk. He picked up one of the pens Bauer had dropped. He had no idea how long it would be before the captain sent someone else to get the safe. No, Chester realized, next time there would be many of them, too many of them.

He wrote quickly, the pen racing across pages as if it knew what had to be written and only needed Bowie to hold nib to paper. He watched his hand flowing back and forth, not fully conscious of the words it was writing. In fifteen minutes he'd filled eight pages with tight script he could barely read. No one came, so he filled another ten, fleshing out his story as best he could remember it. He was sure this would be his last will and testament, all that remained of a life's obsession — these words and the sample in the safe. But it was enough. He had tread in the footsteps of emperors. How many men could say they'd achieved that?

When he felt his hand had written enough, he dialed the safe's combination and stuffed the pages inside, taking what he knew would be his last look at the sample he'd brought back from Africa. It resembled a cannonball, a perfectly round sphere he'd crafted with the help of a blacksmith in Khartoum. He closed the safe and wrote a name along with a cryptic message on the stiff cover of his notebook. He tore the remaining blank pages from the book's spiral binding, and using the lace from his left boot he threaded the spiral and note to the safe's handle. There was nothing else he could do but pray that whoever found the safe would deliver it to the addressee.

There was no need to write where the

man lived. Everyone knew how to find him.

Chester Bowie rolled the corpse of Gunther Bauer under the bottom bunk, trying hard not to notice how the head flexed unnaturally on the broken stalk of his neck. Then he began to shove the safe from its corner, straining at first but seized with such desperation he quickly skidded it across the carpet. He opened the cabin door, peered up and down the hallway, and then shoved the hundred-pound safe toward the stairwell to B deck.

So far no one had spotted him, but downstairs he knew passengers and crew would be watching the New Jersey coastline scroll below the observation windows.

"May I help you with that, sir?"

Bowie froze. The voice came from behind him and he recognized it. From where? His mind raced. Cairo? Khartoum? Somewhere in the jungle? He whirled, ready to fight. Standing before him was the earnest young steward he'd yelled at on the second day of the crossing.

Werner Franz did everything in his power not to recoil when he saw the crazed look in Bowie's eyes, the feral countenance of a cornered rat. While only fourteen, Werner considered himself an experienced airship-man and no lunatic passenger would crack his veneer of professionalism. "May I help you with that?"

"Yeah, er, yes, thank you," Chester stammered. Surely this mere boy wasn't the second wave of Nazis sent to steal the safe. The captain would send mechanics and other officers, big men who'd beat him and hide the safe until tonight's return flight to Frankfurt.

"I overheard the captain," Werner said earnestly as he began pulling at the safe. "The weather's cleared enough for us to make a run for Lakehurst. With luck we'll land a bit after seven. I guess you want to be the first off the ship, Herr Bowie?"

"Er, yes, that's right. I have people waiting for me."

"May I ask what is in the safe? The other stewards think you carry gemstones to a New York jeweler."

"I, ah, no. These are, ah, papers for, ah, an important scientist." *Jesus!* Why had he said that? The boy could just look at the note tied to the handle to see who the safe was intended for. He should have gone with the story the steward had given him.

"I see." Clearly Werner Franz didn't believe him, and for that Chester was thankful. He'd traveled five thousand miles and almost given away his secret in the final minutes.

Together they dragged the safe down the stairway, its weight making the light aluminum steps vibrate with every tread they descended.

"We will leave it out of the way," Werner said and dragged the safe into the observation room. "Crewmen need to lower the retractable gangways when we land, and we can't have them tripping over your safe."

"This is fine," Chester said, panting from the exertion. His face had blanched under his tropical tan and his legs trembled.

"I will help you with your safe when we land," Werner offered.

Bowie said nothing and waved the boy away so he could sit back against the railing protecting the outwardly angled observation windows. In a moment his heart had slowed.

The airship was flying due south and it seemed that every passenger and crewman not on duty crowded the port windows. The starboard observation room was thankfully empty. Without wasting any more time, Chester braced his still-shaky legs and lifted the safe from the floor. Muscles in his back strained under the load and he heard more than felt some tear. Yet he did not drop his burden. He lifted it higher, pressing it against the wall for leverage until he had it balanced atop the railing.

Below the zeppelin, the ground was an endless sea of pine trees and sand broken only occasionally by lonely rutted roads. They crossed over a stretch of cultivated land with a farmhouse situated along the perimeter. The barn was dilapidated and the tractors and machinery looked like toys.

The windows in the opulent promenade on A deck could open but those on B deck were fixed in place. Chester leaned across the railing, his hands tight around the teetering safe, and waited for the right moment. The *Hindenburg* cruised at a thousand feet as she plowed through the overcast sky. Beyond the protective bulk of the airship's hull, rain fell in gusting curtains. Now that Bowie was ready, the airship continued over desolate stretches of pine. From above, the canopy of trees was an impenetrable mass. His whole body shook with frustration. At any moment a passenger or crewman would come by and his plan would be ruined. From above on the A deck promenade he heard someone play a few notes on the lightweight Bluthner baby grand piano.

There!

Another farmhouse appeared at the edge of the forest. Even from this height Bowie could see the place was run-down. The shingle roof sagged in the middle like the swayback of an old horse, while the porch seemed in danger of collapse. Yet there was light in the windows, and a trail of smoke caught the breeze at the top of the chimney and smeared across the landscape. The nearby barn appeared much newer.

The flight path would take the *Hindenburg* right along the edge of a cleared field a quarter mile south of the farmyard. With luck the farmer would find the safe before whatever crop he grew overwhelmed the pasture.

Chester had to do nothing more than let go of the safe. It fell through the angled window with a crash that was quickly swallowed by the roar of wind whipping into the airship. Bowie hadn't been prepared for the blast of rain-soaked air. He staggered back from the rail then whirled away, running back up to his cabin just as the door to the crew's mess opened. He was trailed by angry German voices but no one had seen what he'd done.

Unfortunately, Chester Bowie also couldn't see the safe plummet to the ground. A hundred feet before it plowed into the sandy soil, the note he had so laboriously tied to the handle was stripped away. It stayed aloft in the stormy air for nearly an hour and by then it was shredded to confetti and spread across two counties.

Rain cut forking trails along the gum rubber poncho as drops pooled and poured across the fabric. For nearly eighteen hours the lone figure had remained hidden under its folds, unmoving and nearly unblinking. From his perch atop a hangar he had an unobstructed view of the landing field a half mile away and the metal framework of the mooring mast. From here it looked remarkably like a miniature Eiffel Tower.

His target was twelve hours late, a bit of irony since his hurried orders had forced him to rush into position.

Moving so as not to change the outline of the weatherproof poncho, he brought his rifle up to his eye. The scope was a trophy he'd taken from a sniper during the Great War. He'd adapted it to every rifle he'd ever used. He stared through the optics, centering the crosshairs on the milling throng of the landing crew. They'd just returned to the field after a brief downpour. He estimated there were more than two hundred of them, but such a number was needed to manhandle the giant airship in the face of even a gentle breeze. He let the reticle linger on individuals for a moment before moving on. He spotted the airfield's commander, Charles Rosendahl. The man next to him had to be Willy von Meister, the Zeppelin Company's American representative. Despite the occasional gusts, the sniper could have dropped either man with a shot through whichever eye he chose. A ways off were a radio journalist and a cameraman, both of them checking equipment as everyone waited for the *Hindenburg's* late arrival.

He was about to lower the heavy rifle when everyone on the ground turned at once, raising an arm skyward in what almost resembled the Nazi salute. The sniper shifted a fraction. Out of the pewter sky came the *Hindenburg.*

Distance could not diminish the size of the airship. It was absolutely enormous, a defiant symbol of a resurgent Germany. She was sleek, like a torpedo, with stabilizers and rudders larger than the wings of a bomber. At its widest the zeppelin was one hundred and thirty-five feet in diameter, and inside her rigid frame of duralumin struts were gas cells containing seven million cubic feet of explosive hydrogen. Two-story-tall swastikas adorned her rudders and pale smoke trailed from her four diesel engines.

As the airship approached it grew in size, blotting out a larger and larger slab of the sky. Her skin was doped a reflective silver that managed to glisten even in the stormy weather. The *Hindenburg* passed directly over the naval air station at about six hundred and fifty feet. The sniper watched passengers inside the accommodation section of the ship leaning out the windows and trying to shout to family on the ground. It took fifteen minutes for the leviathan to circle back around for her final approach from the west. A quarter mile from the mooring mast the engines suddenly screamed at full reverse power to slow the airship, and moments later three tumbling avalanches of ballast water spilled from beneath the hull to correct a slight weight imbalance.

Someone in the hangar below had rigged a speaker so the sniper could hear what the radio announcer was saying as the airship made its final approach. The voice was high-pitched and excited.

"Well here it comes, ladies and gentlemen, we're out now, outside of the hangar, and what a great sight it is, a truly one, it's a marvelous sight. It's coming down out of the sky pointed towards us and towards the mooring mast."

The gunman pulled his rifle — a .375 Nitro Express more befitting an African big game hunt than a sniper — to his shoulder and waited. The first of the heavy mooring lines was dropped from the bow. He scoped the windows one more time. Then came the second mooring rope as ground workers began to haul the ship to the mast. They looked like ants trying to drag a reluctant elephant.

"It's practically standing still now," the announcer said, growing more animated as he described the scene. "They've dropped ropes out of the nose of the ship and it's been taken ahold of down on the field by a number of men. . . ."

By moving the rifle barrel an inch the sniper found his target.

"It's starting to rain again, the rain had slacked up a little bit. . . ."

The bullets in the rifle were of his own manufacture. He'd had only a day and a night to construct them and had only fired two as a test at a deserted gravel pit. Both had worked as he'd designed, but he still felt apprehension that they would fail to do the job he'd been assigned.

Herb Morrison's voice on the speaker was reaching a fevered pitch as he described the landing. ". . . the back motors of the ship are just holding it, just enough to keep it from . . ."

The rifle cracked. The recoil was a brutal punch to the shoulder. At two thousand feet per second the bullet took one point two seconds to reach its target. In that sliver of time a coating around the special slug burned away, revealing a white-hot cinder of burning magnesium. Unlike a tracer round, which burned all along its trajectory, the incendiary core of this round only showed in the last instant before it hit.

Hydrogen needs air to burn. A random spark could not have ignited it within the airship's enormous gasbags. Only when hydrogen was released to mix in the atmosphere could something like this round cause an explosion. But the bullet wasn't meant to ignite the gas. At least not directly.

The sniper had fired along the spine of the *Hindenburg.* The intense heat of the bullet scored the zeppelin's doped skin as it traveled down the length of the airship. By the time it reached the tail fin, it had lost enough velocity to hit the dirigible and lodge into the duralumin frame. Just as the magnesium burned itself out, the waterproof paint, a combination of nitrocellulose and aluminum powder, began to smolder. The doping agent on the cotton canvas skin was in fact a highly combustible mixture commonly used as fuel in solid rockets. The smoldering turned into open flame that burned through the skin and sent flaming bits of cloth onto a gasbag. The fire quickly holed the bag and allowed a gush of hydrogen to escape into the growing inferno.

Herb Morrison's voice turned into a horrified shriek. ". . . it burst into flame! It burst into flame and it's falling, it's fire, watch it, watch it, get out of the way!"

The sky seemed to go black, as if all the light at the airfield had been sucked into the explosion above the airship. The stately approach of the *Hindenburg* turned into frantic seconds as time telescoped.

". . . it's fire and it's rising," Morrison cried. "It's rising terrible, oh my God, what do I see? It's burning, bursting into flame and it's falling on the mooring mast and all the folks agree this is terrible. This is one of the worst catastrophes in the world. The flames are rising, oh, four or five hundred feet into the sky."

For seconds the ship hung in the air as the intense heat warped and melted her skeleton. Her outer skin rippled with the concussion then burned away. The roar of burning gas and the intense heat was like standing at the open door of a blast furnace.

She fell stern first, panicked ground workers racing from under her bulk. One of them wasn't fast enough and was engulfed in wreckage as the zeppelin crashed to the earth.

Inside his cabin on A deck Chester Bowie felt the ship lurch as her stern lost buoyancy. He heard screams from the observation lounge and the sound of tumbling furniture as the airship dropped from the sky. The ceiling above suddenly flashed red-orange as the hydrogen exploded above him. The ship dropped further, the thunder of burning gas overriding the terrible screams of twisting metal as her frame collapsed. He remained on his bed.

At first he thought he'd just smile at the irony of it all, but he found himself laughing instead. He knew this was no accident. The Germans were willing to sacrifice their own dirigible to deny the United States gaining possession of what he'd found. They'd chased him halfway around the globe, sabotaged the *Hindenburg* to stop him, and still he was one step ahead. Chester opened his mouth wider, laughing even harder, maniacal now. It was just too funny.

The heat hit him then, a solid wall preceding another gush of flame. He died in an instant, hearing his own laughter above the sound of the fire that consumed him.

The sniper watched for a second longer as the great airship plummeted, its back broken when the bow slammed into the ground. Smoke and flame licked the heavens as the carcass melted, its skeleton bowing under the thermal onslaught and then collapsing into a pile of melted girders and burning flesh.

"It's a terrific crash, ladies and gentlemen. The smoke and it's flame now and the frame is crashing, not quite to the mooring mast . . ." Morrison's voice became a strident, evocative sob that still echoes today. "Oh, the humanity . . ."

Central African Republic Present Day

Cali woke to the mindless frenzy of gunfire.

With her hotel windows open, the sound seemed amplified. She tensed, waiting for return fire from the jungle that would surely come. Instead she heard the steady beat of a heavy rain and then a burst of drunken laughter. The local troops sent to oversee the evacuation of Kivu had been drinking steadily since their arrival. The lone officer sent to control them seemed to be the worst offender. Not even the six Belgian peace-keepers the UN had dispatched bothered to keep the soldiers from the booze or from smoking the potent marijuana called bhang.

Cali remained on the floor where she'd slept. She'd learned her first hour here that the piebald rug was home to far fewer insects than the bed. Mashed breasts were preferable to being eaten alive by fleas and God knew what else. There had been no water in the hotel when she'd arrived late yesterday so she smelled of sweat, dirt, and DEET. A rotten night's sleep had done nothing to relieve her aching body following the torturous drive from the capital, Bangui. She rolled onto her back. She'd slept in shorts and a sports bra with her boots lightly laced. Her tongue was cemented to the top of her mouth, and when she finally got it unstuck she found her teeth sticky.

Dawn was slowly creeping over the town. With the approaching sun the canopy of trees outside her room resolved themselves in shades of gray and silver. Mindful that light might attract a burst of gunfire from the drunken soldiers, Cali left her flashlight next to her bedding, slid her arms into a bush shirt, and cautiously went to the window.

The town clung on the muddy banks of the Chinko River, a tributary of the Ubangi, which eventually flowed into the mighty Congo. Kivu had grown around colonial French plantations that had long since been reclaimed by the forest. While mostly built of round mud huts thatched with reeds, Kivu boasted a cluster of concrete buildings arranged around a central square; one was an abandoned government office that now housed the soldiers, and another was her hotel, optimistically named the Ritz, a two-story structure that was riddled with bullet holes after decades of civil war. A quarter mile upriver lay a dirt airstrip that was still serviceable.

Kivu was a tiny island surrounded by a forest sea, an impenetrable expanse of trees and swamp that rivaled the Amazon. There was no electricity now that the owner of the general store had fled with his family and the town's only generator, no sewer or running water, and the only ready communications with the outside was the satellite phone in her rucksack. Kivu had changed little in a hundred years and it was unlikely to change much in the next century. If it survived the week.

Two weeks earlier, reports had filtered in to the capital that a group of rebels had crossed the border from Sudan and were making their way south in an effort to isolate the eastern third of the country. It was now believed that the vanguard of Caribe Dayce's Army of Popular Revolution was a mere four days from Kivu. From here it was only thirty more miles to the Ubangi River and the border with the Congo. The government of the Central African Republic planned to make their stand there, outside the town of Rafai, however few believed the CAR's meager forces would prevent Rafai from falling to Dayce. Any people still in the region afterward would find themselves under the authority of a rebel who found inspiration in Idi Amin and Osama bin Laden.

Cali muttered an oath under her breath.

The Central African Republic was one of the few nations that even the poorest of third world countries could look to and feel proud of their own success. Most mid-sized American companies had more revenue than the CAR. The average person made less than a dollar a day. There were few natural resources, little infrastructure, and absolutely no hope. Why someone would take the time to carve out a piece for himself defied logic. Caribe Dayce would soon make himself the ruler of a few thousand square miles of nothing.

The rain slashed through a thin fog that oozed up from the river, obscuring shapes and making the first stirrings of the towns-people look like ghosts meandering back to their graves. A driver from a relief organiza-tion opened the door to his big Volvo truck and fired the engine. The first load of refugees for the day would be on their way out in a half hour or so.

With luck Cali would make it the last miles up to where the Scilla River emptied into the Chinko this morning, check her theory, and be back on the road to Bangui by noon.

She turned from the window, first buttoning her shirt, then using a rubber band she kept on her wrist to tame her red hair into a ponytail. A baseball cap hid the rest of the snarls and tangles. She brushed her teeth with bottled water and spit in the sink anchored to the wall outside the toilet cubicle. She teetered over the seat rather than let her skin touch the filthy commode. She didn't want to waste her precious water supply so she made do with a towelette from a foil packet to clean the sleep from her face. Using a hand mirror, she applied spf 30 lipstick. Although her hair was a deep shade of red — thank you, Clairol — she still had the pale complexion of a carrottop, with a generous dappling of freckles to match.

Looking at her reflection in the kind light of the dawn, Cali admitted that even in these rough surroundings she managed to look years younger than thirty-seven. In the past year her work had kept her away from home nearly eight months, in places where she was hard-pressed to find enough food to spend her per diem, so she maintained her shape without becoming a slave to a health club.

Shape, she thought without looking down, a nearly six foot bean pole with B cups, no hips, and a flat ass. She didn't even have the green eyes the red heads in romance novels always seemed to possess. Hers were dark brown, and while they were large and wide-set, they weren't green. Her older sister had gotten those, along with the boobs and the butt and all the other curves that had attracted men since she'd hit puberty.

At least Cali had gotten The Lips.

As a child she'd always been self-conscious about the size of her mouth. Like any adolescent, she hated to stand out. It was bad enough she had hair that shone like a beacon and that she was taller than all the boys in her class, but she'd also been given a mouth much too large for her face and lips that always looked swollen. She'd been teased about it from kindergarten. Then suddenly, in her junior year of high school, the teasing stopped. That summer her face had matured and cheekbones had appeared, graceful curves that transformed her mouth from something oversized into something sensual. Her lips gained a pouty ripeness that continued to spark carnal fantasies to this day.

Cali packed her toiletries in her rucksack,

swept the dim room to make sure she hadn't forgotten anything, and headed down to the hotel's lobby. The eight-room establishment's reception area was an open space defined by arches along three walls. At the back was the reception desk, which doubled as a bar, and a door leading to the kitchen. A collection of mismatched chairs and tables dotted the flagstone floor. Beyond the arches, the steamy rain came down in curtains. The town's dirt square had turned into a quagmire. A group of villagers huddled at the back of a truck for their turn to join the exodus. Their few meager possessions were carried in plaited grass bags or piled on their heads.

Cali took a seat near the back of the lobby.

"Ah, miss, you are awake early." As with many businesses in Western and Central Africa, the hotel's owner was Lebanese.

"You can thank the assault rifle alarm clock," Cali said and accepted a cup of coffee. She eyed the owner, her expression asking the question.

"Yes, yes, yes, the water was boiled, I assure you." He looked out beyond the falling rain. "The troops the government sent are no better than Caribe Dayce's bandits. I think if UN had not send observers the

36

government wouldn't have even come for us."

"I was in Bangui yesterday," Cali told him. "It's just as bad there. People who can get out of the country are."

"I know. My cousins live there. Many believe that Dayce will move on the capital after he takes Rafai. Tomorrow I will join my family and we go to Beirut at the end of the week."

"Will you come back?"

"Of course." He seemed surprised by her question. "Dayce will eventually fail."

"You sound sure."

"Miss, this is Africa, eventually everything fails." He went off to take the order of the truck driver who'd just stepped out of the rain.

Cali ate two of the plantains he'd brought to her table, and left ten dollars. By Kivu's standards the Lebanese was a wealthy man, but she felt the need to give him something extra, maybe just the knowledge that people on the outside still cared.

She'd parked her rented Land Rover under a crude lean-to in a dirt yard behind the hotel. The rain drumming against its tin roof sounded like a waterfall. She kept her head down as she slogged through the clinging mud, so she didn't see the damage until she'd slid under the lean-to's roof. The four bullet holes in the Rover's windshield weren't the problem. Nor were the shattered headlights. She could have even dealt with one of the tires being shot, because there was a spare bolted to the vehicle's rear cargo door. It was the second front wheel lying deflated that did it.

Hot rage boiled. She whirled, looking for a place to vent her anger. The square was quickly filling with people desperate to leave the region. Some soldiers were trying to keep things orderly, while others slouched negligently in doorways out of the rain. None paid her any attention.

"Son of a bitch," she muttered in frustration. She could blame no one or everyone. It didn't matter. Finding who shot up the four-wheel drive wouldn't fix it, and without it she was as helpless as the refugees.

Before she left the States one of the old hands in the office had told Cali an expression that seemed strange at the time but now fit perfectly. Africa wins again. The Lebanese hotelier had said essentially the same thing. Everything fails here. If it wasn't the weather, it was the disease, or the corruption, or the sheer stupidity of drunken soldiers using her truck for target practice. If it hadn't been so pathetic it would have been funny, like a Buster Keaton farce where he keeps knocking himself down again and again as he bumbles through his day.

Well this explains why the shots I heard were so loud, she thought as she circled the Land Rover looking for other damage. The lone spare mounted above the tailgate mocked her.

There wouldn't be a second spare in Kivu so she'd have to hitch a ride to Rafai with the refugees. Not only was Rafai bigger, but the military was there in force and only a handful of businesses had closed. If she got a second tire she could return in an empty truck coming back for the next group of evacuees.

And that would waste a day she was sure she didn't have.

She had landed in the CAR only two days ago, thinking she would have at least a week to get her work done. Then she'd heard about Caribe Dayce's lightning thrust. She'd rushed to Kivu as quickly as she could, hoping she could get in and out before he overran the town. Could she lose a day and still do it? Were Dayce's men far enough out to give her the break she needed?

Cali had no choice. She would have to

chance it. With luck she would be back this afternoon. She'd reassess the situation then and make her decision about heading farther north. She'd phone in her report after first getting herself a place on one of the refugee trucks. From her rucksack she withdrew a travel wallet and tucked two fifties into her shorts.

She dodged out of the lean-to and ran back to the hotel, her boots sucking at the clinging mud with each rushed pace. The truck driver was hunched over his breakfast, shoveling food into his mouth even before swallowing the previous bite. Two empty plates were stacked at his elbow. A carton of Marlboros rested on an adjacent chair. The hotel's owner wasn't leaving anything for Dayce to loot, so everything was going cheap.

She was about to approach when another heavy truck roared into town. Unlike the other vehicles, this one had come in from the north. In the open bed of the six-wheeled diesel were three dozen Africans trying to keep a piece of plastic tarp over their heads. When the truck braked in front of the hotel, the mass of bodies shifted and gallons of water sluiced over the cab just as the driver jumped clear. The full weight of the water poured over his head and ran down his open rain jacket. He looked up through the bed's stake sides and must have made a face, because children suddenly started laughing.

Cali watched as the white driver raked rain from his hair and flicked drops at the children, eliciting more shrieks of delight. She hadn't heard a child laugh since she'd arrived in the country. Judging by the bundles of possessions being handed down from the truck, these people had just fled their homes and somehow this man could make their children laugh. She guessed he was an aid worker and they had known him for some time.

Which meant he knew the situation up country.

She looked behind her. The trucker would be at his meal for a while. She stepped back into the rain and approached the stranger. He paid her no attention as he helped people out of the truck, handing infants to waiting mothers and steadying the arms of old men, affording them dignity while making sure they didn't fall. He was maybe an inch taller than Cali and with his T-shirt stuck to his chest she saw he had a powerful build. Not the grotesque muscles of a weight lifter, but the lean physique of someone who worked hard for a living.

He must have finally felt her presence because he turned. Cali startled. It was the eyes, she realized instantly. The man was handsome, yes, but his eyes, a shade of gray like storm clouds, were riveting. She'd never known such a color existed or could have imagined they would be so attractive.

"Hi," he said, an amused lift at the corner of his mouth

"Hi," Cali replied before gathering herself. "You just came from the north."

"That's right," he said. "Found these people wandering out of the jungle about twenty miles from here. Thought I'd give them a lift."

"You're not an aid worker?"

A lanky farmer passed a caged chicken down to the man. He handed it to Cali, making her part of the human chain unloading the truck. "No. I'm a geologist." He held out a hand. "Mercer. My name is Philip Mercer."

His occupation took her by surprise as she absently took his hand. For the second time in just a few moments, Cali startled. Even wet, his palm was as rough as tree bark, callused so that the skin picked against her own. She felt strength in that fleeting touch, but also something more. Assurance, confidence, kindness, an utter lack of guile —

she wasn't sure which, or maybe all of them. He held her gaze as he let her fingers drop.

"And you are?"

"Huh? Oh, I'm Cali Stowe. I'm with the CDC. The Centers for Disease Control. In Atlanta. I'm a field researcher."

"Believe it or not, disease is the last thing these people need to worry about right now." He was American but had a trace of an accent that Cali couldn't quite place.

"So I've noticed," she said. "Mind me asking what you're doing here?"

Mercer slid a large iron cauldron from the truck and set it on the ground. "Prospecting."

She laughed. "I always picture prospectors wearing union suits with picks over their shoulders and dragging a stubborn mule on a short rein."

"Only ass here is me. I'm here doing a favor for a friend."

"My friends ask me to go shopping or help talk through why their current boyfriend is a total creep. You really have to learn to set boundaries."

It was Mercer's turn to laugh. "Point taken."

"What were you prospecting for?"

"Coltan, colombite-tantalite," Mercer replied. Cali looked disinterested but he

43

added, "It's used in the capacitors for small electronics. Especially cell phones."

"Don't take this the wrong way but I hope you didn't find any. There are already too many of those damned things in the world."

"Amen," Mercer agreed. "And no I didn't. This was a UN-sponsored expedition. Some functionary from their economic development office in Bangui heard about a hunter who claimed he found coltan on the Chinko River. More than likely he'd smuggled it from Uganda or the Congo, but the UN guy saw it as an opportunity to create jobs in the area."

"And get his ticket out of here punched, no doubt."

"Probably. I've spent the past six weeks shifting tons of worthless mud, until I heard slaughter season was starting up again. I waited as long as I dared then sent my workers out. When I packed it in yesterday I found these people along the way."

"Listen, I ah, I'm planning on heading north tomorrow. How bad is it?"

Mercer stopped unloading the truck to give her his full attention. "Since this corner of the world isn't on many tourist maps, I assume whatever you're doing here is important. I won't try to talk you out of it, but if you really need to head upriver, do it today.

Right now."

"I can't," Cali admitted. "Some hopped-up teenager used my truck for target practice this morning. I have to go down to Rafai to buy a spare tire."

"Then forget it."

He wasn't being dismissive, or protective. He was stating a fact as simply as he could. Cali appreciated that, but she also had to ignore his advice. "I wish I could. I have to go."

Mercer pushed wet hair off his forehead. Cali thought he was calculating a price he wanted for his truck. "How far?"

"Sorry?"

"How far do you need to go?"

"There's a village on the Scilla River about a mile from where it empties into the Chinko."

"That's about a hundred miles north. How important is this?"

Cali answered readily. "One of our researchers came across some medical records put together by a missionary in the late eighties. No one had paid any attention to them. It seems the people in this town suffer from the highest cancer rate on the planet. The CDC believes there may be a genetic cause. If we can isolate it, well, you can figure it out for yourself."

"Gene therapy to prevent cancer."

She nodded. "And possibly cure it. I need to get blood and tissue samples."

"And if you don't get there before Dayce, those people are either going to be dead —"

"Or so scattered I'll never find them," Cali finished for him. "That's why I rushed here as soon as I could."

"You're talking about going further than I'd planned, but I'll take you."

"You were going back up there?" Cali couldn't believe it.

"Why do you think I unloaded the truck?" he said. "I passed a lot more people than I could carry on my way down here. The government's not going to get them, so someone has to." His voice went grave. "Just so we're clear, though. We're turning around at the first sign of trouble."

Cali's tone matched his. This was her best, and probably only, shot. "You got it."

"Okay, once I get this beast refueled we're out of here."

"Thank you," she said.

He grinned. "Don't thank me until we come back. Why don't you wait in the cab out of the rain."

Mercer watched Cali slide around the battered Ford but didn't know what to make of her. He was sure that if he hadn't offered to drive her she would have followed her original plan. It was in the stubborn set of her jaw, but mostly it was the intensity of her eyes. Cali Stowe believed in her mission and he couldn't imagine much that could deter her. It was a trait he admired because there were few people left who had it.

One of the refugees he'd driven down pressed two tomatoes into his hand as he fed diesel from the drum lashed behind the cab. Mercer was overwhelmed by the gesture. This man had just lost everything he owned, the home he'd lived in probably since he was a child, but still wanted to thank him with perhaps the only food he'd have for as long as it took to get resettled. Mercer carefully inspected the tomatoes, took the best for himself, and handed the other back. Returning the better one would have been an insult. The farmer touched Mercer's hand and nodded. Behind him his wife smiled her gratitude and hugged her children a little tighter.

Mercer's thoughts turned back to Cali. As a field researcher for the CDC he imagined she'd been in some rough country before, but he doubted she'd seen anything like this. Yet she'd shrugged off her car getting shot up as though it was a mere inconve-

47

nience. That kind of confidence came from experience. He doubted the CDC prepared people for this kind of thing, so he guessed there was something else in her past — military training, perhaps.

That made him feel a little better about driving her north. While he only had one weapon with him, a Beretta 92 pistol, he sensed she wouldn't freeze if he needed to use it. And for all he knew she had her own gun.

The sudden image of her holding a drawn pistol spiked his pulse. It was the capacity for violence juxtaposed with her delicate features and that sensual mouth. Uncharacteristically, he acknowledged how attractive she was. Uncharacteristically because Mercer hadn't thought of a woman in those terms in a long time, not since a woman he'd thought he'd loved died eight months ago.

He then found himself circling the same argument he'd faced since her death. He hadn't told her he loved her until after she was gone, until after there were no consequences to the declaration. He still didn't know what that meant, or if it had meaning at all. He'd talked about it with his best friend. Harry's advice was that he should mourn her for a while, miss her probably forever, but not let his guilt make her more than she was. Usually taking advice about women from Harry was like asking a vegan to name a good steak joint; however this time the old man had a point. Harry knew Mercer better than anyone alive and knew how guilt drove him more than any other emotion.

The truth was it was a fear of guilt that drove Mercer, the fear that he could have done more, but hadn't. That is what pushed him so hard in his professional life. He feared not being able to face the mirror knowing that somehow he had failed at something, really, at anything he attempted. And rather than back down from challenges, Mercer continually set himself tougher and tougher goals. He had no obligation to return north other than his own desire to help those who couldn't help themselves.

Yet like so many men, he avoided the challenges of his own emotional life. Rather than take time following Tisa Nguyen's death, he'd buried himself in work. Soon after her funeral he'd returned to the Canadian Arctic where he was under contract with DeBeers. Then it was off for two months on behalf of the Brazilian government to head a task force investigating illegal gold mining in the Amazon rain forest, and then six weeks consulting in Jo'Burg followed by another couple of months working with geologists at Nevada's Yucca Mountain Nuclear Repository. As he'd known, the distractions hadn't healed the wounds, but he felt the scars were less raw, which was why he could see Cali Stowe as an attractive woman.

A gush of diesel erupted from the gas tank and Mercer quickly shut the hose's valve, his thoughts snapped back to the present. He looked around, chagrined. People were struggling for their very lives while he was rediscovering the first flicker of his libido.

He coiled the hose around the bracket mounted behind the cab and hauled himself into the truck. He slid out of his wet raincoat and stuffed it behind the seat. Cali had changed into a dry bush shirt and had used makeup to cover the dark circles under her eyes and freshen her lips. She was probably in her mid-thirties, but the freckles made her look like a teenager. Mercer smiled at her efforts.

"Yeah, yeah. I know. Typical woman, can't go anywhere without makeup. For your information I've been a field researcher for the CDC for five years in some places that make this look like paradise. My makeup

50

kit weighs exactly six ounces and I don't go anywhere without it."

"With your fair complexion it's a good idea."

Cali stopped and looked at him, her mouth creased upward in a surprised grin. "Thank you. You wouldn't believe the grief I get from some of the men I've worked with."

"I spend seven or eight months a year away from home," Mercer told her. "I know how important the little things can be. I worked with a guy in Canada a while ago who carried the remote from his TV set. He said holding it makes him feel he's back in his living room. Although it really pisses off his wife and kids."

Cali laughed. "What about you? Anything you carry to make yourself feel better?"

Mercer turned serious. "Not to sound dramatic, but this helps." He slid his Beretta from behind his back and set it on the bench seat between them. "I thought you should know I have it."

She nodded. "Let's just hope we don't need it."

The jungle began just five feet from the back of the town's last building, an arcing canopy of greenery that met above the single dirt track so it was like driving through a living tunnel. For the first half hour they passed miserable groups of refugees trudging south toward Kivu. Mercer stopped at each to tell the refugees that if he had room he'd give them a lift on the way back but to hurry nevertheless. None of the locals had seen or heard Dayce's army, but Mercer and Cali remained quiet and vigilant as they continued northward.

The rain started to slacken, and even though the windshield wipers made a sound like nails on a chalkboard with each swipe, Mercer wouldn't turn them off. Too much water was dripping from the trees, and if he had any hope of spotting an ambush, he needed clear visibility.

Two hours into their drive, and an hour after seeing the last group of refugees, they neared the swift Scilla River. The mud brown Scilla was barely fifty feet wide where it swept into the Chinko. A ferry made of empty barrels lashed with wire and topped with corrugated metal was the only way to cross. Mercer was relieved to see that before he'd fled, the ferryman had punctured enough barrels so the flat craft was half-sunk on the near shore. If Caribe Dayce had followed the Chinko down from Sudan, which the rumors said he had, he would have to track east for at least fifteen miles to where the river could be crossed on foot.

"According to the report," Cali spoke for the first time in twenty minutes, "the village I'm looking for is about a mile to the left."

Mercer peered into the jungle. While the area where the two rivers met was relatively flat, the Scilla carved through a series of hills so its banks were steep dirt berms. There was no road in, just a narrow footpath meandering along the bluff that quickly grew to eighty feet in height. He backed the truck next to the ferryman's abandoned hut and killed the engine. It appeared silent for the moments it took for his hearing to return and then he caught the sound of the river, the patter of water dripping from the trees, an occasional bird cry.

"Ready?" he asked Cali.

She eyed him. "Are you taking your gun?"

"Yes."

"Then, I'm ready."

On the approach to the village, Mercer and Cali passed what appeared to be an old open-pit mine carved into the top of the bluff. It was a maze of interconnected trenches that covered at least four acres, one long wall acting as a dam to keep the filthy water trapped within from dumping down into the river. Mercer estimated the workings were at least ten feet deep, but as flooded as they were they could have been deeper. He paused at the lip of the main trench, his back to the steep bank and the river. He dropped to a knee, taking a handful of damp soil in his hands and letting it sift from his fingers. Cali stood rapt at the edge of the trench for a moment before taking a small camera from her knapsack and snapping a dozen digital pictures.

Judging by the erosion, Mercer guessed the site was at least fifty years old, possibly older. As he thought about the incongruity of such a mine, he realized he might be able to pin down the exact year the mine was worked, by whom, and at the same time answer the mystery of the village's cancer rate. He looked more closely at the surrounding topography, noting that the far bank of the river was primarily dark granite while this side contained intrusive basalt.

"I think you can forget your gene theory." Mercer stood, wiping his hand on the seat of his pants.

Cali gave him a wary look. "Why do you say that?"

"I'm not positive. We need to talk to the villagers. Someone old preferably. Come on."

"Can you give me a minute," Cali asked. "I need to powder my nose."

"Powder your — Oh, sorry. Sure."

He stayed at the trench while Cali meandered into the jungle. He called to her. "Don't go out of earshot."

"Peeing fetish," she called back. "Like to listen, do you?"

Mercer could tell she was teasing. "Watch usually."

"Don't worry. I'm not going any farther than decorum requires."

After five minutes Mercer called her name.

"A minute," she answered, her voice strained. "Jesus, what do they call Montezuma's Revenge in this part of the world?"

Mercer kept the instant concern from his voice. "In India I've heard it called Hindu Tush. Egypt it's Tut's Curse or Pharaoh's Fanny. I don't think Central Africa has its own *nom de poop*."

"Cute." Her voice sounded a bit stronger. A minute later she emerged from the jungle. She looked none the worse for her troubles.

"You okay?"

"Yeah. Fortunately when I get the, ah, Congo River Runs, it passes quickly. No pun intended."

"Want me to carry your bag?"

Cali tightened the strap over on her shoulder. "No. I'm fine."

The village sat atop the bluff with a commanding view of the river below. Ten or so acres of jungle had been cleared to raise crops, manioc mostly. Several near-feral dogs roamed the round huts while a pair of staked goats watched Mercer and Cali's approach with disinterest, their bodies as scraggly as their beards. It wasn't until they reached what passed as the village square that the first person came out to greet them, a child of about six wearing an overly large Manchester United T-shirt that fell past her knees. A woman in a print dress dashed from her rondavel and rushed the child back inside. A moment later an old woman emerged from the same hut. Her face was perfectly round and so deeply wrinkled that the only way to see her eyes was by the light reflecting off them. She leaned on a cane made of a tree root and wore a shapeless dress that completely covered her ample figure. She said something in a dialect Mercer didn't know, an accusatory question by the tone. Her voice was a force of nature that startled birds into flight and sent one of the dogs slinking with its tail curled under its belly.

"*Pardon, madam,*" Mercer said in French. "*Parlez-vous Français?*"

She stood as silent as a statue for a moment, appraising the two white people, then grunted something into the hut. The child's mother emerged with the toddler clinging to her shoulder.

"I speak English," the young woman said haltingly.

"Better and better." Mercer gave her his best smile. "We're American."

The matron said something else to the younger woman. She lowered her child to the ground and went back into her hut. When she reemerged she carried a low stool and set it on the ground behind whom Mercer assumed was her mother, or maybe grandmother. With a groan the old woman lowered herself onto the stool. Mercer half expected the chair to collapse as the woman's generous backside enveloped the seat.

Mercer and Cali approached a few paces and hunched down near the woman's bare feet. She smelled of wood smoke and animal dung. In the doorways of other huts Mercer could see eyes watching them — most of them female and all of them older.

"Where are all the young people?" Cali asked.

"Gone into the jungle," Mercer said bitterly. "I've seen this happen before. Other places, other wars. With Dayce on the move, everyone who can takes off, leaving those too old or infirm behind."

"My God that's . . ."

"I know." The young mother must have stayed behind to care for her elder, though Mercer couldn't understand why someone didn't take her baby when they fled. He looked more carefully at the child and understood why. She had a tumor on her neck the size of an orange, an angry reddish mass that if left untreated would soon choke off her breathing. Cancer. Why would someone slow themselves down with a child who would die soon anyway?

"You are very brave to stay," Mercer said slowly.

The woman said nothing, but her wide eyes filled with tears.

"I have a truck near the ferryboat that crosses the Chinko River. I can take you all with me to Rafai." As quickly as the tears welled, they subsided and the woman's stoic expression exploded with a smile. "Tell the others to prepare," he added. "We can leave in a few minutes."

"You are from the government?"

Mercer didn't want to explain to her that her government had pretty much abandoned everyone north of Kivu. "Yes."

The woman shouted out to the villagers, many of whom had stepped from their mud and thatch huts. In seconds they ducked back into their homes to collect anything of value the younger people hadn't already taken when they ran away.

"What do you know of the mine on the bluff overlooking the river?" She didn't respond, so Mercer said, "The holes dug into the hill. Do you know who did it?"

She spoke to the old woman, who in turn gave a lengthy reply punctuated by a wet cough. "A white man came when my grandmother was a child." That put the time frame right in Mercer's mind. "He paid the men to dig many holes then he left with crates of dirt. Some time passed and then more men came. They forced the men of our village to dig more holes and they took away even more dirt."

"Soon after, did the people of your village get sick?" Mercer touched his neck in the same spot where the little girl had her tumor.

The young mother clutched her daughter's hand. "That is what my grandmother says. Many children die and many are born with . . ." She didn't have the words to describe the horrors of newborns deformed by the ravages of acute radiation poisoning, many of whom probably never took a breath.

Mercer turned to Cali. "I think this is

where the United States mined pitchblende during World War Two."

"I thought that came from the Congo," Cali said quickly then stammered, "That is the stuff used in the atomic bomb, right? I saw a special on the History Channel about the Manhattan Project a month ago. I could have sworn they said we got our uranium ore from the Congo."

"I'm not sure," Mercer replied. "But someone mined something from here, and judging by the woman's age I'd guess around the Second World War. Then a short time later the villagers begin suffering what sounds like radiation poisoning. Then it's discovered this place has the highest cancer rate in the world. The guy who did the initial medical survey probably thought the mine was irrigation canals or something and never put the pieces together. Usually pitchblende isn't dangerous. It needs to be refined before radiation concentrations are high enough to cause illness. But not here apparently. The natural concentration of uranium 235 was high enough to cause birth defects and cancer."

The old woman spoke to her granddaughter. She went back into her hut and returned with something in her hands. It slipped when she handed it to Mercer. He picked it up from the ground. It was a metal canteen with a waterproofed canvas cover. The olive-drab canvas was frayed and brittle but remarkably intact. The metal was still bright. It looked government-issue to Mercer. He slid the canteen out of its cover and a scrap of paper fell to the ground. Written on it were the words "Property of Chester Bowie."

He showed it to Cali. "That's an American name if there ever was one. I think the History Channel got it wrong."

The daughter translated what her grandmother was saying. "The first man. He gave this to my grandfather's father." The old woman pulled something from around her neck, a leather thong she wore as a necklace. Hanging from it was a small copper object fastened to the leather by a tiny wire cage. "The second men, the ones who came later, gave her this."

The old woman handed the necklace to Mercer. The pendant was a misshapen bullet. Mercer looked at the woman, confusion written on his face. She hiked up her skirt to reveal one of her thigh-sized calves. The black skin was puckered by a small scar on the outside, and when she turned her leg he saw a much nastier exit scar, the skin shiny and gray even after all these years.

"They killed many of the workers when they were finished with the digging," the daughter translated. "They used fast guns and just a few escaped into the jungle. My grandfather's father and all his brothers died."

Cali looked to Mercer. "I don't understand. The Americans killed the miners to hide what they'd done?"

"I can't believe that," Mercer replied even with the evidence in his hand. "I know the whole project was shrouded in secrecy, but I just can't see Americans systematically killing innocent villagers."

"If not us, then —"

Mercer never let Cali finish her question. It was the brief instant of silence, the absence of the omnipresent jungle sounds that launched him into action. In one swift movement he shoved her into the dirt, covering her body with his own as automatic fire erupted from behind them.

The barrage struck all three generations of women. The old woman took two slugs in her chest, the fat rippling with the impact before she fell back off her stool. Her granddaughter and great-granddaughter were stitched across the stomach and head, both dead before their bodies hit the earth.

Banshee cries and more gunfire followed

as elements of Caribe Dayce's army attacked the isolated hamlet. Mercer caught a glimpse of a teenage rebel soldier with an AK-47 nearly as long as he was tall. His young body shuddered as though he was holding a live wire when he fired the weapon into a hut.

Mercer's first instinct was to save as many people as he could from the onslaught. But with only a single pistol, he knew he didn't have a prayer, so he opted for his second choice and that was to save himself and Cali. The truck was a mile away and it would take the rebels at least ten minutes to satisfy their bloodlust. They had a chance if no one saw them.

He rolled off Cali, grabbed her knapsack, and started to slither toward the old woman's hut. He felt Cali respond to the tug and follow him. The hut's mud walls hid them from the rebels but otherwise offered no practical protection. Once inside, he got to his feet, locked eyes with Cali in the dim light to make sure she was okay, then kicked out the back of the hut. A thin strip of vegetation ran along the crest of the bluff before it dropped to the river. He considered making a dash for the water but there was no cover on the sloping bank. They'd be cut down long before they reached the water, and even if they made it, the river offered no cover. They were trapped between the army of Caribe Dayce and the Scilla. He led Cali into the hedge, not knowing when he'd drawn his pistol but not surprised it was in his hand, a round chambered, the safety off. He'd also given Cali her pack to free both of his hands.

The attack had originated from farther upstream, so Mercer pressed Cali ahead of him. If they were caught from behind he would take the first rounds and hoped his sacrifice would see her clear. They stayed low and Mercer kept a hand on her back to steady her pace. Quick movement would catch the eye of even the least trained soldier.

A gush of smoke overwhelmed them as the rebels put a hut to the torch. Someone within screamed as the thatched roof ignited as though it was soaked in gasoline. The scream was ended abruptly when the roof collapsed in an explosion of sparks. There seemed to be no break in the gunfire. As soon as one weapon went silent, another rebel found a target and opened up.

Mercer didn't dare look at the carnage behind him as he and Cali threaded their way through the thin tangle of trees and ferns. He'd seen it before. He'd been orphaned by such an attack not five hundred miles from here. His hand on Cali's back was as much to steady her as it was for himself.

Fifty yards from the edge of the village the strip of jungle ran out. Mercer and Cali paused, keeping low in the shadows of a tree. Mercer finally looked back. Smoke billowed from several huts, and indistinct figures moved through the haze, some firing weapons, others dropping. No one seemed to be looking in their direction. Dayce had assumed his attack would overwhelm the village so quickly that there was no need to station sentries on the perimeter.

The mine was another hundred yards away. The trenches would provide cover, and beyond it the jungle grew thick and impenetrable. Mercer surveyed the ground, picking his route through the barren land, while another part of his brain dealt with the adrenaline overload that was flooding his system. Next to him Cali seemed to be faring better. Her eyes were wide, her body loose and ready.

"We'll make it," she whispered, adjusting her pack so it rode high on her shoulders.

"I know." He forced confidence into his voice.

They struck out, commando crawling

across the damp ground, and had made half the distance when Mercer saw a pair of rebels cross the dike separating the mine from the edge of the bluff. Dayce *had* sent pickets. The rebels were coming at a jog, anxious to join in the slaughter. They would spot the two prone Americans in a matter of seconds.

Mercer was an expert with the Beretta but he had no chance at this range. There was no cover nearby, nothing to hide them. He had no choice and brought the pistol to bear. His mouth had gone stone dry. He watched them come, two boys with bandoliers crossing their thin chests, sandals made of truck tires on their feet, their AKs battered but serviceable. They were thirty yards off when one finally spotted Mercer and Cali lying on the ground. His mouth opened in a surprised O. His partner saw the duo an instant later and his face went savage. He shifted his weapon to fire.

Mercer had his sight picture and pulled the trigger. The gun bucked. The first rebel went down. The next shot was hurried and Mercer was positive the round went high, but the second rebel dropped his AK-47, clutching his shoulder, and began to wail as he collapsed.

Cali and Mercer were up on their feet

before the youth had fully fallen. They ran stride for stride, accelerating like sprinters out of the blocks, eating distance with each pace. The distinctive crack of the pistol had created an eerie lull in the gunfire behind them. It lasted just long enough for Mercer and Cali to cover another thirty yards before rebels began firing in their direction.

They covered another ten yards before the gunmen calmed themselves enough to aim. Hornet swarms of 7.62-millimeter rounds cut the air around the fleeing pair, stitching fist-sized craters in the dirt at their feet. A round hit something solid in Cali's pack and the force of the impact saved her life. She pitched to the ground as a half dozen rounds sped through the space where her head had been.

Mercer barely broke stride as he dragged her back to her feet then bodily tossed her into the trench now three yards away. She rolled with the impact and fell into the ditch as Mercer leapt over her, hitting the far wall of the eight-foot-wide trench and sliding into the fetid water.

"Are you okay?" he gasped, spitting a mouthful of water.

Cali stripped off her pack, taking just a moment to examine the bullet hole. She tossed it aside and nodded wordlessly, her cheeks flushed and her breathing coming in irregular gulps.

"Come on." Mercer took her hand and began wading through the thigh-deep water. It would take less than a minute for the rebels to reach the open-pit mine. Mercer and Cali had to lose themselves in the labyrinth then find a way back out.

They half-ran half-swam, their feet sliding on the slick mud of the trench's floor. Mercer led her into the interior of the maze so that gunmen at the perimeter couldn't simply pick them off. He had no idea how many of Dayce's men would come, all of them probably, but with four acres of trenches to cover he doubted the rebel leader had enough troops to fully encircle the mine.

The dirt walls were shear and all the corners were still sharp. Their view of the leaden sky was reduced to angular ribbons, like walking through a scaled-down version of Manhattan's canyons. Mercer hadn't taken a close enough look at the mine to know the way out of it, but his acute sense of direction had been honed through years working in the three-dimensional network of tunnels in coal, gold, and diamond mines. And while the sun was hidden behind storm clouds, he could judge its direction and thus maintain his own.

Two minutes after tumbling into the trench, Mercer estimated they were a quarter of the way across. He heard voices behind them, far enough away that he knew the men had just reached the lip of the workings, but close enough to make him quicken their pace. A soldier fired off half of his AK's banana magazine. His cohorts cheered him on. The rebels didn't have a clue where their quarry had gone.

"Do you know where you're going?" Cali asked after another minute.

"Not exactly," Mercer admitted. "But we need to get away from the river, where Dayce is sure to station troops along the main trench. I think our best hope is to get to the opposite side of the mine, nearest the jungle, and hope we can make a break for it."

"Lead on, Macduff."

Some of the trenches were long, straight galleries while others dead-ended or branched into innumerable side channels. As he ran, Mercer scanned the edge of the trenches above them, in case rebels had managed to reach the interior earthworks and were searching for them.

They rounded yet another corner. "Damn."

"What is it?"

"That tree branch leaning against the left wall. We passed it a minute ago. We're circling ourselves." Mercer looked back the way they'd come, then glanced at the sky. He could no longer tell where the sun had hidden itself behind the scudding clouds. It began to drizzle.

He turned around and led Cali the way they'd come, feeling a slight hesitation in her step. He didn't blame her.

The young rebel had already killed three people today, but wanted more. His friend, Simi, would be able to cut six new notches on his AK's already serrated stock. He had managed to jump the outside trench and had been running along the top of the maze in his search for the whites. Suddenly he saw where the normally calm water sloshed against the side of the channel. They were near. He kept running, his rubber sandals mere inches from the lip of the trench. He turned another corner and saw them. They were below him, running in his direction, their legs hidden by the water, their heads down.

He skidded to a stop and was about to fire when something slammed into his shoulder. His feet slid out from under him. As he fell he managed to twist himself and clutch the ground before sliding into the trench, his assault rifle pinned uselessly under his chest, his feet scraping against the trench, trying to climb back out.

Mercer stopped and raised his pistol, yet hesitated to fire at the defenseless, wounded boy. Who knew how many people this child warrior had killed, how many women he'd raped, how much suffering he'd caused? At that moment, it didn't matter. Mercer couldn't shoot him in cold blood. Instead he ran forward and grabbed the boy's skinny ankle. The rebel shouted out to his comrades as Mercer yanked him off the wall.

The boy splashed into the water and before he could regain his equilibrium, Mercer fired a straight right fist into his face. With a broken nose and several loose teeth, the boy would be unconscious for hours. Mercer made sure the kid wouldn't drown, tucked his Beretta into the flat holster sewn into the back of his pants, and took the AK-47.

Who had shot the kid? he wondered. Could there be government troops in the area? Is that who took out the second rebel when he and Cali were pinned in the open? Because Mercer was sure his second shot had gone high.

A shadow passed over his face. He whirled, firing from the hip. The first two rounds blew dirt from the lip of the trench; the other three punched blooming crimson holes in the chest of another rebel. An instant later a third rebel ducked his head over the parapet. Keeping out of view, he swung his weapon and sprayed the trench with a full magazine.

His shots went wild as the assault rifle bucked in his hand. Mercer and Cali raced around the next corner. A moment later came an anguished cry as the rebel peeked over the rim of the mine and saw the cloud of blood forming around the friend he'd just finished off. The rebel and three others jumped into the trench and started after the whites.

Hand in hand, Mercer and Cali ran on, staying in the shorter stretches of trench, trying to keep from being spotted, but Mercer knew their wake was as easy to follow as a trail of bread crumbs. At the next corner, he pushed Cali ahead of him and flattened himself against the wall. The pursuing rebels made no effort at silence, coming on like charging crocodiles. Mercer waited another two beats then rounded the corner.

The AK was at his shoulder and he had

complete surprise. He killed the first before they were even aware they were being ambushed. The second went down an instant later. The third dove flat and Mercer fired his last two rounds into the spot where he'd sunk. The body floated to the surface, two neat holes in his back. Mercer threw the gun aside and took off after Cali.

He caught up with her just as she rounded another corner. Twenty paces away a rebel stood in the center of the trench, a rocket launcher tucked under his arm. Mercer and Cali both dropped into the water as the RPG punched out of the launcher and ignited. A blazing trail of fire and smoke corkscrewed down the trench and hit the far wall. The projectile detonated an instant later, blowing a twelve-foot hole in the dam separating the flooded trenches from the steep riverbank.

Mercer erupted from the water, pistol in hand. The instant his vision cleared, he put two rounds in the terrorist's chest. As he fell back he realized what had happened. With the dam breached by the RPG, the stagnant water began to rush through the opening, worrying at it, eroding the sides so the hole doubled in size in seconds. Caught in the inexorable pull, he and Cali were swept along with the current. Neither could dig their heals into the muck at the bottom of the trench or find purchase on the crumbly walls.

Water swelled through the cleft, a remorseless torrent that bore them like so much flotsam. Mercer cursed and Cali clung to his arm as they were sucked through the opening. They went airborne for what seemed like forever before crashing to the ground, tumbling in the flood, and sliding down the bank amid a batter-thick sludge of water and mud. They cartwheeled over each other and the Beretta was stripped from Mercer's grip.

When they hit the river, they were pushed far out into the stream but were so disorientated they couldn't seize the opportunity to escape. Together they struggled back to the bank, choking and coughing up water with every painful breath. Mercer pushed Cali ahead of him as they floundered back to land. Neither looked up until they'd dragged their upper bodies from the surprisingly cold river.

The man was huge. Six four at least, with a broad chest and a head like a cannonball. He wore fatigues, new boots. A leather vest made of some animal hide was all that covered his muscled upper body. His features were cold and distant while his sunglasses mirrored the pitiable figures at his feet. The holster belted around his waist was big enough to carry a railroad gun. He took an unlit cigar from between his teeth and gave a short derisive laugh.

"Welcome to hell, Mr. CIA Man." The looming rebel removed his sunglasses, revealing deep-set fanatical eyes. "I am General, soon to be Emperor, Caribe Dayce."

CENTRAL AFRICAN REPUBLIC

Bound at the wrists, Mercer and Cali were dragged back up the riverbank to the village and dumped into one of the few surviving huts. The men took everything from their pockets and performed an exhaustive search of Cali's breasts and between her legs. By their expressions, there was little doubt what was in store for her when Dayce was done with them.

Two of the men remained outside the hut while the others went on to continue ransacking the small village to a chorus of screams and rifle fire.

"I think we're going to be okay," Mercer whispered, shuffling across the dirt floor so he could lean next to Cali. Their clothes were soaked, and despite the tropical heat he could feel her shivering.

"Are you out of your mind?" she hissed, her eyes wide. "In an hour or two you're going to be shot and I'm going to be raped to death."

"No, listen to me. I don't think we're alone. The kid who fell into the mine, he'd been shot in the back and the second guerilla who went down just before we reached the trench, I don't think I hit him. I think there's another force out there who took them out, a rival faction or maybe government troops."

"I'd like to think so," she said in return, "but doesn't it make a little more sense that they were shot by their own men? Please be quiet and let me think for a second."

Cali didn't get her second. Caribe Dayce wedged his considerable bulk into the thatched hut, seemingly dropping its temperature by ten degrees just with his presence. He didn't remove his sunglasses in the dim recess of the rondavel. The clouds of smoke wafting from his cigar masked the stench of abject poverty.

Blood dribbled from the bottom of his knife scabbard, forming a black pool in the dirt as he hunkered down to stare at his seated captives.

"The CIA must not think too much of me to send just two of you, and one is a woman." Dayce spoke slowly in English with a deep, commanding voice.

"We aren't from the CIA," Cali said before Mercer could buy a little time by replying in French. "I am from the Centers for Disease Control. The CDC."

"Ah," Dayce said as if he'd heard of the organization. "That is the arm of the CIA that controls disease and spreads it among the people of Africa by pretending to vaccinate our children."

"No. It is not part of the CIA," Cali replied hotly. "I'm here to prevent the spread of disease. I hope to save your children."

He casually backhanded her. Mercer stiffened and Dayce's enormous pistol was suddenly pressed between his eyes. "Next lie I use my fist. You are here to spread AIDS and to give me AIDS, like how the CIA tried to kill Brother Fidel by overwhelming Cuba with pigs."

It took Mercer a moment to realize Dayce's warped sense of history had led him to believe the Bay of Pigs invasion was quite literally an invasion by a bunch of pigs. In another time and place he would have laughed.

"You are assassins sent to kill me and end my revolution." He switched his attention back to Cali. "You carry the disease, yes? I am supposed to want you because you are

78

white? And when we are done you will tell me I have the Slim."

"Yes." Cali scoffed in a display of bravado or idiocy. "We're here to assassinate you with a disease that takes years to kill."

"And you." He turned back to Mercer, never once lessening the pressure of the gun between his eyes. "What disease do you carry?"

At that moment Mercer saw a white man pass by the rondavel's open door. He was dressed for combat and carried a machine pistol slung under his arm. He moved with an easy professional grace, almost like a shadow in the smoke of burning huts. He had to be from the UN, one of the Belgian soldiers on guard in Kivu sent north to hasten the evacuation of the region. And if there was one there had to be more. Mercer swiveled his eyes back to Caribe Dayce and kept all trace of emotion from his voice. "Optimism."

The African guerilla leader rocked back on his heels and laughed. "That is something that you can't spread in Africa."

"I know."

Dayce got to his feet, remaining in a stooped position because the hut wasn't tall enough. He holstered his sidearm. "I think we will not take chances with the two of you. I decree that you are CIA spies and sentence you to death. Execution is at sundown."

"Did you see him?" Mercer asked as soon as Dacye had walked out of earshot.

Tension ran from Cali so her body sagged against his. "Yes, Jesus, I did! Who is he?"

"I think he's a UN peacekeeper and he won't be the only one. They must be getting into position. Get ready to bolt as soon as they attack. Can you get your hands free?"

"I can't even feel my hands."

"Doesn't matter. As soon as they attack we'll kick out the back of the hut and drop straight for the river. The truck's only a mile downstream. All we need is three minutes' head start and we're gone."

They crawled to the back of the hut and braced their feet against the wall. One or two good kicks would likely knock the entire structure down. The tall riverbank was only a couple of yards beyond the hut. For the first minutes Mercer felt adrenaline sing in his veins as he waited for the inevitable assault. But after five his body relaxed as his mind began to wander. The UN soldiers had to have seen their capture. They wouldn't wait until the last minute before attempting an attack. Granted they were outnumbered, but Mercer had taken out a half dozen rebels and he had nowhere near their combat training. More experience maybe, but not training. Even if they didn't attack Dayce's entire force, they must know where he and Cali were being held and could rescue them.

After another couple of minutes Cali pushed back to a sitting position, her lower lip quivering slightly. "We're wrong."

"You can't be sure."

She composed herself and gave him a wry smile while mimicking Caribe Dayce's voice. "You can't spread optimism in Africa." She looked at him levelly. "If there really is a UN force out there, they'll wait until after sundown to attack. That's what I would do in their position, making it a bit late for us."

Her easy grasp of military tactics was at odds with what she'd told him about herself. Again Mercer wondered if she'd been in the military. "Who are you?"

"I told you. I'm with the CDC."

"And before that how long were you in the army?"

"What makes you think . . ."

"No one who hasn't seen combat is as calm as you."

She looked away. "I was captured by

81

Sunni insurgents in Baghdad in 2005. They couldn't pull a Jessica Lynch for me because no one knew I was missing."

"What were you doing there?"

"Medic in the National Guard. I got separated from my unit just before they ran into an ambush. It took three days for our guys to recover our Humvee and realize mine wasn't one of the four burned bodies. Another five days passed before Special Forces got me out."

Mercer was about to ask why the media never picked up the story, but he stopped himself. He imagined that military censors quashed it. The reasons would forever be locked in a file someplace and in her heart.

A tense silence filled the hut. Even the village had gone quiet.

"I wasn't raped," Cali said softly after a minute.

"I'm sorry?"

"I said I wasn't raped. I just wanted you to know. I'm scared shitless right now but the Iraqis didn't touch me and I'm relieved that Dayce's men won't get to me either."

"I'm grateful for that too," was all Mercer could think to say.

Although it put his wrist in an awkward position, he reached out as much as the binds would allow and took Cali's hand.

She returned the grip and together they waited for a rescue that seemed less likely with each passing second.

A half hour before the sun set on the overcast day, the final flicker of hope vanished when the white soldier they had seen crossing the camp suddenly stepped into the hut. In the glow of the lantern he carried, they could see he was as large as Caribe Dayce and equally muscled. His features were Eastern European, with thinning blond hair and thick, slack lips. One of his eyes was hidden by a black patch that couldn't cover all of a scar that ran from his temple to his nose. His other eye was watery blue and small, but held dark malevolence. Whatever had taken his eye had damaged the tear ducts because the patch was moist and he wiped at it with a finger absently as he regarded the two prisoners.

Mercer knew the type. He'd even run across a few. The man was Special Forces from the former Warsaw Pact, now turned mercenary. Spurned by the countries who'd trained them to be killers, many elite soldiers had sold their skills on the open market. While Western governments concentrated on keeping Russian nuclear scientists from trading their skills with terror organizations, ranks of highly specialized soldiers had gone to the very same terror groups to train the next generation of fighters. While the fear of a nuclear device falling into the wrong hands was very real, a perhaps more immediate threat was thousands of fundamentalists with skills rivaling the best Special Force troops in the world.

Caribe Dayce entered the room and slapped the mercenary on the shoulder. The man whirled. Dayce recoiled. He had an army of soldiers at his command, a reputation of brutal savagery, and the confidence that came from his huge size, and still he feared the mercenary.

"What have they told you?" The mercenary's accent was thick, Slavic or Russian, and his voice was as deep as Dayce's.

"There is nothing they can tell us," the rebel leader said with a touch of deference. "We will find what we find, as I said."

"I do not like that they are here when we arrived."

"I don't either, Poli," Dayce agreed. "My men saw them enter just before the attack. Whatever they learned will die with them here."

"We do not know who sent them."

"They are American. It must be the CIA."

The mercenary looked Mercer up and down then gave Cali the same scrutiny. He didn't appear impressed by what he saw. "I do not think they are CIA."

"Then torture us and find out, you stupid son of a bitch." Cali's outburst startled all three men. Mercer tightened his grip on her hand to steady her, but she continued. "Jam bamboo shoots under our nails. Cover us in hot coals. Do whatever you want. In the end you will know that I work for the Centers for Disease Control in Atlanta and Mercer is here on behalf of the UN. In case it escaped you, your little revolution has caused a humanitarian crisis that has killed God knows, no *you* know, how many people, and forced thousands to flee their homes."

Poli regarded her for a moment as Cali struggled to get her breathing under control. He said nothing and backed from the rondavel. Dayce followed him out and a moment later four teenage guerrillas stormed into the hut. Since Dayce's pronouncement earlier, Mercer and Cali had known this was coming, but now the moment of reckoning was here. Cali screamed and Mercer struggled to his feet. He kicked the gun from one rebel's arms and threw himself bodily at a second, knocking the skinny youth to the ground and landing on him with his full force. The teen's breath exploded in Mercer's face, a rank combination of stale liquor and rancid meat. Mercer head-butted him to keep him down and was just getting his legs untangled from the youth's when a third soldier rammed the stock of his AK-47 into his kidney.

Mercer recoiled from the strike, searing agony radiating from the blow. The guerilla tried to repeat the attack. Mercer managed to roll enough so the wooden butt slammed into the back of his thigh, deadening his leg. He continued to roll as the soldier rained blows, swinging the assault rifle like a club. Mercer came up against the hut's wall and frantically tried to kick his way through. It was a test of endurance between the rondavel's rickety walls and his ability to absorb punishment, but as fate would have it the wall was the hut's strongest, and a particularly sharp blow to the back of his head knocked Mercer momentarily unconscious.

The rebel clubbed Mercer once more for good measure, then he and his partner hauled him to his feet. Cali had been subdued in the first seconds of the melee with a rifle butt to her lower abdomen that nearly ruptured her bladder.

They were both dragged outside, where several excited soldiers waited in the village's central clearing. Only two huts remained; the rest were smoldering piles of ash. A short line of men waited outside the second hut. They joked with each other with nervous jibes and toothy grins as they waited their turn with whoever was alive inside.

Two wooden poles had been rammed into the loamy soil behind an odd stone pillar. Mercer was dimly aware of the strange column's size, about seven feet, and how it was shaped like an obelisk, before he was turned and thrust up against one of the poles. Cali fell as she was pushed against the second one. A rebel hauled her to her feet while another tied her bound wrists to the pole. Mercer tried to fight off his two guards but was eventually secured as well.

Dayce ambled over to them, examining the glowing tip of his cigar in the fading light. There was no sign of the mercenary.

"Any last requests? Sorry but I can't spare one of my cigars. Maybe one of my men will give you a cigarette instead."

"General Dayce," Mercer began. He was about to beg for their lives and he stopped himself. Dayce's bemused expression showed he'd been in this position countless times and enjoyed the entreaties for mercy. Mercer wasn't going to give him the satisfaction. If he was going to die, he wanted it at least partially on his terms. "I want to give the order to fire."

Dayce's expression changed slightly. He nodded and gave a deep, barking laugh. "You are a man, I see. I respect that." He shouted to the four men milling a short distance off. The firing squad. One of them gave Mercer a thumbs-up gesture.

"I'm no man," Mercer said. "Not like you think."

Dayce patted Mercer's cheek.

"In that case, die well, No Man."

"What the hell are you doing?" Cali whispered as Dayce moved off to form up his troops.

"When the shooting starts, drop to your butt."

"What?"

"Do it."

"Think we can dodge the bullets like in that *Matrix* movie?"

"You never know."

The four troopers had formed their firing line. Caribe Dayce stood to their right and slightly behind. He had his big pistol in hand to administer the coup de grâce. Poli, the mercenary, stood a dozen or so yards behind them, idly wiping a tear from under his eye patch.

"Make your count."

The men held their weapons low at their waists, their eyes bright with the prospect of killing two more people. Mercer glanced at Cali's profile. Her face was rigid while her chest heaved. "Mercer," she cried softly. "I don't want to die."

"Drop to the ground like I said." Mercer looked beyond the firing squad, even beyond the mercenary, where shadows played at the edge of the jungle.

"Make your count, No Man, or I will do it for you."

As loudly and with as much authority as he could muster, Mercer shouted, "At the ready!"

In unison, four Kalashnikovs snapped to port arms. All around them the rebels watched the proceedings with fascination. Most of them had left their weapons outside the hut they used to rape any of the women they'd captured.

Cali began to whimper.

Mercer waited as long as he dared, never taking his attention off Dayce, judging the man's impatience to the second. Just as the guerilla was about to speak, Mercer whispered to Cali, "Don't forget what I said." Then, tensed for the inevitable, he shouted "Take your aim!"

Guns came up to shoulders, the men settling into their stances as their fingers sought triggers. Mercer flicked his eyes to the jungle perimeter then back to Dayce. He opened his mouth wide to fill his lungs.

Fire erupted from all quarters of the jungle. The four men making up the firing squad were scythed down like wheat. Caribe Dayce was stitched from thigh to head from two different directions, his body exploding under the onslaught. The men who'd preferred to keep their place in line at the hut rather than enjoy a ringside seat at the execution were taken at the same instant, shot through the head with a pistol by a figure dressed in black who had materialized behind them. The assassin slipped into the hut and two more shots rang out.

Any of the rebels holding weapons were targeted next. One managed to counterfire and was gunned down with half his neck vanishing in a gout of blood. Next came any soldier who made for his rifle. Some dropped to the ground to crawl to the cache while others ran doubled over. It didn't matter. The unseen gunmen found their marks and the guerillas died. Those that tried to flee into the jungle were shot in the back. Those that turned to beg for mercy were shot in the front.

At the instant of attack, Poli was far

enough from the mass of rebel soldiers to escape immediate detection. Rather than run and draw attention to himself, he eased to the ground and edged toward the river embankment, crawling so slowly that in the fading light he looked like nothing more than a faint breeze blowing through the undergrowth. When he reached the steep hill, he slowly rolled over the precipice and slid down the unprotected face, keeping his arms and legs spread to maintain a slow pace. He allowed himself to roll into the water without making a splash, filled his lungs with as much air as his powerful chest could hold, then struck out underwater for the far shore.

He surfaced near a felled tree and drew himself from the water with the patience of a crocodile stalking a shore animal. Despite his exposure, he crawled slowly and steadily, knowing a sniper with a night scope could easily pick him off. But he reached the top of the escarpment and faded into the jungle. By the time the firing in the village stopped, he was a half mile away and eating ground with every pace.

Mercer hadn't told Cali about seeing the shadowy figures encircling the village, because he wasn't sure if he'd really seen them himself. They were like wraiths, hints of movement rather than solid form. He hadn't wanted to give her false hope again. His whole charade about wanting to give the command to fire was his way of helping his rescuers if they really existed.

As soon as the first rounds raked the firing squad, he dropped to his backside and leaned as far over as he could, trying to present as small a target as possible. He couldn't shout to Cali over the din of automatic fire but he saw she had followed his lead. She'd even managed to flatten herself to the ground using some double-jointed maneuver.

The one-sided firefight lasted less than five minutes, dwindling to silence as the unknown force picked off the last of the rebels who'd fled into the night. In all, one hundred and forty-eight well-armed guerillas had been massacred. The mysterious attackers had done what neither the Central African Republic's army nor the UN had been able to do.

When it was over Mercer stood on shaky legs. He'd hoped for this but the aftermath left him drained. Cali didn't bother to stand. She lay back against her pole, her eyes shut.

"You knew they were out there?" she finally asked.

"I suspected."

"You weren't going to tell me?"

"I didn't think you'd believe me."

"You're right. I would have thought it was a lame attempt at being gallant, and I would have died thinking you were a misogynist jerk."

"And now?"

She finally looked over. "Well, you're not a misogynist." And then she rewarded him with a tired smile.

A few seconds later Mercer felt someone behind him. He stiffened before feeling a knife slice through the ropes securing his wrists. When he tried to turn to face his rescuer, strong hands clamped the sides of his head.

"Do not turn around." The voice was pitched low and expressionless, as if masking an accent. Keys rattled next to Mercer's ear. "These were in Dayce's pocket. The two men he sent to search for your vehicle have been dispatched. Take your woman and go. Never return here." The man thrust the keys into Mercer's hand along with two other items. "You dropped these." It was the canteen and the necklace made from the bullet that the old woman had worn.

"Who are you?"

"That is not your concern. Go."

"But —"

"You leave in five seconds or die in six. We give you this chance for our own reasons. Take your woman's hand." Cali was moved next to Mercer, her fingers locking with his, their palms tight. "Walk straight forward until you reach your truck, then drive to Rafai. Tell them Dayce is dead and then never come back to this area again."

As soon as the unseen man released Mercer's skull, an accomplice racked the slide on a pistol to emphasize his point. Cali and Mercer needed no further urging. As if they were soldiers on parade, they marched in lockstep from the ruins of the village, bodies rigid, eyes straight ahead.

Only after they'd made their way along the dike separating the mine from the riverbank and climbed up from the cut left by the RPG did Cali finally ask, "What the hell just happened back there? Who were those guys?"

Mercer noted they were still holding hands. "I don't know. That wasn't another rebel faction. They fought like commandos and the guy who spoke sounded white, although not American."

"Could they have been UN?"

"If they were, why not let us go with them? No, this is something else. That warning about not returning to the area. They were here to protect something and I don't think it's coincidence that they got here the same day as Caribe Dayce."

"Or us for that matter. Do you think they were here all along, keeping watch over the village?"

Mercer thought it over. It was possible, with one glaring exception. "If they were here to protect the village, why allow Dayce to slaughter everyone and rape the few that survived? It's something else."

"The old mine?"

"I can't think of anything else."

"But why?"

"That's something I plan on finding out."

"Well, this is kind of out of both our purviews."

"Not mine," Mercer answered.

She glanced over, startled by the mettle in his voice. "How so?"

There was never any easy way for Mercer to explain his part-time position with the government without sounding like he was boasting. He usually just told it straight. "Two years ago I was hired as a consultant to the President of the United States. My title is special science advisor. Because my work, like yours, takes me to some pretty hostile places, I act as an intelligence

95

gatherer for anything that could threaten the United States."

"You're a spy?"

"No, not like that." Mercer reconsidered. "Well, kind of. If I come across anything out of the ordinary when I'm in the field, I write it up and forward it along to a deputy national security advisor named Ira Lasko. Truth be told I've only passed on a couple of things in the two years since I agreed to take the job, and nothing's ever come of them."

"And you are going to follow up on this."

"Cali, we just saw a village butchered and then some other mystery group come out of nowhere and annihilate the vanguard of a rebel army. How could I not follow up on it?"

They had reached the truck. It was almost dark. The jungle canopy was a silvery gray and the waters of the Chinko River ran black. They spied curious puffy white shapes milling around the battered cargo truck. Mercer held out a hand to take Cali's wrist and lower her to the ground. A pair of figures stepped from the far side of the vehicle. Mercer cursed himself for not retrieving his Beretta. It was hard to make out details, but both people carried something long in their hands. Weapons?

One of the figures brushed aside one of the odd pale shapes and it protested with an angry bleat. They were sheep. As soon as Mercer realized it, the details came into focus. It was a man and a woman. They had just forded the river with the twenty-five or so sheep to flee Dayce's army. The animals must represent the sum of their wealth. As Mercer and Cali watched, a pair of naked toddlers joined their parents. The mother lifted the youngest to a hip and allowed him to slide her breast from her blouse and begin to feed.

"What do you think?" Cali asked.

Mercer was pretty sure that all of the men with Dayce were dead, but he couldn't take the chance a few were still out in the jungle. He couldn't leave these people here, vulnerable. He stood, holding his arms wide in a friendly gesture as the family's father saw him and lowered his staff as if to joust. It was all just too bizarre, but that was Africa. Mercer chuckled. "I think we're making our escape from the CAR with a frightened family and a flock of wet sheep."

It took Mercer and Cali three days to get from Rafai to the capital, Bangui, and from there a flight to Lagos and finally to New York's Kennedy Airport. To Mercer it seemed the closer to home she got, the more withdrawn Cali Stowe became. He suspected it was a defense mechanism to distance herself from the horrors of the past days. She had compartmentalized the episode and was slowly building a wall around the memory, locking it deep in her soul so it would only return as nightmares, and given time even those would fade.

Mercer recognized the technique. He'd done it himself dozens of times. He'd seen savagery on a scale Cali couldn't possibly conceive. Not the slow death by international apathy someone from the CDC would witness in refugee camps or in rural AIDS clinics, but wholesale violence for violence's sake. He'd seen wars on four continents, regional dustups that barely made the evening news but left thousands dead; he'd rescued enslaved miners in Eritrea, and he'd held a woman he loved in his arms as she died.

Harry White had been in a particularly philosophical mood one night not long after Tisa Nguyen's death and told Mercer that God didn't place a burden on a person that He felt couldn't be handled. Look at Job, Harry had said by way of example. The guy had it all when God took it away — family, money, friends, health, the whole magilla. But God also knew old Job could take it.

You soldier on, Harry had continued; you take the shit life tosses at you and keep on going. There's really only one alternative.

"Yeah, I could turn into a bitter drunk like you," Mercer had replied, "hanging out in a bar twelve hours a day waiting for some dupe to pick up your tab."

Harry had grinned at that, his lopsided grin that turned the eighty-year-old rogue into an eight-year-old scamp, if only for an instant. "That's exactly the alternative I'm talking about."

But in a way, Harry had a point, and his words had stuck. Mercer did soldier on. Maybe what he'd seen and done in his life clouded his once crystalline beliefs, forced him to search through the shades of gray, but the core was still there, the ability to find the good amid the rotten, and hold on to it while the rest eroded with time.

He sensed that Cali worked the same way. In a week or a month she'd look back and recall an episode from her trip, maybe their profanity-laden struggle to load twenty-seven damp sheep into the truck, and she would smile. That would also bring back the panic she'd felt in the village and the smile would fade, but so too would the intensity of that fear. In six months or a year she'd still smile at the sheep and maintain just a vague unease about the rest.

In order to do all that, she needed distance, distance from Africa and distance from Mercer. He understood, and as she waited with him at the US Airways counter, they exchanged phone numbers and made indeterminate plans to stay in touch. Both knew they wouldn't; however, there was comfort in the ritual.

"Well, good luck with your search," Cali said stiffly.

"And I'm sorry about yours." She shot him a puzzled look. "Your cancer research. It had sounded promising."

"Oh. I think I got carried away when I first read about that village and ignored the number one rule in medical research. There are no shortcuts."

"Where will you go next?"

"That's up to the CDC. Though I won't be putting in for any new assignments for a while. I think I'll stick to a desk until . . ." Her voice trailed off.

Mercer took both her hands, made sure she was looking into his eyes, then leaned in and kissed her gently on the corner of her mouth. It was perhaps a bit more intimate than he intended, but he had to feel the texture of her full lips, if even just a sliver. They were softer than he'd imagined.

"Good luck, Cali Stowe."

"Good luck, oh my God, I can't remember your first name. I've just been calling you Mercer."

"Don't worry." He smiled. "Everyone does."

Their eyes remained locked, steady. He held on to her strong fingers a moment longer, and she let him. Both knew this was the last they'd see of each other. It was awkward, but charmingly so. Had they met at another time, in another place, they'd have been making plans for a date, not saying good-bye forever.

Just before he released her, Cali impulsively returned his kiss. Her lips didn't linger and she turned, her red hair flaring, catching sunlight and reflecting back like spun copper. "Good-bye."

She was swallowed immediately by the throng of commuters and tourists.

A few moments later an elderly woman in line behind Mercer tapped his elbow. Her hair was a white bush, her eyes blue and friendly. "It's none of my business but I think you should go after her, young man."

Mercer looked to where Cali had vanished. "I think you're probably right, but such is life."

"Yes, I suppose. Making mistakes is how we learn."

Mercer smiled at her. "You think I'm making a mistake letting her go?"

"Only you can answer that." She pointed. "There's a spot open at the counter."

Mercer grabbed the bag he'd bought in Lagos containing Chester Bowie's canteen and the mashed bullet the old woman in the village had shown him. He took one step toward the counter then turned suddenly. "Thank you, ma'am, you go ahead."

He dashed out of line. He moved quickly through the terminal, hoping to spot the flash of Cali's hair above the crowd. Already he was composing what he'd say to her. "This is stupid. I think we're attracted to each other and I don't think it's right that circumstance should bring us together only to force us apart. I know you want to put everything behind you, I do too, but I also think one date wouldn't kill us. I can be in Atlanta the day after tomorrow. I just have to file a report with my contact at the UN, Adam Burke."

If she said no, she said no. It would only cost him an hour's delay until the next flight to Reagan National, but if she said yes then maybe it would help heal a little of the loneliness that had dogged him for the past six months.

With Atlanta being their hub, he assumed she'd made reservations for a Delta flight. He'd stepped out of the airport and begun searching for a skycap to ask where their terminal was located, when he saw her across the traffic-choked street. He was about to call her name when she reached a black Town Car.

She didn't look back or even acknowledge the driver holding the door as she ducked into the backseat. Mercer waited until the Lincoln was rolling before dashing out into traffic. A cabbie leaned on his horn and a traffic cop shouted. Mercer ignored them, angling so he could see the vehicle's license plate. The white background and black letters were distinctive, and suddenly a great many things came clear, while even more became confused.

The Town Car was registered to the United States government.

Arlington, Virginia

It seemed to Mercer that the block of brownstones on his street was the last stretch of what had once been a charming suburb. Arlington had grown in the decade since he'd bought the three-story row house. It was now mostly anonymous high-rise apartment towers and office parks, with a few box stores thrown in to complete the sprawl trifecta.

Mercer's street was lined with identical buildings, red stone structures with dressed block entrances, narrow windows, and shade trees along the curb. Traffic was generally light outside rush hour, and it wasn't unusual to see mothers allowing their kids to play outdoors. It was almost as if time had left the street alone for the past sixty years.

Usually Mercer felt a calming wave as he entered his house. He owned the entire building and had remodeled the space so an

104

atrium lofted to the third floor and a circular staircase spiraled down to the first. On the second floor were a niche library, two spare bedrooms, and a room outfitted with a five-stool mahogany bar, matching wainscoting with brass accents, and clubby leather furniture. It was a space designed to evoke a nineteenth-century gentleman's club, and other than the plasma TV and the 1950s-era lock-lever refrigerator behind the bar, the effect was perfect. The master suite took up the entire third floor. Bathed by a pair of skylights, Mercer's bedroom was larger than most apartments in Arlington, and the marble bathroom was the only he knew of that had a urinal tucked in beside the toilet.

He strode through the front door and made straight for his home office on the ground floor. He felt no sense of homecoming, nothing but the hot anger that had been with him since seeing Cali get into a government car. He wasn't going to allow himself to speculate until he was sure, but now that he was within minutes of knowing, all kinds of scenarios played out in his mind. None of them were very good.

He snatched the phone from his desk and dialed information. He heard a female voice and was about to ask for the number of the CDC in Atlanta when he did the acoustical version of a double take. He listened to the voice more carefully.

"God, Harry, you are so big. I don't think Chantelle and I can take you but we're willing to try. You just have to promise to be gentle."

"What the . . . ?"

"We're both still virgins you know, Harry. You'll be our first time."

"Who the hell is this?" Mercer demanded. Before the woman could reply, Mercer heard the sound of snoring through the open line. "Son of a bitch," he muttered and killed the connection.

He left his travel bag on the desk and mounted the circular stairs to the second floor. Just as he thought. Harry White was sprawled on one of the couches, the cordless phone lying on his chest, rising and falling in time with his snoring. The nearby coffee table was covered in so many water rings left by highball glasses it looked like it had been mauled by a squid. The cut crystal ashtray atop was overflowing. Harry wore faded chinos, an over-laundered white shirt made of some indestructible synthetic, dark socks, and sneakers. His ubiquitous blue windbreaker was thrown over the back of one of the bar stools, a dog leash uncoiling from a pocket.

On the opposite couch, in an equally sprawled position, was Harry's dog. The obese basset hound lay on his back so that his belly sagged in avalanches of fat. While one ear dangled almost to the floor, the other was spread across the leather like a mangy napkin. The dog lifted one bloodshot eye, spotted Mercer, and tried to wag his tail. The effort seemed too great, so he went back to sleep, snoring just a shade softer than his master.

"*Et tu,* Drag?" Mercer said to the mutt. He snapped off the portable phone on Harry's chest and tapped the old lecher on the shoulder. Harry gave a startled grunt and his eyes flew open.

"Phone sex, Harry? At your age you get a hard-on only during leap years and you waste it on phone sex."

The old man ran his tongue around his mouth and was obviously repulsed by what he found. "Hi, Mercer." Harry's voice rang with the lilt of a train wreck. "I wasn't wasting it. I just wanted to see what it was all about."

"Since you were asleep, I can tell it worked wonders. How long were you on for?"

Harry looked at his watch, his wrinkled face pulling taut with concentration. "Holy shit, it's four thirty. Hey, I gotta go. I told

107

Tiny I'd be back by now."

"How long, Harry?"

"I'm not sure. I think I fell asleep around three thirty."

"Two bucks a minute?"

Harry looked away, not because he was embarrassed by what he'd been doing, but because he'd been caught. "I think they said something about four dollars but I can't be sure."

Some friendships develop over many years; some are mere conveniences because of job or neighborhood. Some defy explanation. Harry White was fast approaching his eighty-first birthday, more than twice Mercer's age and yet they had been friends from the moment they met at the dive down the street called Tiny's. A few who knew them assumed Mercer saw a father figure in the octogenarian, especially since he'd lost his parents at a young age. Others thought Mercer helped old Harry as though he were a charity case. Neither explanation was even close. Mercer had analyzed their relationship a few times and the best he could figure was that the two of them were the same person, just separated by a few decades.

Harry White had fought for his nation during World War Two, never bothering to get veterans benefits afterward because he'd done it out of a moral obligation and wanted nothing back for his service. He gave everything and asked only for loyalty in return. He knew firsthand that no matter how blurred the line between right and wrong, there was still a threshold that couldn't be crossed. He believed that actions and words were of equal importance and that a favor asked was a favor granted. He personified what it meant to be part of the Greatest Generation.

Without consciously knowing it, Mercer had held himself to the standard set in those days and lived by a similar code. So in fact Mercer and Harry were from the same generation, men who had known deprivation in their youth, who had survived combat, who still mourned friends, and who still believed in the rightness of their deeds.

Harry suddenly became indignant. "And anyway you weren't supposed to be home until the end of the month."

Mercer slid around the bar and poured himself a vodka gimlet using Jamaica Gold, lime juice, and Ketel One. He put together a Jack and ginger for Harry, adding just enough ginger ale to make the whiskey tingle. "Nice to know you care, you bastard. The Central African Republic is in the middle of a civil war, or haven't you been following the papers?"

"I've stolen your paper every day since you left." Harry found his customary place at the bar and took an appreciative gulp before lighting up a Chesterfield, his blue eyes vanishing into folds of skin to blink away the smoke. "But if it ain't a headline or on the crossword page, I don't pay attention." A tiny trace of concern edged into his booze- and butt-ruined voice. "Everything okay? I mean nothing happened to you?"

Before Mercer told his story he grabbed the cordless from the couch. Drag whimpered in his sleep. In the months since Harry had found the basset bawling at the Dumpster behind Tiny's trying to get food, he and Mercer had come to the conclusion that the dog couldn't be dreaming of rabbits. Snails, maybe, or arthritic sloths were more his speed. Mercer dialed information and got the number for the CDC in Atlanta.

After dealing with a Byzantine automated answering system, Mercer managed to get an operator and request the personnel office.

"Human Resources, John speaking. How may I help you?"

"Hello, John. My name is Harry White. I just got back from Africa and I think the airline gave me a piece of luggage belonging to one of your people."

"The name." It sounded to Mercer as if John took his social cues from the automated system.

"Stowe, Cali Stowe." Mercer spelled it.

"We don't have anyone — oh wait." There it was, the pause Mercer feared he would hear. "Um, yes. Let me transfer you to Mr. Lawler."

"That won't be necess—" John had already started to reroute the call.

A moment later a guarded voice came on the line. "This is Bill Lawler. I understand you're asking about Cali Stowe."

"No, Mr. Lawler. I just want to make sure that if I send a piece of her luggage mistakenly dropped off at my house by the airline that she would get it. She mentioned that she worked for the CDC when I met her on a flight today."

"Ah, yes, she is an employee. You said she was on a flight today? May I ask from where?"

"So she works there. Great. I'll put her bag in the mail first thing in the morning. Thank you." Mercer cut the connection before Lawler could ask any more questions.

"What the hell was that all about?" Harry cocked one bushy eyebrow. "And more

111

importantly, if I find her bag does that mean I can go through her underwear?"

"There is no bag," replied Mercer, his voice filling with frustration and exhaustion. "I met Cali Stowe in Africa. She told me she worked for the CDC but when she and I split at JFK I spotted her getting into a government car."

"And?"

"And the guy I just talked to at the CDC seemed pretty interested in why I was asking about her. I think she uses them as a cover for something else. Cali's name shows up on their computer but it flags whenever someone tries to get information about her."

Harry ground his cigarette into an ashtray and drained the last half of his drink. He spoke while Mercer rummaged through a drawer behind the bar. "Any suspects on who signs her paycheck?"

"Dozens of suspects but no clue." Mercer found a blue pushpin and pressed it into the CAR on the world map hanging behind the bar, adding one more to the dense forest of pins studding the framed chart. There were easily eighty other gaily colored tacks denoting the places Mercer had traveled for work and pleasure. There were almost a dozen clear ones, showing places where he had been involved in covert actions. His eyes lingered on the transparent pin stuck into the island of La Palma, part of the Canary chain. It was all he had of Tisa.

Harry noted the tension creeping into Mercer's neck and saw the shadow lingering in his storm gray eyes when he turned from the map. "You were attracted to her."

"She was attractive," Mercer admitted.

"Quit dodging. That's not what I asked."

No matter how much Mercer wanted to avoid the issue, he knew his friend wouldn't let him. "Yes, I was attracted to her."

"She's the first since Tisa and now you feel guilty about it."

"Yeah."

"Six months is an eternity and it's a blink of the eye. I can't tell you how to feel about this but I will tell you that being attracted to another woman is not a bad thing. You do realize that since Tisa died you've held yourself to a standard most married men can't touch. Guys find women attractive every damned day and you can bet that not one of them feels the least bit guilty. But you, you see it as an act of deepest betrayal. This isn't mourning, Mercer, it's self-inflicted punishment."

"What if I can't help it?"

"You've always found a way in the past."

"What do you mean?"

Harry lit another cigarette, gathering his thoughts. "You beat yourself up every time something in your life goes wrong. You blame yourself whether it's your fault or not. Most people don't take responsibility when they screw up but you do even if you don't. This isn't a character flaw, or maybe it is but not a bad one to have, except each time it costs you a little more to find your center again and come to grip with whatever just happened. It's been six months since you lost Tisa and you're no closer to putting her death behind you."

Mercer's anger flared. "I won't put her behind me."

"Not her, you dope, her death. You haven't put her death behind you. There's a distinction and maybe that's where you're stuck."

"What do you mean?"

"I bet you relive her death every day but don't relive her life." Mercer didn't deny it so Harry continued. "You've turned her into the symbol of some perceived failure, a memory where you can unload all the guilt you carry around. You don't celebrate the short time you were with her and that's not very fair. To her I mean."

Mercer was rocked by what Harry had said. In a rush he realized it was all true. Tisa's memory had become a wound he would reopen just so he could revel in the guilt he was certain he deserved. This *wasn't* mourning. It was self-flagellation and was actually a little sick. He'd made her death about him and in doing so reduced her life to something he could blame himself for.

"So how do I put my life back together?"

Harry leaned back on his stool, jetting smoke from his nose. "How the hell should I know? It's your life. Ask that Cali woman out on a date. Or maybe spend a week at a resort watching honeys parade by."

Mercer hadn't been to a beach in years and couldn't imagine himself sitting around leering at bikini-clad hardbodies, nor did the prospect of dating Cali hold much interest, not at least until he found out who she was and who she really worked for. That thought reminded him that he needed to contact Admiral Lasko. He dialed Ira's cell, ignoring the red light indicating that the handset's batteries were low.

"You're being back early can't be good news," Lasko said in greeting, having finally mastered caller ID. Ira Lasko was a former submariner who then transferred into Naval Intelligence. John Kleinschmidt, the President's national security advisor, had tapped him shortly after his retirement from the navy to work for the White House. Lasko possessed a mind that could think on both strategic and tactical levels and intuitively understand the link between the two. He was below average height and had a slight build but he more than compensated with a commanding voice, boundless energy, and a pugnacious attitude to go along with his shaved head.

"No and no," Mercer replied. "No, I didn't find any coltan. I'll call Burke at the UN tomorrow then fax him a formal report later this week. And the second no is because I found something else that isn't good news."

"You want to get together?"

"I think we should. I've got a couple of items that need to be analyzed."

"I'm stuck in the office until eight. I'll meet you at that Thai place I like near the Pentagon City Mall."

"Eight thirty at Loong Chat's. Got it." After some of the swill Mercer had been eating over the past weeks, the idea of Thai food sent a spasm through his guts. He'd grab a sandwich before the meeting.

"I'm off," Harry announced. "Drag, get up."

The dog didn't even lift an eyelid.

"Drag, up. Walk time."

The basset rolled onto his side, his back

to Harry, an annoyed growl rumbling from deep in his chest.

Harry walked over, favoring his prosthetic right leg, which always bothered him when he napped with it on. He shook the hound, causing waves of fat to ripple under the dog's loose skin. Drag finally righted himself, his stubby legs barely able to keep his belly from rubbing the couch's leather. He managed to get a single wag from his tail before it sagged like a deflated balloon.

Harry clipped the leash to his collar and, as his name implied, had to drag him from the couch and toward the library and the curving stairs beyond. Mercer smiled as he heard Harry tug the recalcitrant dog across the tile foyer to the front door. Harry called up, "If you finish with Ira before midnight I'll be at Tiny's."

"I don't think so."

"Okay then, I'll see you tomorrow."

Ira was already at a table when Mercer stepped into the trendy Thai bistro. A trio of women sipping cosmopolitans at the bar eyed Mercer as he entered the room carrying a never-used gym bag. He didn't see them but spotted Ira at a table near the back. Ira already had a pair of drinks waiting. Lasko had removed his suit jacket and

117

loosened his tie, but couldn't shed his thirty years in the military. He sat straight, with his fingers laced, while his eyes never rested.

"You look beat," the deputy national security advisor said by way of greeting. They didn't bother to shake hands.

"You have an eye for the obvious. The past few weeks and especially the past five days are something I wouldn't mind forgetting."

"I thought this was supposed to be a slam dunk. You go in, find some minerals to make the CAR rich. The UN gets to look good and a little rubs off on us."

"Problem is the minerals aren't there, which I suspected all along, and whatever riches the CAR might eventually have are going to line the pockets of warlords."

"I read a brief about someone coming down from Sudan."

"Caribe Dayce. Charming fellow. All muscle. Favors a machete. He's dead."

Ira didn't show surprise. "You?"

"I wish." A waiter came to take their orders. Mercer demurred. The sandwich he'd had earlier lay like a stone in his stomach. Ira ordered enough food for two. Mercer continued when the young Asian had stepped away. "Dayce actually had me and a woman named Cali Stowe staked out for a firing squad when this group of" —

Mercer wasn't sure what to call his rescuers — "soldiers came out of nowhere and gunned down all of his men."

"Locals? Peacekeepers?"

"Neither. I don't know who they were. They just came out of nowhere, did their thing, and warned me to never come back."

"Who is Cali Stowe?" Ira rarely made comments until he had all the facts.

"That's one of the things I'd like you to find out for me. She claimed to work for the CDC but when I called I got the impression she was using them as a cover. Also when we parted ways at Kennedy I saw her get into a government car. If she's on Uncle Sam's payroll I'd like to know why she happened to be the same place I was."

"I can make a few calls. Anything else?"

Mercer plucked Chester Bowie's canteen from the gym bag and set it on the table. He then withdrew the misshapen bullet from his pocket. The copper glinted in the restaurant's dim lighting. "I'd like these looked at by an expert. Especially the bullet." Mercer took nearly a half hour to tell him the story he'd heard from the old woman and lay out everything that had happened from the moment Cali had approached him in Kivu. Ira jotted a few notes on a napkin.

"White mercenary. Eye patch. Pauly or Poli. Eastern European accent. Got it." The admiral set his pen aside and pushed away the near-empty plates. "So what's your take?"

"At first I thought that village was where the U.S. mined its uranium for the Manhattan Project, but I can't believe we'd kill off the witnesses."

"Agreed. But where does that leave us?"

"It's gotta be the Germans," Mercer answered quickly. "They had a pretty sophisticated nuclear program during the war. Somehow they learned about a vein of incredibly concentrated uranium ore and sent out an expedition to get it."

"And Chester Bowie?"

"It's just a guess but maybe he was the prospector the Germans used to find the uranium. From what the woman told me it was just a few weeks or months after he left that a bunch of other white men arrived. If he got word to the Nazi high command, it would take about that long to put together a team and get them on the ground."

"So he's a traitor who helped the Nazis during World War Two?"

"Possibly. Or maybe he was coerced or didn't know who backed his original exploration. That's what I want to find out."

"How?"

"I entered his name in a search engine and came up with over a hundred thousand hits. Bowie State University. Bowie, Maryland. Jim Bowie. Bowie knives. Teen sluts with big bowies. But I have a better plan to track him down."

"Okay, I'll leave you to that. What about the town now? Is the old mine still dangerous? I mean could someone go there and dig up their own concentrated uranium?"

"I doubt it. From what I saw it looks played out. Whoever mined it took everything. And as of three days ago the village no longer exists. In my report to Adam Burke I'm going to recommend that a team from the International Atomic Energy Agency go in once things calm down, just to make sure."

"With Dayce dead, shouldn't it be quiet now?"

"It'll take a few weeks or months. With Dayce out of the way there will be a dozen or more petty warlords fighting to take over the remains of his army."

Ira was quiet for a moment, furrows on his forehead extending up to the crown of his shaved skull. "How did Bowie find it in the first place?"

Mercer leaned back, a smile on his lips.

He'd known Ira would get to the real mystery about the whole affair. "That's the question nagging me since Cali and I got out of the CAR. The village isn't even a blip on the map. The geology in the area doesn't look conducive for uranium and yet sixty-odd years ago this guy walks into the jungle and starts to shovel overburden as though there was an X on the ground with a sign saying 'Dig here.' "

"You have any idea how he did it?"

"Either he was the greatest prospecting geologist I've never heard of or the luckiest SOB in history."

Ira motioned to the waiter that he wanted the bill, then stood. "I'll call as soon as I learn anything."

"What parts of this story do I keep out of my report to the United Nations?"

Ira didn't have to think. "As much as you can. I told them about you as a favor to the President. It doesn't mean I want you sharing any secrets with them. In fact, ax your recommendation about sending in a group from the IAEA."

Having seen firsthand a number of UN failures in Africa and elsewhere, Mercer was inclined to agree. "I'll contact Connie Van Buren at DOE." Constance Van Buren was the secretary of energy, a longtime friend of

Mercer's. "I'll see if she can send some of her own inspectors."

"I'd wait on even that," Ira said guardedly. "Let's dig a little on our own before you contact her. You said the place is too dangerous now anyway."

Ira Lasko had also picked up that there were elements to what had happened that didn't add up. The admiral paused for a second, looking down at Mercer, who was sliding a credit card from his wallet. "What's your sense of the group who took out Dayce and his men?"

"Don't ask me how or why but I think they knew about the mine and had gone there to make sure Dayce didn't discover it."

"If the mine's played out like you said, what's the point?"

Mercer had no answer. But he would find it.

New York City

The Upper East Side co-op had a commanding view of Central Park and the apartment towers beyond. It had four bedrooms, a study, and a small suite for a live-in servant. The dining table could seat a dozen. The owner stood on the balcony, the first brush of a spring breeze blowing through his dark hair. He wore black linen slacks, a black silk shirt, and black shoes. He scanned the park like a hawk eyeing an open meadow, as if he too were searching for prey. In one hand he held a slim cell phone. In the other he cradled a snifter of seventy-year-old cognac.

The man was in his mid-forties, unmarried but handsome enough to rarely want for female companionship. He hadn't earned the money to buy the co-op, that had been earned generations earlier. His older brother ran the family's empire, a far-reaching conglomerate with interests on four continents. A lesser man might have been jealous of the power his brother wielded, not only over the company but over the family as well. Yet because of the career path he'd chosen and what he'd done with the contacts he'd made, he was close to reaching a pinnacle of power his brother couldn't even conceive.

The roots of the operation came from within his own family history, from a story he'd learned from his grandmother, so in a sense he'd been planning it since childhood, although he'd never told a soul. This was to be something he alone would accomplish. His brother needed an army of lawyers and accountants to keep the business running, while he was about to change history with a select few.

The cell phone rang. He answered it quickly. "Hello?"

"It's me, darling, I was wondering if you'd reconsidered my proposal."

It took him a moment to recognize the voice — Michaela Taftsbury's, an international attorney from London currently working in New York — and to recall her proposal — a weekend at a bed and breakfast in Vermont.

"Michaela, I told you I can't leave the city."

"It's a weekend, not a fortnight, lover. I haven't seen you in so long."

Best to end it now, he decided. While she was a passable conversationalist and highly charged in the bedroom, she was becoming bothersome. "And you won't see me for even longer," he warned, "if you keep pestering me."

"Pestering? Pestering! Screw you. I thought we were having a little fun. If I've become a pest then to hell with you." She hung up.

But the phone rang almost immediately. *Damn it.* He shouldn't have dumped her before he got the call he was waiting for. Now he'd waste precious time assuaging her feelings so he could get her off the phone. He'd only break up with her later. He checked the phone's caller ID feature. It was an international call with a country code he didn't recognize. This was it!

"Poli?" he asked when he opened the connection.

"No names!" the one-eyed Bulgarian assassin hissed.

The man in New York ignored the rebuke. He was about to hear the news he'd waited for all his life. "Was it there?"

"At one point maybe it was and maybe it wasn't."

"What are you talking about? Was it there?"

"If it was there someone beat us to it a long time ago."

"It's gone?"

"I didn't stick around long enough to explore the entire region, but it is safe to say that I believe it is all gone."

"You didn't 'stick around'? I am paying you a great deal of money to more than merely 'stick around.' "

"You've *promised* me a great deal of money," the killer reminded sharply. "And I didn't stay because they showed up."

The disappointment was too much. The whole thing could have been wrapped up in a couple of days. Now he was being told the ore was gone. And then Poli's statement finally cut through the man's frustration. "Wait, 'they'? Who are 'they'?" But he knew. All too well, he knew, but still he persisted. "My God, man, you had an army behind you. Caribe Dayce's men are more than ample protection."

"Dayce's dead and so are a lot of his men, so you can forget about paying him the other half you owed to get me to that village. I barely got out myself. This happened five days ago. It's taken me this long to reach Khartoum." A note of professional respect crept into Poli's voice when he added, "You warned me the opposition was good. I had no idea a fire team could move like that."

"They've had centuries to refine their craft. What of the American who was in the area?"

"Which one? There were two. A man and a woman."

"I know nothing of the woman," the man in New York admitted.

"In either case, I don't know what happened to them. I was running the first instant the opposition showed up. Last I saw of the pair they were staked out and about to be executed by Dayce. It's possible they were killed in the cross fire. I don't know."

"I will make inquiries. You'd best come to New York. I have a feeling you'll be needed here."

"My flight's in two hours."

Mercer knew exactly how he'd find Chester Bowie, and he began his search with the optimism of the fatally misguided. He worked under the logical assumption that Bowie wasn't the luckiest SOB in history and that he was a trained geologist, and a damned good one at that. He also assumed that a guy older than fifty wouldn't trek into one of the remotest spots on the globe without a support team. Placing the excavation at the village sometime in the early 1940s and working backward Mercer guessed that Bowie would have graduated from college no earlier than 1913. He gave himself a cushion of another five years and decided to begin his search in 1908.

The next step was simple and that was to search the electronic database for Academics Who's Who for the years between 1908 and 1945. The computer search took less than a second and came up with no Chester Bowies. Not yet concerned, Mercer pushed the search back to 1900, the oldest records on the database, and still came up empty.

He leaned back at his desk and wondered if Bowie hadn't been a good student in college or, worse, if he'd been a self-taught geologist. Mercer was so sure of his investigative technique, he hadn't considered either alternative. He idly brought up Bowie's name on the search engine again and for a fruitless hour called up and scanned random entries.

He wouldn't let go of the idea that Bowie had formal training. No one could have found the uranium deposit without it. He phoned the alumni office of a dozen schools with preeminent geology departments. No Chester Bowie. He called all the major mining schools and still no Bowie, even going back to 1900, which would have made Bowie at least sixty when he went to the CAR. He ate lunch hunched over his computer and let his answering machine pick up the twenty incoming calls. Dinner was Chinese delivery, which he also ate at his desk, and he finally called it a night past one.

He was at his desk at six the following morning, the coffee at his elbow strong enough to take the enamel off his teeth. He continued on with the search engine until nine, when he called the company that ran the Who's Who Web site. He talked his way past two secretaries and finally got the chief archivist on the line. She introduced herself as Mrs. Moreland. From the frailty of her voice he guessed that she might have graduated a couple of years before Chester.

"How can I help you, Dr. Mercer?"

He thought it prudent to use his title, and to embellish the story somewhat. "I'm a field geologist, Mrs. Moreland, and I've just returned from Central Africa, where I came upon a grave in a remote village. The headstone said that the man who was buried

130

there, one Chester Bowie, died in 1942. A village elder remembered the man was also a geologist who had come to the region by himself and that he was mauled to death by a lion."

"How awful," the elderly librarian said.

"Yes. He went on to say that the village has experienced nothing but bad luck ever since, cattle diseases, drought, and the like. He believes that because Bowie's family doesn't know how or where their ancestor died that his spirit still haunts them. It sounds a little strange to us, but animism is the prevalent faith in this part of Africa."

"Dr. Mercer, I'm from New England. I know all about ghost stories."

"I promised the headman that I would try to contact the Bowie family to tell them what happened to Chester."

"And you think I can help?"

"It's a hunch but I believe he was a rather gifted geologist and it's possible that you have records of his academic career. Your records online go back only to 1900 and I was wondering if you could dig back a couple more years."

"No digging required. We are about to load the years 1890 to 1899 onto the site. Give me a moment." She typed so slowly that Mercer spelled out the name in his head. "And here we are. Chester T. Bowie, class of 1899 from Keeler State in New Jersey."

He knew it. "Thank you, Mrs. Moreland. I can contact the college. Hopefully they have records going back that far that give some family history."

"I'm not sure if that will help."

Her tone sent a stone plummeting to the base of Mercer's stomach. "How so?"

"It indicates here that this Chester Bowie graduated summa cum laude with a degree in ancient Greek history."

"Excuse me?"

"I don't think this is your man. He wasn't a geologist. He was a historian."

Mercer cursed and immediately sensed Mrs. Moreland's disapproval over the phone. He apologized, thanking her for her time. He stared into space for a minute, his hand still holding the portable phone. "What the hell," he said and dialed information for the small New Jersey college.

"Our records go back to the day the school was founded by Benjamin Keeler in 1884," a perky coed named Jody in the alumni office assured Mercer when he asked.

"I'm looking for information about Chester Bowie. He graduated in 1899."

"Oh sure," Jody said as though she knew the man. "Bowie the booby."

"Excuse me?"

"Oh, it's a nickname he had. He is sort of, like, a legend here."

"How so?"

"He was a student here and then became a teacher. I guess he was a real whack job. He vanished in the 1930s or something."

The timing could fit had Mercer been wrong about the African woman's age. "Why do you say he was a whack job?"

"I'm not sure. Students here use his name if someone does something stupid, like you know 'pulling a Chester.' It's just, like, a thing we say."

Mercer had thought using the word "like" so often had died out a decade ago. "Is there anyone in the office who could give me a bit more information?"

"Um, not really. I'm here by myself and I don't know when my boss is coming back. She's on maternity leave." Jody went quiet before perking up once again. Her voice jumped several octaves. "But hey, there was like this book written a couple years ago. This woman wrote it and she had a section about Bowie the booby. She gave a couple of signed copies to the school. There's one here someplace." She fumbled through a bunch of drawers, slamming them so the metal rang in Mercer's ears. "Yes! I found it. *Science Beyond the Fringe: Alchemy to Perpetual Motion and Those who Sought the Free Lunch* by Serena Ballard."

Mercer was more than a little intrigued that a historian of ancient Greece was in a book about junk science. He thanked Jody and hung up, typing the title on an Internet bookseller's site.

And there it was: *Science Beyond the Fringe* by Serena Ballard. The book had been published three years earlier and by the looks of it hadn't done well. There were no readers' reviews and the site indicated the book was already out of print.

Next he typed the author's name onto a search engine and came up with an uninspired Web site dedicated to the book. As the title implied, the book chronicled pseudo-scientists in their bizarre quest to invent the impossible. On the single-page site were short paragraphs about some of the stranger folks — a dry cleaner from New York who tried to patent his interstellar telephone, a mechanic from Pennsylvania who spent his life trying to draw usable power from static electicity, and another from California who was convinced he'd deciphered the language of humpback whales.

Mercer got the sense that the book was written with tongue firmly planted in cheek and thought it might make an amusing read. At the bottom of the page was a link where he could e-mail the author so he dashed a quick note to Serena Ballard explaining his interest in Chester Bowie and giving his telephone number.

To his astonishment his phone rang in less than a minute.

"Hello?"

"Dr. Mercer?"

"Yes. Is this Serena Ballard?"

"It is. I can't tell you how surprised I was to get your e-mail."

"About half as much as I appreciate you getting back to me," Mercer said. She had a beautiful throaty voice.

"According to the Web counter on that old site you just doubled the number of hits since it went online."

"I have the feeling the book didn't do as well as you'd hoped."

She chuckled. "The publisher lost my princely advance of one thousand dollars. In truth, *Science Beyond the Fringe* was a labor of love. I sent it to publishers on a lark."

"Still, writing a book is a hell of an accomplishment."

"I did it for my grandfather. If you saw the Web site you might have noticed the bit about the guy in Pennsylvania who tried to harness static electricity."

"Your grandfather?"

"He was inspired by a machine he read about in Ayn Rand's *Atlas Shrugged* and knew he could make it work. He spent every night and weekend in his garage tinkering away. He burned it down once and spent a week in the hospital after nearly electrocuting himself. He got a chance to read my book before he died, but never knew that I managed to get it published. You indicated you wanted some information about Chester Bowie."

"What can you tell me about him and what did he do to merit a mention in your book?"

"Bowie taught ancient history at a place called Keeler College here in New Jersey."

"You're in New Jersey?"

"Yes, I'm the marketing director for the new Deco Palace Hotel and Casino in Atlantic City. It's great. Have you ever been here?"

"No, but I have a friend who considers Atlantic City his third home."

"Third home, wow."

"Not that impressive because he uses my place as his second. Anyway back to Bowie."

"Chester Bowie taught ancient history at Keeler. From what I recall from my research he was a real flake. He muttered to himself all the time and always wore a cape around campus."

"And what did he do to merit a mention in your book?" asked Mercer.

"Well he wasn't a scientist but he *was* a crackpot. That's why he's in there. He was convinced that the creatures from Greek mythology actually existed."

"You mean griffins, Medusa, and giant three-headed dogs?"

"Yup."

"I guess that would certify him as a crack-pot."

"It's not as bad as that," Serena admitted. "What Bowie believed is that ancient Greek farmers plowing their fields discovered bones from animals that went extinct in the last ice age. Not knowing how the skeletons fit together, he believed they created all kinds of fantastic monsters from the bones, mixing and matching as they went along and then inventing stories about their creations."

Mercer absorbed what she'd just said and

couldn't find any quick flaws in Bowie's theory. It was a simple, elegant answer to a question he'd never considered, but it got him no closer to explaining how Chester Bowie came to be at a high-grade uranium deposit in Central Africa where he presumably vanished in the mid-1930s.

"He had no other interests? Geology for example?"

"Not that I'm aware of." Serena paused. "I hate to say this but I don't remember much about him. I wrote the book a few years before I got it published, and Bowie was only a couple of paragraphs. I still have boxes at home with some of my old research material. There might be something in one of them. I could look through it and mail you anything I find."

Mercer considered her offer. He doubted he was on the right track even though the dates somewhat corresponded with what he knew. This could very well be the wrong Chester Bowie. However, he had nowhere else to turn. Pressed by a vague sense of urgency, he asked, "Would it be possible for me to come up and get them?" He sensed hesitancy. "I assure you I'm not a stalker or anything. I can even meet you at the hotel." Mercer knew he'd have to bring Harry. The old bastard would pout for weeks if he knew

Mercer had gone to a casino without him.

"Well, I suppose so. I can go home at lunch and grab the stuff. I'm pretty sure I know which box it's in. Are you in New York?"

"No. D.C." Mercer checked his watch. "How about five o'clock in the lobby."

She gave a small laugh. "This hotel is huge. We'd never find each other. How about the Bar Americain. It's right next to the casino's main entrance."

"Bar Americain it is it is. Five o'clock. And, Serena, thank you."

"I'm glad I can help. I'll even see what I can do about getting you a room comped." Then she added as an afterthought, "I never asked. What's this all about, anyway?"

"I'll tell you when we meet. Suffice it to say that Chester Bowie found something and it sure wasn't minotaur bones."

Mercer checked the time again and decided it was still too early for Harry to be at Tiny's, so he called White's apartment. When he got no answer he tried Tiny's but even the owner, Paul Gordon, wasn't there. He climbed the back stairs up to the rec room to refresh the inch of tar-thick coffee fused to the bottom of his mug. Harry was slouched at the bar, pen poised over the *Washington Post* crossword, a Bloody Mary within easy reach.

"Morning," he growled.

Mercer shook his head slowly. "Help yourself to my paper and booze."

"Already done, my boy, already done."

"Feel like going for a ride?"

"No." Harry didn't look up from the puzzle. "Tiny's getting some guys together for a poker game tonight. I'm gonna crash on your couch this afternoon to rest up for it."

"I'm going to Atlantic City."

Still Harry remained slouched, but he didn't miss a beat. "Drag, get your leash. You're spending the day with Uncle Tiny."

The dog raised himself over the back of the couch to regard his master through bloodshot eyes. His head was bowed so that his ears dangled past his long gray muzzle. He gave one soulful bawl.

"Sorry, pooch, I'm exchanging your crap for a game of craps today."

"We're getting a room for the night. Go home and pack. I'll pick you up in an hour."

"I'll be ready in fifteen minutes."

ATLANTIC CITY, NEW JERSEY

The tires of Mercer's Jaguar convertible gave a slight chirp as he pulled into a spot near the top floor in the parking structure adjacent to the Deco Palace Hotel and Casino. He killed the engine but could do nothing to stifle the excited monologue Harry had kept up since getting off the Garden State.

"Then there was this time I was here, oh, must have been eighty-eight or eighty-nine with Jim Read. You remember Jimmy? For some reason he and I drifted apart when he got sober."

"You drifted apart for the same reason feminists don't hang out with pornographers," Mercer said sarcastically.

Harry ignored his remark. "Anyway, we came up here and I have never seen someone as hot with the dice. Not Jimmy. I swear to God the dice would land on their edges for him. No, it was this little old biddy, well, she was probably five years younger than I am now, but could she roll. She must have gone on —"

"The way you're going on now?" Mercer interrupted.

"Give me a break, will you. I haven't been to a casino since you were in Canada."

"That's what, seven months, Harry?"

"Five. Tiny and I came up when you went back to finish your contract with DeBeers."

Mercer unlimbered himself from the sports car. "And you took my Jag, no doubt."

Harry held a Zippo to his Chesterfield and arched his brows at Mercer. "No doubt."

From the elevator a moving walkway glided them through a long tunnel lined with advertisements for shows, restaurants, and of course, the gaming tables. Keeping with the hotel's Art Deco theme, big band played over hidden speakers. The other guests riding with them were mostly older New Yorkers uniformly dressed in nylon sweat clothes in neon colors with gold chains resting on fleshy breasts for the women and mats of graying hair for the men. None of the couples spoke to each other. They seemed intent on getting to the games with as little distraction as possible.

The conveyor ended at the lobby. The

expansive space was themed after the old iron-and-glass railway stations seen in hundreds of movies from the thirties and forties, but with Art Deco accents on the walls and numerous columns. The reception desk ran along one wall with a commanding view of the boardwalk and the ocean beyond. Opposite was a real locomotive, puffing ersatz steam, connected to a pair of beautifully restored Pullman cars. There were forests of potted palms and all the staff were dressed in period uniforms.

"There it is," Harry said, pointing across the vast lobby to the Bar Americain.

"Leave it to you to find the bar." Mercer checked his watch. They were a half hour early but he could use a drink.

They ducked into the bar, which was remarkably intimate despite its size. The room looked like it had been the set for Rick's Café Americain from *Casablanca*. There was even a black piano player at an old upright, and while he was probably named Jamal or Antoine, his staff badge identified him as Sam.

Harry muttered, "I feel I should be wearing a tux and drinking champagne cocktails."

They sat at the alabaster-topped bar. Harry ordered a Jack and ginger while

Mercer asked for a gimlet.

"Of all the gin joints in all the towns in all the world . . ."

Mercer recognized the voice at once, but couldn't believe it. He swiveled on his bar stool. Cali Stowe wore a black suit with flared slacks and a cream silk shell. Her ruby hair danced and tangled to her shoulders. Her lips were such a bright red that he had trouble dragging his eyes to hers. There was humor in them that sparkled into a smile. She'd looked beautiful in Africa, unwashed and dressed in wrinkled safari clothes. Here she was absolutely stunning and it took Mercer a moment to get over his shock.

"Here's looking at you, kid," he finally stammered and saluted her with his glass.

"Buy a lady a drink?" She didn't wait for an answer and addressed the bartender. "Dewar's rocks with a water back."

"Don't get me wrong," Mercer said, "but you are about the last person in the world I expected to see here. To what do I owe the pleasure?"

She took a sip from her drink. "I'm a compulsive gambler. Can't stay away. Mortgaged the house, sold the car, the works. I live in a Dumpster out back."

"I'm in love," Harry said, then stood to

introduce himself. "Harry White, at your servicing."

She chuckled at his quip and they shook hands. "Hi, Harry. I'm Cali Stowe."

Harry shot Mercer a glance before saying, "She was the one in Africa?"

She too gave Mercer an appraising look. "And now I'm here. What *are* the odds?"

"Pretty even if you're meeting Serena Ballard."

"Head of the class for the guy in the Armani sports coat." She took the stool next to Mercer, forcing Harry to lean over the bar so he could ogle at her. "She and I spoke this afternoon, and imagine my surprise when she told me she already had a meeting to discuss Chester Bowie today."

Still not over his shock, and delight, at seeing Cali, Mercer asked, "So are you going to tell me who you really are? Because I know you don't work for the CDC. Their human resources guy nearly choked when I asked about you."

"Ever heard of NEST?"

"Part of the Department of Energy, isn't it?"

"It stands for Nuclear Emergency Search Team. I'm a member. Our main function is to act as a rapid response force in the event of a nuclear bomb strike or an attack at a nuclear plant. Back in 2003 our charter was changed slightly after President Bush went before the country in his State of the Union address and made a serious boo-boo by saying Saddam had gone uranium shopping in Africa. Because of that gaffe NEST has also been tasked with finding and securing previously unknown sources of uranium. There are ten of us on a team searching the world for old uranium mines, and places where uranium might be found."

"So you weren't lying about how you found that village."

A shadow passed behind her luminous dark eyes and she took a quick sip of her Scotch. Some of her freckles blurred into an angry flush. "Sort of but not exactly. Someone at the CDC contacted me about that village having the highest cancer rate on the planet. When I took that info to my bosses they played around with it for a while, talked it over in a dozen meetings and committees, and finally shelved it, saying, and I quote, 'There are more pressing matters.' "

"Let me guess," Harry chimed in, "you went out on your own?"

Cali nodded, her good humor returning. "If you noticed I'm sitting kind of funny, it's because most of my ass was chewed off when I got back to our field office in New York."

Unbidden, Mercer's mind conjured up the image of her backside. He was in little hurry to force it away but he remarked, "I saw you getting into a Town Car."

"The head of NEST, Cliff Roberts, came to get me personally. That's when the butt chewing began. Part of my left cheek is still in that Lincoln." Cali tossed hair from her forehead in a simple gesture that held Harry entranced. "They bluffed about firing me, then about suspending me. In the end I was ordered to take a week's worth of personal days and come back," she deepened her voice to an approximation of her superior, " 'with the proper attitude of a team player.' I envy you, Mercer, for not having to deal with government BS."

"One of my first jobs was working for the USGS. It wasn't bad as bureaucracies go but I knew I'd never make it there for long." He thought back to their time at the village, making certain connections now that he knew her true purpose in being there. Some discrepancies came to light. "When you stepped into the bush for a little privacy . . . ?"

"I was checking a Geiger counter. If you were anyone other than a geologist, I could

147

have done it in the clear and made up a story. You would have seen through the ploy in a second, forcing me into the jungle with tales of diarrhea."

"Sorry to cause you the embarrassment. Now that I think of it you weren't all that pale coming back and you made a miraculous recovery."

She grinned. "I'm not a method actor and I wasn't kidding about having an iron stomach."

"So what did the Geiger tell you?"

"There wasn't much radiation above normal ambient. However large the lode was, it was all cleared out back in the thirties or forties and erosion would have carried away any contaminated soil long ago."

"I'm leaning toward the 1930s," Mercer told her. "Not long after Chester Bowie made his discovery."

"And then the Germans came to mine what Bowie left behind?"

"That's my guess. From what little Ms. Ballard told me about Bowie, I doubt he was a traitor, so I think someone caught wind of his find later on and came back to clear out the vein." Mercer ordered another round. Sam/Jamal/Antoine, the piano player, must have thought there were enough patrons in the bar to start in on a pretty good rendition of "As Time Goes By." He must have played that song a dozen times a day. "So how did you find Bowie?" Mercer asked. "I traced him through his schooling."

"IRS database." Cali sucked on an ice cube and both Harry and Mercer paused to watch her sensual mouth in action. She noticed the scrutiny and quickly crunched down on the cube. It was an absentminded habit that drew more attention than she intended. "In matters of national security, NEST can access some pretty powerful databases. Since I'm out sick, I had one of my teammates do the search. He led me to Keeler so I called the school's president and he passed on the information about Serena Ballard's book. I called her *et voilà,* here I am.

"What I don't get," she continued, "is what that mine has to do with a loopy classics professor. Serena filled me in a little about Bowie's theories and it doesn't jibe at all with what we found. If he went out playing amateur archaeologist to prove his theory about ice age bones, he would have gone to Greece. How did he end up in Africa?"

"With luck Serena's notes might shed a little light on the subject."

"That reminds me," Cali said quickly.

"The president of Keeler is ticked at her. She was supposed to have returned her research material to the school years ago. So make sure I tell her that it all has to go back."

A lone woman in her forties entered the dim bar. Unlike the tourists ebbing and flowing into the room, she wore a business suit and carried a briefcase. She had long blond hair and a chubby round face. Mercer put her height at about five three and her weight somewhere around his own. He guessed that there was Pennsylvania Dutch not too far down her family tree. She spotted the trio at the bar and made her way across the room. It had to be Serena Ballard.

"Dr. Mercer? Ms. Stowe?"

"You found us," Cali answered.

"Hi, I'm Serena Ballard."

"Please call me Cali." Even seated on the stool, Cali was almost a head taller than the casino executive.

"And people generally call me Mercer." He shook her hand, noting that her eyes were cornflower blue. "This is my friend Harry White."

Harry didn't repeat his servicing joke again. His instincts had been spot-on that Cali would see the humor. He didn't think

Serena Ballard would. "Pleased to meet you."

Serena looked first at Mercer and then to Cali. "Three years after my book comes out and not one but two people suddenly show an interest."

"Mercer and I are working on the same problem from different perspectives and came to the same conclusion — you. Can we get you a drink?"

"Just a diet Coke. Why don't we grab a booth away from the piano." She hoisted her bag. "I brought everything I could find. Actually there is a lot more than I remembered and it reminded me that I was supposed to return it all to Keeler College."

Cali grabbed up her and Serena's drinks. "The school's president asked me to ask you about that." She then quipped, "He made it sound as though there was a long line of scholars clamoring for the Chester Bowie files."

Once they were settled at a corner booth, Serena emptied the contents of the collapsible briefcase onto the table. There were about ten musty notebooks, several old manila folders, and clutches of loose papers. Mercer, Harry, and Cali started leafing through the notebooks. It was clear from the eager look on her face that Serena wanted to help but had little to add. "There isn't much I can tell you. I looked through some of this in my office but I'm afraid it didn't jog my memory. As I told you over the phone, I wrote the book a long time ago and Chester Bowie wasn't a very big part of it."

"How did you first hear about him?" Cali asked over the top of a brittle notebook.

"My father-in-law went to Keeler. He was the one who told me about him when I was working on the book. Even though he vanished sometime in the 1930s, students still talked about Bowie the booby when my father-in-law was a student. I just contacted the school and told them I was writing about Bowie. They sent me everything they had in their archives."

Cali continued to press. "You hadn't come across his name in any other source?"

"No, sorry." Serena sipped at her soft drink. "What is this all about?"

Mercer set aside the notebook he was thumbing through. "We found a canteen in a small village in Central Africa that once belonged to Chester Bowie. An old woman there remembered him from her childhood. She also told us that shortly after Bowie left, other white men came and killed a number of people."

"My God, that's awful. Why would they do such a thing?"

Mercer just shrugged, since she didn't need to know about the uranium mine. "We don't know. We hoped that this material might provide a clue."

Serena bit her lower lip. "Are you two looking into this for yourself or is this some kind of government thing?"

"I work for the government," Cali replied. "I'm sorry I can't tell you in what capacity. Mercer's a civilian consultant."

Mercer tried to suppress a smile. Cali had put just the right hint of intrigue in her voice for Serena Ballard to make her own inference and also to make the offer without being asked. "I was going to let you keep this stuff overnight so I can return it to Keeler, but if this is something official you should keep it until you're done with it. Just get it back to me so I can forward it."

Mercer gave her his best smile. "I'll do you one better. I'll send it to Keeler myself, with the promise that we'll keep you informed as best as we're able."

Serena beamed at being included. "I can't ask for anything more." She stood. "Oh, and good to my word I got you some rooms compliments of the Deco Palace Hotel. You should be in the system already. Just give your names to one of the receptionists."

"And don't you worry," Harry said, shaking her hand, "the hotel will more than make up the cost by the time I'm through tonight."

After Serena had gone, they received their room cards at the reception desk. Harry dumped his overnight bag on Mercer with the vague promise to be back before they left Atlantic City in the morning. He gave his cane a jaunty wrist flick with each pace as he headed for the craps tables. Their rooms were on different floors, so Mercer gave Cali half of the documents Serena had provided and kept the other half for himself. They made arrangements to meet for dinner at eight.

Mercer decided against a quick shower and instead sat himself in a club chair in his room and began scanning Chester Bowie's notebooks. After leafing through just a dozen pages he was convinced that Jody, the alumni receptionist at Keeler College, was correct. Bowie was a whack job. His writing style rambled from subject to subject with no discernible pattern. In one paragraph he railed against Sir Arthur Evans's work on Minoan culture at Knossos and in the next he gave scientific reasons why the sun couldn't have melted Icarus's wax-and-

154

feather wings. He wrote that the boy must have blacked out from hypoxia and crashed into the sea, as if the mythological story was fact.

Once he'd established in his mind that the bones of ice age creatures were the basis for demons and monsters, Chester Bowie treated all the ancient myths as if they were real and sought to explain them logically. Or at least as logically as he could. He believed that the famous Gordian knot was simply a hedge maze at the entrance to Phrygia and Alexander the Great merely chopped it down with his sword.

Mercer was well into the third notebook when the phone rang. "Hello?"

"I forgot what room you are in," Cali said breathlessly.

"1092."

"I'll be right up. I found it."

A minute later he opened the door to Cali's insistent knock. She blew into the room, her eyes alight. She'd removed her blazer and he could see the shape of her small breasts and how they moved under the silk of her shell. "Chester Bowie was certifiable but he was also a genius."

Mercer found himself immediately caught up in her enthusiasm. "What did you find?"

"Adamantine."

"Huh?"

She threw him a teasing smile. "Not the geologist you thought you were?"

"Always suspected I wasn't," Mercer replied. "What's adamantine?"

"In Greek stories of creation, after the gods had fashioned the earth," she glanced at a note card, "Epimetheus and his brother were given the job of fashioning all the animals. Some were given wings, others claws, some got speed, some got strength. Unfortunately Epimetheus gave out all the best attributes, so when it came to man he had nothing left in his bag of tricks and he asked his brother for advice. The brother told him what would make an appropriate gift to man so Epimetheus went up to the heavens and lit a torch from the sun and bestowed fire to man, making him superior to all creatures. As you might imagine this wasn't what Zeus, chief god of all the gods, had in mind. In anger —"

Mercer finished the story. "In anger Zeus had Epimetheus's brother, Prometheus, chained to a mountain where birds ate his spleen."

"Exactly." Cali checked her card again. "It was Mount Caucasus and it was his liver, actually. The chains were reportedly made of unbreakable metal called adamantine that

Jupiter himself had mined. Only Hercules' strength was enough to break the links and free Prometheus."

"So what does this have to do with Bowie?"

"Don't you see? Through his research he thought he had found Jupiter's secret adamantine mine. He went to Central Africa to prove that adamantine really existed, just one more step in proving that everything about ancient mythology was real. But instead of some legendary metal he discovered a vein of naturally enriched uranium."

Mercer shook his head. "Hold it. He trekked into the most remote part of the world because he thought he'd found the mother lode of an imaginary metal."

Cali grinned at his skepticism. "I'll do you one better. He got a grant from Princeton in the fall of 1936 to go looking for his adamantine mine."

"Princeton? Princeton backed this lunatic?"

"To the tune of two thousand dollars. Not large by today's standards but in the 1930s that's not chump change." She handed him a memo on Princeton letterhead. The letter, from a Professor Swartz at the Institute for Advanced Study at Princeton, stated that indeed Bowie had been given two thousand dollars to pursue his work on procuring "the elemental metal you outlined in your grant request." Mercer read the short note a second time, as if not believing his first reading. He looked up. Cali had a smug look on her face.

"Why the hell would someone fund this guy? He was off his rocker."

"Apparently this Professor Swartz didn't think so. Since I found our link, you're buying dinner."

Mercer didn't acknowledge her. There was something about the date that struck a chord. Princeton in the 1930s. What was happening at Princeton in the 1930s?

"Did you hear me?" Cali noted the faraway look in Mercer's eyes.

And then Mercer remembered. Not what was happening at Princeton in the 1930s. The question was who. Without thinking he reached across and drew Cali to him, kissing her hard. "You are a genius!"

Flustered, but not disturbed by the sudden kiss, she asked, "What? What did I do?"

"Do you know who happened to be at Princeton in the Institute for Advanced Study in the 1930s? Hell, he was there until he died in the fifties." Mercer didn't wait for an answer. "Albert Einstein, that's who. And while he didn't send that letter to

President Roosevelt until just before the war detailing how his theories could create an atomic bomb, he must have suspected that Bowie was on to something and had this guy Swartz fund the expedition. Einstein knew Bowie hadn't found adamantine, but believed that he might stumble on highly concentrated uranium, maybe a source with naturally occurring isotopes of U-235, which is usually refined from the more common U-238 in centrifuges. That's what they needed to sustain a chain reaction."

"Einstein sent Bowie to find the uranium?"

"That's the only theory that fits the facts." Mercer spoke faster and faster. "Somehow, God knows where, Bowie found something in his studies that mentions the location of Zeus's adamantine mine. Maybe he made the connection to uranium or maybe it was someone else, but his idea eventually gets Einstein's attention. Einstein knew that Fermi and a couple of others were working on creating a nuclear chain reaction at the University of Chicago. He believed that Bowie's adamantine might just be the uranium isotopes the team needed for their experiment, so he gets Princeton to fund the expedition."

"So what happened? The first sustained

chain reaction didn't occur until 1942."

Mercer was surprised she knew the date but had to remind himself that Cali wasn't a medical researcher, as she'd once claimed. Instead she was a trained nuclear specialist and would surely know the history of her chosen field. "The girl at Keeler told me he vanished. Chester Bowie never made it back from Africa with his samples, leaving Fermi's group to enrich their own uranium."

"Let's not get ahead of ourselves. We can't be sure that he found a vein of U-235."

"Come on, Cali, it was strong enough to kill dozens of people over the years from acute radiation sickness. I've never heard of a case of natural uranium doing that, especially since their village is a good half mile from the mine. You need proximity to radiation to feel its effects."

She conceded the point with a nod. "So what happened to Bowie?"

"No clue. He could have been eaten by crocodiles on his way out. Eaten by a rival tribe for all I know. If he died out there, then he's carrying a sample of whatever the Germans came back to take later on."

"There's no way we're ever going to find his body after all these years."

It was Mercer's turn to admit his enthusiasm was getting the best of him, but he wasn't going to admit defeat. "I won't let the trail just die here. There must be something. Maybe there are archives at Princeton. Letters between Bowie and Einstein. I think I read someplace that he kept pretty complete records of his correspondence."

"Should be easy enough to get," Cali said. "Princeton's not that far. If we leave early enough we can get there when they open tomorrow."

"You're on. I'll book this room again for Harry. He and I can head back to D.C. the day after. We should finish reading Bowie's notebooks first. There may be other clues."

"Agreed, but not before you buy me dinner. It's near enough eight now." Cali suddenly became aware that her nipples were pressed against the silk of her sleeveless shell. She'd long ago admitted she didn't have much in the way of breasts, she also knew men would look no matter the size. She gave Mercer high marks for not leering. "I'm just going to run down to my room for a minute. I'll meet you at the elevators in the lobby."

Cali finally came down from her room fifteen minutes later, and while the effects were subtle, she'd taken the time to apply some makeup and fix her hair. Mercer felt like a slob for not showering earlier. They dined at a restaurant in the hotel called Margeaux, and despite the urgency they'd felt up in Mercer's room, they took their time over crocks of onion soup, Dover sole and Beef Wellington, and thick wedges of Black Forest cake. Mercer had left the wine selection to Cali since his only knowledge of the vintner's art was to avoid anything that comes in a box. When they were finished their meal, the bottle was empty and the restaurant was nearly deserted.

It wasn't until their conversation drifted into a companionable silence and lingering glances that the guilt slammed into Mercer like a sledgehammer blow. He hadn't known the exact moment their working dinner had become a date, his first since Tisa, but that's how he felt about it now and the delicious meal turned sour in his stomach. He thought he'd given no outward sign but somehow Cali picked up on his distress.

"Are you okay?"

Lying is what he should have done, blamed eating too much, and moved on. It would have been easy and he could have kept Tisa's memory locked away, barely reined, but still under control. But before he could open his mouth, the idea of lying faded. Tisa's memory wasn't under control. It was controlling him. It wasn't reined; it rode free across his mind, and until he exorcised it, it would always be there.

"I lost someone very dear to me six months ago." Cali had to lean across the candlelit table to hear him. "Tonight was the first time since then I've had dinner with a woman. This dinner wasn't a date, but sitting here with you it was easy to imagine it was. I was overwhelmed by guilt."

"Thank you for sharing that. I know it couldn't have been easy."

"I have a tendency to keep stuff locked away."

"What man doesn't?"

Mercer gave a low chuckle. "True. I guess it's just easier than admitting there's something wrong. You pretend you can handle the pain, and usually you can, but sometimes . . ."

"Sometimes you need to talk."

"Talk or just admit to yourself it's okay to have feelings."

"Women often complain about men shutting them out," Cali said. "I've had my share of that, but I also came to realize that men's silences can be just as cathartic as when women vent. The dangerous guys, the ones you have to look out for, are the ones that don't even allow themselves the silence. I've never lost anyone close to me, so I can't imagine how it feels. I will say that you seem to be handling it pretty well. I think we had a good time tonight. I know I did. Had you not been dealing with her death, you wouldn't have allowed yourself even this."

Cali let that sink in before setting her napkin on the table. They stood and made their way back to the elevator. "Why don't we meet here at seven?"

"Okay. Sorry to end the night on a down note."

Her smile was the most charming he'd ever seen on her. "You ended it perfectly." When her elevator reached her floor, she gave his cheek a gentle kiss. "See you in the morning."

Mercer held the elevator open until she was in her room. He thought he'd come off sounding like a morose dolt pining for an unrequited love, and she thought the night had ended perfectly. He repeated to himself something Harry was fond of saying: "The only thing you'll ever truly understand about a woman is what she'll let you understand."

ATLANTIC CITY, NEW JERSEY

Two minutes on the Internet would have saved Mercer and Cali about six hours but would have cost them a bucolic ride and a self-guided tour of Princeton's campus. The Institute for Advanced Study wasn't affiliated with the Ivy League school. It had been started in 1930 with money from Newark department store magnate Louis Bamberger as a place for theoretical mathematicians and physicists. The small institute did not archive any of their most famous thinker's papers. In fact, Einstein's home was merely another piece of property for faculty housing.

A harried staff member, who had answered the same question for countless people, told them that all of Einstein's papers had been bequeathed to the Hebrew University of Jerusalem. In conjunction with Caltech, they were making much of the material available online.

Back in Mercer's room at the Deco Palace, he handed her a beer from the minibar and opened one for himself. The sun was setting and the hotel cast a long shadow over the boardwalk. Cali checked that she had a connection with the hotel's Wi-Fi and quickly located the archive. They found that there was a document of some sort in the collection from a Ch. Bowie; however, that particular piece of writing couldn't be accessed through the Internet.

"What time is it in Israel?" Cali asked, reaching for the phone. "Never mind, it doesn't matter." She dialed a long number from memory, and when it was answered she asked for Ari Gradstein.

"Who is Ari Gradstein?" Mercer asked.

"The deputy director for Israel's Demona nuclear research facility. We've worked together a few times on responses to nuclear terrorism," Cali replied, then picked up the conversation with the Israeli when he came on the line. "Ari, it's Cali Stowe from NEST." She paused, listening. "Good, how are you? . . . Excellent. And Shoshana? . . . Great. Listen, Ari, I need an official favor. I'd like you to cut through the bureaucracy for me at the Hebrew University in Jerusalem. I can't tell you what it's about yet other than to say I highly doubt the state of Israel is at risk. I'm researching an American who wrote to Einstein, and all his papers are archived at the university. . . . Yeah, I know. It surprised me too. I wasted a couple of hours at Princeton thinking they were there.

"Could you call over there for me and clear the way? I'm going under the assumption that as soon as I identified myself as someone from the DOE, all sorts of red flags would go up and it would be weeks before I got an answer." Cali rattled off her e-mail address and then the university's reference number for the document authored by Ch. Bowie. "Thanks, Ari, I owe you one. Bye."

Mercer was impressed. "Even if I had a contact in Israel, I never would have thought of that. You were brilliant."

Cali smiled at the compliment. "And sometimes knowing your way around a bureaucracy isn't a bad thing."

Harry returned to the room while they waited for an e-mail from Israel. He was bleary-eyed and his cheeks were prickled with silver stubble. It was the first Mercer had seen of him in nearly twenty hours.

"Well, well, well. Look what the cat dragged in. Have you been gambling this whole time?"

Harry lowered himself to the bed with an

exaggerated groan. "God, no. I stopped for breakfast this morning."

"And how'd you do?" Mercer asked, knowing the answer by Harry's dejected look.

Harry propped himself against the pillows, his eyes closed. "Never ask a gambler that until he's done."

"That bad, eh?"

The old man suddenly leaned forward and pulled thick bundles of cash from both pockets of his windbreaker. He spoke mildly, as though it were no big deal. "Actually I think I did all right for myself."

"Holy shit!" Mercer and Cali exclaimed at the same time. "How much?" Mercer asked.

Harry roared in triumph. "Thirty grand, my boy! I crushed 'em. I was unstoppable. I even told them I was staying at Trump's so they'd comp me a suite last night to keep me here."

"You wily son of a bitch," Mercer muttered in astonishment.

"Congratulations," Cali added. "What are you going to do with all that money?"

Harry eyed her as though she were an idiot. "Gamble it away tonight, of course."

Cali looked like she was going to try to dissuade Harry from blowing his winnings.

Mercer knew better. Her laptop pinged and all thoughts of Harry's windfall vanished. It was an e-mail from the Hebrew University. The archivist who sent it wasn't happy about answering a request past midnight but said they'd found what Cali had asked for. "This is it," Cali said and opened the attachment. It was a telegram sent to Einstein in April of 1937 from Athens, Greece. Mercer read over her shoulder:

May I inquire as to your health, sir? It has been seven weeks since I left. I have spent my vacation near Lake Como. My hotel reminds me a little of that monstrosity Hearst built. At least there is plenty of sunshine and fresh air. I've found some trinkets you'd enjoy and plan to ship soonest. I could not find the Gibson print of Drake's Golden Hind you so wanted. I did locate that recording by Stephan Enburg you asked for. In my opinion that is a small success, but I can't imagine why you liked it. Too much oboe, not enough flute.

Ch. Bowie
PS fail fall ball bill fill pill poll
pall pail pain gain

Cali was the first to voice her assessment.

"What the hell is this? It's meaningless. Lake Como? He was in Africa, and that bit about seven weeks. Bowie'd been gone for months. How did he end up in Athens? And what's with the postscript?"

"It's got to be code," Mercer said. "Maybe he and Einstein had some prearranged signal concerning the expedition. He says he had a small success. The name Stephan Enburg could mean something specific, like that Bowie found the mine. Had he not found it, maybe it would have been a different name."

"Maybe, maybe, maybe. Damn it." She blew a frustrated breath.

"Let me see that," Harry called. Mercer swiveled the laptop so Harry could read the telegram.

"Gibson's print of Drake's Golden Hind?" Cali questioned aloud. "What is that?"

"Drake is Sir Francis Drake," Mercer replied, "an English admiral and privateer around the time of Queen Elizabeth the first. The *Golden Hind* was his flagship. My knowledge of art ends with dogs playing poker, so I'm guessing that Gibson was an artist who created a famous portrait of him. When Harry's done, we can search it on the Internet along with a composer named Stephan Enburg. It might give us a clue what Bowie meant.

"Don't bother," Harry said, looking up from the computer. His blue eyes were alight with a devilish spark. "The real question you need to answer is if Chester Bowie made it aboard the *Hindenburg* like he planned."

"What are you talking about?"

"Give me a pen and a piece of paper and I'll show you." Cali handed him some hotel stationary and her Montblanc. "The clue's in the postscript. That line Bowie wrote is called a doublet, a word game invented by Lewis Carroll, the guy who wrote *Alice in Wonderland.* The object of the game is to transform one word into another, usually with the opposite meaning, by changing one letter at a time and using as few words as possible. Bowie turned fail into gain using eleven words including the original."

"Oh I see," Cali exclaimed. "Change an I into an L and fail becomes fall, then change the F to a B and you get ball."

"And so on. Except Bowie messed it up and it was deliberate."

"How so?" asked Mercer.

"It's obvious that he knew the rules of a doublet since he wrote one out, but he used eleven words when you can change fail into gain with only four." And he wrote: fail pail pain gain.

Mercer nodded at what Harry had done. "This is all well and good and I'm sure provides hours of entertainment to the gaming set, but how does this get us to Bowie being on the *Hindenburg?*"

"Eleven words when four would do. I guessed eleven is the key to the telegram, and when you count out every eleventh word you get . . ." Harry wrote out the secret message: May seven Lake Hearst air ship Hind Enburg. Success oboe. "Bowie was telling Einstein that he was returning to the United States aboard the airship *Hindenburg* and to have him met on May 7 in Lakehurst. Success is obvious, but I don't know what that bit about oboes means."

"I do," Mercer and Cali said at the same time and exchanged a grin. He indicated for her to explain. "Obo is a large town in the Central African Republic. It's pretty close to where we found Bowie's canteen."

"He was telling Einstein the approximate location to the uranium deposit," Mercer summed up.

"Didn't everyone die when the *Hindenburg* blew up?" Cali asked the men, but she was looking at Harry.

Harry edged his chin toward Mercer. "Ask

him. He's the expert."

Mercer demurred. "I'm no expert. I was fascinated by airships when I was young, so I've read a few books about the disaster. A couple of years ago I managed to buy a piece of a girder from the wreck. I hate to say it's been in a closet ever since. And to answer your question, sixty-two of the ninety-seven on board got out of the zeppelin alive. If Bowie was on her that fateful day, there's a one-in-three chance he survived. The man we need to talk to is Carl Dion. He's the real expert and the guy who sold me the girder."

Mercer's near-photographic memory failed him. He knew Dion lived in Breckenridge, Colorado, but couldn't remember the number. He got it from information and dialed the retired aerospace engineer.

"Hello?" a timid woman answered after the seventh ring.

"Mrs. Dion?"

"Yes."

"Mrs. Dion, my name is Philip Mercer. I'm an acquaintance of your husband. Is he there?"

"One moment please."

Three full minutes went by before Carl Dion came on the phone. "Hello. Who is this?"

"Carl, it's Philip Mercer."

"Oh, hello, Dr. Mercer. My wife doesn't hear so well and she told me it was my friend Phyllis Matador, a friend, I needn't point out, I don't have. What can I do for you?"

"I need a little information about a passenger on the last flight of the *Hindenburg*. His name was Bowie, Chester Bowie."

The aviation expert's reply was as instantaneous as it was damning. "No such passenger, I'm afraid."

Tension flooded Mercer's shoulders even as he felt his body deflate. He collapsed into a chair. "Are you sure? I have a telegram from him saying he was going to be on the flight."

"Sorry, but there was no Bowie listed on the passenger manifest. He wouldn't have had a difficult time booking passage. The flight from Germany wasn't even half-full. The zepp's trip back to Europe was, however, fully booked by people going to a coronation."

"Think, Carl; this is important. Is there any way he could have gotten on? Stowed away, perhaps, or under an assumed identity."

"Now that you mention it, there was an anomaly." Mercer's fist tightened around the phone as if physical strength would draw out what he wanted to hear. "A German couple, Professor and Mrs. Heinz Aldermann, were to have been aboard but never showed up in Frankfurt for the flight. However, their luggage did make the crossing. If I recall, there was a substantial amount of it."

"Enough so it could cover the weight of a stowaway?"

"Oh, yes, four or five hundred pounds."

"Then someone could have been in their cabin?"

Dion became a little more excited. "Now this is pure rumor, mind you, but witnesses claim there was a foot found in the debris after the crash that didn't correspond with any of the bodies. This has been widely discredited as, oh, what do you call them, an urban legend, a tidbit to make the disaster just that much more horrifying."

Mercer wasn't sure if this was good news or bad. It brought Bowie that much closer to home, but if he'd died as a result of the crash then the trail went cold again. "But if the rumor was true, then it could belong to Chester Bowie."

"Like I said, it's a rumor."

"What happened to the luggage?"

"Oh, gosh, what little wasn't burned

175

beyond recognition was returned to its rightful owners or their heirs. Mind you not much made it out of the blaze, though. I don't know specifics about the Aldermanns' luggage"

"And the stuff that wasn't claimed?"

"Shipped back to Germany, actually. There were a few bits and pieces carted off by the curious, like that small piece of dur-aluminum you bought from me, but the *Hindenburg's* skeleton and everything else went back and was recycled into fighter planes for the Luftwaffe. Göring was never a fan of airships and detested Dr. Eckner, the head of the Zeppelin Company."

"Dead end." Mercer sighed. Harry had turned on the television and Mercer waved at him to lower the volume.

"What's this all about?" Dion asked.

"Oh, nothing, Carl. This guy Bowie might have been carrying some important geologic samples. I'm trying to track them down."

"I see. Well I have another rumor for you and take it for what it's worth, which I believe is nothing. About fifteen years ago, right after the publication of my book on the disaster, I received a letter through my publisher from a gentleman in New Jersey who claimed to have a safe thrown from the *Hindenburg* on the afternoon she crashed."

"A safe?"

"Yes. He even included a photo. Smallish affair, totally unremarkable. He claimed his father found it a few days after the wreck when he was plowing a field. Because there were no tire prints around the safe, he said it must have been thrown from the airship and wanted to know if I wished to buy it."

"How much?"

"This was when zepp memorabilia was at its peak. He wanted fifteen thousand dollars and would provide no provenance other than what his deceased father had told him. I spoke to him once. Very disagreeable fellow. I didn't even make an offer. I believed then, and I still do, that the man is a shyster and the safe is something he, or his father, had bought in a pawnshop."

"Do you have his name?" The chances the safe was real or that it had belonged to Bowie were so remote they were off the chart and into the realm where early cartographers wrote "beyond here there be dragons," but Mercer was desperate.

"I knew you'd ask. I'm searching for it now. I remember what you're like when you want something. You were after me for years to buy that piece of the *Hindenburg*. I certainly hope you have it prominently displayed."

"Er, yes," Mercer lied. "It's on a credenza next to my desk."

"Ah, here we go. He still lives on his family farm in Waretown. Believe it or not his name is Erasmus Fess."

"Mercer!" Harry shouted from where he was reclined against the bed's headboard.

Mercer didn't turn, just held up a finger for Harry to wait. "Erasmus Fess?"

"That's right." Mercer wrote out the address Dion rattled off.

"Goddamn it, Mercer!"

"Hold on, Carl." He covered the phone. "What?"

Harry was pointing to the television. Mercer looked. On the screen cops and a medical team were swarming around a small suburban house. Mercer tuned into the reporter's voice. ". . . this morning by a neighbor who describes the scene inside as a slaughterhouse. While the body has yet to be found, sources have been unable to locate Miss Ballard and the amount of blood in her house indicates foul play."

Mercer went numb and the color drained from his face. He cut the connection without saying good-bye to Carl Dion. "Serena?"

"Yes."

Another few seconds ticked by as the trio

watched the news change to another story. Cali was the first to pull herself together. "We have to get out of here. If they tortured her, they know we're staying at the hotel. Probably the room number too. Mercer, do you have a car?"

"Yes," he said, his mind spinning faster and faster. "It's in the garage."

"Mine too. That's where we should head." Cali had already closed her laptop.

"Bad idea. If they're already here they'll have it staked out. Harry, do you still have that suite?"

"Sorry, the room they gave me is reserved tonight. They're giving me another but it won't be ready until seven."

Mercer just nodded at the news. "Okay, then we'll just slip from the hotel, amble down to the next casino on the boardwalk, and hail a cab. If we can get that far without being spotted, we're clear. Cali, any chance you have a gun?"

She shook her head. "In my desk drawer at the office I've got a Glock, but that doesn't help us here."

"My spare Beretta's in my bedside table," Mercer admitted, handing Cali her computer case and casting an eye around the room for anything important. "Ready?"

Harry and Cali nodded.

Mercer opened the door and peered quickly down the long hallway. It was deserted but that didn't mean someone wasn't lurking in the elevator vestibule. With Harry in tow the stairs weren't an option. He motioned for them to hold still and he took off down the hall, moving so his shoes made the barest whisper against the carpet — a sound easily masked by the hotel's humming ventilation system. There was no one hiding by the elevators so he pressed the button and motioned for Harry and Cali to join him. On the odd chance the people who murdered Serena Ballard arrived on the next car, the three of them had better odds using surprise to overpower them than had Mercer waited alone.

His stomach was calming after the first jolt of adrenaline at seeing the news piece, and he began to wonder what they had stumbled into. It was no coincidence that Caribe Dayce was operating near Kivu at the same time Cali was searching for a potential uranium deposit. The key had to be the one-eyed mercenary, Poli. Mercer's thinking about what had happened in Africa was backward. Dayce hadn't hired Poli to work with his troops. Poli was paying the African rebel to secure the lode of highly radioactive ore.

Answering that question to his satisfaction left Mercer with another. How the hell did they know about the uranium in the first place? He glanced at Cali. Was it possible she wasn't who she claimed to be? Mercer discounted that idea even as it formed. Too many bullets were flying in her direction for her to be working with Poli and Dayce. The answer lay someplace else.

The light above one of the Deco elevator doors popped on with a discreet chime.

The instant before the doors opened, Mercer heard the distinct sound of an automatic pistol being cocked inside the elevator car. They had less than a second before the gunman saw them, not nearly enough time to run more than a few feet. And if they had their weapons drawn, Mercer could forget about overpowering the assassins. Their only chance was to hide in plain sight. The gunmen were looking for two men and a woman. But not a couple and another man.

Harry stood closer to Cali than Mercer, so he pushed his friend into her arms and hissed, "Kiss her."

Mercer was sure Cali understood what he had in mind but felt confident that Harry would just give in to his natural lechery. As the elevator doors slid open, the two wrapped their arms around each other.

"Oh, thank you, John," Cali squealed in a little girl voice and pressed her lips to Harry's.

Mercer had turned away just enough so it was evident he wasn't with the May/December couple.

The three men who stepped from the elevator held their pistols under their coats. Each gave Harry and Cali a passing glance, and as their eyes swiveled to Mercer, he bent as if to tie his shoe. Mercer didn't recognize two of the men, but the third was indelibly imprinted on his brain. Poli wore a black turtleneck and suit, and rather than give him a piratical air his eye patch made him all the more menacing.

Cali made sure she kept Harry between herself and the gunmen as she and Harry strode into the elevator.

"Room 1092," one of the assassins said, studying a plaque screwed to the wall. He motioned to their left. "This way."

Mercer felt Poli's eyes burning into the back of his skull but remained calm as he stood erect and casually moved into the elevator behind Cali and Harry. Harry pressed the button for the lobby. "How's your luck holding out, chum?" he asked Mercer, playing the part of strangers.

The elevator doors began to whisper closed. "Just fine," Mercer replied and began to turn to face the front of the car.

Poli stood rooted in the vestibule, ignoring his men as they moved down the corridor toward Mercer's room. His single eye went wide as he recognized Mercer, and his mouth split into a rictus of anger. He lunged for the elevator doors, trying to prevent them from closing, but he was a second too slow.

"Holy shit," Cali gasped as the car began to plummet for the lobby. "How did he escape the counterattack in Africa?"

Mercer didn't have an answer and knew now wasn't the time to worry about it. "We have just a few seconds once we reach the lobby," he said, then added grimly, "or no time at all if Poli has more men and a radio."

"What's your play?" Harry asked.

"Can you get around okay without your cane?"

Harry smiled, understanding what Mercer really wanted. "I think I'll be all right." He handed over the polished wood cane that Mercer had given him for his eightieth birthday.

Mercer had commissioned the cane from one of the finest knife makers in North America. He took the walking stick from

Harry and pressed a hidden button to release a two-and-a-half-foot-long rapier. The blade was as sharp as a scalpel, and while Mercer had no formal fencing training, the barest touch would split cloth and skin. He gave the black walnut scabbard to Cali.

"Clubs and swords against pistols?"

"Desperate times," he replied with a smirk.

Mercer's hands were slick on the silver handle and he rubbed the sweat against his pants, leaving a damp smear. He kept the blade tucked behind his leg while Cali held the baton across her chest and under her suit jacket. They remained silent as they watched the indicator lights fall inexorably toward the lobby.

Before the doors opened, they could hear the chimes and bells from the slot machines, and the noise grew as the doors hissed apart. Mercer ducked his head around the door and spotted nothing out of the ordinary. No one was rushing for the elevators and it didn't appear that anyone was listening to a radio or cell phone.

"Come on." He led them out of the car.

The elevators were off-limits to nonguests, and a security guard checked to see that people approaching the banks of lifts had room keys. Mercer noticed that the paunchy guard had an automatic pistol belted around his ample waist. Just beyond the velvet rope was the casino floor, a dazzling display of lights and sounds unlike anything else in the world. Hundreds of people were clustered around the green baize tables or seated behind ranks of gleaming slot machines, their expressions rarely changing no matter how well or poorly they were doing. Waitresses in skimpy black outfits danced between the patrons, their trays laden with complementary drinks while dealers and pit bosses watched the action with inscrutable eyes.

The atmosphere was designed to pump up the players and keep them gambling long after they should quit. For Mercer it was just a distraction. His scanned the crowds, watching for anyone not enthralled by the experience.

"See anything?" he asked.

Cali shook her head. "Not unless Poli's guys are disguised as a bunch of widows bent on blowing their late husbands' life insurance."

Mercer glanced back at the elevators just as they reached the guard's desk. One set of doors were opening.

"Shit!"

Poli raced from the car followed by his two henchmen. All of them carried their pistols in plain view. They shoved aside a couple waiting for the elevator, and the man shouted angrily, drawing attention. A woman saw the guns and screamed. The security guard tried to twist in his seat to see the commotion, but years of inactivity had tightened his muscles.

Mercer reached for the guard's gun, snapped the thumb lock off the holster, and pulled the weapon free. The guard hadn't even realized he'd been disarmed. Mercer racked the slide, noting that Cali had pushed Harry behind an ornate column.

Poli got the first shot off, and Mercer counterfired. Neither had aimed. Poli's round blew the strobe light from a slot machine while Mercer's embedded itself in an elevator door.

Before either could fire again, someone began shooting at Poli and his men from across the casino. They dove for cover. Mercer took the seconds-long distraction to grab Harry and Cali and begin running for the exit. He assumed the gunfire had come from casino guards, but as they raced toward the big steam locomotive near the Bar Americain he saw a pair of armed men dressed in dark suits, not uniforms. Their attention was focused solely on Poli and they barely gave Mercer a passing glance.

The crowds had quickly turned into a panicked mob. Shouts and screams had replaced the bells and the clanging of coins falling in hoppers. It was all Mercer could do to keep his grip on Harry and Cali. He bulled his way through the throng until they could flatten themselves against one of the locomotive's massive drive wheels. Dry ice provided the faux steam that leaked from around the pistons and rocker arms.

"How are we doing?" he asked, his throat suddenly tight and dry. Cali nodded sharply. "Harry?"

"Fine," the octogenarian wheezed. "Just get us the hell out of here."

"Working on it," Mercer replied.

Keeping their backs to the train and their eyes out for more assassins, they maneuvered their way down the length of the locomotive to the first car, a dining car that had been restored to its full glory. Normally a hostess stood at the bottom of the stairs to take reservations for what the Deco Palace Hotel touted as one of its most unique dining experiences. Mercer had read in the hotel brochure that the rail car was equipped with flat panel displays that were lowered over the windows, and hydraulics made the train feel like it was in motion. Each night a computer controlled what scenic trip the diners experienced as they ate. One night they traveled through the Rocky Mountains and on another they crossed the California desert and on yet another the passengers were made to feel they were crossing the Florida Keys on Henry Flagler's famous Overseas Railway.

"Get aboard," Mercer said, pushing Harry and then Cali up the steep steps. He was just about to follow her when a gunman broke out of the crowd. He cradled a silenced machine pistol, and as soon as he spotted Mercer he sprayed a deadly stream of rounds. Mercer dove up the stairs, feeling the searing heat of a bullet passing through the loose folds of his pants.

"Go!"

Harry slid open a beveled glass door and Cali and he began hobbling down the length of the dining car. Mercer fired two rounds to keep the gunman from charging and went off after his friends. The dining car's leather booths were set with elegant crystal and special Deco Palace Railways china. The silverware was sterling.

Outside the train, the gunman saw the figures through the windows and hosed the car with the remainder of his magazine.

Cali had glimpsed the assassin a moment before he fired, and she'd shouted a warning. They hunched down but didn't slow as glass exploded all around them and the air came alive with ricochets and copper-jacket rounds. The hand-carved paneling was splintered and the sophisticated electronics that controlled the liquid crystal screens began to spark. The car filled with the smell of burned plastic, ozone, and smoke.

As soon as the firing stopped, Mercer shoved aside one of the tables, sending the dinner service to the floor in an expensive cascade. The gunman had a fresh magazine in his weapon and was in the process of ratcheting the bolt when Mercer double tapped him in the chest. Out on the casino floor a pitched battle was under way, with at least a dozen men firing at one another. While one group seemed intent on minimizing civilian casualties, Poli's men fired indiscriminately. With just a quick scan Mercer saw a half dozen hotel guests either wounded or dead.

Harry and Cali waited for him at the end of the railcar and together they raced through the next. It was the restaurant's gleaming kitchen, disguised in a Deco-era Pullman car. A few waiters and cooks cowered behind the stainless steel appliances. One door at the end of the car opened out onto the lobby but there was a second door in the side of the train for bulky food deliveries.

Mercer led Cali and Harry through this second door and across a commercial loading dock. Unfortunately there were no trucks unloading goods for the hotel. One of the dock doors was open and the smell of the nearby Atlantic mingled with diesel fumes and the stench of old garbage.

"Why not hide around here?" Cali suggested, swiping blood from her cheek where she'd been hit by flying glass.

"Because it will take them about thirty seconds to realize where we've gone."

"Hate to admit," Harry panted, "but I'm about done in. One of the straps on my peg leg has shifted so my stump's killing me."

Though Mercer had known Harry had lost his leg decades earlier, he rarely walked with a limp and usually used his cane for ornamentation, so Mercer had forgotten the pain his old friend was going through. Mercer slowly turned in place, tapping into the mental map he'd created of the casino in the twenty-four hours he'd been there. It was an unconscious skill honed over his years working in the labyrinthine world of hard rock mines. He could discern the layout of almost any building after a brief tour and knew intuitively where he was at any time.

"Don't worry," he said once he had his plan. "The main entrance is outside the loading dock and around the corner. It's no more than seventy-five feet. At this time of the evening there's got to be a lot of people checking in."

Cali picked up on his idea. "Which means a lot of cars waiting for the valets to park them."

"Precisely." Mercer handed Cali his gun and caught Harry's eye. "Firemen's or piggyback?"

"Aw shit, Mercer, I can make it."

Mercer didn't ask him again. He bent low and flipped Harry over his shoulder. He was already running even as he settled the weight, Cali at his side. "If you fart, Harry, I'm going to drop you."

"I'd worry more about my occasional incontinence," Harry cackled.

Outside the loading dock was a dark parking lot, but once they rounded the corner they saw the neon glow of the Deco Palace's porte cochere. Liveried valets bustled between the ranks of cars. Most of the automobiles were ordinary sedans and SUVs, but there were a number of stretch limos and a Ferrari parked so that people driving to the casino would be sure to see it. It didn't appear that the pandemonium on the casino floor had spilled outside, but it was only a matter of time.

They hustled up the access road. Because the entrance was so congested, they needed to reach the head of the line of automobiles if they were to make their escape. Few paid them any attention as they danced through the throng.

"Mercer!" Harry shouted. "Behind us."

Cali reacted faster than Mercer, whirling around but keeping her weapon out of sight. Mercer saw them too. Poli and two of his men had just emerged from the loading dock. They paused, studying the parking lot, trying to spot movement. Mercer ducked as much as his knees allowed and still keep Harry's weight centered. He danced between cars and people, ignoring the few grumbles from guests he shouldered aside.

"They're on to us," Cali announced as they reached the head of the line.

The first car wasn't what Mercer expected or hoped for but it was their only option. The car was a work of art, a 1954 Rolls-Royce Silver Wraith with Hooper coach-work. It was painted in dove gray with dark blue fenders that swept gracefully over the wheels. With a wheelbase over ten feet long, the car was the epitome of stateliness and class. Although powered by a four-liter in-line six-cylinder engine, the vehicle was hopelessly underpowered because of its weight. Mercer could only hope they could vanish before Poli and his men reached their own car, because there was no way the British automobile would win any races.

"Cali, you drive," Mercer said as they approached. A distinguished man with the look of a television news anchor had just stepped from the passenger door. Mercer bulled past him so he could unceremoniously dump Harry inside. "And give me the gun."

She tossed it over the roof as she ducked into the driver's seat. The passenger's protest at what was happening died on his lips when Mercer caught the automatic pistol one-handed and pegged him with a flat stare. Just then a crush of people burst through the hotel's multiple doors. Many of them were screaming and all wore masks of fear. Like a tidal wave they crashed into the lines of cars, surging around the vehicles and shoving anyone who got in their way.

Mercer jumped into the back of the Rolls. The rear bench seat was covered in soft

Connolly leather and the burled woodwork gleamed in the light cast by the Deco Palace's marquee. Cut crystal highball glasses were laid out on a folding tray and the decanter next to it held a rich amber liqueur. He knelt against the seat and peered out the rear window. One of Poli's men was limping but they were coming on fast.

"Mercer?"

"Not now, Harry," he snapped without turning. "Cali, go!"

"I can't," she cried. "The car's right-hand drive!"

Mercer twisted around and saw that Harry sat behind the wheel. Rather than an export model modified for the American market, the classic Rolls had been built for the roads of England, so the driver sat on the right. Poli and his men were seconds away. They kept their guns from view, but as soon as they were in range Mercer had no doubt they'd open fire.

ATLANTIC CITY, NEW JERSEY

"No time to switch seats," Mercer shouted. "Punch it, Harry."

Harry mashed the clutch and forced the car into first gear, laying on the horn, which sounded a majestic, almost apologetic tone. The Rolls didn't exactly shoot from its mark, but in seconds they were outpacing Poli and his men. Mercer watched as the gunmen reached the head of the queue of waiting cars. Poli snatched a young woman out of the seat of her Geo Metro, the next car in line to pull away from the hotel. The gunman with a limp lowered himself into the passenger seat, waving his pistol at the second tattooed young woman who had been about to settle in for their drive home. Poli mouthed an order to his third man and gunned the little car. The three-cylinder engine screamed and the front wheels squealed as Poli took off after the Silver Wraith.

"He's following us," Mercer said and smashed out the rear window with the butt of the automatic. He checked the magazine, and was startled to find only two rounds.

Harry glanced into the rearview mirror. His eyes widened slightly when he realized the tiny blue car was what Poli had stolen. "He's driving that thing? Braver than I thought."

"Just for the record I've got two shots left, so if I don't get lucky you're going to have to outdrive him."

"No problem," Harry said breezily as he turned onto Atlantic Avenue. "You forget Tiny and I come up here whenever you're out of town."

"And take my car," Mercer added.

While Mercer hadn't been impressed by Atlantic City's boardwalk, with its T-shirt shops, psychic readers, and saltwater taffy stands, it was infinitely better than the rest of the city. Just a block from the glitzy multimillion-dollar hotel-casinos the neighborhoods were some of the poorest in the nation. Abandoned houses were covered in graffiti, yards were choked with weeds, and teens loitered in hunting packs like wild animals. Smashed bottles littered the gutters and few of the streetlights still worked.

The pall of apathy and despair was over-whelming.

"Cali, honey," Harry said as they flashed through an intersection. "I need you to focus on the road about a hundred yards ahead. My night vision isn't what it used to be."

She nodded grimly and tightened her seat belt.

They had enough of a head start that Harry could keep one turn ahead, but the Rolls was so slow on acceleration that he couldn't shake the little Metro. He broke out onto a long street and revved the engine, winding out the old six-cylinder until it shrieked and managed to gain a few pre-cious yards.

Mercer watched the Metro wheel around the corner, side-swiping an abandoned sedan. The range was too much for him to waste one of his precious bullets, but Poli's man had no such shortage. He steadied his pistol out the passenger window and cycled through the magazine. Most of the rounds went wild thanks to the potholed macadam, but two hit the Rolls. One blew off Cali's side mirror and the other slammed into the trunk, burying itself in a pair of matching Louis Vuitton suitcases that the valet hadn't had the time to remove.

There was a convenience store on the next corner. Many of the lights in the metal canopy above the gas pumps were out but the place was still open. Neon signs hung in the store's windows and a tricked-out Honda Del Sol was pulled up to the curb.

Though Mercer had never smoked, he had developed the habit of always carrying a couple of disposable lighters in his pocket. It was the old Boy Scout training, and having them with him had saved his life more than once.

"Harry, get ready to cut through that gas station."

Mercer pulled the stopper from the decanter of liquor, and stuffed one of the linen napkins that the highball glasses were sitting on into the mouth.

"Hey, I smell booze," Harry said. "Save me some."

"Sorry, old boy." Mercer upended the bottle, soaking the napkin in what smelled like a very good single-malt Scotch. "When we drive through the gas station, I want you to take out one of the pumps."

"Are you crazy?" Cali shouted.

"Like a fox," Harry said with delight. He had supreme confidence in Mercer, so he was actually enjoying himself.

Harry slowed slightly to lure the Metro,

and then jerked the wheel to the right. The big car bottomed out as it shot over the crosswalk, kicking up a shower of sparks. Cali screamed as he nearly ran over a homeless man sitting on the curb drinking from a large bottle of malt liquor. Like a juggernaut the Rolls raced across the lot, Harry aiming unerringly at the second pump in line. Mercer lit his improvised Molotov cocktail. The alcohol-soaked linen caught fire instantly.

In a maneuver that taxed both his strength and dexterity Harry tweaked the wheel to miss one of the steel columns holding up the canopy, drove the car up onto the island curb, and sent the front fender crashing through one of the old pumps.

The deceleration was brutal. Cali snapped forward, her head missing the dash by inches. The pump was sheared off at its base, tumbling end over end while the gasoline still in the lines splashed to the ground in a dark stain. Mercer pulled himself from the floor where he'd sprawled, the Molotov cocktail held high as if he were an outfielder clutching a ball he'd dived for.

The Metro was twenty yards back and coming on hard. He could see Poli's one eye shining with hatred. His partner had reloaded and was just reaching out to open fire again. Harry regained control of the car and brought it off the curb, aiming for the next cross street. Mercer shoved himself half out the side window, took aim, and heaved the fiery bottle back toward the pump. It hit just in front of the hole in the concrete island where gas was fed to the pump from a huge underground tank. The cut crystal shattered and for a sickening moment he thought the Scotch hadn't caught fire. But it had, burning with a clear flame that quickly reached the flash point of the pulsing waves of gasoline fumes spewing from the tank.

Like a rocket motor, the gas ignited, sending a coiling jet of fire fifteen feet into the air. It licked, then blackened, the underside of the canopy. Poli had closed the gap to twenty feet from the back bumper of the Rolls when the gasoline detonated. It exploded almost directly next to the Geo, forcing him to crank the wheel hard over. His car smashed into the rear of the lime green Del Sol, kicking the sports car across the pavement and tearing off its rear fairing. The Honda's alarm shrieked over the combustive roar of the flames.

Harry accelerated away from the conflagration, shifting smoothly through the gears. Built in an age long before airbags and automatic seat belts, the Rolls' thick metal skin had protected the engine's vital areas, and other than a wrinkled fender the luxury car was none the worse.

"That ought to buy us some time," Mercer said with satisfaction.

"I see a sign for the Atlantic City Expressway," Cali said.

"Where?" Harry asked, peering through the windshield.

"Straight ahead."

"What, that green blur above the road?"

Cali smiled. "Yeah. It's actually the right-hand green blur."

In moments the big car made its grand entrance onto the expressway, the main artery out of Atlantic City and back to the mainland. The Garden State Parkway was only a couple of miles ahead. Traffic on the inbound lanes was heavy but fortunately there were very few people leaving the city. Harry edged the Rolls up to seventy.

Mercer continued to glance behind them in case Poli somehow managed to get the Geo running again. He was about to dismiss a fast-approaching vehicle until he noted the distinctive paint job. The Honda Del Sol had to be doing a hundred and twenty as it barreled down the expressway, cutting through traffic with the effortless grace of a slalom racer.

"Will this guy ever quit?"

"What is it?" Cali asked. She looked over her shoulder and saw the fast-approaching sports car. "Jesus."

"What do you want me to do?" Harry asked. They were outgunned and were no match for either the Honda's speed or its agility.

Before Mercer could come up with another plan, Poli's teammate began firing again. Unlike before, the smooth asphalt gave him a steady shooting platform, and rounds found their mark.

"Cali, do you speak French?" Harry growled.

"Huh?" She wasn't sure if she'd heard right, or if Mercer's friend had lost his mind.

Harry kept one eye on the rearview mirror as he drove. His jaw was set firm and there was the barest trace of a smile on his lips. He kept watching the Del Sol edge up to within ten feet of the back bumper. "I want to know if you speak French because I'm gonna ask you to pardon me using it." He paused for another second, judging angles and speed, then shouted, "Fuck you, buddy!"

Standing on the brake pedal didn't have the dramatic results Harry had expected. As if ignoring the driver's wishes, the heavy car merely rocked forward on its suspension in what could be described as a stately deceleration. The maneuver forced Poli to apply the Del Sol's brakes, tricked out discs that could have stopped the nimble sports car on a dime. Sensing an opening, he raced alongside the Rolls to give his partner a clear shot into the Silver Wraith.

This is what Harry had been waiting for. He spun the wheel in an attempt to crush the light Honda between the Rolls and the guardrail. He could see Poli almost smile at the vain attempt, as he applied more brake to tuck in behind the Rolls-Royce once again. But Harry had another trick up his sleeve. He reached for the hand brake and gunned the engine to build up enough RPMs to slam the transmission down into third gear. The big car shuddered at the insult to its machinery, but it complied. This time the deceleration was almost instantaneous, as the big in-line six-cylinder engine quickly lost power. Poli was also quick, but not quick enough. The Rolls pinned his Honda against the guardrail and held it there effortlessly. A shower of sparks, torn metal, and fiberglass spewed from the Del Sol as it was relentlessly smeared against the metal barricade. Its right front tire blew and its steel belt ripped through the fender like a grenade going off, and still Harry kept up the pressure, all the while laughing demoniacally.

"Harry," Cali screamed. "Gun!"

Poli's partner had recovered enough to try to fire into the Rolls while Poli fought to keep the disintegrating car from climbing the railing.

Harry shoved the hand brake back into its recessed slot and swerved away from the Del Sol. He slid the transmission back into fourth and watched in his rearview mirror as the little Honda slid to a stop in a cloud of smoke. There was a lick of flame from the blown tire, and steam erupting from the crushed radiator. Harry caught Mercer's eye in the mirror and repeated what Mercer had said moments earlier. "Now, that ought to buy us some time."

Mercer squeezed Harry's bony shoulder. "You drive my Jag like this and I will kill you."

Harry chuckled. "I have a confession to make."

The tone made Mercer nervous. Even Cali picked up on it. "Yeah, and what's that?" Mercer asked with trepidation.

"Tiny and I have been pulling your leg about me driving when we come up here. I haven't been behind the wheel of a car in years." He craned his head around to look at Mercer. "But, hey, it's like falling off a bike. Do it once and you never forget."

"Eyes on the road please."

"I don't think we should use the Garden State," Cali said. "Even though the police are going to be busy at the Deco Palace, there's sure to be a description out of a stolen Rolls-Royce."

"Good thinking," Mercer said.

"So where are we heading?"

"Get onto 9 North. We're going to have a chat with a guy named Erasmus Fess about a safe his father claimed fell from the *Hindenburg* not long before it exploded."

It took forty-five minutes to reach Waretown and locate the home of Erasmus Fess. The sweep of the Rolls's only working headlight revealed that the property had once been a farm. There was a one-story farmhouse with a shed roof overhanging a sagging porch. At some point the original support columns had been removed, and now the whole affair was supported by unpainted two-by-fours. The sofa on the porch was the bench seat of an old car mounted on a metal stand. The forlorn house was covered with a fur of peeling and cracked paint. Flickering blue light spilled from the front window. The Fesses were home watching television.

Behind and to the right of the house was a metal-roofed barn that looked even more neglected than the yard. There were half a dozen cars parked randomly around the house. Most were rusted heaps sitting on flattened tires, with smashed windshields and rumpled fenders. A flatbed tow truck stood watch over the vehicles, "Fess Towing and Salvage" written on its door above a phone number. Behind the barn was a corrugated metal fence that stretched out into the darkness. The gates were open, and inside was a sea of abandoned cars lined up in meandering rows. A large forklift sat just inside, its steel tines thrust through the side of a Volkswagen like the lance of a knight through the armor of an enemy.

"Jesus," Harry breathed as he shut off the engine. "If we see a kid playing the banjo or someone comments on how pretty my mouth is, we're outta here."

"Amen, brother, amen." Mercer stepped from the car and tucked the automatic pistol behind his back. A cat raced off the porch and vanished under one of the dilapidated cars.

With Harry and Cali behind him, Mercer mounted the sloping porch. A screen door hung awkwardly from its broken hinges. The torn screen was loose and showed signs of being clawed by the cat. Mercer shouldered it farther aside and rapped on the main door. When there was no response he hit it again, a little louder.

"Get the goddamned door," a male voice shouted from inside, almost loud enough to rattle the windows.

"I'm busy," a woman shouted back. From the sound of it, both were seated in the front room no more than a few feet from each other. Harry hummed the theme from *Deliverance.*

"Jesus, woman! I'm watching *Wheel.* Go see who it is."

"Fine."

A moment later the front porch light, actually a naked bulb hanging from its wiring, snapped on. In seconds it had attracted every insect within a five-acre area. The woman who opened the door had a cigarette dangling from her slack mouth, and a bovine expression. She wore a housecoat that showed off her thick, blue-veined calves. Her feet were shod in slippers and Mercer could see that her toenails were cracked and yellow, more like horn or the rough body of a beetle. Her eyes were watery behind the cigarette smoke, an indeterminate color, and small. She was as thick as she was wide and probably tipped the scales in the two-hundred-and-fifty-pound range. The shadow of a mustache on her upper lip was inky black.

Behind her was a short hallway and the kitchen. The old metal sink was piled with dishes, and the fly strips above it were blackened with their victims.

"Mrs. Erasmus Fess?" Mercer said, hiding his revulsion. He put her age anywhere between fifty and a hundred.

"That's what it says on the marriage license." Her high-pitched voice and brusque manor made her sound like she was screeching rather than talking. "What do you want?"

"I would like to speak with your husband."

"Who is it, Lizzie?" Erasmus Fess shouted from the living room just off the entrance.

She turned to face her husband. "How the hell should I know? He wants to talk to you."

"Tell 'em we're closed. Come back in the morning if he wants a car or a tow." He then cajoled the contestants on his television. "Come on. Big money. Big money!"

"You heard him. Come back tomorrow."

She began to swing the door closed but Mercer shot out his foot to stop her. She continued to press on the door for a moment, not understanding why it had stuck.

"Mrs. Fess, this isn't about a car or a tow job. My name is Philip Mercer and this is Cali Stowe and Harry White. I'm here because of the safe your husband once offered to Carl Dion."

At that, a furtive look flashed behind her close-set eyes. "You're here about the *Hindleburg* safe?"

Mercer didn't bother correcting her pronunciation. "That's right. We came up from Washington, D.C. Does your husband still have it?"

"Have it? Hell, he don't get rid of nothing. He's still got the bite marks from his first case of crabs." She turned to yell at her husband again. "Ras, they're here about the *Hindleburg* safe."

"Ain't for sale," Erasmus Fess shouted back.

"Yes it is," Lizzie said hotly. "I told you back when to just give that damned thing to the feller from Colorado." She turned to address Mercer and the others again. "Ever since Ras's father found it we've had nothing but bad luck. After he dragged it home ain't been no kids born in the family. I got seven brothers and sisters and Ras had eight. Don't make sense we never had children."

"Could be the crabs," Harry muttered.

Cali silenced him with a look. "How about cancer?" she asked Lizzie Fess. "Does your family have a history of cancer?"

"Sure do. Ras's daddy and younger brother both died of the cancer. And me and one of his sisters had our titties cut off 'cause of it."

Given the amount of fat she carried and the shapeless coat she wore, it was understandable that no one had noticed she'd undergone a double mastectomy.

"Had they lived in the house after the safe was found?" Cali asked

"Sure did. That's why I said the safe brought bad luck. Ras's oldest brother didn't get along with his father none and moved away before they found the safe, and he's fit as a fiddle and has twelve kids and a whole mess of grandkids."

Cali whispered to Mercer, "Sounds like we're on the right trail. Elevated cancer rates, sterility. Remind you of anywhere?"

Mercer's mind had already cast back to the isolated village along the Scilla River in Central Africa. Chester Bowie must have brought a sample of the uranium ore with him on his return to the United States, but just before the *Hindenburg* met its fateful end he had tossed it from the airship in a safe. What astounded Mercer even more than the sample's bizarre odyssey was how it had remained radioactive enough to cause cancer at the farm and sterilize at least one if not both of the Fesses.

The *Wheel of Fortune* theme music reached its crescendo and then the television was shut off. A moment later Erasmus Fess approached the door. Unlike his wife, he was rail-thin and raw-boned. He wore a pair of oil-stained coveralls with his name stitched over his chest. His hair was sparse and gray and he had dandruff the size of Corn Flakes. He wore thick glasses that magnified his bloodshot eyes and he sported five days' worth of silver stubble. He belched a cloud of beer breath and held out a ropey arm to Mercer.

"Erasmus Fess."

"Philip Mercer." They shook hands.

"Why are you interested in the safe?" Fess asked.

"What difference does it make?" Lizzie hollered at her husband. "He wants to buy it."

Mercer hadn't come out and said that he wanted to buy the safe, but he nodded anyway.

A speculative, almost feral look came over Erasmus Fess. "Twenty thousand. Cash."

Fess wanted five thousand more than he'd offered Carl Dion, but that wasn't an issue for Mercer. He would have bought the safe, and its contents, for anything Fess asked. The problem was he just didn't have that kind of money on him. He could write a check for that amount easily, but he knew Fess would never accept it, and there was no way the scrap man would want the paper trail from a credit card transaction. Mercer hated that they'd have to wait until morning for a bank to open, but he saw no alternative. Then he remembered Harry's winnings. He shot his friend a look. "Easy come, easy go, old boy."

"Huh?"

"Empty your pockets."

"What?" Harry finally got what Mercer wanted and his face turned red. "Forget it. I won that money fair and square."

"Relax," Mercer said soothingly. "I'll pay you back when we get home." He would then turn around and present a bill to Deputy National Security Advisor Lasko.

Lizzie and Erasmus Fess's eyes bulged when Harry withdrew two thick bundles of hundred-dollar bills from his windbreaker. He handed the stacks to Mercer. "I should ask for a receipt."

Mercer presented them to Fess but didn't hand them over. "I want to see the safe first. And I want you to throw in a working car. We sort of borrowed that Rolls outside."

Fess peered out into his driveway at the elegant car. He cast a practiced eye over the luxury car, paying particular attention to the ruined fender and dented doors. "I'll give you a car so long as you forget where you parked that one."

Mercer had hoped to return the Silver Wraith to its rightful owner and thought he could call the police as soon as they were safely back in Washington, but he knew the Rolls would be a bundle of parts by the time they hit the Maryland border. Tomorrow would just have to be a bad day for some insurance company.

"Deal."

"You should give him the papers too," Lizzie said to her husband.

"Papers?" Cali asked. "What papers?"

"Ras's father had the safe opened back in the fifties. Don't know what else was in it, but there were a bunch of papers. A note or something. He made a copy of it and locked the originals back inside. Ras, where did they get to?"

"God, you talk too much, woman," Fess

groused. He ran his fingers through his hair and unleashed a blizzard of dandruff. "They're in the office file. Bottom drawer. Behind the paperwork for them airplane engines I bought five years ago."

Mercer wasn't surprised that Fess knew where the papers were. He suspected that the salvage yard owner could put his hand on any piece of scrap in his sprawling yard.

"Let's go," Fess growled. Harry said he'd wait on the porch, and he'd talked Lizzie into giving him a drink by the time her husband grabbed a flashlight from the tow truck's cab.

"You ain't no collector like that writer fella from Colorado," Fess said as he unlocked the chain link gate guarding his scrap yard. "What do you want with the safe?"

"There's a chance it belonged to my grandfather," Cali said before Mercer could come up with a lie. "He was returning from Europe on the *Hindenburg.* He always carried a safe with him. He was a jeweler."

At that Fess stopped short and shone the light in her eyes. "Ain't no jewels in the safe, I can guaren-damn-tee you."

"Do you recall what was in it?" Mercer asked.

"I was fightin' in Korea when my pappy had it opened. He said there wasn't nothing in there but the notes and a shot put."

"A what?" Cali and Mercer said in unison.

"A shot put. Like athletes use. Said it was nothing but a round ball o' metal."

He led them deep into the salvage yard, past ranks of demolished automobiles and trucks. Mercer spotted a burned-out fire engine, several boats, and the boom of a large crane. There were countless tarry patches of oil dotting the sandy ground, and a tire pile that had to be twenty feet tall. Night animals scattered at their approach, and shiny eyes watched them from the darkness.

Near the back of the yard was a metal shed. Fess used another key from his jangling ring to open the door. He stepped inside and pulled the chain to a single bulb dangling from the ceiling. Why the junk on the shelves that lined the shed needed protection from the elements was something Mercer couldn't understand. Most everything looked like valueless hunks of rusted metal.

"I keep the good stuff in here," Fess said.

Mercer wasn't going to ask what exactly qualified this to be "good stuff."

Fess shoved a transmission from out of a corner and bundled up a filthy piece of canvas to reveal the little safe. It was about a foot and a half square and made of dark metal, with rust on the prominent hinges. On the single door were an offset dial and a small handle.

"Be right back," Fess said and scuttled from the shed.

"The shot put has to be an ore sample," Cali said as soon as Fess was out of earshot.

"No other way to explain it," Mercer agreed. "Remember the old woman said Chester Bowie sent crates of dirt away by river, but he must have kept some ore with him. He refined it and must have put it in the safe to block the radiation."

"But enough has leaked to affect Erasmus and Lizzie." Cali thought for a moment. "I'm going to have to report this site to my bosses at the Department of Energy. We need to get a NEST team down here right away. We need containment." She looked around the shelves. "God knows how hot all this junk is."

"Might have a turf battle with the EPA," Mercer quipped, "considering all the oil that's leached into the ground."

A moment later Fess returned to the shed with a gardener's cart. The tires were flat, but it would be easier using the rusted handcart than to try and carry the safe. Mercer manhandled the safe into the cart, pausing as he heard the distant beat of a helicopter. His senses were hyperacute from the adrenaline overdose, and he became suspicious.

"Any flight paths around here?" he asked Fess.

"That chopper's nothing. Hear 'em all the time. It's big shots from New York going down to Atlantic City."

The explanation seemed reasonable but Mercer remained on edge. The quicker they were on their way to Washington, the happier he'd be. He settled the safe toward the back of the cart and swung around to take the handles. It took considerable effort to get the flattened tires rolling, but once he had a little momentum it became easier. Fess didn't seem to be in any great hurry, so Mercer ignored him and made his own way out of the salvage yard, relying on the map he'd unconsciously drawn of the facility.

"Sure you know where you're going?" Cali asked as she paced him with her long legs.

"God, you talk too much, woman," Mercer said with a dead-on impression of Fess's redneck accent. Cali pantomimed smoking a cigarette and blowing the smoke in his face.

They reached the gates and Mercer set

down the cart's handles. He didn't know which vehicle Fess would give him, so he waited for the irritable scrap man. "Why don't you go check on Harry?" he asked Cali. "I'll load the safe once our pal Erasmus ambles along."

She stepped onto the sagging porch and knocked on the door. A second later she was inside. Fess finally emerged from the salvage yard. He locked the gates and motioned Mercer over to a late-model Ford sedan. The tires looked bald and the right front fender was dented but otherwise the car would be fine. Fess opened the rear door and grabbed the keys from under the back bench seat.

"Thieves always look in the sun visor or under the driver's seat. Never in the back." He used the key to pop the trunk and stood far enough back to let Mercer know he wasn't going to help him lift the safe into the car. Mercer braced his legs and lifted what had to be a hundred pounds of dead weight. He balanced the safe on the rear bumper then rolled it inside. He clearly heard a heavy metal ball rattle inside the safe as it crashed into the trunk.

"There," Fess said, holding out his calloused hands. "You got your safe and car. I want my money."

Mercer handed him the two bundles of hundred-dollar bills. "Twenty grand."

But Fess didn't hand over the keys. He turned and started back for his house, mumbling, "I gotta count it."

Without realizing it Mercer balled his hands into fists as he felt his blood pressure spike. It was a struggle to keep the anger from his voice. "Mr. Fess, we're in a bit of a hurry."

The old man whirled. "Listen, sonny buck. I don't know who you are or what you're really after but I don't trust you as far as I can throw you. So you're just gonna have to cool your heels until Lizzie and I count the money."

If Mercer wasn't sure he'd give the codger a heart attack, he would have pulled the pistol still tucked behind his coat. "Fine," he said and seethed. He was about to follow Fess into his house when he became aware of the helicopter again. It sounded much closer. Too close.

Someone flying from New York to Atlantic City would surely stick to the coast or run along the barrier islands. They wouldn't be five miles inland. Then Mercer willed himself to relax. He'd left Poli stranded on the AC Expressway, and the rest of his team was still back at the Deco Palace. There was no way they could have tracked the three of them to Fess's house or known about the call to Carl Dion that led them here.

Mercer looked into the darkened sky but could see nothing but a few stars. The sound of the helicopter continued to rise. It was coming fast. Despite what logic was telling him, a sense of urgency swept through him. He started sprinting after Fess when the dark chopper cleared a copse of pine trees fifty yards from the farmhouse. Mercer caught a glimpse of the open side door an instant before autofire rained down from above. The gunman first concentrated on the Rolls-Royce. The right side tires were shredded and a steady stream of rounds shot through the grill until radiator fluid poured from the car like its lifeblood.

Mercer reached Fess just as he was about to mount the steps onto his porch. He tackled the old man and together they tumbled through the front door an instant before the porch caught the second volley from the chopper. The money had come loose from its paper strapping and littered the floor.

"Sweet Jesus Christ," Fess roared over the deafening fusillade.

Mercer ignored him and peered around a grimy window, not recalling that he'd drawn his weapon, but it was in his hand neverthe-less. How? he thought. How in hell did Poli find them? It was impossible. Poli hadn't had time to put a tap on the phone back in Mercer's room at the Deco Palace and Mercer was certain no one had followed them from Atlantic City.

The chopper came lower, its blades mere feet from the trees. Four figures jumped from the open door and the pilot pulled up. A fifth person remained in the helo with an assault rifle in his hands.

Mercer pulled his cell phone from his jacket and flicked it to Cali. "Dial 911," he ordered. "Tell them the men who shot up the Deco Palace are here." He then grabbed Fess by the collar of his overalls. Lizzie was holding her hands over her ears and scream-ing in the living room. "Do you have any weapons?"

Mercer had to give Fess credit. He quickly gathered his wits, his eyes losing their manic glint. "Goddamn right I do. I'm an Ameri-can, ain't I?"

"And there I was thinking you were barely sentient," Harry remarked and took a swig of whatever liquor he'd coaxed out of Liz-zie.

The entire house rattled as the chopper hovered overhead. The precarious pile of dishes mounded in the kitchen sink crashed to the floor, and pictures danced and blurred on the walls. Erasmus Fess went to the back of the house and returned a moment later with a semiautomatic rifle, two shotguns, and an enormous revolver tucked between the buttons of his overalls. He handed Mercer one of the pump-action shotguns. Cali took the other.

"They're both loaded." He placed the box of shells he'd tucked under his arm on the coffee table and checked the extended magazine of his Ruger Mini-14, a civilian version of the weapon the army had used during the early years of the Vietnam War. "Lizzie," he shouted. "Cut your wailing and get the ammo from the dining room."

Mercer was back at the window. He recognized Poli leading his team as they slowly advanced on the house. They moved like seasoned professionals, never exposing themselves for more than a few seconds as they crossed the yard. When Poli reached cover behind the big flatbed tow truck, he motioned for his men to take flanking positions. He spoke into a walkie-talkie and the chopper banked away.

"Can you hear me?" the mercenary then shouted.

Mercer said nothing, watching as two of

Poli's men took positions to the left and right of the house. He could take out one of them, but the other had gone far enough around the building that Mercer could no longer see him.

"I know you can hear me, Mercer," Poli yelled. "Tell me why you came out here and I might let you live."

"He's here for a safe that fell off the *Hindenburg*. It's in the trunk of that Ford Taurus out there," Fess shouted back before Mercer could stop him. "You just take it and leave us be."

"Shut your mouth," Mercer hissed at the junk man. Fess remained defiant.

One of Poli's men broke cover and ran to the brown sedan. He peered into the open trunk without slowing, then found cover behind another wrecked car. "It's in there," he yelled across to his team leader.

A shadow flitted across the window where Mercer stood. One of Poli's men was on the porch. The front door wouldn't last a second under the onslaught of their automatic weapons. Mercer craned his head to see the gunman, but he must have flattened himself against the wall. Mercer looked out toward the flatbed, knowing Poli would give the signal at any second.

Mercer wasn't going to wait. He had only

one chance to catch the man on the porch by surprise. He aimed carefully and fired. The twelve-gauge bucked in his hand and he had another round chambered before he knew if he'd hit the target. The fully choked barrel prevented the steel shot from spreading more than a couple of inches at close range, so the full load ripped through the two-by-four propping up one end of the porch roof. The piece of lumber disintegrated and its partner on the other end of the porch quivered then snapped with a sound heard over the nearby chopper. As if hinged, the entire porch roof pivoted downward. The gunman wasn't quick enough. He'd tried to lunge off the deck but the roof smashed into him, tossing him back against the house until the section of plywood and shingles crushed his body against the stout wall.

Poli and his men opened fire, spraying the front and sides of the house with a continuous barrage. Windows vaporized and Lizzie's cheap curtains were torn to shreds. Mercer tried to return fire, the shotgun roaring over the staccato cracks of the assault rifles, but the fire was pouring in too heavily. The high-powered bullets bored through the farmhouse's aluminum siding, through the rotted insulation and the lathe and plaster, with barely a check in their speed. Plaster dust and bullets filled the air in the living room. Everyone dropped flat as the air seemed to come alive.

Many of the lights were blown out, plunging the living room into near darkness. The couch took a long fusillade, stuffing and fabric spilling like cotton waste. A bullet found an electrical outlet in the kitchen and started a fire that quickly grew.

The sound was hellish, unworldly, a continuous din that pounded at eardrums and threatened sanity. And there was no letup. As soon as one of the gunmen drained his magazine he inserted a fresh one, seemingly without pause. Chunks of plaster were falling off the walls and the fire in the kitchen grew so Mercer could feel its heat through his clothes. A round found the television and it blew with a searing pop.

Smoke was growing thick. Pressed flat to the floor by her husband, Lizzie Fess began to cough.

Mercer caught Cali's eye. Her face was ashen with fear, her beautiful lips parted as she tried to draw precious oxygen from the reeking air. He peered over his shoulder toward the kitchen. The entire room was engulfed in flame. He didn't know if the Fesses cooked with natural gas, but if they did it was only a matter of time before the heat or a bullet ruptured the gas line and blew the house off its foundation.

And just as quickly as the barrage had started, the firing ceased. Mercer's ears rang so loudly and the fire roared so powerfully that he only knew Poli had stopped firing because there were no new holes appearing in the walls. As his senses returned, he heard Poli's chopper once again. The heavy beat of the rotors told him that the Jet Ranger was taking off.

Poli had used the cover fire so he could grab the safe and radio the helicopter for a quick evacuation. What Mercer couldn't understand was why Poli and his men were leaving before making sure everyone in the house was dead. It was the first mistake he could see that Poli had made.

Fearing a trap, that Poli had left behind a sniper, but pushed by the urgency to get out of the burning building, Mercer crawled across the broken glass and debris littering the floor and approached one of the ruined windows. He tossed Erasmus Fess's singed copy of *TV Guide* outside, and when there was no gunfire he chanced a momentary peek. He saw nothing out of the ordinary and gave the yard a longer look, peering as deeply into the shadows as he could.

Light caught his eye and he understood why Poli had retreated. He glimpsed the flashing red and blue lights of a string of police cars through the pine trees. They were racing for the salvage yard, and the lead vehicle was only seconds away.

Unable to use the front door because of the ruined porch roof, and with the back engulfed in flame, Mercer led everyone out the window, making sure that Erasmus and Lizzie went first. Harry demurred to going next, so Cali could throw a long leg over the sash and duck outside. She helped Harry onto the ground and Mercer slithered through after him. He herded them to the far side of Fess's tow truck, and there he and Cali fell into fits of coughing as they gulped at the fresh air.

For some reason Harry and the Fesses weren't as affected. Harry took out his pack of cigarettes, lit three, and handed one to Erasmus and one to Lizzie.

Through a wreath of tobacco smoke, Harry said, "Years of building up my immunity finally paid off."

The New Jersey State Police cruiser slid to a stop, kicking gravel across the yard. The officer threw open the door and emerged with his pistol drawn, making sure he was protected by the bulk of his car. "Hands up where I can see them, assholes!" he shouted, hopped up on adrenaline and the thought of a promotion in his near future. "Anyone move and you're dead."

The five of them did as ordered, while more cars careened into the driveway.

Before the next officer could cover them, the back of the house collapsed in a shower of sparks and the flames danced ever higher. Lizzie turned to her husband and said matter-of-factly, "Ras, we're movin' to Florida."

ARLINGTON, VIRGINIA

Mercer swirled the last of his vodka gimlet and downed the remainder in one gulp. He was on his third, contemplating his fourth. Harry slouched next to him on his favorite stool at Mercer's home bar. Both of them were raw-eyed and exhausted, but neither was ready to call it a night.

It had taken more than eight hours, and the direct intervention of Ira Lasko as well as a shadowy figure from Homeland Security who vouched for Cali Stowe, before the New Jersey police and FBI realized they hadn't captured public enemies numbers one through three. Lizzie and Erasmus had spent no more than an hour making their statement before being released. Ira assured Mercer that the junk man would be fully compensated for his losses.

Cali had left before Mercer and Harry, whisked away by the Homeland Security agent in a government car, while Mercer was allowed to return to the Deco Palace to retrieve his Jaguar. It was a long drive home.

Harry had shown up at his place a couple hours after Mercer had dropped him at his own apartment, Drag in reluctant tow. They'd ordered Chinese food but neither was in the mood to eat. Each was pre-occupied with his separate thoughts.

"Well at least one mystery's been cleared up," Harry said after a healthy slug of his Jack Daniel's.

"What?"

"The car."

The police who'd searched the Rolls-Royce they'd stolen from the Deco Palace found that the car had been fitted with a LoJack tracking device. The man Mercer had seen Poli leave behind at the entrance of the hotel had grabbed the driver and made him reveal his personal identity number. The tracking service led Poli and his men straight to the Fesses' salvage yard. Fortunately the car's owner hadn't been killed, but three people inside the hotel were dead and another eight wounded.

While Mercer knew their murders weren't his fault, they still lay heavy on his conscience. He especially felt Serena Ballard's death. There was no way around the fact that had he not contacted her she'd still be alive. All of those people would.

"I do have something to cheer you up," Harry said after a long silence. He shuffled over to his windbreaker and tossed some papers onto the bar.

"What's this?"

"The copy of the notes from the safe Lizzie Fess gave me."

Mercer looked at him incredulously. "Why didn't you tell me earlier, you bastard? You've let me sit here thinking we're at a dead end while you've had this the whole time."

"Hey, sorry," Harry replied. "I wanted to translate all of it first, but seeing your face hanging lower than Drag's made me reconsider."

Mercer read the first couple of paragraphs.

Deer and the antelope play. That damned infernal song will not leave me. Were there ever any antelopes in America? I ask you, Albert, what games did they play? What merriment the rams and ewes all enjoy? I remember once being sane and I think I should go back there. But then again how does anyone really know what is madness. And are there many who really care? I no longer do. Burned out, I fear this trip has changed me in sick and disturbing ways. I no longer recognize the reflection in the mirror. And within this safe is the key for more madness to follow. Nick of time I thought when I boarded this massive airship. I escaped all those who pursued me — the Carmines, and their minions. But I have paid a price. My eyes appear kohl darkened, like a pharaoh's. My hair, what little I started with, has fallen out in stiff tufts and my body aches in unholy ways. Other passengers turned away when we boarded. I indeed am a wreck. To recall what I've endured in the past weeks and months makes me think that even before I left I was more than a little mad. But I had to find out. I was obsessed, I suppose, unable to forgo my ego's needs to always be correct. I barely had the strength to rise each morning on the zeppelin and now I sit here trying — forcing myself to write this story.

Second tea into cup in six.

But I did it. I had to show the world that at least one of my theories was worth pursuing. And I have learned that they all were. By ships, automobiles, trains and donkeys I've allowed my obsession to drive me deeper into hell.

I've been so wracked with fever I chipped a tooth shivering. At one point my fight with malaria was so bad my urine turned the color of wine. I think what my brother nick endured in the Great War and I know I have surpassed his suffering. My journey had all the elements of a great quest, Odysseus's odyssey. Only mine will not end in the dew-covered fields of my Ithaca in the arms of my beloved Penelope. I could not vanquish the suitors. And while I didn't want to believe they exist I know even now they are plotting against me. I have become paranoid, but I fear I am not, in fact, paranoid enough. I lack the Hero's cunning and I lack his strength. Guile is not in my nature.

"This has got to be in code like the note Cali and I got from Einstein's archives," Mercer said when he finished the cryptic paragraphs. "It makes sense on one level but there has to be more. Do you remember the code? How many words to skip?"

"Every eleventh word," Harry said at once.

Mercer grabbed a notebook and a pen from a drawer behind the bar and began counting out words. After a few moments he set the pen down and read aloud what he'd deciphered. "Leave you and I really care has recognize the thought of but like fallen ways." He looked to Harry. "What the hell does that mean?"

Harry chuckled. "It means you're an idiot," the octogenarian said mildly. "You didn't count the first word."

Mercer turned the pages over to his friend in frustration. "You're the one who loves puzzles and cracked the first message. You do it."

"I already did. The first ten words are 'Deer me Albert ewes should know I changed the key.' When you clean it up a little you get 'Dear me, Albert, you should know I changed the key.' "

"Shit." Anger crept back into Mercer's voice. "So how do we find the new key? Is there a clue?"

"Yeah." Harry pointed to the second paragraph, a one-line non sequitur that Mercer had glossed over when he read the text. "This line here. *Second tea into cup in six.* I'm pretty sure it's another doublet. Change tea into cup in six words and the second word is a clue. I scanned the rest of letter and found five more doublet clues."

"Can you figure them out?" Mercer asked anxiously.

"Might take me a while, but sure."

Mercer slid Harry's drink out of his reach. "Then get to work."

After making a pot of coffee strong enough to melt a spoon, Mercer sat next to Harry as he began writing out words. There were literally hundreds of combinations and they wouldn't know if they were right until all five had been figured out.

"Damn," Harry muttered after a minute. "I'm beginning to hate Chester Bowie."

"Why?"

"You only need four words to change tea into cup. It goes: tea, tap, cap, cup. The other two are just filler and I don't even know where to put them. I could make it tea pea pet put pup cup or it could be tea sea sep sap cap cup."

"Wait, what's sep?"

"Abbreviation for separate. General rule for doublets is if it's in the dictionary you can use it."

"Well I'm not as good at these things as you but why don't you give me the second hint and I'll see what I can do."

Harry leafed through Bowie's note to Einstein and read out the next doublet. " 'Fourth games into balls in nine.' Changing only one letter at a time, turn the word 'games' into the word 'balls' in nine words. The fourth word's our clue. After that we have: 'fourth gout into full in ten, second east into west in four,' and finally there is 'third dire into fine in four.' "

Mercer wrote out the first and last word of the second clue on a piece of paper, realized how much harder it would be with five-letter words versus three, and silently switched papers with Harry to give him the more difficult puzzle.

"Just for that I want my drink back," Harry said without looking up.

Mercer slid the highball glass back to his friend and together they set to work.

At eleven o'clock they compared notes. Mercer had filled line after line on his paper but had made no progress, while Harry was pretty sure he had three of them, albeit they were the easiest. He'd deciphered the last two, coming up with west, lest, last, east and dire, dive, five, fine. Seeing that one of the clue words, "five," was a number, he'd cracked the first doublet and came up with tea, ten, tan, tap, cap, cup.

"So we have ten, something, something, lest, five," Mercer said, emptying Harry's overflowing ashtray into a metal bucket he kept for that sole purpose.

"It must be a math problem. Ten plus something lest five, or ten minus something less five."

"Ten times?" Mercer suggested.

"Genius," Harry shouted and bent to his paper again. "Games into balls." He spoke aloud as he wrote out "Games, dames, dimes, times, ah, tiles, tills, fills, falls, balls. Perfect."

"Way to go, Harry," Mercer applauded. "Figure out the last one and we're in business again. You know the fourth word has to be a number."

"Give me a minute." A few minutes passed. Harry finally looked up. "You realize that Bowie wrote this just before he tossed the safe."

"Yeah, so?"

"Just think what kind of mind he had to create the doublets and then write out the letter to Einstein making sure he kept his word count straight. He could do this stuff in his head without really thinking about it. And from the sound of it he'd been through hell and back."

"From what I've gathered, he was an eccentric, that's for sure," Mercer said. "And from the tone of this letter it sounds like he was on the verge of a nervous breakdown."

"Oh, I'd say he'd crossed the verge and was deep into la-la land."

Mercer asked Harry for Drag's leash so he could take the mangy basset for his last walk of the night. From long years of experience, he knew Harry wouldn't leave until he'd solved the code, and even then he'd sleep on the leather couch rather than return to his dingy one-bedroom apartment up the block.

Mercer dragged the old basset to the circular stairs, and once he got him going the dog made good progress, the fat of his belly rippling as it scraped over the stair treads. He even waddled across the polished marble foyer. Usually Harry had to drag him to the door but for Mercer he was a little less stubborn.

Mercer had just reached the front door when the doorbell chimed. He automatically checked the TAG Heuer strapped around his wrist. It was quarter past eleven. No one visited at this hour unless the news was bad. He thought for a moment about running upstairs for the Beretta nine-millimeter he kept in his bedside table, but he caught a glimpse of his visitor through the door's side lights. He smiled and opened the door.

Cali Stowe wore jeans and a black tank top with a man's white oxford shirt thrown over it. Mercer got the impression she'd dashed over in a rush. She wore no makeup and her red hair was a little disheveled, but still she looked beautiful, in that vulnerable way men love but women never understand.

Then three things struck Mercer at once. Cali hadn't returned his smile, he'd never given her his home address, and there were two men standing behind her.

"Sorry," she said sadly. "They didn't give me much choice."

One of the men showed Mercer the pistol he held to Cali's back.

Anger came in hot black waves. "Who are you?" Mercer demanded.

"Why don't we step inside, Dr. Mercer," the gunman said.

Both men had dark hair and dark complexions, with thick mustaches, but they appeared more Mediterranean than Middle Eastern. The one with the gun was Mercer's height and had a slender build and an angelic face that belied the weapon in his hand. The other was older, his mustache and hair shot with silver, and shorter, five seven or so. While both wore conservative dark suits, Mercer had the impression that the shorter man was the leader.

"Are you okay?" Mercer asked Cali as he stepped back from the door.

"I'm fine," she said.

He couldn't see any bruises on her and she wasn't limping, but Mercer knew that in front of these two Cali wouldn't tell him if she was hurt. She was too brave for that.

"What do you want?" Mercer demanded of the one he thought was the leader.

"I am here to deliver a warning, Dr. Mercer, nothing more." The man had an accent Mercer couldn't place and spoke gently, almost like a priest.

"Warn me about what?"

"You must stop your search for the Alembic of Skenderbeg. The more you look the more you help others who are also searching for it."

If one of them didn't have a gun in his right hand, Mercer would have laughed at them. "Friend, I don't have the foggiest idea what you're talking about. I don't know what an alembic is or who Skenderbeg is, so why don't you leave and we'll pretend this never happened."

"It is much too late for that."

"Jesus!" Mercer recognized the voice, and his reaction suddenly tripped Cali's memory too. She blanched.

"That was you in the village," Mercer said. "You saved Cali and me."

"Had I known you would continue your quest," the man agreed, "I would have delayed my attack and let Caribe Dayce kill you."

"We're not on any quest," Mercer said, somehow feeling more in control. Had these two wanted them dead they wouldn't be talking, and the gunman had lowered his weapon, which Mercer realized was the first gun he'd seen in a long time that wasn't firing at him. "We're trying to find out what happened to the uranium that was mined near that village almost seventy years ago. This has nothing to do with your Allergy of Skinbag, or whatever it is."

"The Alembic of Skenderbeg." He said it almost reverently. "You don't even know what you're searching for, Doctor, but I must tell you to stop. We have saved your life twice."

"That was you last night at the casino?" Cali asked.

He nodded. "Yes. A mercenary has been hired to retrieve the alembic and we have managed to follow his movements. We tracked him first to Africa and then to Atlantic City last night. But at the casino we underestimated the size of his forces and didn't know he had rented a helicopter." He turned his gaze to Mercer. His eyes appeared haunted, like he knew too many secrets. "You led them to a clue they would have never found. What was it by the way?"

"A safe," Mercer said, guilt edging into

241

his voice as he again thought about Serena Ballard and all the others. "A classics professor brought back ore samples from Africa. He had gone there believing he'd found the source of the metal Zeus used to forge Prometheus's chains. What he found was a vein of unusually powerful uranium, not the mythical adamantine."

The two men exchanged a look when Mercer said the word "adamantine," as if they knew of it. "Was there anything else?"

"The safe's owners said there was nothing else in it but the ore samples," Mercer lied, praying that Harry wouldn't come out to the library overlooking the foyer. "The mercenary —"

"Poli Feines," the man with the pistol offered.

"He stole the safe before I had a chance to verify, but I have no reason to doubt what the owners said. They knew nothing beyond the fact that the safe had been tossed from the *Hindenburg*."

Again the two men glanced at each other. "Interesting," the leader said at last. "But it changes nothing. I came here to warn you. You are caught up in an ancient battle you can't possibly understand. I beg you to end your investigation now. You have been lucky so far that I have been in a position to save your life. The next time you might not fare so well."

The two men backed toward the door, the one holstering his pistol. Cali and Mercer remained where they stood. "And know this, Dr. Mercer, if I could find you and Ms. Stowe so easily, Poli Feines will be able to do so as well."

"Who are you?" Mercer asked before they disappeared into the night.

The leader paused, considering the question. He searched Mercer's eyes and found whatever it was he was looking for. "Janissaries," he said at last and closed the door.

It was as though the room had been dark and suddenly there was light. Mercer took a deep breath and stepped close to Cali. He rested his hands on her thin shoulders and looked her in the eye. What he saw was anger rather than fear. "Are you okay?"

"I'm pissed," she answered and stepped back just a bit. Her freckles stood out in relief against her smooth, pale skin and her small ears were reddened. She didn't need comforting. She needed to vent. "They came in through a supposedly alarmed window right into my bathroom. I was a soldier for God's sake and I didn't even hear them. They turned on the light and I just kept on sleeping. They had to shake me awake. Which I will admit was one of the scariest moments of my life. You can imagine what I was thinking. But, Jesus, then they never said a goddamn thing. That was the worst part. They held out clothes for me and motioned me to get dressed. Weird thing was they shielded their eyes so they could only see my feet when I got out of bed, so I figured they weren't going to rape me.

"Then they led me to their car and just started to drive. I had no idea what was going on until you opened the door. What is it with you, anyway? First it was Africa and then Atlantic City and now tonight. Do you go anywhere where there aren't armed goons gunning for you?" Her raised voice alerted Drag. He ambled over and flopped onto his back in front of Cali, instantly defusing her anger. She bent to rub his ample belly. Looking up at Mercer, she said, "For some reason I never pictured you with a dog."

"Drag's not mine. He's Harry's."

"Harry's here?"

"Upstairs working on Chester Bowie's damned word games. This one's a little more complex than the first one we got from the archive. Why don't you head up.

I've got to walk Drag. I'll be back in a second."

"Do you think those men . . . ?"

"They're gone. I believed him when he said he just wants to warn us off."

"And did he?"

Mercer's eyes tightened for an instant then he smiled. "Not by a long shot."

Cali straightened and kissed Mercer softly on the cheek. "Sorry about blowing up like that. I was just —"

"Don't worry about it."

Mercer returned to the brownstone after Drag had sniffed at every car tire, lamppost, and fire hydrant in a two-block radius before finding one worthy of peeing on. When he opened the door, he heard Cali's ringing laughter from the bar and he silently thanked Harry for dispelling the last of her misgivings.

Harry had poured her a stiff Scotch and was showing her the codes. When Mercer came into the room, Harry cast him a wicked look. "Cali told me what happened. I told her she has it all wrong. You hired those guys just so you'd finally have a woman in your house."

"Desperate times," Mercer shot back. He moved behind the bar to pour himself another cup of coffee, only this one he laced with a generous dram of brandy. "Has he shown you the codes?" he asked Cali. "Or has he just been besmirching my character?"

"He cracked the last one."

"I think," Harry said. "Gout into full; gout, pout, pour, four, which is our clue by the way, then foul, fowl, bowl, boll, bull, full."

"So the key is?"

Harry checked his notes. "Ten times four lest five."

"Forty minus five," Mercer said. "Thirty-five. Have you started looking for the words?"

A shadow crept across Harry's blue eyes. "Yeah and I may be all wrong. It doesn't make a whole lot of sense to me."

"What do you have?"

"Counting every thirty-fifth word gives us this."

He showed the paper to Mercer: "Deer Albert nick cola was right trains urine nick elements dew exist in nature."

"See what I mean?" Harry said, waving away a cloud of cigarette smoke that was drifting toward Cali's face. "Bunch of gobbledygook if you ask me."

Mercer read the sentence again and again, speeding up, slowing down, and inserting random pauses. Two words kept thrusting themselves to the forefront of his mind. Nick cola. Nick . . . cola. Nickcola. Nickola. Nikola. "Holy shit!"

"What?" Cali and Harry cried in unison.

"Tesla," Mercer said and suddenly the rest of the sentence became clear. He blanched. "We're in trouble."

"Damn it, what does it mean?"

"Dear Albert," Mercer said, still grappling with what Chester Bowie had discovered. "Nikola was right, transuranic elements do exist in nature."

"Oh my God," Cali gasped. Mercer wasn't surprised she understood right away. She was a nuclear scientist after all.

Harry still didn't get it. "So what?"

"Transuranic elements are elements above uranium on the periodic table," Mercer replied. "They can only be produced in a lab by a nuclear reactor. Most of them decay in a few seconds but there's one that lasts years — hell, millennia. Chester Bowie's adamantine isn't naturally enriched uranium, it's fucking plutonium. And raw plutonium doesn't need expensive refining with centrifuges and a staff of scientists to be made into a weapon. Its stuff is ready to go. Instant dirty bomb. A terrorist's wet dream come true."

"I have to call my boss at NEST," Cali said at once. "We have a national emergency on our hands."

"In due time," Mercer cautioned. "I want us to get everything together first. Figure out what we know and determine what we need to find out. Once we're ready, you can present it to your nuclear response team while I'll go to Ira Lasko at the White House."

Cali looked uncertain.

"Besides," he went on, "it's almost midnight. We should be able to put a report together by morning if we work through the night."

She relented. "Okay."

"Harry?"

"What the hell," the old man said. "I'll get plenty of rest when the big sleep comes."

"Thanks, I owe you a favor."

"Actually you owe me twenty thousand

favors, but who's counting?" He set to work on Chester Bowie's thirty-page letter to Albert Einstein.

Mercer made a less sadistic pot of coffee for Cali while she slipped into the guest bedroom to clean herself up a bit. When she came back her eyes were clear and bright and her hair was tucked into a ponytail. She'd applied lip gloss which accentuated her generous mouth.

"Mind my asking why you have women's toiletries in your guest bathroom?" she said teasingly.

"They're Harry's," Mercer deadpanned. "Old letch is a crossdresser."

"Something's bothering me," Cali said, taking a seat at the bar. "Actually everything's bothering me but what I don't understand is how can there be naturally occurring plutonium. That's physically impossible."

"Not at all. Traces of it are found all over the planet. What's more difficult to explain is a large concentration of it and I think I know the answer. Ever heard of Oklo, Gabon, in West Africa?" Cali shook her head. "In the early seventies a French team discovered unusual ratios of isotopes in a bunch of uranium deposits. The discrepancy was tiny but important. Something had happened to the uranium.

"At first they thought the sample had been contaminated in the lab or at the site, but they ruled it out. The only logical conclusion was that at some time — and they later figured out it was about two and a half billion years ago — the natural uranium deposit had gone critical."

"And started a chain reaction," Cali finished. "I *have* read about it. A natural nuclear reactor that operated just like one in a power plant. It had all the elements, fuel in the form of concentrated uranium-235. There was plenty of water to act as a moderator so the chain reaction didn't turn into a runaway explosion, and there weren't any neutron absorbers in the rock to prevent the mass going critical in the first place."

"That's exactly right. The water that seeped down to the uranium deposits was high in calcium, which acted just like the control rods of a nuclear power plant. The water also kept the reactor cool enough to allow for a sustained chain reaction."

"How long did it burn, do you know?"

"Estimates range between five hundred thousand and a million years."

"Wow."

"And just think — no one around to protest it," Mercer joked.

"Do you think the ore Chester Bowie discovered came from another natural reactor like Oklo?"

"With one critical difference. Bowie's didn't go critical until much more recently; otherwise the plutonium would have decayed. It has a half-life around twenty-four thousand years, so the size of the reactor and the ratio of remaining plutonium-239 would determine its age. But if I were to hazard a guess, I'd say it couldn't be more than a couple million years old, which in geological terms is yesterday."

Cali was impressed. "I hadn't thought about that. Is it possible there are other natural reactors, young ones I mean?"

Mercer shook his head. "I doubt it. And even if there were, chances are they're buried deep in the crust."

Cali became thoughtful. "It's weird to think my original hunch about elevated cancer rates in Africa led us to a natural source of plutonium."

"And something else tipped off someone else."

Cali cocked her head. "What do you mean?"

"Poli. When we saw him in Africa I assumed he was a mercenary hired by Caribe Dayce to help in his revolution. Now it's more likely that Dayce was the muscle hired to protect Poli and help him find the deposit."

"That's right! Damn, I hadn't seen the connection. Poli's been on the trail of the plutonium all along. Which leaves us with tonight's visitors. What did they call themselves?"

"Janissaries," Mercer answered. "You just knew this would end up involving Middle Eastern terrorists."

"Who or what are Janissaries?"

"During the Ottoman Empire they were elite soldiers bound personally to the sultan. They were some of the fiercest fighters in history. Totally ruthless. If I remember correctly they grew so powerful that some sultan in the 1800s organized another army and massacred the Janissaries to a man."

"And now they're back."

"I doubt these guys have any legitimate claim. They're just using the name."

"You know, though, they didn't act like any terrorist I've dealt with over the course of my career. They aren't wild-eyed jihadists ready to blow themselves up at the drop of the Koran. Think about it. They saved our lives in Africa and again in Atlantic City. And tonight, other than scaring me to death, they didn't hurt me. They were actually kind of respectful. I sleep in the nude and when I got out of bed they averted their eyes."

"Cali, devout Muslims wouldn't want to look at your naked body." Mercer couldn't stop such an image of her flooding his mind. He was sure she knew exactly what he was picturing and turned away. He added hastily, "Besides, they had guns."

"First of all, a year in Iraq taught me that men are men all over the world. They'll cop a feel or sneak a peak any chance they get. Muslim, Jew, Christian — it's all the same. But these guys didn't and why try to warn us off? Why not just kill us and be done with it? If I was a terrorist that's what I would do."

Mercer considered her point and admitted it had merit. Poli Feines and company obviously didn't care about human life. From what he'd seen they looked like they enjoyed taking it, but the two Janissaries hadn't hurt Cali tonight and hadn't even threatened them. The leader just warned them that if they kept investigating they might get caught in the cross fire. What was it they thought he and Cali were looking for? The Alembic of Skenderbeg. Mercer still didn't know what that meant.

"Any idea what they thought we were

after?" he asked her. "The Alembic of Skenderbeg?"

"No clue," Cali admitted. "Do you have a dictionary?"

From down the bar Harry said, "An alembic is a device once used in distilleries to purify booze."

"Figures you'd know that," Mercer remarked sarcastically. "What about Skenderbeg?"

Harry returned to his notes. "Couldn't tell you."

Cali followed Mercer down to his home office. He brushed his hand against a bluish rock on a credenza near the office door. It was a personal talisman, a piece of kimberlite, the lodestone of every diamond mine in the world. This particular piece had an exquisite diamond embedded on its underside and had been the gift of a grateful mine owner from South Africa.

"I haven't had the chance to tell you," Cali said as Mercer fired up his computer. "Your home is beautiful."

"Thank you," Mercer replied. "I travel so much that I needed to make my home more of a retreat." He accessed the Internet, found a search engine, and typed in "Skenderbeg." He read silently for a few moments then said, "Looks like Skenderbeg was an

Albanian general who revolted against the Ottoman Empire."

Cali interrupted. "Ottoman connection again." She'd retreated to the leather sofa against the wall, throwing the steamer robe that was folded on the arm over her lower body.

"U'huh. He died in 1468. Seems he held off a Turkish army five times the size of his and managed to keep Albania independent for twenty-five years. He's considered one of their national heroes. Sort of a medieval George Washington."

"What about an alembic?" Her eyes were closed and Mercer could tell she was moments from falling asleep.

Mercer's fingers blurred across the keyboard as he tried several variations on his search but came up empty. "Nada."

When Cali didn't respond, he looked up. Her breathing was shallow and even, her lips slightly parted. She was out. He came around from behind his desk to stand over her. Despite her considerable height she'd managed to turn herself into a tight ball with one hand under her cheek.

He couldn't help but think of Tisa again, although there was no similarity between her and Cali. Tisa had dark sloe eyes and delicate Asian features and the small body of a gymnast. Cali was all-American with her red hair and freckles, which Mercer could see covered her upper chest, and he suspected the rest of her as well. She was tall and lanky, more angles than curves, but she moved with an athletic grace that softened her hard edges. And, Mercer admitted, she was the first woman he had been attracted to since Tisa's death.

In truth they had spent very little time together, but under the intensity of the circumstances he had come to understand her — the way she thought, the way she reacted, and most importantly, what she thought of herself. She was confident and self-assured, characteristics that Mercer found appealing above everything else.

But now wasn't the time for any of these thoughts.

He had to resist the urge to brush a wisp of hair from across her forehead. He straightened the blanket instead, pulling it up so it was just under her chin, and re-moved her shoes. Her feet were long and narrow, with delicate bones and skin so pale he could see where veins came close to the surface. She made a little sound then sighed as she drifted deeper to sleep. He gave her one last look, smiled, then left the office, turning down the lights to a faint glow so if she woke during the night she'd be able to see a bit.

Mercer made sure all the doors were locked before heading up to the master suite on the third floor. The Beretta 92 in his nightstand was probably the fifth or sixth one he'd owned. Some he'd lost in fights, while others were in evidence lockers. It was a reliable weapon and he knew its capabilities as well as he knew his own. He knew the nine-millimeter was loaded but checked it anyway. There was a round in the chamber and the safety was off. He safed the pistol and stuck it behind his back. He doubted Poli would come tonight, but he wasn't going to take any chances. He'd make sure that starting tomorrow Harry stayed at his own place, while he would ensure that Ira Lasko got him and Cali into a safe house.

Back in the bar Harry was snoring on the couch, a deep rumbling that sounded like the dying gasps of a bear. Drag was curled around Harry's prosthetic leg, his nose near where the leg was strapped to the stump so he could spend the night smelling his beloved master.

Mercer didn't adjust Harry's blanket.

He took a seat at the bar and saw that Harry hadn't finished his work yet, so he set aside Harry's notes and instead read the lengthy letter to Einstein to keep himself awake through the long night.

At noon the next day Ira Lasko's secretary led Cali and Mercer through to Lasko's office in the Old Executive Office Building adjacent to the White House. Ira came around his big desk to shake Cali's hand as Mercer made the introduction.

"So you're the lady Mercer met in Africa à la Stanley and Livingstone?" The top of his bald head barely reached her chin. "When he called me from New Jersey night before last he mentioned you're with DOE."

"I'm a field investigator with NEST."

"Nuclear response team. Your boss is Cliff Roberts, then?"

"That's right."

"He's an ass."

Cali grinned, warming to Lasko's directness immediately. "That he is."

"He's ex-navy like me. I spent a year with him at the Pentagon. He has the imagination of a kumquat and half the brains. He only got his gig at NEST when Homeland Security was created after 9/11." He indicated they should take the chairs in front of his desk, while he slid around to his seat.

The office was large and comfortable, with wainscoting and a plush green carpet. There were only a few framed pictures and papers on the walls, as well as an American flag. Ira also wore a flag lapel pin. There was a model of a submarine on a credenza, an old Sturgeon class that Lasko had served on as executive officer before moving over to naval intelligence.

He turned to Mercer. "So what's so hellfire important that I have to give up a golf game with the chairman of the Joint Chiefs?"

"A couple hundred pounds of plutonium that's been missing for seventy plus years." Mercer explained about the naturally occurring nuclear reactor at Oklo and his theory of how what they thought was an unusually concentrated uranium deposit was in fact the remnants of a much younger reactor that hadn't fully decayed.

"What are the chances there are other such reactors?" Ira asked when Mercer finished.

"Cali asked the same thing last night. Remote. I think this is probably the only one like it in the world."

"So how did that guy find it? You told me at dinner the other night that he was either the best geologist in the world or the luckiest."

"Chester Bowie was his name," Mercer

said, "and he wasn't a geologist at all. He taught classics at a small college in New Jersey. He wasn't looking for uranium or plutonium. He was searching for a mine out of Greek mythology."

"Lost me."

"According to mythology Zeus chained Prometheus for defying him and giving fire to humanity. The chains were made from an unbreakable metal called adamantine. Bowie thought he knew where the adamantine had come from. He ran into a little problem of funding his expedition and talked it over with a colleague from Princeton, hoping the Ivy League school might see merit in his research."

"Not likely," Ira growled.

"On the contrary. Someone at Princeton was very interested. None other than Albert Einstein himself. From what I gather, Nikola Tesla, the Croatian-born genius who invented the alternating current electrical system we use today, had contacted Einstein in the mid-1930s with the theory that there were elements higher than uranium on the periodic table. Remember this was six or seven years before Enrico Fermi created the first sustained chain reaction at the University of Chicago and four or five before Einstein wrote his famous letter to

Roosevelt indicating the theoretical possibility of an atomic bomb.

"Bowie didn't know how Einstein became aware of his grant request, but he did, and agreed to have Princeton fund his trip. Einstein warned Bowie that what he might find wasn't adamantine from his mythology but a new and potentially dangerous element. Bowie was certain Einstein and Tesla had it wrong and was eager to prove himself to two of the greatest minds of his generation."

"Was Bowie well regarded in his field?" Ira asked.

Mercer chuckled. "The guy was a total flake. A real zealot when it came to his theories. He refused to believe anyone but himself."

"He sounds deranged."

"He was. Obsessive-compulsive, arrogant, you name it." Mercer picked up the story again. "So he went to Africa and using his research into Greek mythology he found the mine. He mentions in his journal that there was an ancient stele there to mark the site."

"Wait. What's a stele?"

"A carved stone obelisk used by the Egyptians usually to mark a military victory or some important event."

"So this goes back to the Egyptians?"

Mercer held up a hand. "That's getting

ahead of the story, but Cali and I both remember seeing it in the village square. It was about seven feet tall and very weathered. Anyway Bowie hired some locals to help him dig out samples of the ore. And as you know, ever since then the natives have been suffering from long-term radiation exposure. He crated up about a thousand pounds worth of dirt and made his way to the port city of Brazzaville. That's where he realized that he wasn't the only person looking for the ore. In fact it seemed there were a couple of groups interested in what he was doing in the interior. He was pretty sure his guide had betrayed him to some German agents.

"I'm sure you're aware that the Nazis had a thing for the occult and had sent out teams of agents to find certain ancient relics. Hitler needed them to legitimize his claim about pure Aryan stock and all that crap. That's how they came into possession of the Spear of Longinus, the weapon purportedly used to pierce Christ's side."

"I've seen the movie," Ira said. "Lost ark and all that. Besides that fits with what you told me about others showing up at that village a few years after Bowie to mine the rest of the ore."

"And gunning down most of the villag-

262

ers," Mercer added. "Anyway Bowie managed to get the crates of ore samples onto a tramp steamer called the *Wetherby,* with orders that it go to Chicago, where Einstein believed Fermi should study it to see if they really were transuranic elements."

"Why didn't Bowie stay with the ship?"

"Paranoia, plus he had just spent several weeks around plutonium without any kind of protection. He realized he was suffering from radiation poisoning and was also wracked with malaria and a few other fun tropical bugs. There's a line in his diary that goes something like 'For three days my bowels ran like the River Styx.' "

"Lovely."

"The day after the ship sailed he was almost killed by a pair of men he believed were Germans. They tried to muscle him into a car but two other men dressed in dark suits came out of nowhere, shot the Germans, and vanished."

"Who were they? Did he know?"

"He didn't but we do." Mercer's statement invited an explanation.

Cali said, "Last night two men in dark suits showed up at my condo and forced me to go with them. They took me to Mercer's, where they warned us to stop searching for something called the Alembic of Skenderbeg."

"They were the same guys who wiped out Caribe Dayce and his army in Africa and took on Poli Feines at the Deco Palace," Mercer added. "They called themselves Janissaries and said we were caught up in an ancient conflict we couldn't possibly understand."

Ira held up a hand. "Hold on. Are you saying that the men who saved Bowie in Brazzaville are the same two who took out Dayce?"

"No, but I think they belong to the same organization, a secret group that's been around for at least seventy years and may have roots going back to the 1400s. Skenderbeg, who's real name was Gjergi Kastrioti, was an Albanian-born general in the Ottoman Army, a Janissary who eventually revolted against Sultan Murad II. He captured a key town in Albania and, with a force never exceeding twenty thousand, managed to keep the Ottomans' quarter million men at bay for twenty-five years. He had close diplomatic ties and financial support from the Vatican because he was defending Christendom from Islamic invaders.

"What's interesting, and why I mention all this, is that the name Skenderbeg is a local translation of the Ottoman, Iskender Bey or Iskender the Great. We know him as Alexander the Great. This morning I got in touch with an Ottoman history teacher at George Washington University to get some more background on Skenderbeg. It's accepted conjecture that Skenderbeg was given this title because his military skill matched that of Alexander's, but there's another story, one that can't be verified. It was rumored that he possessed a talisman of some sort that Alexander carried into battle against his greatest foe, Darius, at the Battle of Arbela in 331 B.C., and it was this talisman that allowed both men to defeat armies ten times the size of their own."

"What sort of talisman?"

"The professor didn't know, but I assume it's this alembic the Janissaries mentioned. The professor said the real expert on Skenderbeg is a Turkish historian named Ibriham Ahmad. I tried calling him in Istanbul but just left a message."

"We have a theory," Cali said. "Before his final battle against Darius, Alexander invaded Egypt and overthrew the Persian governor. According to history the people welcomed him openly and paved the way for the construction of the city of Alexandria, home to the famous library. During his stay in Egypt he went to the temple of Zeus-Ammon someplace in the Libyan desert. It was there that the oracle revealed to him that he was the son of Ammon, Egypt's chief deity, and was thus a god himself. A year later he defeated Darius."

"With you so far," Ira said.

"What if Alexander received something else when he visited the oracle, like how to procure a great weapon fit for a god? Trade along the North African coast was well established by this time. It's possible the priests had learned about magic rocks that could incapacitate an army and told Alexander where to find them."

"What we think," Mercer said, "is he sent a column to Central Africa, to the site near the Scilla River. There they mined some of the plutonium ore and erected a stele to commemorate their visit."

"We think Alexander went into battle against Darius using an improvised radiological bomb," Cali concluded. "We checked and the Battle of Arbela was carefully staged. Both Alexander and Darius knew when and where they were going to meet. It's possible that in the days leading up to the battle Alexander had radiological dust spread around Darius's encampment. His people would need little more protection than rags tied around their mouths so they didn't inhale the plutonium, which is the only way plutonium is fatal by the way, while Darius's men would suffer radiation poisoning. Nothing lethal but enough to incapacitate them and allow Alexander's smaller army to wipe them out."

"Now jump forward seventeen hundred years to Albania," Mercer added, "and you have a general who holds off a huge army for decades using a talisman that once belonged to Alexander the Great. We think Skenderbeg used his alembic to dose the Ottoman Army with enough radiation to make them too sick to fight."

"What happened to Skenderbeg?"

"He died in 1468 of natural causes," Mercer said. "His men held out for another decade but eventually they were overrun."

"And his alembic?" Ira had a dubious look on his pug face.

Mercer shrugged. "I'm hoping Professor Ahmad in Istanbul can answer that."

"Admiral Lasko," Cali said, "I know this all sounds like a bit of a stretch but there's a line in Chester Bowie's journal that ties it together somewhat. He left Brazzaville right after the abduction attempt and made his way across Africa to Alexandria. In his journal he wrote that given a couple of days he could have found Alexander's hidden tomb. He knew there was a connection between Alexander the Great and his work."

"From there," Mercer went on, "he caught a steamer to Europe, where he did the one thing the Nazis would never suspect. He knew he was dying and wanted to reach America as fast as possible to tell Einstein what he'd discovered. He sent Einstein a telegram from Athens and Einstein wrote him back telling him to contact Otto Hahn, a nuclear physicist who would eventually win the Nobel Prize for being the first person to split a uranium atom."

Cali interrupted. "Hahn wasn't a Nazi, and he refused to work on Germany's nuclear bomb program, so when Einstein contacted him about Chester Bowie he made arrangements for Bowie's return to the United States the fastest way possible — the airship *Hindenburg*."

"Are you telling me he was on the *Hindenburg* when it exploded?"

Mercer nodded. "Which makes me think that maybe the conspiracy theorists are right and the zeppelin was sabotaged. Only it wasn't about discrediting the Nazis, but about preventing Bowie from giving the sample of plutonium to Einstein."

"Jesus," Ira exclaimed. "Who? How?"

"My money's on the Germans themselves and here's why. In the last few pages of his diary Bowie said an officer came to his cabin. He killed the officer, believing that the Germans had found out who he was and weren't going to let him off the airship. That's when he wrote down his story and tucked it in the safe. He tied Einstein's name to a tag on the outside and heaved it out the window. But what makes me think it was the Germans and Bowie wasn't being paranoid is that the airship was delayed coming into Lakehurst because of a storm. But what if the captain was ordered to wait because the Nazi higher-ups were trying to think of a way to destroy it? I don't know if you're aware, but after the *Hindenburg* blew up the Germans refused to let anyone help clean up the debris. They sent over teams themselves to haul the zeppelin's skeleton back to Germany. That could have been cover to find Bowie's safe in the wreckage, only he was a step ahead of them and heaved it over the side above Waretown, New Jersey."

"I think it was the Janissaries," Cali offered. "I think they realized they'd made a mistake letting Bowie go in Brazzaville, somehow learned he was going to be on the *Hindenburg,* and had someone in the United

States in place to take it out."

Ira scratched his bald head. "I might have a third candidate, one that might squirrel all your theories." He reached into the middle drawer of his desk and placed an item on the blotter.

Mercer recognized it at once. "That's the bullet the old woman gave me in Africa."

"I sent it to the FBI lab at Quantico," Ira said. "This, my friend, isn't a German round but a 7.65-by-25 shell casing from either a pistol or a PP Sh submachine gun, which if you aren't aware, was the standard automatic weapon for the Soviet Army during World War Two."

"The Soviets?" Mercer and Cali said as one and then fell silent.

Mercer hadn't expected this at all. He was certain that it was the Germans who were after Bowie. As far as he knew the Soviet Union didn't even have a nuclear program until spies infiltrated the Manhattan Project in the 1940s, so why would they want plutonium five years earlier? He was about to mention this when Cali spoke up.

"It makes perfect sense," she said. "We know the Soviet Union had spies at Los Alamos, which is how they got the plans for the bomb. Stalin knew more about it than Truman when they met at Potsdam and the

President mentioned we had a weapon that would end the war. What has never made sense to me and a lot of people who studied the history was how the Soviets were able to create their own bomb so soon after the Japanese surrender. Rather than the decades we expected to have nuclear dominance, we lost it in just four years.

"The entire western third of Russia had been devastated by the war," Cali went on. "Whole cities were destroyed and millions of people were left homeless. The Soviets didn't receive any of the aid we gave to Europe to rebuild. In fact they had to spend money to shore up their holdings in Eastern Europe. I know Stalin was a ruthless tyrant, but the economics don't pan out. They didn't have the resources to keep their people from starving while trying to rebuild their own country, occupy Eastern Europe all the way to Germany, and spend a hundred billion dollars building their own bomb. Even with the plans provided by Stalin's spies, it takes a tremendous amount of sophistication and resources to refine fissionable materials." She caught Mercer's eye. "But what if he already had those materials? If the Russians had some of the ore, it would dramatically reduce the amount of time and the cost it would take to build an atomic bomb. They could easily do it in four years and still do everything else I mentioned."

"Makes sense," Ira said thoughtfully. "I've got a lot of contacts in Russia, and since the collapse they've been pretty forthcoming with information from the bad old days. I'll ask around to see if what you surmise is true." He looked at Mercer. "What about you? Where do you want to take this?"

"Cali spoke with her supervisor at NEST. We've got them tracing the disappearance of the *Wetherby.*"

"How do you know she disappeared?"

"Simple. Nowhere in the history books does it say Enrico Fermi experimented with plutonium ore in the 1930s, so he must have never received the samples, ergo the *Wetherby* vanished. Also I think someone should take a look at that stele Cali and I saw in Africa. There could be clues on it about how much ore Alexander's people mined."

"Is that important?" Ira asked. "I mean come on, we're talking ancient history."

"If we're only right about Alexander possessing a radiological bomb or dispersal device, then I'd agree, but the Janissaries who nabbed Cali last night act as though the alembic is lying around for someone to find."

"You told me over dinner that you think that part of the Central African Republic is still pretty hot. I don't want to send a team in there unless you're sure it's important."

Mercer silently cursed Ira, though he didn't believe his old friend was deliberately putting the responsibility for a potentially dangerous operation on his shoulders. He was just being cautious. But Mercer knew the ultimate responsibility would fall on him if something went wrong. Like Serena's death and the others at the casino. Like Tisa's and dozens more — he felt the weight of it all pressing down on him. It would be so easy to just tell Ira to forget it, that he didn't need to send a Special Forces team into the middle of a war zone. He could crawl out from under a little of his guilt. But Mercer also knew it would be wrong.

It didn't matter if the stele turned out to be nothing more than a marker saying the equivalent of "Kilroy was here." He had to know, no matter the cost.

"Yeah," Mercer finally said. "It's important."

"Consider it done," Ira replied with finality.

BUFFALO, NEW YORK

Mercer opened the door of the Cessna Citation executive jet as soon as the wheels stopped rolling. Mist that was almost rain swept Buffalo Niagara International Airport, making the runway lights blur into the distance. Dawn was just a ruddy promise hunkered low against the eastern horizon. He grabbed his leather hand grip but didn't bother pulling up the hood of his North Face rain jacket. As soon as he stepped from the aircraft, water glittered like jewels in his thick hair.

"Dr. Mercer?" a man's voice called from the rear of the airport's general aviation gate.

"I'm Mercer," he replied and strode across the tarmac, paying scant attention to the multimillion-dollar jets parked all around. A throaty roar swallowed the man's next sentence as a Boeing 737 hauled itself into the dark sky. "What was that?" Mercer asked as he reached the protection of a glass enclosure that led into the building.

"I said you have a car waiting to take you to the docks."

"Thank you," Mercer said and followed the executive jet service employee through the lounge. They walked across the quiet airport and eventually reached an exit. A black Town Car idled at the curb, its driver waiting expectantly in the front seat.

Mercer didn't wait for the chauffeur to open the door. He did it himself, then tossed his bag into the back and swung himself into the front seat. "Morning," he said in greeting to the startled driver. "I'm not important enough for the full chauffeur treatment so I'll ride up front with you."

"Guy gets off a private jet and says he's not important don't know his place in the world, but it makes me no never mind." The driver eased the big Lincoln into gear and headed out of the airport complex. Soon they were on Route 33 headed west toward an area of industrial warehouses along the Niagara River.

As the car eased between two metal buildings and onto the dock, Mercer saw a tight cluster of people huddled around the gangway of a large flat-bottomed barge. Above them a street lamp cast their faces in heavy relief. Sitting atop the barge was a crane with a modified smooth silhouette. It reminded him of the low-slung turret of a modern battle tank rather than a lifting derrick. It was tied to a small tug with side-mounted exhaust, so the vessel was no more than ten feet high from the waterline to the top of its radar dish.

Mercer recognized Cali Stowe standing with the people. She stood several inches taller than all of them. When he got out of the car, she looked over and waved. She wore a dark windbreaker and her hair was covered in a baseball cap. Her jeans were just tight enough to outline the lean shape of her legs.

Mercer grabbed his bag, thanked the driver, and approached the group. The drizzle had stopped and dawn was fast approaching. The air remained crisp with the smell of Lake Erie.

"Welcome to Buffalo," Cali greeted.

It was the first time they'd seen each other since the meeting with Ira Lasko four days earlier, and he had to resist the urge to kiss her cheek. Had they been alone he would have done it.

"Let me introduce you around," she said. "Philip Mercer, this is my boss, Cliff Roberts." Because Cali and Ira had a low opinion of the director of the Nuclear Emergency Search Team, Mercer knew he wouldn't like him either. Roberts had mouse brown hair and indistinct features, except for a pursed mouth that looked as if he'd just swallowed something sour. His stance made certain that his trench coat was open enough for everyone to see it was a Burberry. He didn't meet Mercer's eyes when they shook hands, and his grip was limp.

"Pleasure to have you with us," Roberts said with little warmth. It was obvious he resented Mercer's presence in what was to be NEST's highest profile operation when or if word got out about what they were doing.

"I'm glad to be here," Mercer replied neutrally. "When Admiral Lasko wanted an observer I happened to be available."

Roberts said nothing so Cali piped in, "And these two characters are Jesse Williams and Stanley Slaughbaugh. They're part of my regular NEST team. Stan's a Ph.D. from Stanford and Jesse joined our outfit after babysitting nukes for the air force."

Mercer shook their hands. He eyed Jesse Williams. "Didn't you play for the Air Force Academy?"

"Good memory, man." Williams grinned. "That was fifteen years ago. Missed the Heisman by five votes."

"I have a friend who, well, he's a bookie." Mercer was talking about Tiny. "He said the most money he ever won on a game was when you upset Michigan State in the Cotton Bowl."

Williams's smile faded just a tic. "Same game I blew my ACL and any chance of a pro career."

"And finally this is Lieutenant Commander Ruth Bishop from the Coast Guard," Cali said, not wanting to hear another insufferable football conversation. "Ruth's here to ensure we follow the Coasty's regulations concerning the salvage and she'll act as liaison with her Canadian counterpart since the *Wetherby* is pretty close to the border."

She was a short woman in a Coast Guard utility uniform. Her hair was streaked with silver and there were lines around her mouth and bright blue eyes. Mercer had the impression they were laughter rather than frown lines. She glanced at Cali before saying hello, which made Mercer think the two women had talked about him prior to his arrival.

"Just think of me as your den mother,"

she said with a toothy smile that made her glow with warmth. "When you're not sure about something ask me for permission before you do it."

"So when I have to pee-pee?"

Her smile deepened. "Ask me and I'll give you a hall pass. Just don't make on the Canadians. They're touchy about that."

Mercer laughed. "Yes, ma'am."

"Ruth is also a bit of the local expert on the *Wetherby*," Cali added. "She's made four dives down to her over the years."

"Not for a few years now," Lieutenant Commander Bishop admitted.

"What's her condition?" Mercer asked. Before Ruth could answer, he asked another question. "First of all, why don't you tell me what happened to her and what kind of ship she was."

"Okay. First, the *Wetherby* was a tramp steamer, what's called a stick ship. She was only two hundred twenty feet long and thirty feet at the beam. She was coal fired, had a single stack, and from what I've been able to learn hadn't seen a moment's maintenance after she put to sea." Bishop corrected herself. "That's not entirely true. She served admirably during World War One on convoy duty but after that she was a derelict waiting to happen."

"So what happened when she reached Buffalo?"

"The *Wetherby* put in here on the night of August 9, 1937, where she was picking up some machine parts headed for Cleveland. She was then supposed to go on to Detroit, Milwaukee, and finally Chicago, where Cali said the cargo you are interested in was destined."

"That's right."

"Early morning August 10 she unloaded some fuel oil barrels she'd picked up in Montreal that were supposed to have come down the St. Lawrence on another ship. During the transfer a fire started in the hold. Since no one physically inspected the wreck because she sank, investigators had to go along with eyewitnesses who claimed she was struck by lightning."

"There's a problem with their story." It was a statement more than a question.

"It *was* raining that day but no one other than the crew in the hold recall any lightning in the area. It's possible a static charge built up and its discharge ignited one of the fuel barrels, but I'm putting my money on either a longshoreman or a member of the crew smoking in the hold. A dropped match in some spilled bunker fuel and voilà." She made the motion of an explosion with her hands.

"How many men were killed?"

"Six in the hold, including the *Wetherby's* second officer, Kerry Frey. Another man was killed on the dock, a local vagrant well known at the time. Another body was recovered from the river about a mile downstream but he was never identified."

"No idea who he was?"

"None. Everyone was accounted for. A lot of people said he had nothing to do with the *Wetherby* because his body wasn't burned, but I think it's too much of a coincidence."

Mercer glanced at Cali. She was already looking at him. "Janissary," he mouthed but she just shrugged. He turned back to Ruth Bishop. "Go on."

"As the fire raged out of control, a crane operator on the dock panicked. When he jumped from the cab of his crane, he hit a lever that sent a pallet of fuel drums plummeting back into the blaze. When they exploded a second later, it blew out the side of the *Wetherby* as if she'd been torpedoed."

Mercer didn't say it aloud but he was sure she had told this story many times; her sense of dramatic timing was too good not to be practiced.

"The *Wetherby* rolled right there against the dock, parting her mooring hawsers as she turned onto her side. Another stevedore was injured by one of the heavy ropes when it snapped back toward the dock. He lost his hand but went on to make a full recovery. In fact his niece is a lieutenant commander in the Coast Guard."

It took Mercer a second to process that bit of information. "Ah, so that's how you became interested in the disaster?"

"Uncle Ralph told me this story so many times I had it memorized by the time I was ten," Ruth admitted.

"So the *Wetherby*'s on fire and capsized?"

"That's right. The current took hold of her before she could settle, and she started drifting down the Niagara River toward the falls. Because she was on her side she slipped under the railroad bridge that spanned the river between Fort Erie and Buffalo and also under the nearby Peace Bridge. Eyewitness on the Peace Bridge said that it looked like the river was on fire as she passed underneath, and people at the falls saw the burning oil slick going over and thought it was part of a show. By the time the *Wetherby* reached Grand Island, where the Niagara splits into the Chippawa and American channels, she'd grounded herself a couple of times, once for nearly two hours before enough water had piled against her upstream side to push her farther toward the falls.

"She finally came to rest just above the northern tip of Grand Island in the Chippawa Channel, and as luck would have it she settled into the deepest trough on the river, a sixty-foot sinkhole left over when the glaciers retreated and created both the river and the falls."

That reminded Mercer that Niagara Falls had only been in existence since the last ice age, some twelve thousand years ago. That wasn't even a blink of an eye in geologic terms.

"What was she like when you dove on her?"

"She's lying on her side and, like I said, in sixty feet of water. The part of her hull facing the surface is in good shape. Freshwater isn't as corrosive as salt but she's taken a beating from logs and other flotsam coming down from Erie on the way to the falls. Last time I went down, and that was a good ten years ago, she had an oak tree embedded in her forecastle."

"What are diving conditions like?"

"Hell," a voice called out.

"Mr. Crenna." Cali greeted the stranger

then turned to the little group. "This is Brian Crenna from Erie Salvage and Dredging. He'll be in charge of the salvage barge and support ship." Cali made the introductions.

Crenna was a plug of a man standing about five foot six with a hard, round gut and a snarled black beard. He wore company coveralls and steel-toed boots, a hardhat tucked under one of his muscular arms. When Mercer shook his hand, he realized Crenna was missing his pinkie. He also realized that Crenna wasn't particularly happy about being here.

"Why do you say the conditions are hell?" Mercer asked.

Crenna spat. "Because about a hundred and seventy-five thousand cubic feet of water come down the Niagara River every second. That's twelve thousand tons. Some places the current runs two knots, some it runs eight. Some days the winds come from Lake Erie, which increases the flow ten or twenty percent. Others it's off Ontario which slows things a bit. And some days it changes every couple of hours so you never know what you're going to get. Then there's the fact that last winter saw some heavy snows so the river's still in flood. And that sinkhole where the *Wetherby* got herself lodged is loaded with back currents and whirlpools. If you know anything about diving then you'll know what I'm describing is hell." He waited for anyone to speak. When no one did, he added, "And don't forget if you get into trouble the damned falls are only a couple miles downstream."

"Yes, well thank you," Cliff Roberts said in his best bureaucratic voice.

"I named a crazy price to agree to this job," Crenna said, addressing Roberts, "and you said you'd pay it but don't for a second think I agree this is a good idea. We should wait until the spring runoff ebbs and we know we'll have a few good days of weather."

Roberts pulled himself to his full five foot seven. While he managed an inch on the tow boat operator, he fell far short of intimidating him. "You've been hired by the United States Government for a very important mission. We are paying you for your expert advice concerning the salvage operation. Anything else you have to say is merely your opinion and quite frankly I don't care about it. Do your job."

Mercer expected Crenna to turn around and walk off again. Placed in a similar circumstance, Mercer would have, after a few choice words. Crenna stood his ground, his dark eyes never leaving Roberts's, and it was almost as if Mercer could see his mind at work. But in the end he must have decided the money was more important to him than his own feelings about working for a martinet like Roberts.

"You coming with us?" he finally asked.

"No," the director of NEST said as if the question was absurd. "I'm needed back in Washington."

Crenna spat again. "Good 'nuf."

"Why don't you tell Mercer the plan?" Cali said to dispel the tension and cleanse the air of testosterone. "Mercer just arrived and hasn't been filled in yet."

Crenna shot Mercer a dark look. "You another one from Washington?"

"Don't hold it against me but that's where I live. I'm a prospecting geologist."

"Noticed the hands when we shook," Crenna remarked and glanced at Roberts. "Figured you've done some work in your life."

Mercer knew the type. It was inevitable in his line of work. When on a consulting job, he usually spent equal amounts of time with mine managers and the miners themselves. While most understood the other guys had a job to do, there were always a few on both sides who carried a chip on their shoulder about their own importance. There was nothing wrong with being proud of what you did. Mercer applauded it. What he didn't like, and what he saw in Roberts as well as Crenna, was disdain for the other side of the management/labor symbiosis.

"So what is your plan, Mr. Crenna?"

"Captain."

"Captain it is."

"As soon as my crew arrives," Crenna began, "we'll tow the crane under the bridges and downstream to the site. As you can see she's built low because there isn't much clearance under them bridges. Once over the *Wetherby* I'll deploy the hydraulic anchors to keep us in position, then I'll send for you all. I don't want you on the barge until it's secure." Cali made to protest but Crenna cut her off. "I've got liability issues as it is, so no argument. Once you're aboard I'll send down a couple of divers to assess the wreckage and determine the best way in."

"You're not going to try to lift her?"

"Can't risk it if the current picks up," Crenna said. "The hulk would produce enough drag to pull the anchors off the river bottom."

Mercer nodded. Crenna seemed to know his business. "Most likely you'll have to cut through the hull to find the crates."

"Which shouldn't be too difficult," Crenna agreed. "With a little luck we'll get her open by tomorrow and have your crates on the surface the next day or so. Provided they're still aboard. It's possible they were thrown from her when she was being dragged downriver. Which case they're in the sinkhole at the base of the falls which is deeper than the falls are high."

Mercer had considered that when Cali first told him she'd found that the *Wetherby* had sunk on the Niagara River. But even with the possibility that the crates of plutonium ore lay scattered at the base of the largest waterfall in North America, he still considered her discovery the first break they'd had in the investigation.

Professor Ahmad in Istanbul hadn't returned Mercer's repeated calls and Ira was making slow progress with the Russian authorities concerning their operation into the CAR. It was also taking time to assemble a team to investigate the stele. Ira had explained everything to his boss, national security advisor John Kleinschmidt, but so far neither had had any luck persuading the Pentagon to dispatch a Special Forces unit into Africa. And now State Department officials were getting involved, citing all kinds of sovereignty issues. Ira had told Mercer that they would probably have to tell the President and have him issue an executive order.

But they got lucky when it came to the *Wetherby.* Cali had done the research and quickly discovered that the ship had sunk in the Niagara River just north of Grand Island. The wreck was well known in the Buffalo area, and when she'd asked the local historical society, she was given Ruth Bishop's name as an expert on the wreck. A call to the Coast Guard confirmed that Ruth was the person she needed to speak with.

Ruth told her of her diving experiences on the wreck and helped locate a salvage master willing to take on the job. Cliff Roberts had used his influence to clear the bureaucratic hurdles that cropped up, and just days after learning the *Wetherby*'s location Cali had everything in place to salvage Chester Bowie's ore samples.

Mercer marveled at how effortlessly she seemed to pull everything together. Usually an expedition as complex as this, especially so close to a foreign border, would have taken months if not years. He shot her another glance. Now that the sky was growing brighter he could see the red swelling under her eyes and a little furrow between them. She noted his scrutiny and shot him a tired smile, then a saucy wink.

Mercer made a phone call as Crenna's crew of four arrived, and fifteen minutes later they cast off the tugboat amid a roar of blue exhaust. The international railway bridge was a short distance down the river and from Mercer's vantage it looked like the tug wouldn't fit, but he had to trust the captain to know what he was doing.

"Well, I'm off," Cliff Roberts said as if someone was going to miss him. "Cali, I expect reports every hour once the crane is in position." He nodded to Mercer and Ruth Bishop and shook hands with Williams and Slaughbaugh. "Good luck to you all."

He headed for one of a pair of identical rental cars parked next to a black Suburban with tinted windows that Mercer suspected belonged to Cali's NEST team. Its large cargo area was doubtlessly filled with their equipment. The fourth car was a minivan that had to belong to Ruth Bishop.

"What a wanker," Stan Slaughbaugh said as soon as his boss was out of earshot.

"You said it, my man," Jesse Williams agreed.

"Think what you want," Cali said, "but we wouldn't be here if he hadn't pulled a lot of strings."

"So what do we do now, Boss?" Stan asked, wiping absently at his horn-rimmed glasses.

"I had expected we'd be going out with the barge and staying on site," Cali replied. "I guess we find a hotel. Any recommendations, Ruth?"

"Who's picking up the tab?" she asked.

"Uncle Sam."

"Hyatt's about the best in the city."

"Then the Hyatt it is." She turned to Mercer. "Sorry about having you fly here so quickly. I really thought we'd be going out with the crane."

"That's okay. I wasn't making much progress back home and Harry's been driving me nuts wondering when he can come back and start drinking my booze again."

They drifted to their vehicles. Ruth said her good-byes and said to call her tomorrow if they needed anything, while Mercer set his heavy hand grip into the rear of the rental. Stan and Jesse had driven the NEST Suburban from Washington.

Cali got behind the wheel and told Jesse to follow her. She found the Hyatt on the car's trip computer and started out. "I don't think it was the Janissaries who attacked the *Wetherby.*"

"You said in Ira's office that you believed they took out the *Hindenburg*. If they had the ability to blow an airship out of the sky to stop Bowie from delivering a small sample to Einstein, it's not too much of a stretch for them to destroy the freighter hauling the bulk of the plutonium ore he'd mined."

"I thought of a problem with my idea that the Janissaries destroyed the *Hindenburg*," Cali said with a trace of concern in her voice. "If Bowie took the fastest mode of transportation available at the time to return to the United States, how did a Janissary beat him here so he'd be in place to cause the explosion?"

"Carl Dion told me when I called him that tickets weren't hard to get on that particular flight. It's possible that a Janissary was on the voyage."

"Then why blow it up? All he needed to do was kill Bowie and heave the safe out a window when they were over the Atlantic. It doesn't make sense that he'd allow Bowie to keep the safe during the flight and then destroy the *Hindenburg* when she was getting ready to land."

"Okay, so there wasn't a Janissary on the flight," Mercer said.

"Back to my point. How did the Janissaries get someone to America faster than the fastest way possible?"

"Maybe they had agents here."

"I considered that but I don't buy it."

"Okay, tell me why."

"As far as we know this outfit is strictly interested with protecting the Alembic of Skenderbeg. And all our research so far points to them being confined to Africa and Europe. It wasn't until Bowie came along that they had a threat from the United States. There is absolutely no reason for them to stage assets here. Not unless the organization is huge, like the Masons or something, and it's not or we would have heard about it by now. I can see a small secret society lasting a couple of centuries undetected. Not some large-scale organization with recruiters in North America." She shook her head decisively. "Doesn't wash."

"So if there wasn't a Janissary on the *Hindenburg* and they didn't have someone here, then was it the Russians or the Germans?"

"I don't know. We know the Russians were involved somehow, so it could have been them. They had all kinds of spies in the United States during the thirties. Same with the Germans. Either one of them could have radioed someone to shoot the *Hindenburg* down."

"You couldn't destroy the *Hindenburg* with anything smaller than a shoulder-fired rocket," Mercer told her.

"Are you nuts? It was loaded with millions of cubic feet of hydrogen. A small spark and instant firecracker."

"Au contraire," Mercer said, sure of his subject. "Hydrogen needs oxygen in order to burn and the ratio is very narrow. Too much or too little O2 and it won't catch fire. There would have to have been a sustained leak in one of the gas cells in order for hydrogen to be the culprit, and that would have been noticed by the officers in the control car. Also you can't see a hydrogen fire. It's like pure alcohol. It burns clear, and if you've ever seen footage of the explosion you can clearly see the flames from the very beginning.

"The latest theories concerning the destruction of the *Hindenburg* focus on the waterproofing dope used to cover the skin. It was basically a paste made of the same chemicals found in rocket fuel. Some experts believe that a spark from one of the engines landed on the envelope, causing a small fire that quickly grew to encompass the entire airship. It was only then that the hydrogen detonated."

Cali was silent for a moment, digesting

Mercer's words. "Ah ha," she said with a wicked grin. "Incendiary bullets."

"Did they have them back then?"

"Absolutely."

It was Mercer's turn to think through the scenario. He could find no flaw in her reasoning about the Russians or Germans or about a sniper using incendiary bullets to ignite the airship's explosive skin. "You know," he said at last, "they're going to have to rewrite a lot of history books by the time we're done."

NIAGARA RIVER, NEW YORK

Mercer, Cali, and her NEST team met Brian Crenna's support boat at a pier on Grand Island. A chilled mist clung to the fast-flowing river and obscured the forest on the Canadian side. In the middle of the channel sat Crenna's barge, the crane's telescoping boom rising into the fog like a spindly finger. The tires hanging from the side of the barge looked like oversized portholes, and they could clearly see men on her deck.

The support vessel was an old cabin cruiser that had seen better days. The once white fiberglass hull had yellowed with age, and the red strip along her waterline had faded to the color of old brick. Crenna brought the boat in fast, cutting a tight circle at the last moment to lay the cruiser against the dock, barely squeezing the rubber fenders. The three fishermen readying their big Bertram sportfisher farther down the jetty looked up when the wake made their vessel bob, but they didn't say anything about the breach of maritime etiquette.

"How'd it go?" Cali called after a deckhand had tied the craft to the wooden dock and Crenna had idled the engine.

"No problem. We've got the crane anchored just upstream of the *Wetherby.*" He pointed to the stack of black trunks on the dock. "What's with all the gear?"

"Just some scientific instruments," Cali said. "Plus a pair of dry suits. The water's freezing."

By her evasive tone Mercer realized that Captain Crenna hadn't been informed exactly what was in the crates they hoped to recover. He supposed it didn't matter. As he'd told Ira, plutonium isn't particularly dangerous unless ingested or inhaled. As long as the crates maintained their integrity, Crenna and his crew weren't in any danger.

"Oh," Cali said as if she'd just remembered, "and a bunch of gas masks."

Crenna's scowl deepened. "Gas masks? What the hell for?"

"Asbestos from the *Wetherby.* Given her age, she's going to be loaded with it. When we bring up the trunks, you and your crew are going to have to wear them. Sorry, it's an EPA regulation."

Crenna shook his head. "Damned government regulations. All right, load up and let's go."

"Nicely done," Mercer whispered to Cali as they started helping Jesse and Stan transfer the matte-black trunks onto the cruiser. He made sure no one touched the big leather hand grip that hadn't left his side since Washington.

As the cruiser pulled from the dock, Mercer tossed a casual wave at the three fishermen who were still puttering around their boat. Two waved back and the third, a large black man wearing a Greek fisherman's cap, gave him an ironic salute.

The barge wasn't as new as the crane sitting at its stern. Rust showed in streaks through worn paint and scaled the railings. Equipment bins overflowed with coils of rope, lengths of chain, and various tools. There was a compressor for refilling the scuba tanks that looked like Crenna had either just bought it or had rented it for the job.

"The crane used to be mounted on a truck," Crenna explained. "I put it on this barge a couple of years ago when I was hired to salvage a fishing boat that sank on the other side of Grand Island. It cost the owner twice what the boat was worth, but I wasn't complaining. So who's diving?"

"Mercer and I," Cali replied.

Jesse Williams looked up from one of the trunks. "I thought I was going."

"You will when we set the burn charges. Mercer wanted to check out the *Wetherby* for himself."

The former college football star looked at Mercer. "You know what you're doing?"

After years of procrastination Mercer had finally gotten his dive certification a few months earlier, although he'd dived countless times before. While he'd only ever gone down wearing a wet suit or just swim trunks, when he'd asked Cali for the chance to see the *Wetherby* she'd told him the dry suits were just more cumbersome. "I'll be fine," he'd said.

They were ready to go an hour later. Because she had more experience, Cali would carry the dive computer strapped to her wrist as well as a waterproofed gamma ray detector.

Mercer's OS Systems Nautilus dry suit was a little snug around the crotch because he was taller than Jesse Williams, but otherwise it felt comfortable. Jesse helped him into his tanks, buoyancy compensator, and weight belt while Stan checked over Cali's gear. Jesse went over procedures for filling and venting the suit during the dive and made sure Mercer's knife and the steel pry bar were secure.

"You're sure about this?" Williams asked before fitting the helmet.

"Piece of cake."

Mercer popped his jaw to equalize the pressure when the helmet was sealed.

"How do you read me?" Cali asked over the integrated communications net.

"Loud and clear."

Together they waddled over to the rear of the service boat where a gate had been opened. Cali jumped first. Mercer waited until her head bobbed up before following her into the water.

Even with the protection of the dry suit and thermal underwear, he could feel the close presence of the cold waters, but it was the current he noticed most. It ran about three knots, powerful enough to sweep him downriver if he wasn't careful. Visibility was no more than twenty feet and would diminish when they reached the wreck.

Captain Crenna had lowered an anchor down to the *Wetherby,* its line vanishing into the murky gloom. Cali put one hand on the rope and dumped air from her suit, allowing herself to glide into the depths. Mercer followed, adjusting his suit as the water pressure caused a fold of the tightly woven nylon to dig under his arm. The morning fog had dissipated but there was a lot of sediment in the water, dramatically cutting visibility. Mercer snapped on his dive light when he saw that Cali had slowed her descent.

Just like Ruth Bishop had said, the *Wetherby* had settled into a trough in the river bottom where she was sheltered from the worst of the current. She lay on her port side with her classic champagne-glass stern pointing upstream. Her hull was continuously scoured clean by the river, although there were still thousands of cut fishing lines streaming from her rails and superstructure. The ship was doubtless home to a lot of salmon and walleye, and local anglers paid the price for fishing on her with snagged lines. Her superstructure had been battered over the years, first when she drifted and sank and later by flotsam flowing down toward Niagara Falls. At some point the tree Ruth mentioned had been ripped free, leaving a gaping hole.

Cali and Mercer attached safety lines to her stern bollards and finned the length of the vessel. Her funnel was long gone and silt had built up around her bow where powerful back eddies had formed. One of her forward hatches was still secured, while the other was open, a yawning square that revealed her darkened hold. Because she rested on her port side there was no evidence of the explosion that had sent her to the bottom.

"What do you think?" Cali asked as they held tight to their lines just outside the open hold, the current pushing at them like a stiff breeze.

Mercer flashed his light into the hold but its beam could barely cut the gloom. "Let's belay the line and take a look inside."

They tied off their ropes to give them some slack, making sure that the tough nylon wouldn't scrape over any sharp surfaces. They were both well aware that a mistake here could mean certain death plummeting over the falls just downstream. The floor of the hold, which was actually the *Wetherby*'s port side, was littered with barrels and crates lying in a disorganized heap. Mercer again had to adjust his suit as the pressure squeezed it against his body. He checked his depth and saw they were at fifty-seven feet. The water was markedly colder even through the protective clothing.

Here they could see evidence of the deadly explosion. Hull plates had been blown out by the blast and hammered flat by the ship's tumble down the river. Ruth's uncle had been right. It did look as though the *Wetherby* had been torpedoed.

Cali examined a couple of the crates. "Do you think any of these are the ones we're looking for?"

"No," Mercer answered confidently. "Bowie's crates were loaded months before the *Wetherby* reached Buffalo. The captain would have tucked them out of the way because he wouldn't need to reach them until they got to Chicago. This hold looks like it was used for cargo they'd need to access quickly."

He swam aft and found a hatchway that led to the next hold. The door had been warped by the explosion but when he tried to open it farther he found it frozen by time. He loosened the pry bar from its Velcro holster and rammed it into a seam. He placed his feet against the wall and heaved back on the hardened steel, slowly building pressure until his spine felt like it was going to tear through the muscles of his back. The door refused to budge. Mercer repositioned the bar closer to the most damaged hinge and again drew back the metal rod.

A kaleidoscope of colors exploded behind his tightly closed eyes as he strained against the unyielding door. He was about to give up when he felt metal sheer under the pressure. The hinge pin broke with a sudden pop and the pry bar slipped free. Mercer tumbled across the deck, caught immediately by the current that swept the hold. Cali screamed when she saw him rush by, and for a panicked second he was sure he'd be swept out of the ship.

He came up tight against the safety line just at the main hatch coaming.

"Are you okay?" Cali asked as Mercer swam back down into the hold.

"Bruised my ego a bit."

The door hung from one hinge, and by pressing his back against the bulkhead and his feet against the door, he managed to swing it open, the shrieking protest of grating metal muted by the water. The hold beyond was even darker, a stygian void that seemed to swallow the beam of his dive light.

"Stay here and make sure my line doesn't foul," he told Cali and swam into the darkness.

This hold was the same size as the first and a huge amount of cargo had come loose from its pallets and lay against the port-side hull. He saw rotted sacks of what he thought was cotton, smashed crates that held the remains of dishes and glasses, and cases of wine bottles, although all the labels had been washed away. He also noted that there were hundreds of lengths of wood, and when he touched one his heart quickened. Despite seventy years of immersion, the board was still as hard as iron, with no trace of rot. He wasn't sure of the species, but it had to be some kind of African hardwood. And if cargo in this hold had been loaded in Africa, it stood to reason that Bowie's crates were in here as well.

"I think we caught a break."

Cali waited by the hatch, her light like a muted beacon. "Did you find them?"

"Not yet but there's a bunch of wood from Africa in here. I'm sure Bowie's crates are here as well. Tie off our safety lines again and give me a hand."

Before replying, Cali checked her dive computer and air gauges and asked Mercer the pressure in his twin Luxfer tanks. "We've got another twenty minutes, less if we exert ourselves," she said when she joined him inside the hold.

"Okay."

Working in the narrow confines of their dive lights, it was a daunting task, looking for four specific crates amid the jumbled mass of debris but as they began moving junk out of the way they realized that the timber made up the bulk of the load and there were only about forty crates they had to check. Cali took out the gamma ray detector and slowly pirouetted in the still water, her gaze never leaving the device. "I'm getting readings above ambient background but it's hard to tell which crates are emitting the gamma rays. The water's absorbing the particles."

Cali began sweeping individual crates with the detector. As soon as she was certain a crate wasn't one they wanted, Mercer would shove it aside to reveal other crates in the pile, making sure he didn't dislodge anything from the precarious stack. It was like the child's game of pick up sticks, only a mistake here could trap them under tons of debris.

Mercer heard the detector spike before Cali called out they'd found one. The crate was made of the same dense wood that the *Wetherby* had been transporting. Most likely Bowie had bought a few planks on the spot and had a carpenter in Brazzaville fashion the chests. The box was three feet square and nailed together, and the joints had been further protected with a layer of pitch that had hardened so the crate looked like it was striped in obsidian.

"How are the readings?" Mercer asked.

"We're fine. I suspect Bowie shielded the inside with metal."

Knowing what they were looking for made finding the other three a snap. Together they wrestled the heavy boxes closer to the hatch leading to the next hold.

"We've brought protective bags in case the crates had rotted," Cali panted, "but we're not going to need them until we get these to the surface. When I come back down with Jesse, we'll hook the boxes directly to the crane and just drag them out. Let's head back up."

They swam into the exposed hold, untied their lines where they'd belayed them, and made their way out into the river. The current hit like a hurricane gale, having doubled in the twenty minutes they were inside the wreck. They had to climb their way against its force, first scaling the length of the *Wetherby* to where the ropes were secured to the bollard, and then hand over hand ascending to the dive boat. It took them longer than they'd expected and Mercer's tanks were deep into the reserve by the time his head broke water.

Jesse and Stan were there to help him onto the dive platform and remove the eighty pounds of gear. "Well?" Stan Slaughbaugh asked when Mercer got his helmet off.

"Found them on the first try." He held his hand out to Cali and plucked her from the river.

"Hot damn. I can't wait to get the samples to a lab. I'm going to have a career just analyzing it."

"Well done, boss," Jesse Williams said to Cali.

"How'd it go?" Brian Crenna called from the deck of the crane barge.

"We found all four crates," Cali said, raising her voice over the wind. "After I've warmed up and we've refilled the tanks, Jesse and I can go down with a cable from your crane. We'll need to drag them out of the hold first, so I'll need to set up a block-and-tackle system so you can have a clean lift."

"Which hold are they in?"

"The second one. We have access from the first, though."

"I can extend the crane's boom almost a hundred and fifty feet. That should put it on the far side of the hold and I can drag them back without using tackle."

"That sounds like it'll work."

"Call me when you're ready." Crenna turned away to continue some maintenance work with his men.

Cali ate an MRE and rested in the cabin

while Jesse and Mercer filled the tanks with the compressor on the barge. Mercer noticed that the fishing boat he'd seen earlier was still tied to the dock. Two men stood at the transom holding fishing rods, while the black man in the cap lolled in the cockpit a few steps up from the rear deck.

It was eleven thirty by Mercer's watch when they were ready for the second dive. They'd cleared a spot on the barge's deck where they'd laid out large rubberized bags to contain the crates. Stan had told Mercer the bags' carbon fiber underlayment had been designed by NASA and was nearly indestructible. It could absorb the shock of a bullet at point-blank range and would deflect a knife thrust.

Cali gave Crenna a walkie-talkie dialed in to the dry suit's radio frequency so they could coordinate the lift. The wind had calmed again and the sun was trying to break through the overcast once more. A bass boat with a huge outboard roared past the barge, the four men aboard studying the craft as they raced to the next fishing hole.

"Dinner's on me tonight," Mercer said as he helped Cali back into her gear. He spoke low enough so only she heard.

She grinned up at him. "I take it that offer doesn't include Stan and Jesse."

"I'll buy them some buffalo wings before we go."

"It's a date."

Mercer had actually asked her out for a date. He was thankful she'd put on her helmet just then, so she couldn't hear him exhale a nervous breath. "Once more into the breach," he muttered, not sure if he knew what he was doing, but glad he'd done it.

Jesse and Cali dropped into the water as Crenna powered up the crane. He extended the telescopic boom until it reached far down the length of the sunken ship. The barge listed heavily, so that the chop lapped against the base of the forward rail. He shouted to his deckhands to reset the hydraulic anchors to compensate for the shift in the vessel's center of gravity.

Mercer saw Cali and Jesse's bubbles for only a few moments before they were borne away by the current. With Crenna refusing to let him on the barge until the crates had been swung aboard, and only the one radio to eavesdrop on the dive, there was nothing for him and Slaughbaugh to do but wait. Stan held a Ph.D. in nuclear physics, so the two of them talked about Mercer's theory concerning plutonium's origin.

After ten minutes Crenna began to lower

the hook into the water. Cali and Jesse must have reached the hold. A minute later the crane rotated a few degrees and another twenty or so feet of steel cable disappeared into the river.

"They must be hooking onto the crates," Mercer said.

"Won't be long now." As if to punctuate the statement one of the deckhands came over to the barge's rail and looked down onto the cabin cruiser. "They're about ready to lift. Your boss said we should put on the gas masks now."

"Oh right." Stan rummaged through one of his trunks and came away with an armful of NBC (Nuclear/Biological/Chemical) hooded gas masks. He tossed them up to the deckhand and took out two more for himself and Mercer.

"What happens when we get them to the surface?" Mercer asked.

"We'll bag them, and get them back to the dock. We have a hazmat truck standing by."

"Not planning on warning the people of this fair city that you're hauling a thousand pounds of plutonium through their streets?" Mercer teased.

"Please. On any given day there are a couple of tons of radioactive material on

311

the roads. Only reason why there hasn't been an accident is because we don't advertise it and invite out all the wackos."

The crane's big diesel bellowed and Mercer saw the drum at its rear begin to turn ever so slowly. "They've got them."

He could imagine Cali and Jesse in the dark hold making sure the crates didn't snag or smash against anything as the crane dragged them out. For another five minutes the crane spooled back cable in a delicate balance of horsepower, wind, and current. Then everything came to a standstill. Mercer couldn't understand it. He looked across and could see Crenna in the crane's cab. He leaned far back in his chair and had his arms crossed.

"They must have the crates out of the hold," Mercer said, finally understanding. "He wants Cali and Jesse topside before he brings them up, in case there's a problem."

Moments later Cali and Jesse Williams bobbed to the surface at the rear of the cabin cruiser. Stan and Mercer quickly helped them aboard. When Crenna saw that the divers were safely out of the water, he started drawing back cable and retracting the telescopic boom to reduce tension on the crane's hydraulic systems. In moments the crates emerged dripping from the river and hung suspended over the barge's deck.

The roar of the crane's diesel masked another, deeper sound until it was almost at the work site. The powerful outboard on the bass boat that had gone by earlier sent an arcing fountain of water into the air as it approached the barge at nearly forty miles per hour. Mercer had been busy helping Cali off with her equipment and only sensed the fast-moving craft when it entered his peripheral vision. He saw that the four men in the sleek boat were focused on the barge, and three of them brandished automatic weapons.

"Down," he shouted, shoving Cali to the deck. As he whirled he saw the Bertram fishing boat that had been tied to the pier suddenly come alive, a boil of froth at her transom as the captain slammed the throttles to their gates.

Mercer had kept his hand grip close at hand the entire day. He ripped open the zipper, fumbling for a frantic second, and pulled out an MP-40 Schmeisser. The weapon was the standard German submachine gun during World War Two. Mercer had bought it from Tiny, who'd taken it in trade on a gambling debt. He jammed a thirty-round magazine into the receiver and racked the slide. He stuffed six more magazines into his jeans pockets. While not the most accurate weapon, the gun's high rate of fire made it devastating at close range.

The fast-moving bass boat was still twenty yards from the barge when the three gunmen opened up with their Kalashnikovs. Crenna's crew fell flat to the deck and Crenna himself leapt from the crane. He dove behind the big air compressor as rounds pinged and ricocheted off the barge's metalworks. He tore off the gas mask and sat there panting.

Ducking behind the cabin cruiser's gunwales, Mercer shoved the grip to Cali. "There's a Beretta in there."

"How did you know?"

"I didn't. I just wanted to be ready." He addressed Stan Slaughbaugh and Jesse Williams. Both were huddled at the transom and neither looked like he'd ever been on the receiving end of an ambush. "Go forward into the cabin. Fire up the engines then stay down." The two NEST scientists complied wordlessly.

The bass boat continued to roar up the river, the sustained automatic fire popping over the throb of the big outboard. It looked to Mercer as if they were going to jump onto the far side of the barge. He chanced looking over his shoulder. The Bertram fishing boat had crossed half the river and was coming on strong, her blunt bows buried behind a creaming froth of water. The captain was in the high bridge while the other two were stationed on either side of the stern deck. They both carried weapons — Heckler and Koch HK-416s, the German arms manufacturer's latest assault carbine. The compact weapons fired NATO 5.56-millimeter ammunition and were fast becoming the popular choice among the world's elite military units.

Cali saw where Mercer was looking and gasped. They were trapped. Even if they untied from the barge, the Bertram would easily outrun them. She drew a bead on one of the sport fishermen with her pistol when the vessel was fifty yards out. Mercer had turned back to see the bass boat decelerate as it came abreast of the barge. The men were still firing, although Mercer couldn't see Crenna or any of his deckhands. A snap burst from one of the gunmen hit the hydraulic controls that anchored the barge to the river bottom. Hydraulic fluid pumped from the reservoirs like lifeblood. Mercer looked back and was about to tell Cali to stay put when he saw her about to fire on the Bertram.

"No!" he shouted and pushed her hand

into the air.

The Bertram was thirty yards away, close enough for Mercer to see the look of concentration on Booker Sykes's face as he drove the boat across the river. Mercer didn't know the two Special Forces operators with him. They hadn't been part of Sykes's Delta Force team when they escorted Mercer into a Tibetan monastery once run by Tisa Nguyen's father. Calling Sykes to provide security had dredged up fresh memories of the events leading to her death, but Mercer wouldn't let his pain hamper the ongoing investigation.

"They're with me," he said. "They are Delta Force commandos. The commander's name is Sykes. Cover me."

Mercer eased over the gunwale and onto the deck of the barge. He could feel that the hydraulic system had failed and the barge was responding to the wind and waves, but so far he couldn't tell if it was caught in the Niagara River's relentless current.

The bass boat was so low to the water that he couldn't see it on the far side of the barge. He found cover behind a chain locker and waited for the gunmen to expose themselves again. Sykes arced the Bertram well behind the barge and was about to engage from the Canadian side of the river when another bass boat appeared around the north tip of Grand Island. Mercer counted four men in it as well, bringing the total number of attackers to eight. When he looked back to the first bass boat, he caught a fleeting glimpse of one of the men lunging onto the barge.

His initial plan if they were attacked was to wait until he and Sykes could take out all the gunmen in a surprise counter ambush, but the sheer numbers made that option untenable. Another gunman raised himself over the low flank of the bass boat. His classic Middle Eastern features told Mercer two things. One was that the gunmen had probably received training in some terrorist camp in Iraq, Syria, or Saudi Arabia. The second thing he knew was that they were here to fight to the death.

The Arab was exposed for only a fraction of a second but it was enough time for Mercer to bring the Schmeisser to bear. The old submachine gun bucked in his hand like a living thing as he fired off a five-round burst. Four of the rounds went wide but the fifth blew the gunman off the barge in a spray of blood.

The counterfire from the other three terrorists was swift and sustained. The sound of bullets striking the chain locker was horrific. It felt like the noise would shake Mercer's teeth loose from his jaw. But even over this racket he heard Sykes and his team engage the second bass boat, their assault carbines adding to the gun battle raging across the width of the river.

Mercer waited until the firing stopped to blindly fire a few rounds over the chain locker and scamper to better cover near the crane. He nearly tripped over the prone form of Brian Crenna. He was huddled partially under the crane with one of his deckhands.

"What the hell is going on?" Crenna shouted over the roar of automatic weapons.

Mercer ignored the pointless question. "Where are your other two men?"

"Billy jumped over the side." He pointed out over the water. Mercer could see a man swimming toward Grand Island. "He's a good swimmer. He'll make it. I don't know about Tom."

The second bass boat raced around to their side of the barge, Sykes's big Bertram trying to keep up with the faster and more nimble craft. While one of the gunmen fired at the Bertram, two more raked the cabin cruiser. Several shots went wide and slammed into the crane's turret, forcing the three men to cower further, as if trying to burrow into the steel decking.

"Listen," Mercer said when the outboard faded. "I'm going to cover you. Get to the cabin cruiser and get out of here."

He changed out the half-depleted magazine for a fresh one, waited a moment for Crenna and the deckhand to get ready, then ducked under the extended boom and cut loose with the Schmeisser. He raked the far side of the barge in a continuous sweep from stem to stern. The gunmen were out of sight so he nodded to Crenna. The two men took off in a loping run, covering the thirty feet to the side of the barge in seconds. Both vaulted over the rail and onto the cabin cruiser's deck.

Even as he concentrated on finding a target, Mercer noticed that the far bank of the river was moving ever so slightly. When the last round had cycled through the gun, Mercer ducked back under the crane, and as he changed out the magazine he looked at the near bank. Intellect overcame the adrenaline surging through his veins and he realized the land wasn't moving at all. The hydraulic anchors had failed completely and the barge was at the mercy of the Niagara River. And in the few seconds it took to reload the Schmeisser he realized the barge was accelerating. The wind had picked up again and he estimated they were going six knots.

Mercer was certain the cabin cruiser didn't have the power to tow the barge against the current. He needed to get to the tug moored to the far side of the craft if he was going to prevent them all from plummeting down the falls. Failing that, he had to get the crates of plutonium ore into the special bags so they wouldn't smash open when the barge went over.

"Cali," he shouted. "We're adrift. Cast off and get out of here."

"What about you?" she shouted back without revealing herself.

"Sykes can pick me up." For the moment, though, Mercer didn't know where his friend was. The Bertram and the second bass boat had gone upriver. He would just have to trust that Booker Sykes would take out the second group of terrorists and return before it was too late.

Cali and Crenna spoke for a second and she covered him as he inched his way to the controls of the cabin cruiser. Cali wanted Crenna to use the cruiser to push the barge to shore so he opened the throttles and put the rudder hard over. The ropes securing the cruiser to the barge strained as the tired motor roared. To Mercer's surprise and delight it seemed like her plan was working. The nine-hundred-ton barge slowly rotated and seemed to be heading for the Canadian side of the river. The gunmen on the bass boat hadn't expected such fierce resistance so it was taking them a few seconds to regroup, but when they heard the cruiser they opened fire again. The windshield and side windows exploded, covering Crenna in a shower of glass, while chunks were ripped from the cruiser's upperworks. It was a fluke shot that hit the cleat securing the cruiser's bow to the barge. The boat slewed away from the metal side of the barge before Crenna could bring the wheel over or throttle down the engine. The tension on the rear cleat was too much and it gave way, tearing a large section of the transom in the process.

The gunmen continued to fire as the two craft separated. The rear deck was chewed up by the barrage, forcing Cali to dive into the cabin. Greasy smoke began to boil from the engine cowling and the motor started to sputter. As soon as Crenna drove them out of range, Cali mounted the four steps to the cockpit. "We have to go back."

"Forget it, lady. You ain't paying me enough for this. I'm going to pick up Billy and call the Coast Guard."

"Mercer will be dead by the time they get here."

"That's his problem."

Cali cursed herself for emptying the Beretta. She wouldn't have shot Crenna but she certainly would have threatened him. "Okay, I'll drop you off at the dock but I'm going back."

"Not on my boat you're not. Bad enough I might lose my tug and the crane if she don't ground."

Cali exploded in rage. "Those crates we raised are filled with plutonium," she shouted. "If they fall into the hands of a bunch of terrorists I'll make sure you're charged with treason and shot."

He looked at her. Cali's eyes blazed with fury and her breath came in heaving gasps. Just as he was about to agree, a wave of heat washed over them. They turned in unison. The rear of the boat was a wall of flame. A bullet had severed the fuel line and the raw gasoline had ignited. "Jesus," Crenna yelled. "Everyone off the boat. Now!"

Stan, Jesse, and Crenna's third mate scrambled from the cabin. More familiar with watercraft, the mate knew instantly that the boat was going to burn to the water line, so he threw himself over the side. Stan and Jesse saw that Cali and the captain were crawling out through the shattered windshield and they jumped into the swift-flowing river.

Cali grabbed a pair of flotation rings that hung just below the windscreen and jumped into the water with Crenna right behind her. The shore of Grand Island was only a hundred yards away, and once everyone was together and holding on to one of the rings, they struck out. The boat drifted past. The fire had already spread to the cabin and flames shot from the cockpit. Tears of frustration stung Cali's eyes. By the time she reached shore and found another boat it would be too late.

Mercer needed to cross twenty feet of open deck to reach the little towboat. The gunmen were well covered and fired at him from the protection of their boat. Their only exposed flank was from the water, and since Sykes and his team were still upriver fighting the other boat, they could afford to be patient. Mercer was effectively pinned. He had yet to figure out their plan or spot the last member of Crenna's crew, and time was quickly running out. The barge had drifted at least a mile from where it had anchored over the *Wetherby* and was fast approaching a series of rapids.

He couldn't wait for Sykes any longer. He had to end the standoff and get to the tug. He checked his ammo. The magazine in the Schmeisser was fresh and he had two more in his pockets. He fired a quick burst to keep the terrorists' heads down and sprinted for the forty-foot tugboat. As he ran he watched for movement and as soon as one of the gunmen looked over the side of the barge he triggered another three-round burst. The bullets went wide but the terrorist ducked from sight.

Mercer had just another couple of paces to go when the barge struck a rock as the river began to shoal. He was thrown flat and the barge spun on its axis, grinding across the hidden boulder until water pressure shoved it free. The crates of ore still suspended over the deck on the end of the crane pendulumed dangerously but didn't fall.

Mercer scrambled up just as the three terrorists recovered and let loose with their Kalashnikovs. He fell from the barge and onto the deck of the small tug, bullets exploding all around him. He lay flat for a moment and glanced back toward the gunmen when the firing stopped. One of them stood upright, a long tube resting on his shoulder. It was an RPG-7, a venerable Russian-made tank killer. The rocket popped from the launcher a second later, its motor engaged, and it streaked across the barge. Mercer threw his hands over his head just as the rocket-propelled grenade slammed into the tug's wheelhouse. The explosion shattered the big windscreen, allowing most of the blast to vent away from Mercer, but the overpressure wave was a crushing weight that seemed to suck the air from his lungs and left his ears ringing. He could no longer hear the roar of Niagara Falls only a mile or two downstream.

Mercer slowly sat upright. He hadn't been hit by any debris, however the pilothouse was ruined. There was no way now to stop the barge from going over the falls and he had just minutes to get the crates into their protective bags. He looked down the river. There was a structure of some sort jutting into the water from the Canadian side. It was the water intakes for a massive hydroelectric power plant. The barge had drifted too close to the American side for it to be drawn toward the intakes. Instead it was steering for the rapids that preceded the most powerful waterfall in North America.

A movement caught Mercer's eye. He couldn't believe what he was seeing. A man in a black jumpsuit had just landed on the center of the barge, his parachute billowing before he cut it away. A second man landed a moment later. Above them a dark helicopter began to descend toward the barge. The gunmen must have thought Mercer had died when the tugboat was hit because they cheered and ran up to embrace one of their comrades. The second parachutist, who was Caucasian rather than Arab, made straight for the crates.

Mercer steadied his submachine gun on the edge of the tug, took careful aim, and fired. His rounds stitched through the group. One of the parachutists was hit across the hips and collapsed, screaming in agony as bright blood pumped from his femoral artery. Two of the gunmen were raked across the chest because no matter how Mercer fought his Schmeisser, he couldn't stop the barrel from climbing. The last gunman and the second parachutist dove for the bass boat. Mercer didn't give them time to recover. He charged across the deck shouting incoherently. He was halfway there when the barge slammed into another rock and stopped dead. He staggered but didn't fall. He reached the edge of the barge and was about to fire into the bass boat when he realized there was no point. It had been caught between the barge and the rocks and had been crushed flat. Only the big outboard had survived the impact and to Mercer's eye even it looked a little narrower than normal.

The river kept the barge pressed tightly to the rock, and as Mercer stood over the ruined bass boat, panting, it seemed like it was jammed solid. A few hundred yards away he saw a billowing cloud of mist as the river dropped nearly two hundred feet to the gorge below. He checked the gunmen. All were dead with the exception of the man with the shattered hip, but he had already slipped into a shock-induced coma as he bled out. Mercer wasted no more time with them.

The helicopter the two men had parachuted from came within two hundred feet of the barge and Mercer opened fire. He missed at that range but the big chopper pirouetted in the air and thundered over the Canadian border and out of view.

Having logged hundred of hours running everything from a twelve-thousand-ton walking dragline to a compact skip loader, Mercer had little trouble deciphering the controls to Crenna's crane. He retracted the boom and lowered the crates until they were a few inches from the deck. He jumped from the cab and carefully arranged the bags so he could close them around the wooden chests. He was about to lower the crates that last little bit when he felt the barge move again. The current had found a tiny angle to exploit and started swinging the craft around the rock. The deck began to move and the grind of metal against stone reached a fierce crescendo as the barge came free and was again drawn toward the falls.

Mercer hurriedly lowered the crates and ran back out to the deck. He scanned for the helicopter as he wrestled the first crate into place and began closing the bag. There were four different seals. First there was a wide adhesive strip, then Velcro, and then a heavy-duty zipper. Those took seconds. It was having to lace the bag closed with wire that took several minutes.

The barge continued to hit against rocks. It would hold steady for a minute or two then continue downstream while the flat bottom constantly scraped against the shallow bottom. Three shots in rapid succession made him drop flat and pick up his Schmeisser. He looked around. There was no one. Then he looked upstream and saw Booker Sykes standing at the stern of the Bertram, his assault carbine resting on a cocked hip. The Bertram was a wreck. Part of the bow was smashed in and the hull was riddled with bullet holes. Mercer could just imagine what was left of the second bass boat.

Sykes had fired three shots into the air to get Mercer's attention.

Mercer waved over at him then shrugged his shoulders as if to say there was nothing the Delta operator could do to help. Then he went back to work. He had the second bag secured when he started to feel the spray from the falls sprinkling like a light rain, but it quickly grew to a torrential downpour as the barge edged closer and closer.

The sound of the hull scraping bottom set Mercer's teeth on edge and water began to surge over the deck as it succumbed to gravity. With the third bag sealed, Mercer glanced over. Booker was still on station watching the scene through binoculars. Behind Mercer the Niagara gorge began to yawn open. He could see the city of Niagara and the arching span of the Rainbow Bridge beyond the thundering mist.

He had two minutes or less and still hadn't thought of a way out of his predicament. There were no large boulders he could jump to between the barge and the edge of the falls, and if he tried to swim to one he'd be sucked over the precipice. The crash of so much falling water echoed in his head and made concentrating difficult. He had the first three seals in place and had just started to lace the bag when Booker fired again. Mercer looked up just as he was hit from behind in a blind tackle that sent him tumbling. He'd recognized the black jumpsuit as belonging to one of the parachutists, when he was kicked under the chin. The parachutist had somehow survived when the bass boat was crushed, possibly by being close to the engine, and had taken this long to extricate himself.

Mercer's head snapped back and slammed the deck. He fought the dizzying wave of darkness that washed through his mind and rolled clear just as the man tried to smash his heel into Mercer's nose. The empty hull of the barge echoed with the impact. Mercer grabbed the man's ankle with both hands and twisted savagely. The man went down and Mercer used his fall to lever himself into a sitting position. He smashed his elbow into the man's groin as hard as he could and staggered to his feet. The barge had stopped right on the edge of the falls where the water was remarkably only about three feet deep. Niagara Gorge was a void that seemed to stretch forever.

He whirled again as the assassin got to his feet. Mercer recognized him. It wasn't Poli but one of the men with him when they attacked the Deco Palace Hotel. Mercer's Schmeisser was on top of the crates and too far, so he simply charged. The two crashed together and fell into the water sluicing across the deck. The water was only a foot deep but the current was relentless. Mercer lost traction on the slick hull plates and shot twenty feet toward the bow before he could dig in his heels and stand. The leading edge of the barge was suspended over open air and the hull continued to grind against the bottom.

That's when he saw his only chance of salvation. The parachutist had also gotten to his feet, but the wind had been knocked out of him. Mercer splashed to the crates and grabbed up his weapon. The white mercenary reached for a pistol hanging in his shoulder holster, but he wasn't quick enough. Mercer fired one-handed, the heavy weapon bucking in his hand, and a pair of nine-millimeter slugs slammed into the man's chest. He fell and was instantly grabbed by the current. Mercer dropped the Schmeisser and lunged for the body, grabbing at the man's hair just before he went over the bow. He dragged the corpse against the current and in the lee of the crates managed to unhook the man's reserve parachute.

He hadn't done enough skydiving to know if he'd put it on properly, but there was nothing he could do about it. The stern of the barge began to rise with the current as it edged toward its tipping point.

Mercer's biggest threat now wasn't that he was so high above the gorge. The problem was he wasn't high enough. While a hundred and eighty feet was a great height, it was nowhere near high enough for a parachute to deploy. It would be no different than jumping without one. Mercer ran to the crane again, spun it on its turntable until it was facing aft to shift the barge's center of gravity in his favor, hit the levers that raised the boom to its maximum height, and started the hydraulics that would extend it to its fullest length. By doing this he bought himself another hundred feet.

There were ladder rungs welded to the top of the first section of the steel boom, and even as it continued to rise, Mercer started to climb. The next three sections didn't have any handholds so he had to rely on the strength of his hands to shimmy up the slick boom like a monkey.

He reached the top just as the world began to tip. The barge was going over. The crates slid across the deck and vanished over the falls. Mercer popped the drogue chute and held it in his right hand as the barge slipped farther. He paused for a heartbeat, waiting for the boom to reach vertical. The Niagara Gorge was a narrow gash through the forests and farmlands, while in the distance Lake Ontario looked like polished glass.

With a last rending squeal the barge tipped, and just before it shot out from under Mercer he threw himself from the crane, tossing the drogue chute over his head. He and the barge and the water all fell at nearly the same speed, but the pressure against his stomach told Mercer he was accelerating. There was nothing to do but pray as he plummeted down the face of Niagara Falls, his body sodden by the constant spray. He couldn't see the surface of the river or the rocks below because of the mist, and perhaps it was for the best.

But fate wasn't going to be that kind to him. As he fell the mist cleared a bit. He could see the boiling surface of the river, the tons of rocks that had eroded off the falls, and even the plucky sightseeing boat called the *Maid of the Mist*. Mercer could feel the chute start to pull from the pack, drawn out by air resistance against the drogue. There wasn't enough room.

Mercer closed his eyes.

And jerked them open when the main chute deployed, yanking the straps so far into his groin he was certain his testicles had ruptured. The wind off the falls caught the chute and pushed him just past the mounds of jagged boulders as the barge augured in. The crane snapped from its mounts and nearly hit him as he drifted a few more yards before plunging into the river. He went deep and felt the current snatch the chute, dragging him farther downstream.

Mercer fought and clawed his way to the surface, his lungs near bursting as he got there and gulped great drafts of air. He managed to find the chute release, and once it was gone he could tread water. The *Maid of the Mist* cut across the narrows, passengers in blue ponchos cheering when they saw Mercer had survived. A few minutes later a pair of deckhands helped him onto the lower deck.

"Have you got a death wish or something?" one of them asked.

Having no pithy retort on hand, Mercer rolled onto his side and promptly threw up.

Mercer sprawled on the leather sofa in the rec room wearing the loosest pair of sweatpants he owned, a bag of frozen peas pressed to his groin and a vodka gimlet within easy reach. From the floor, Drag regarded him through droopy, bloodshot eyes, indignant that he'd been evicted from his favorite spot.

Cali and Ira Lasko sat on the other couch facing Mercer, while Harry and Booker Sykes were at the bar. Burgers and fries from a fast-food restaurant littered the coffee table and bar top.

When the *Maid of the Mist* returned to its dock and it was determined that Mercer didn't need a hospital, he was given a ride to the Niagara Police Department and booked on numerous charges. Like after the shoot-out in New Jersey, Ira had to step in with local authorities to get him released. Sykes had picked up Cali and her team from Grand Island and abandoned his boat so no one knew of their involvement. Ruth Bishop from the Coast Guard was to lead the investigation into the gun battle, coordinating with her Canadian counterparts to find the helicopter that had dropped the paratroopers and was most likely going to haul away the crates. So far word of their contents had not spread thanks in a large part to the money Brian Crenna was being paid to keep his mouth shut. He'd have a new tugboat and floating crane by the end of the week. His missing crewman had been found on the Canadian side of the border, so with no civilian fatalities this was being heralded as a thwarted terrorist attack on Niagara Falls power plants. Mercer, NEST, and Sykes's team weren't part of the cover story and were sworn to secrecy.

Because none of the terrorists' bodies had been recovered, Mercer, Cali, and Sykes's Delta team had spent the day with the FBI's counterterrorism unit going over hundreds of pictures of known terrorists in hopes of identifying the men who'd attacked the barge. One of the bass boats had survived the ordeal and was found packed with enough explosives to sink a cruise ship. As Mercer had noted during the battle, the terrorists were Middle Eastern. He recognized four of the men from the photo lineup. Two were Iraqi and two were from Saudi Arabia. The Arab paratrooper, a former captain in the Iraqi Republican Guard, was well known to the Pentagon, but none of the others were particularly high up in the Al Qaida chain of command. There was nothing in any database on the Caucasian parachutist.

Ira made sure that Homeland Security would keep him in the loop as they tracked how the men entered North America and where they had gotten their weapons. They would also provide twenty-four-hour guards for Mercer's house. That was his price for cooperation. He didn't want to take up Ira's suggestion of moving to a safe house.

With his genitals sufficiently numb, Mercer set the peas on a dishrag next to him and wiped a smear of ketchup from his lips. He'd just finished telling Harry the story of the fight and his dive off the falls.

"I think that makes you the twelfth person who's gone over the falls and lived," Harry remarked. "However, technically you didn't go over them. You parachuted, so it really doesn't count."

"Technically, my ass," Mercer spat back and hobbled to the bar for another drink. "I may not be able to talk about it but in my mind I went over the falls and I've got the swollen stones to prove it." He turned to

Ira. "I've forgotten to ask. How's it going with the recovery of the crates?"

"Coast Guard's on it now with Cali's teammates, ah, Slaughbaugh and Williams. They managed to recover two of them pretty easily from the *Maid of the Mist* Pool below the rapids, but the other two are directly under the falls, where the water is deeper than the falls are tall. The good news is there's no trace of radiation in the water, so we know they didn't break open."

"And security?"

"Airtight this time," Ira said solemnly. "What made you invite Booker along?"

"Poli's been a step ahead since Africa. He has the original manuscript from Chester Bowie's safe, which gave him the name of the freighter Bowie used to ship the crates to America. And as Cali proved finding what happened to the *Wetherby* wasn't too tough. What I hadn't anticipated was the number of men he'd employ and the sophistication of the assault given the short amount of time he had to plan it."

Booker Sykes spoke up. "An operation like he coordinated would have taken weeks, maybe months for training and he pulled it off in just a couple of days."

"That tells us," Mercer continued, "that he's got a lot of assets in the States."

"And you're sure he wasn't with the assault team?" Ira asked.

"Positive," Mercer said bitterly. More than anything he wished the mercenary had been there when the barge went over the falls. "I did recognize the white paratrooper from New Jersey. He was taking the potshots at us while Poli was driving. I suspect the Qaida fighters on the bass boats were just cannon fodder in case the barge was protected."

"That's why all the explosives," Booker added. "Suicide run if you had a Coast Guard escort. I figure the Iraqi who 'chuted in was the terror cell's leader but they were working for Poli."

"Who ultimately works for someone else," Cali said.

"Someone we don't have a bead on yet." Mercer returned to the couch and settled the frozen peas over his groin again. "But it's got to be Al Qaida. How else could he get their men? For Poli it's all about the money. Guys willing to die in a suicide attack do it for politics or faith."

Ira finished his burger and crushed his napkin. "You think this is Al Qaida's attempt to get the radioactive material they need for a dirty bomb?"

"What else could it be?" Cali answered.

"We all know they've wanted to get their hands on nuclear material for years. And despite what the media thinks, NEST and other groups are doing a damn fine job closing conduits from the old Soviet republics and any other source imaginable." She glanced at Mercer almost as if what she was about to say was his fault. "What no one anticipated was finding a cache of natural plutonium that seems to have been lost for a couple thousand years. Using what Chester Bowie rediscovered is Al Qaida's only chance if they want a dirty bomb."

"I don't get something," Harry said. "If you guys could recover the crates without any problems, what's the big deal with a dirty bomb anyway?"

Cali met his frank gaze. "It's a terror weapon. More people would be killed in the initial explosion than would suffer radiological effects, but that doesn't matter. The mere mention of radioactive contamination would be enough to cause nationwide panic. Remember the anthrax attacks and how many people were hoarding Cipro?"

"Unfortunately," Ira interrupted, "competition in the media has forced them into using scare tactics in order to sell ad space. A story like a dirty bomb attack would turn the media into a feeding frenzy of doom and gloom that would actually help the terrorists in spreading fear. You have to know that our press is no longer free. And it's not some vast right wing, or even left wing, conspiracy that's destroyed its objectivity. It's our own consumerism that has allowed the media to be co-opted by Madison Avenue in order to sell lingerie and cheaper computers. You just know there are editors and news directors out there who are anxiously awaiting a terrorist attack or a plane crash or a celebrity murder so they can pump their circulation and raise their ad rates. So long as advertisers subsidize the media, the press will always find the negative. It's human nature."

"What's the alternative?" Harry asked. "In countries where the state supplies the news, you get nothing but propaganda."

"I don't know," Ira admitted. "But it pisses me off that when there's no real news to report they go out and find some horror to exploit. Thousands of teenagers die every year but it's only during a lull in the news cycle that one death gets turned into a national tragedy. And this happens not because we value that teen over any other but because the constant exposure to the details creates a feedback loop of interest."

"Pretty cynical," Harry remarked. "And I

can't deny it."

"Sad, huh?" Ira said tiredly.

Mercer leaned forward. "We're getting off topic."

"Sorry." Ira scratched at his bald head. "I spent the morning with our media consultants building the cover story around the attack. Leaves a bad taste in your mouth."

"We've secured the bulk of the plutonium Chester Bowie mined," Mercer stated. "I'm not even going to worry about the little bit that was in the safe. That still leaves the Alembic of Skenderbeg, which we're still trying to hunt down, and what the Russians mined after Bowie left Africa. Have you gotten anywhere with them?"

"Actually I have." Ira opened the briefcase at his feet and withdrew a folder. "That's how I spent my afternoon. I got this from Grigori Popov, a guy whose career mirrors mine. He was a sub driver in the Pacific Fleet who moved to naval intelligence. He's now a deputy in the Ministry of Defense. I've known him for years, and while I don't trust him as far as I can throw him, we've been dealing with each other long enough to know when it's time to put all our cards on the table."

Ira glanced at his notes. "We were pretty much right when we spoke in my office a few days ago. The Russians had stolen the designs for our atomic bomb but knew they wouldn't have the resources to enrich uranium for at least a decade, and plutonium production would take even longer. As World War Two came to a close the KGB created something called Scientific Operations headed by a shrewd cookie named Boris Ulinev."

Mercer sat bolt upright, color draining from his face. "Jesus. Department 7."

"You've heard of it?"

"Don't you remember me telling you about my involvement when Hawaii almost seceded and the whole plot to blow up the Alaska Pipeline?" Lasko nodded. "Both of those were old Department 7 operations."

"That's right!" Ira exclaimed. "I knew it sounded familiar when Greg was telling me about it."

"You know their last director is still on the loose out there," Mercer said with ill-disguised anger. "Ivan Kerikov's his name. I wonder if he's mixed up in all of this."

"I doubt it," Ira told him.

"Ah, guys?" Cali interjected. "Little help for those of us who don't know what you're talking about."

Mercer explained. "Department 7 was created during World War Two as the Russians were advancing into German-occupied Eastern Europe and then into Germany herself. Their sole mission was to assimilate captured technology. The Nazis had some pretty advanced stuff on their drawing boards at war's end and the Soviets stole as much as they could get their hands on. Plans for jet aircraft, powerful radar systems, next-generation missiles, even the world's first infrared scopes. It was Department 7's job to take this technology back to the Soviet Union and integrate it into their military. That's how they were able to produce jet fighters so quickly after the war. The MiG-15 was basically a copy of a German aircraft." He looked back to Ira. "It makes sense they'd be involved with this if Bowie was right and it was German agents after him."

"He was and they were," Ira said. "When Heinrich Himmler, the head of the SS, learned about the Alembic of Skenderbeg, he personally dispatched a team to search for its power source. Two of them were killed, we know now by Janissaries, while a third returned to Germany with a sketchy report about Chester Bowie and his crates. The Germans didn't send another team back to Africa, believing they could enrich uranium themselves, and the whole affair was shoved into an archive."

"And in waltzes Department 7," Booker said from the bar, a plug of tobacco shoved against his right cheek.

"Exactly. While the Nazis shipped a lot of their nuclear program to Japan at the close of the war, there was enough left in Germany for Department 7 to figure out there might be a natural source of nuclear fuel. Unlike the Germans the Soviets scoured parts of Africa until they found the cache in the Central African Republic in 1947, which was a French Colony at the time. Oh, and Greg Popov denies any massacre took place."

"Naturally," Mercer smirked.

Ira gave him a wry smile. "He did say that they mined several tons of ore, the entire lode in fact."

"So what happened to it?" Cali asked. She pursed her lips around her straw to sip some of her Coke. It was a sensual gesture that caught every man's attention and delayed Ira's answer for a beat.

"Ah, Greg told me they used up half of it before they began to enrich their own uranium in 1950."

"So their early bombs were fueled by the plutonium," Harry said.

"Appears that way."

Mercer asked, "What about the half they didn't use?"

"Thought you'd bring that up." Ira reached into his briefcase again and tossed two airline tickets onto the coffee table. "You and Cali are going to go see it for yourselves. The Russians have it stored in an old mine in the Ural Mountains with a bunch of other artifacts left over from Department 7. I've already cleared it with your boss, Cali."

Cali couldn't believe it. "The Russians just left it sitting there?"

"You know better than most how poorly they secured their nuclear material during the Cold War. And when you think about it, until the last decade or so it didn't matter. There wasn't anyone interested in getting their hands on the stuff. Of course today is a different story, which has forced them to play catch-up. Our government has funneled billions to Russia and Ukraine to consolidate and better guard their stockpiles, but it takes time."

"I know." Cali shook her head. "It's just frustrating. I've spent my career trying to prevent a nuclear attack and no matter how good I am, or the rest of NEST, it only takes one mistake by us and a city's wiped off the face of the earth. Meanwhile you've got the

Russians leaving nuclear material lying around in mines and warehouses or in the craters of old nuclear bomb tests they never bothered to clean up or even refill.

"And what happens if we do get hit? Sure we'll condemn the terrorists and lob a few smart bombs, but then we'll spend years investigating our own intelligence failures and never once address the real culprits, the assholes who made the material available in the first place. I agreed with taking out the Taliban after 9/11 but then we should have rolled right across Saudi Arabia. It's their government that allowed bin Laden and his followers to fester; only the Saudis were smart enough in the beginning to ship them all to Pakistan and Afghanistan."

"Course now they're coming home to roost," Ira added.

"And it's only when bombs started going off in Riyadh that they took an interest in fighting terrorism, and even now their attitude is still pretty permissive. On the one hand they track down and execute a few extremists while on the other they continue to pump money into the Wahabi schools where future terrorists are trained, because if they stop, the whole movement will turn against them."

"We know invading Saudi Arabia isn't an

option," Mercer said. "So how do we get out of this mess?"

Again Cali shook her head. "The Saudis are actively exporting terror because they can afford to. It won't stop until they're broke. Take away their oil wealth and they're just another backwater third world country that can't feed its population. We stop them by finding other sources of oil and eventually finding an alternative to it altogether."

"In other words," Harry rasped, "we keep taking it on the chin for as long as it takes to pump the bastards dry."

"And that's just what's going to continue to happen," Cali agreed. "They'll keep funding fanatics who will still try to fly airplanes into buildings or detonate a dirty bomb or simply strap on suicide vests and blow themselves up in malls and movie theaters."

"This has turned grim," Booker said, helping himself to a beer from Mercer's retro fifties era lock-lever bar fridge.

"Unfortunately that's the state of the world," Ira replied. "I see more shit crossing my desk at the White House than you can imagine, but I do agree with Cali that fundamentalism is the single greatest danger today and there are no easy fixes either. We're like the Russians playing catch-up with their nuclear materials. It will take us years to find a way to neutralize the Saudis' influence by making oil obsolete."

"In the meantime we have more pressing concerns," Mercer said to get the conversation back on track. "What's the plan once Cali and I get to Russia?"

"Grigori will meet you in Samara, an industrial city on the Volga River. From there you'll take a military chopper to the mine. He'll have a hazmat team on hand to make sure the plutonium ore is handled properly. They're taking it to a weapons depot about a thousand miles from anywhere, in the middle of Siberia. Just so you know, that facility is the newest and best in the country, courtesy of the U.S. taxpayers. Once you verify that the plutonium is safely in the depot, your mission is done."

"Not even close," Mercer said sourly. "We still have Poli and the Janissaries running around, as well as the Alembic of Skenderbeg to deal with." He turned to Booker Sykes. "Are you up for a little trip?"

"Depends," the Delta commando drawled.

"Ira, I take it you're still not having any luck getting the Pentagon to send a team to check out the stele?" Lasko nodded. "Then, Book, how'd you like an all-expense-paid trip to the worst hellhole I've ever seen?"

"To do what exactly?"

"There's an obelisk in the village where Cali and I found the mine. It was placed there by order of Alexander the Great. Cali and I both remember there was writing on it. I need to know what it says. I'm hoping that it will give us some clue as to where the alembic was stashed."

"You just want pictures or the whole damned thing?"

"A couple of Polaroids and you're out of there. Two days on the ground tops."

"I recommend a digital camera," Ira suggested.

"Figure of speech," Mercer replied. "Don't forget I'm a Luddite. I got my first cell phone last year."

Sykes said, "The two guys with me on the boat, Paul Rivers and Bernie Cieplicki, both have to rotate back to Fort Bragg tomorrow." He grinned. "I'll see they come down with a case of the creeping cruds and spring them for the trip."

SAMARA, RUSSIA

By the time the Lufthansa Airbus from Frankfurt touched down at Samara's airport, Cali and Mercer had spent fifteen hours in the air, and thanks to Mercer's upgrading of the tickets from the coach Ira had provided to first class, they had enjoyed their time together. Cali had teased as they ate *petit filets* and asparagus with *sauce Béarnaise* over the Atlantic that this didn't count as their date and Mercer still owed her a meal. And when she grabbed his hand when a crosswind slewed the aircraft just before touchdown at Samara, Mercer felt his heart trip.

For him it was almost like the beginning of a high school romance where the tiniest gestures came loaded with significance but were also fraught with pitfalls. Was it too soon after losing Tisa? Was he even capable of giving himself again? Each step forward came at a price of self-doubt. He wanted to believe that his burgeoning feelings weren't merely a physical reaction to a beautiful woman. Yet when he looked into himself to find the truth, he saw nothing but a hollow, an empty void where once there was confidence. He felt paralyzed by a guilt he was trying to convince himself he didn't deserve.

Cali gave his hand a squeeze as the plane began to taxi to the long one-story terminal building, then she let go. Mercer's palms retained her nervous warmth.

They were met at Customs by a pair of men. One was short and handsome, with blond cropped hair and the insignia of an army captain on his uniform collar. The other was older, stooped, with haunted blue eyes and a large skull covered in wisps of gray hair. His suit was wrinkled and his shirt had an ink stain at the bottom of the breast pocket. He had the look of a muddled academic.

"Captain Aleksandr Federov," the soldier said by way of introduction. He spoke with just a trace of an accent and smiled brightly. "Please call me Sasha. This is Professor Pavel Sapozhnik, of the Ministry of Defense. I will be leading your military escort. Professor Sapozhnik and his team are the disposal experts."

"Mercer. And this is Cali Stowe of the

Department of Energy." They shook hands all around while the Customs inspector frowned. Federov said a few angry words to the inspector then asked Cali and Mercer for their passports. They were quickly stamped and returned.

"Sorry about that," Federov said as he led them to a closed-off section of the airport. "Samara was a closed city until the collapse. Customs still likes to give visitors a hard time. It's not unusual for tourists to be denied entry for no reason, which makes it especially tough since Samara's newest export is mail order brides. A lot of lonely German and American men have come here to meet the love of their life only to return more frustrated than before."

Mercer chuckled, warming to the officer immediately.

"Of course, Ms. Stowe, you put all our brides to shame."

She smiled at the compliment.

"I thought Grigori Popov would be here," Mercer said.

Federov threw his hands up in a universal sign of annoyance. "Bureaucrats. He said he was detained in Moscow and will be here tomorrow or the next day. Most likely he will not come. Samara is not, how you say, a favorite destination. It is like your Pittsburgh without a good sports team." He paused outside a restroom door. "We have another two-hour flight. You might want to avail yourselves."

While Cali used the facilities, Mercer learned that Federov had studied languages during his military service and spoke French, German, and Ukrainian. He had been assigned to nuclear materials protection because so much of that work was carried out by foreign specialists. Professor Sapozhnik ignored them while they chatted, preferring to stare off into space rather than join in.

"Do you know anything about the mine Department 7 used as storage?"

"We did not know the facility existed until your superior's call to Popov," Sasha Federov answered candidly. "It is a sad state that we can misplace nuclear materials so easily but that is the fact we must deal with. The old system was so secretive that the right and left hands didn't even know the other existed.

"It is like a story about an incident in the 1970s when one of our attack submarines almost fired a torpedo at a ballistic missile submarine returning to its port at Vladivostok. You see the two branches of the navy were in a bitter rivalry for additional funding and refused to divulge their patrol schedules. Catastrophe was avoided when the sonarman on the attack sub realized the computer was giving him a false reading on the boomer's identity. He'd served on her a few years earlier and recognized her tonals."

Professor Sapozhnik snapped at Federov in Russian. The younger man answered back just as hotly and an argument flared for a moment. Sapozhnik finally nodded and turned to Mercer. "Forgive me," he said in a deep, mournful voice. "Old habits die hard. We have nothing to hide from our Western benefactors any longer."

"No apology necessary," Mercer said and smiled. He recognized Sapozhnik as from the old guard who believed the nation was better off under a Communist dictatorship. "No one likes to have their dirty laundry aired in public."

"Anyway," Sasha said smoothly, "it is an abandoned gypsum mine. There is a single road that leads to it as well as a railroad line. It was abandoned in 1957 because of flooding in the lowest levels. We now know that Department 7 commandeered it soon afterward to consolidate their warehouses of leftover war material."

"Is the road and rail line still usable after all this time?"

"Yes. In fact we're going to use a train to haul the, ah, ore to Siberia." Even with no one around he was reluctant to use the word "plutonium." "It's much safer than the roads. The train has already left the main freight yard here in Samara but won't reach the mine until tomorrow."

Cali returned from the bathroom. Mercer dashed in quickly, urinated, and washed his hands and face. Rather than risk drinking the water, he dry swallowed a couple of painkillers. The swelling in his groin had gone down significantly and the pain was little more than the discomfort of sitting so long.

They reached an exterior door that Federov opened theatrically for Cali. On the tarmac loomed a military helicopter, a massive MI-8 transport chopper, perhaps the most successful rotary wing aircraft in history. At eighty-two feet long and eighteen high it dwarfed the men lounging next to the open door. They snapped to easy attention when they saw Federov approaching.

The Russian captain gestured for Mercer and Cali to take seats along the starboard wall and showed them how to fix their helmets. "Sorry they do not have radios, but they will protect your hearing."

Seated along the flanks of the helicopter's

cargo deck were six soldiers kitted out for combat with AK-74s and a pair of RPG-7 rocket launchers. There were also five others aboard, and while they wore olive green jumpsuits, Mercer believed they were the civilian scientists under Sapozhnik. In the back of the utilitarian hold were crates for tents, food, water, and biohazard equipment.

Federov took his seat and jacked his helmet into the helo's intercom. A moment later the onboard APU wound up and ignited one of the Klimov turboshafts. The second engine roared to life and the helicopter began to buck under the strain of her own power plants. The pilot engaged the transmission, and the five sagging rotor blades began to beat the polluted air. They vanished into a blur and the shaking increased so that Mercer had to clamp his jaw. He felt Cali's hand find his. It nestled into his palm like a little creature seeking safety in its den.

The shaking suddenly eased as the pilot gently lifted the eleven-ton chopper from the crumbling apron.

Mercer peered out the yellowed Perspex window as the helicopter gained height. The city lay under an industrial pall from dozens of huge factory complexes as it clung to the shores where the Samara River dumped into the Volga, the largest river in Europe. Although the Volga was many times the size of the Ohio or Allegheny, Mercer had to admit the city of three million did look a bit like Pittsburgh.

The flight to the Samarsskaya Gypsum Mine was monotonous. The steppe slowly gave way to ugly hills of fractured granite, worn smooth by time so they looked bald, denuded. The valleys weren't particularly deep and what timber had once grown in the region had long since been harvested, so the trees remaining were stunted and gnarled. The land was muted shades of gray and dun and the sky was particularly cheerless.

As Federov had predicted, it took two hours to reach the mine. For the last twenty minutes of the flight they flew directly over the rail spur that serviced the installation. The rails were shiny streaks in the otherwise murky landscape. The mine's machinery and headgear, the crane that raised and lowered mine cars into the depths of the earth, were perched near the top of a long valley. The mine shaft itself was a black square in the gray stone that descended into the mountain at a shallow angle. About a quarter mile from the headgear was a clutch of small buildings, administrative offices and housing for the miners when the mine was in operation. Now they were abandoned and crumbling.

The facility had been a bleak, forlorn place even before the ravages of decades of neglect.

Near the valley floor was the rail depot with ore-loading hoppers straddling the tracks. A half-mile-long metal chute connected the two parts of the complex. A broad dirt road switchbacked down to the valley floor, occasionally passing below the ore chute. The train Federov had said wouldn't be there until the following day was backed into the depot. There was a bright orange TEM16 diesel-electric locomotive from the Bryansk Works and a string of eight boxcars. Pale blue smoke vented from the engine's exhaust and a few men milled around the locomotive. Several more worked near the open door of one of the boxcars.

Mercer glanced at Sasha Federov and didn't like the puzzled look on his face. He looked back at the train, at Federov again, and quickly unbuckled his seat belt even though the chopper was making its landing approach in a large open area adjacent to the mine's towering headgear.

"That's not your train," Mercer shouted at the Russian. "It's a trap."

Federov nodded grimly and yelled into his microphone at the pilot.

The missile came from behind, a perfect blind ambush. While a notoriously inaccurate weapon beyond two hundred yards, the RPG-7 lifted from its tube less than seventy yards behind the hovering MI-8 just as it reached its most vulnerable position. Covering the distance in less than a second, the five-pound warhead should have impacted squarely under the helo's tail boom, but Mercer's instincts and the pilot's quick reaction heeled the chopper over just enough so the projectile slammed into the fixed landing gear. The explosion came a microsecond later.

Most of the detonative force blew away from the chopper, but enough blasted into the MI-8 to tear a sizable hole into her rear cargo compartment. Hot gas and molten aluminum from the helicopter's skin ripped through the men and women inside the compartment, killing the two soldiers at the end of the bench seat outright and severely injuring three more. Something sheered the drive shaft to the aft rotor because suddenly its contra-rotating force was gone. The chopper begin a dizzying spin through the sky.

Mercer had been tossed across the cabin when the pilot threw the MI-8 onto its side and now was pinned up against Professor Sapozhnik and two of his scientists. The world outside the small portholes whirled by as the chopper corkscrewed from the sky. Cockpit alarms blared over the roar of her engines and the cabin was quickly filling with smoke.

Over the din of screams and the lingering effects of the explosion that had partially deafened him, Mercer heard the ping of small arms fire against the helicopter. Whoever had sprung the trap wasn't taking any chances. In the fleeting seconds before the big cargo chopper plowed into the earth Mercer's mind turned to the perpetrator. He knew it was Poli who'd ordered the helicopter shot down. What he didn't know, what had nagged at him repeatedly since first crossing the mercenary in Africa, was how he was always a step ahead.

"Crash positions," Sasha screamed.

Most of the passengers were too paralyzed to move. A few of the soldiers wrapped their arms around their knees and ducked their heads. Just before they hit, Mercer saw Cali do the same and smiled. She'd doubled her chances of survival by protecting the fragile bones of her neck from the shearing forces of a crash. Mercer snaked his arm into Sapozhnik's safety belt and held on as the blades ripped into the gravelly soil above the rail spur, not far from the mine's entrance. The tips threw up a cloud of dust before they disintegrated. The pilot managed to torque the chopper ever so slightly so she came down not on her side but at a slight angle.

The damaged landing gear collapsed as it took the helo's weight, and the blades gouged deeper into the soil until they blew apart, thrown like javelins across the mine site. The MI-8 slowly rolled onto its side, burying one of the air intakes for her Klimov engines in the ground. It sucked up rock and dust and debris, choking off the turbo shaft. The engine bellowed for a moment then fell silent. The second engine cut off almost immediately but smoke continued to thicken in the hold.

For the moment Mercer couldn't hear automatic weapons ripping into the chopper's thin skin, and even if Poli still had them in his sights the chance of aviation fuel catching fire was too great to use the helo as a redoubt.

Mercer stood shakily. Bodies lay strewn

across the cabin and for a panicked moment he thought he was the only survivor, but he soon saw slow movement. He looked to Cali. With the helicopter on its side, she was on her back, still strapped to her seat. She was pale and there was a smear of blood at the corner of her mouth where she'd been struck by the soldier next to her, but her defiant expression told him she was all right. Mercer was on Professor Sapozhnik's lap. He looked at the man's face. His mouth was slack, his eyes open and sightless. His neck was clearly broken. The scientist next to him was also dead. A boulder had punched through the MI-8's side when it rolled over, and crushed the back of his skull. His head lay in a thickening pool of dark blood.

Mercer looked up to where Sasha Federov dangled from his safety straps. He was alive and working to release the belt's catches. Trusting that the Russian officer would open the cargo door, Mercer moved closer to Cali. "Are you okay?" he asked, using his finger to gently wipe the blood from her full lips.

"They're going to be even puffier after this." She coughed. The smoke was as dense as Tiny's on a Saturday night.

"I'll think only pure thoughts." He unsnapped her belt and helped her to her feet.

The uninjured soldier was already checking on his comrades. He was wasting precious seconds on a man who was clearly dead. *"Nyet,"* Mercer shouted at him. When the soldier looked up, his young face was a mask of uncomprehending fear. He'd never been in combat. Mercer pointed at the cache of weapons and made a grabbing gesture. The boy had been conditioned by the army and seemed thankful to be given an order even if it came from an American civilian. He crawled over the corpses of his friends to retrieve several AK-74s and one of the RPG rocket launchers. He handed them across to Mercer just as Sasha slammed the door back on its roller stops. The acrid smoke boiled out the opening like a volcano, but the sudden influx of fresh air also caused the small fire smoldering at the rear of the helicopter to flare up.

"Come on," Sasha shouted in Russian. He grabbed Cali's hand and helped her crawl up the hold. When she reached the door he said, "Jump as soon as you're outside and run fifty meters straight ahead. The mine is behind us, so they won't see you." He handed her his AK-74. "Round is chambered. Is okay?"

Cali nodded. "I'm familiar enough."

Sasha helped her climb out the open door

and she immediately disappeared from view. Next came the two uninjured scientists, a man and a woman. The man was frightened and shaking so badly he was ready to topple over. The woman, with her thick body and Slavic features, looked as imperturbable as a babushka. Sasha repeated his order and was about to give an automatic pistol to the man when he thought better of it and handed it to the woman instead.

He had to struggle to push her ample backside out the door.

Mercer checked the rest of the passengers. The pilot had already escaped through the shattered windshield. The copilot was dead. The only other survivor was a pretty girl from Sapozhnik's staff with a broken collarbone. She screamed when Mercer probed it gently with his fingers. She said something in keening Russian. *"Stolichnaya,"* Mercer said. "Ah, *mir.*" Having exhausted his Russian, he unstrapped the girl and got her to her feet. She cradled her arm against her chest. The soldier was coming forward carrying a bundle of weapons and haversacks of ammunition over his shoulders.

Sasha gave his orders to the soldier and together they tossed most of the weapons out through the door and onto the ground. Then the soldier scrambled up and out of the helicopter. Mercer shot Federov a scathing glare, thinking the girl should have been the next one out.

"I need him to catch her and cover for her. I also heard automatic fire."

They used one of the AK-74 assault rifles as a step and boosted her up. She paused on top of the chopper, fearfully looking down at the young soldier outside.

"Go," Sasha hissed and reached out to shove her.

A sustained burst of autofire slammed into the underside of the helicopter, opening dozens of sizzling holes in the aluminum skin and sending ricochets whizzing through the hold whenever a round struck something solid. There was no mistaking the sound of several of the bullets punching through human flesh. Either the girl or the soldier or possibly both were dead. Cali had found cover behind a hillock some fifty yards from the downed bird. From there she quickly silenced the gunfire with a pair of three-round bursts.

Knowing that jumping out the hatch was suicide, Sasha and Mercer scrambled for the cockpit, and as the echoes of the exchange faded, Cali screamed, "RPG!"

They dove headfirst through the remains of the windshield and hit the ground running. The rocket veered slightly at the last second and hit the tail rotor. The explosion blew the boom from the body of the chopper while the concussion knocked Mercer and Federov off their feet and into a drainage ditch. A moment later the remaining fuel went up in a boiling cloud of orange flame and black smoke that lit the stark landscape like the hellish glow of a blast furnace.

"Who's out there?" Sasha Federov panted as he checked over his AK-74.

Mercer inspected his own weapon and said, "A mercenary named Poli Feines. I don't know what you've been told but the plutonium we're here to secure is naturally occurring. It was mined in Africa back in the late 1940s. Feines was in the village where Cali and I found the old mining operation, again in New Jersey while we were tracking a clue about an American who first discovered the lode. Two days ago one of his men and a bunch of Arab terrorists attacked us in Niagara Falls, New York."

"How is it he's here?"

"Million dollar question," Mercer said. He made sure the Yarygin nine-millimeter pistol he'd shoved behind his back was secure. "I suspect there's a leak within the organizations I've been dealing with." It was the first time he'd given voice to the nagging thought that had been with him almost since the beginning. If true, the ramifications of it were chilling because the only people who knew the truth were himself, Cali, Ira Lasko, and Harry. He trusted Harry and Ira with his life and Cali had been shot at enough times to disqualify her as a traitor, so the theory didn't make sense. But there were no alternatives, either.

He poked his head above the rim of the drainage ditch. He spotted Cali behind a mound of boulders. The two scientists were with her, and the young soldier had found cover behind a pile of mine tailings. The body of the pretty female scientist had been immolated when the helicopter exploded.

The building that housed the headgear machinery was four stories tall and covered in corrugated metal. The seams were streaked in rust, creating a patchwork effect. Around it were several smaller buildings, offices, and workshops. Also littering the mine were piles of machinery — old ore cars with broken wheel bogies, small electric shunting locomotives, pumps, and hundreds of other items. Most of the old machinery had rusted together over the past decades and thorny weeds grew around everything. But there were two trucks backed to the gaping mine entrance. They were UAZ-5151s, rugged little four-wheel drives that resembled jeeps. Poli was here to steal the plutonium and transport the ore from the mine down to the train with the off-roaders.

Mercer spotted a dozen men around the trucks, more than half of them armed. As he watched, a forklift emerged from the mine, a single barrel lashed to a pallet it carried. Its driver wore a gas mask and protective suit. At least the Soviets had taken a few precautions, Mercer noted. The barrel was massive and obviously well shielded, and when the forklift lowered it into the bed of the truck, the suspension sagged under the load. He looked at the other vehicle. Its tires were still fully inflated which meant they hadn't been loaded yet. This explained the train, however. The trucks couldn't handle the crumbling Russian roads carrying such weight.

The guards didn't seem intent on hunting down Mercer's party. They just wanted to keep loading their trucks so they could leave. Mercer turned to Sasha.

"Do you have a radio or satellite phone?"

The Russian shook his head. "Radio was on the helicopter and I've never even seen a satellite telephone."

"This just gets better and better." Mercer

plucked a sleek cell phone from the inside pocket of his leather jacket. There wasn't a cell tower for a hundred miles but he tried anyway. When he didn't get a signal, he slid it back into his coat. "It's up to us."

"You seem like you can handle yourself," Sasha said. "Cali, too, but that leaves us just four against eight or more."

"Five. That other woman looks capable." Mercer's eyes went hard. "But it doesn't matter. We don't have an option. We can't call for help, and once they get those trucks on the train we'll never be able to stop them. They'll be beyond Russia's borders by the time anyone comes to check on us."

Sasha nodded grimly. "All right."

Mercer turned back to study the terrain and come up with a plan. A frontal assault was out of the question. Poli's force was too large. They could circle around the building, but there was a lot of open ground to cover, and if Poli was smart, which Mercer knew he was, he'd have sent a couple of guards to cover his flanks as soon as he saw people escape the chopper crash. The best way would be to circle even wider, climb up the hill rising above the mountain, and attack from above. It would take time but Mercer saw no other way. He turned to run his plan by Sasha but the Russian was gone.

He looked down the length of the drainage ditch. Federov was crawling away, and for a fleeting second Mercer wanted to put a bullet in his back. Then he realized that Sasha was getting into a better position to attack from the opposite flank, behind a row of abandoned ore cars. From there he could find cover behind the steel pylons that supported the ore chute.

Sasha would still need cover to get into position. Mercer inched his way out of the ditch, crawling across the cold ground. The forklift disappeared into the mine once again as a man emerged. One of the others used a hose attached to one of the trucks to douse his suit with water before he took off his gas mask. Even at two hundred yards Mercer recognized the bald head and eye patch.

Uncontrollable rage made him bring the AK to his shoulder, not caring that the counterfire would catch him exposed. He wanted the son of a bitch dead. He centered Poli's broad chest in the weapon's iron sites and eased the trigger. The instant he fired, Mercer rolled to his left several times and lurched to his feet, racing toward where the young Russian soldier had found cover as Poli's men chewed up the ground at his feet with a steady barrage. He reached the pile of crushed rock and ducked his head around the slope. Mercer cursed.

Poli was directing his men and there wasn't a scratch on him. Mercer was a fair shot with a rifle but he was unfamiliar with the AK and hadn't compensated for the wind's effect on the light 5.54-millimeter bullet.

Mercer glanced back and saw that Sasha had reached the first row of small mine cars and settled his rifle on the side of one. He fired, picking targets who were covered from Mercer's position but exposed to his. He dropped two of them before half the force swung their aim and raked the ore car. He ducked behind it as rounds ricocheted off the thick metal. Mercer and the young soldier named Ivan opened up, hosing the trucks with little regard to how much ammo they were using up. Ivan had managed to keep his rucksacks of magazines as well as the RPG-7.

Poli's men sought cover behind their trucks as Cali and the heavy-set Russian woman, Ludmilla, added their guns to the attack. Three of the terrorists were down, two dead, and one had half his jaw shot away. Using all the cover fire, Federov ran from behind the train car, eating ground to reach one of the ore chute's support pylons.

The forklift emerged from the mine once again. Judging by how the truck had settled, Mercer believed this was the last barrel Poli would load on it. He thought about using the rocket grenade but he only had the one, so he could only take out one truck, not both, and he had no idea how many barrels had already been loaded onto the train.

Poli's men had no such shortage. A pair of RPGs streaked from behind one of the trucks and exploded on the far side of the gravel pile where Mercer and Ivan crouched. The fifty-foot-high mound of mine waste absorbed the twin explosions as though they were nothing, but a moment later the top of the pile shifted and a hissing avalanche barreled down the slope. It came down so fast that Mercer didn't have time to shout a warning as he jumped out of the way. Ivan looked up and screamed as a towering wall of fist-sized rocks pounded into him. The sheer weight of rock crushed him flat and the rough edges tore away his clothes and flayed great sheets of skin from his body. He was dead before he was fully buried, but that didn't stop Mercer from trying to reach him as more rock shifted and slid down the hill. Mercer recklessly waded into the avalanche, getting buried up to his knees in seconds and up to his thighs in just moments more. But there was nothing he could do. The barrel of the RPG launcher poking up from the ground was all that marked the young Russian's grave.

Another RPG arced from behind the truck. Mercer watched its path as it slashed through the cold mountain air. Sasha Federov was behind one of the pylons and had just a couple of seconds to run before the rocket exploded against the metal stanchion. He was thrown fifteen feet by the blast, landing in a tangle of loose limbs, and when the smoke cleared he wasn't moving.

Mercer fought to lift himself from the avalanche debris, tearing at the stones with his bare hands until his fingers bled. He heard the trucks' engines fire. With Cali so far to the left, Poli had a clear path down the hairpin road to the railhead. The convoy would pass no more than twenty feet from Mercer, and if he didn't get himself free he was dead.

Frantic now, he kicked and struggled, his heart hammering painfully in his chest. The trucks grew louder as they started across the facility. They fired barrage after barrage in Cali's direction to keep her pinned. Mercer had seconds at most, and rather than loosening, the rubble seemed to be solidifying around his legs. What a stupid way to die, he thought fleetingly — standing thigh-deep in a pile of mine tailings so trained gunmen could use him like kids with BB guns going after soda bottles.

In one desperate heave he managed to free one leg. He lurched to his right, painfully wrenching his trapped knee to tear it from the earth. The lead truck rounded the massive pile as Mercer dove flat. His movements caused the heavy aggregate to shift again, and a small wave of rock slid down the mound and buried him under a foot of loose stone.

The trucks roared by, doing forty miles per hour, and while a couple of the terrorists noticed the rock slide, none saw the man hiding under the veneer of rubble. Moments later the vehicles turned down the first hairpin and vanished down the hill.

Mercer began to heave himself from under the rock, moving slowly because his body had taken a beating by the stones. He was almost free when Cali raced up to him, the two Russian scientists in tow. The man was catatonic, while the woman scanned the grounds warily.

Cali threw herself into Mercer's arms, tears on her cheeks. "I thought you were dead."

"The boy is," Mercer said grimly, holding

her tight. He wanted nothing more than to stand there forever, forget about Poli, the plutonium, and everything else and simply surrender to the embrace. Pulling his arms from around her neck took a force of will. "Sasha?"

"We haven't checked."

"See to him. I'm going after Poli."

"How? They'll have the barrels loaded before you get halfway to the train."

Mercer looked over his head. "Like hell they will."

He grabbed the RPG from where it stuck up from the tailings, checked that it hadn't been damaged, and slung the long tube over his shoulder. The steady growl of the locomotive at the bottom of the valley deepened as the engineer made ready to pull from the ore depot.

"What are you doing?"

"I going to catch a train."

The pylons supporting the ore chute had integrated ladders so workers could access the half-mile-long slide for maintenance. The metal was scaled with rust and the paint was badly flaked. With the RPG and an AK over his shoulder, Mercer climbed the ladder, wincing with the pressure of each step on his strained knee but thankful it would take his weight.

No sooner had he cleared the ground than he felt movement below him. Cali was climbing on his heels. He wasn't going to make any chivalrous remarks. He could use all the help he could get.

The support column was eighty feet high and it took them nearly two minutes to climb. Their hands were cramped from the cold metal rungs, and Mercer's eyes teared up because the wind was gusting to thirty miles an hour.

From the top of the stanchion they could see the ore-loading hoppers and the train far below, although their vantage wouldn't let them see what was happening on its far side. The twisty road down to the depot looked clear. Poli would have had more than enough time to reach the rail spur.

Mercer helped Cali up onto the small platform next to the chute. "You sure about this?"

She threw him her trademark saucy grin. "As sure as you are."

The chute was more than twenty feet wide, with curved sides to prevent ore from tumbling to the ground. The decades of rain and snow hadn't rusted the metal. It was still bright from years of being polished by ore headed to the hoppers down below. Mercer repositioned the RPG so it was across his chest and cinched the AK-74's sling around his arm before he and Cali climbed over the rim. The angle was steep and they had to hold themselves in place by planting their rubber-soled boots and holding on to the edge. Just before he sat, Mercer saw the locomotive lurch and heard the rail car's couplings crash together as the train started to leave.

"Shit! Come on."

When they sat, their view was blocked by the sides of the chute so it was like looking down a ski lift or a bobsled run. Mercer could feel gravity sucking at his chest as his eyes adjusted to the vertiginous scene. He took Cali's hand and they eased their feet off the bottom of the chute. They began to slide immediately, slowly at first but the speed built quickly. Too quickly. Mercer tried to apply pressure with his feet to slow himself. Cali did the same and for a moment it was working. Then her shoe caught a seam in the metal chute and she flipped head over heels. As Mercer made to grab her, Cali careened into him and he too began to tumble out of control.

They somersaulted down the chute for fifty feet before Mercer managed to grab Cali's collar. The move vaulted him over her prone form and he slammed into the chute hard enough to make it vibrate, but the maneuver stopped her from flipping again. Now flat on his back, Mercer eased his heels against the metal, careful to lift when he neared a seam, and had himself slowed enough to regain control of the slide.

"Are you okay?" he called over his shoulder, feeling Cali's presence right behind him.

"I think so," she answered.

"We're almost there." Mercer was glad she hadn't asked about his condition. His back ached from the impact and he'd have a bump the size of an egg on his forehead if he survived the next few minutes.

They'd descended two thirds of the way to the ore hoppers, and now that they knew how to handle the slide, they rocketed downward, crisp wind whipping at their faces so their eyes streamed tears. With thirty feet to go, they could see the top of the train through the open hopper. It was still moving slowly but the last car was halfway through the loading trough. They had seconds or they'd drop twenty feet to the hard rails below.

"Hurry," Mercer shouted and he and Cali took their feet off the chute completely.

They shot down the last section of the ore slide like arrows, the metal walls becoming a blur as they focused on landing atop the last rail car. Cali pulled slightly ahead.

The ore hopper was a long metal trough with steeply angled sides and an open bottom that allowed the crushed rock to stream into rail cars. Cali braced her feet when she reached the end of the slide, slowing herself just enough so when she was launched off the lip she didn't crash into the far side of the hopper. The impact was still brutal, but she absorbed the blow and fell easily to the roof of the rolling boxcar.

Mercer had to contend with the RPG-7 as he came to the end of the chute, tugging the weapon back over his shoulder at the last second. He was in an awkward position when he shot off the end of the slide. Cali screamed his name. He slammed into the opposite side of the ore hopper, knocking the air from his lungs in a painful explosion of breath. He looked down to see that the rear of the train was almost past him. He pushed off from the hopper and fell through empty space.

His timing was a fraction off. He dropped clear of the chute and hit the very end of the boxcar, further bruising his aching ribs. With his legs dangling off the edge of the train, he struggled to find something to grab, but there were no handholds and he began to slide off. He looked down. Railroad ties emerged from under the car like an ever-lengthening ladder as the locomotive accelerated down the valley.

He slid farther, clamping onto the edge with just his elbows, his legs bicycling against the rear of the car as he fought to find purchase. He couldn't support himself much longer — his body had taken too much punishment and he just wanted to let go. Instead he fought harder, kicking at the rear of the boxcar with his steel-toed boots, using his chin and the muscles of his neck to give him an ounce more leverage. Cali was running toward him. He had to hold on for a few more seconds, but he wasn't sure he could.

A head emerged between their boxcar and the next one in line. Mercer saw it through Cali's long legs. Then he saw a torso and an assault rifle.

"Behind you," he gasped. Cali kept coming. Mercer managed another hoarse bellow: "Behind you!"

She barely slowed as she whirled around, flipping her Kalashnikov off her shoulder and under her arm in a fluid, almost well-practiced motion. She fired from the hip, sweeping across the gunman's midsection, and continued to spin so she was still running toward Mercer. The three bullets that hit the gunman passed clean through, tumbling as they transited his body and tearing fist-sized chunks of tissue from his back. He fell between the two cars and hit the tracks.

Mercer glanced down as he felt Cali's hands on his jacket collar. The gunman had landed across the tracks and the train's steel wheels had sliced his corpse into three pieces.

"Hold on," Cali panted, struggling to haul him back aboard the boxcar.

"If you insist," Mercer said, knowing she had him. She heaved and he rolled over the edge of the car and onto his back, not caring that the RPG's pistol grip was digging into his flesh.

Mercer gave himself just a second before getting to his feet. Poli wouldn't just post one man to guard the train's roof. And with the train continuing to accelerate down the valley, they didn't have much time to stop it before it was going too fast for what he had in mind.

"Are you okay?" Cali asked. She'd seen Mercer wince when he put weight on his bad knee.

"Doesn't matter," he said grimly. "Come on."

In a crouch they padded forward, and as they neared the coupling to the next rail car Mercer cautiously poked his head over the gap. It was clear. They leapt in unison and continued forward. The train was starting to vibrate as it sped past twenty miles per hour.

"Watch our backs," Mercer said, fearful now that one of Poli's men could still emerge from between the cars.

They leapt four more cars without seeing anyone and were a quarter of the way down the sixth car when three men began to climb up from between it and the next car. They spotted Mercer and Cali instantly. Mercer opened fire and saw an explosion of pink mist blow away in the wind as one of his rounds found its mark, but the other two men vanished back into the gap. Without cover, Mercer had to turn back and run. He grabbed Cali's arm and they raced to the end of the car, scrambling down the ladder before the gunmen at the front of the car recovered. This situation was exactly what Mercer didn't want. It was a standoff, and every second that passed meant the train was going that much faster.

He didn't think through his decision. He just went for it. He handed Cali his AK-74 and hung the RPG from a tear in the

383

boxcar's skin. "Act like we're both still here. Fire both weapons and weave back and forth so it looks like two people pinned here."

"Where are you going?"

"Outflank them."

Mercer ducked around to look up the length of the train. With the exception of the big door in its middle, the side of the railcar was a featureless wall of steel. The tracks ahead ran straight down the valley floor, boxed in by mountains on both sides.

"They'll see you on the side of the train if they look around the corner," Cali said, desperately trying to stop him.

"I know."

Without another word, he climbed the rest of the way down the ladder and crawled onto the heavy coupling securing this car to the next. The tracks were only two feet below him, a blur of wooden ties and gray ballast stones. He ducked lower still and peered under the railcar. Beyond the bogie trucks that anchored the wheels was a series of girders and beams that gave the boxcar its strength. It would be difficult but not impossible.

Mercer moved the Yarygin pistol from his back into the front of his jeans and slung himself under the coupling. An occasional weed growing between the tracks whipped at his head. Ignoring the distraction, he reached forward and grabbed the bogie truck, feeling the power of the train's engine through the cold metal. He shifted his weight, using the muscles of his legs and stomach to keep his body from sagging onto the ground, and slowly inched himself into the space above the axles.

He heard Cali fire a couple of shots as he eased himself above the whirling axles. Grease coated everything, but the railcar was so old it was sticky rather than slick. He flipped onto his stomach to jam his feet against one of the longitudinal beams and hold on to the other with his arms. Inch by inch he shimmied down the length of the car, his stomach quivering with the strain of holding his body in a shallow arch. The ground whizzed by a foot under his nose. He could no longer hear Cali because of the noise generated by the boxcar, but when he reached the forward set of bogies he caught the sound of the gunmen. He torqued a leg over the top of the bogie assembly, felt the axle spinning against his skin, and yanked the leg back. One hand slipped from the beam and for a precarious moment he was suspended over the tracks by one hand and a foot and felt himself tipping over.

Mercer scrambled to right his grip and keep his heart from exploding from his chest. He took a couple of breaths before trying again. This time his foot landed on one of the axle's supports and he managed to awkwardly climb onto the truck. The front of the car was only a few feet away. He could clearly hear the men shooting back at Cali, precisely timed shots that made him think they had ammunition to spare.

He eased forward again and was reaching for the coupling when he felt the mechanism vibrate. One of the gunmen had jumped off the ladder and onto the coupling. Hanging one-handed like a gibbon, with his shoulder no more than an inch from the wooden ties, Mercer pulled the Yarygin pistol just as the gunman got on his knees to see if he could pull off the same trick Mercer just had.

In the microsecond of shock, Mercer saw he was Middle Eastern, hadn't shaved in a couple of days, and had perfectly capped teeth. He put a bullet through the man's skull and swung out of the way as his body fell onto the tracks and vanished.

The gunman still on the ladder heard the shot and looked down just as Mercer swung back, extending the pistol over his head. He fired as fast as he could, absorbing the recoil with a stiff elbow to keep the barrel pointed at the assassin. He had to give the man marks for courage, because even as a wall of lead flew around him he tried to bring his gun to bear. He had the barrel pointed downward when he ran out of time. One of the nine-millimeter rounds entered his stomach just below the diaphragm and shredded his left lung before emerging out the top of his shoulder, nearly severing the arm. The next two hit him in the upper chest as he lost his grip on the railing and started to fall. Another punched through his head as the Yarygin locked back empty.

The gunman hit the coupling and rolled off to follow his partner as so much litter on the tracks.

Mercer heaved himself up and climbed the ladder. He waited while Cali fired off a three-round burst and then he shouted, "Cali. All clear."

"What?"

He thought to himself that if he was calling out to her she should realize it meant he'd made it and it was clear to come forward. "It's clear. I got them. Bring the RPG."

He looked up as she scrambled onto the

roof of the boxcar and he too climbed up. "Hurry," he urged and she broke into a run.

"God, you're filthy," Cali said when she reached him. She gave him back his half-empty assault rifle.

"Yeah, but you should see the other guy."

She made a face. "I'll pass, thanks."

On the last car before the locomotive, Mercer stopped and set his AK onto the roof. Hot exhaust spewing from the locomotive stung their eyes and made the air difficult to breathe.

"This is close enough," Mercer said. Ahead of them they could see the tracks running down the valley. The rail spur was so straight that it looked like they could see forever.

He checked over the RPG, making sure he knew how to use it. "I think the train's clear so why don't you start back."

"What are you going to do?"

"Blow the tracks a couple hundred yards ahead of the train and derail the whole thing. We can jump off the back."

She looked him in the eye. "We go together."

Mercer made to argue, but every second saw the train going faster and faster. A leap off the back of the train was dangerous enough. It would be suicide if it was traveling much faster. In fact just to be safe he would need to give the engineer time to slow down to avoid hitting the destroyed section of track.

Without a word he hoisted the rocket launcher onto his shoulder, aimed at a spot three hundred yards ahead of the train, and pulled the trigger. The eighty-five-millimeter missile shot from tube and an instant later the motor ignited, blasting Mercer and Cali with a wave of hot gasses. The fins deployed as the missle rocketed ahead of the train, zeroing in exactly on the spot Mercer had aimed for. He had already dropped the tube and was turned to start the mad race to the end of the train when he saw the rocket motor cut out and the missile drop like a stone. It hit the tracks and exploded less than two hundred yards in front of the speeding train, sending up a shower of loose ballast stones and tearing one of the rails off the ties.

He and Cali started to run, lurching slightly as the engineer slammed on the brakes, creating a keening screech like nails across a blackboard amplified a thousand-fold.

Mercer ignored the pain in his knee, sprinting on his toes, his lungs pumping in time with his pounding heart. Next to him Cali ran with the grace of a natural athlete, her head high, her lips only slightly parted. He knew she could have run even faster but she was determined to keep pace. They took the leap onto the next car like a pair of Olympic hurdlers, with barely a check in their speed.

Behind them, the locomotive barreled on toward the ruined track, her antiquated brakes fighting her massive inertia. It was a losing battle. The one-hundred-and-eight-ton TEM16 diesel-electric hit the broken rail doing twenty-seven miles per hour. When the right side wheels hit the ground, they dug into the hard earth, plowing a deep furrow for thirty feet before the entire locomotive tipped onto its side. The coupling to the first car in the train was wrenched to one side and the car jack-knifed, splitting in half as it slammed into the back of the engine.

Cali and Mercer leapt onto the next car, feeling the vibrations of the destruction behind them through their feet. Neither dared look back.

The second car came loose and rode up and over the first, tumbling it like a log as the locomotive's belly tank ruptured and the four thousand gallons of diesel fuel she carried spread out in a small lake.

They continued even faster, running

beyond what either thought they were capable of, the sound of the awful destruction behind them never seeming to recede as they ran from it.

Even with the train slowing, they jumped to the second car from the end an instant before the one they left slammed into the pileup. That car had a structural flaw of some kind because when it hit, the front of it accordioned, metal shearing and tearing as though it was paper.

The gaps between the trains were only about four feet but as Cali and Mercer neared the rear of the car Mercer shouted jump with five feet to go.

Cali did as he ordered, and as they launched themselves from the car, it hit the one before it. The coupling to the last car broke free as the second boxcar was pulled off the tracks and onto its side, falling as if in slow motion, spreading ballast stones in an arc as it tore into the ground.

They landed hard on the last car, both of them knocked off their feet by the impact. Mercer looked back. With the preceding car pulled bodily from the tracks, the last of the rolling stock had a clear path to the tangle of destroyed train cars. It had slowed enough so he threw an arm over Cali and together they held on as it hit. Most of the energy of the collision was absorbed by the squashed cars in front, so it felt like nothing more than a mild bump.

Cali and Mercer shared a surprised look then burst out laughing.

"I think this is our stop," Mercer quipped and Cali laughed even harder.

But their laughter was cut short when both smelled burning fuel at the same time. They scrambled to their feet and ran to the rear of the car. Cali descended the ladder first, with Mercer right behind, hooking his feet outside the rungs so he could slide down the ladder like a submariner. They ran for a couple hundred yards before turning back.

The railcars were piled three high in places. Two of them were flipped over on their roofs, and as Mercer and Cali watched, the spreading pool of diesel consumed the wreckage in a wall of flame that grew to a hundred feet.

Mercer put his arm around Cali's slender waist and she snuggled into him as they watched the inferno mutely, confident that Poli was dead.

Poli Feines had been behind the wheel of the Russian jeep for twenty straight hours, yet the predatory gleam in his single eye hadn't faded. His drive from the mine to the Black Sea had been over torturous back roads and old smuggling routes, and it was only when he reached the M-27 motorway near the port city of Novorossiysk that he encountered asphalt.

While this part of the Black Sea was famous for its resort beaches, his destination was a small working-class fishing village on the other side of the Bay of Zemess called Kabardinka.

Blind rage had erased any memory of the first part of his journey. First Africa, then New Jersey, and Niagara Falls, and now this. Though he hadn't seen him, Feines was positive that Philip Mercer was behind the attack at the mine, just as the helicopter pilot had described him as the man on the barge in upstate New York. Even after twenty hours of thinking about his losses, acid jetted from his stomach and scalded the back of his throat. He'd served with Gavrail Skoda for more than a decade in the Bulgarian Army and had partnered with him numerous times when he'd gone freelance. Feines had five brothers, one of them an identical twin, but he'd loved none more than Gavrail and now Skoda was dead, killed by Philip Mercer on a barge on the Niagara River.

Feines admitted that they hadn't had enough time to plan that mission properly, but he and Skoda had pulled off far more elaborate capers with less time than they'd had. And the men with him were combat-hardened veterans of Afghanistan and Iraq. That they were willing to martyr themselves for the cause only made success more certain.

And now Mercer shows up again. Poli's hands tightened on the wheel until his knuckles went white and the bones threatened to erupt from the skin. He welcomed the pain, for it reminded him what he would do with Mercer when their paths crossed again. Feines was a professional. He never let his contracts affect his personal life. But this was different. When he'd discharged his obligation to his client, he would hunt Mercer down, kill everyone close to him, then torture Mercer so slowly that he'd beg for death.

The lights of Poli's vehicle showed the sign for his turnoff. He exited the deserted highway and drove slowly through the fishing town. The smell of the sea, which tinged the air, was overwhelmed by the stench of rotted fish and diesel fuel. North of the town a road ran parallel to the sea. He could see the bright lights of Novorossiysk across the bay. There were several supertankers lined up to load oil transported on the new pipeline from Kazakhstan. And out on the still waters of the Black Sea, more ships could be seen headed into or out of the port. The laden tankers would need to transit the full length of the Black Sea and pass through the Bosporus Strait at Istanbul, one of the busiest shipping lanes in the world, where on average there is an accident every three days. Before reaching the Mediterranean, they also faced the navigational nightmare of crossing the Aegean Sea.

The headlights revealed a small fish processing plant built on pilings over the water. The parking lot was deserted but for two cars, a luxurious Audi A8 W12 and a limousine. The lights were on in the office trailer at the edge of the parking lot. Alongside the plant was a long wooden jetty where an eighty-foot commercial fishing boat was moored. Poli could see the glow of navigation equipment through the broad bridge windscreen.

He parked the UAZ jeep next to the black Audi. He reached over his shoulder to touch one of the barrels. It was warm but not yet hot. The heat was a by-product of the exchange of subatomic particles from one barrel to the next. By themselves there wasn't enough ore in any one of the containers to start such a chain reaction, but two in close proximity created a critical mass. In the mine the barrels had been stored well away from one another, but in the confines of the truck it was almost as if they were calling to one another in a deadly siren song. Left unchecked, the plutonium would eventually explode in a shower of deadly dust that would contaminate several city blocks or more, depending on the wind.

Two men emerged from the office trailer and he sensed movement on the fishing boat.

The older of the two walked up to Feines and hugged him while the other held back at a distance. Poli didn't return the embrace. The man released him. He was of average height, with thick salt-and-pepper hair. His mustache was tell tended, and below his arched brows were arresting blue eyes that even in the dim light of the parking lot possessed a devilish charm. "First of all," he said in Russian, "are you okay?"

"I'm fine. But I think all the Arabs sent to help me were killed."

"What happened, Poli?"

"You didn't give me enough time," Feines snapped.

"I couldn't stall the Americans any longer," Grigori Popov said. "Ira Lasko was about to go over my head. If that happened there would have been an investigation and it would have been my ass on the line. As it is I'll have a lot of explaining to do. I can only hope to convince my superiors and the Americans that the timing was a coincidence or perhaps there is a leak within Lasko's office. Tell me what happened."

"We were loading the last barrels when the chopper appeared. We were ready for it but somehow the stupid raghead missed. It was a MI-8, for Christ's sake, as big as a barn, and the damn fool only managed a glancing shot with an RPG. From the amount of fire we got after it crashed, I estimated most of the soldiers survived, so rather than get into a pitched battle I ordered us out."

"But you decided not to go with the train?" Popov asked slyly.

Poli remained grim. "As was my plan all along, just in case something happened to the train. I wanted to make sure I got some of the plutonium here. I heard the train wreck as I drove out of the valley, and saw the fire. Even if I went back, there's no way we're going to recover those barrels."

"How many did you manage to bring with you?"

"Two."

Popov nodded. "More than enough for their current operation."

"Good, because I am done with this operation," Feines remarked.

"You're not going after the alembic?"

"This operation has been a lot more than I anticipated," Poli admitted. "I thought I'd find what I needed in Africa, only to learn your army beat me to it by a half century. Then I thought I had it from the samples the American recovered and shipped home on the *Wetherby.* I have the pictures I took of the stele, which might reveal the alembic's location, but your information about the old depot led me to complete the project. I'm out of it now."

"I don't blame you," Popov said. "I'm glad

my only part in this thing was giving you information about the cache in Samarsskaya."

"You mean selling me that information."

Popov shot him an oily smile. "We've known each other for a lot of years, Poli, but business is business and helping you smuggle nuclear material out of Russia, well let's just say my conscience needed a little help accepting it. In truth I wouldn't have given that information to anyone but you, because I know you couldn't let these crazy bastards do anything to us."

It sounded like a question to Poli. In truth he had just a vague notion of what the people paying him were going to do with the plutonium, and given the amount of money he'd receive, he really didn't care. He doubted the little village in Bulgaria he planned to return to was a terrorist target, so nothing they did would affect him personally. Let them nuke the States and then face her wrath. It wasn't his problem anymore. "What about Mercer and the other survivors at the mine?" he asked.

"Federov reports directly to me. I am supposed to be there tomorrow when the real train arrives. I will tell the engineer and his crew that Federov needs more time. They'll be isolated for a few days at least."

"Good." Feines considered driving back up there with a sniper rifle and at least killing Philip Mercer, but he didn't want to rush his hunt. He would make certain he and Mercer met soon enough.

Popov motioned for the other man to join them. "I don't believe you two have actually been introduced formally. Poli Feines, may I present the deputy oil minister of Saudi Arabia, currently stationed at the United Nations overseeing charitable contributions from the cartel, Mohammad bin Al-Salibi, your employer."

Al-Salibi shook Feines's hand but there was a cold reserve behind his handsome face. "I understand that you ran into a setback." He spoke with a slight British accent from having prepped and gone to university in England.

"Philip Mercer."

"Not the Janissaries this time."

"No, it was Mercer."

"Resourceful man."

"A man on borrowed time."

"He's not a priority to me," the Saudi ambassador said.

"This is personal," Poli snarled.

"Let's go into the office," Popov suggested. "A little coffee is in order, I think."

The fish processing plant's office was as

unkempt as the plant itself. It stank of fish oil, and the furniture in the reception area was stained from years of supporting the backsides of dirty fishermen. Popov got the coffee machine brewing and poured when it was ready.

"How much ore do you have?" Al-Salibi asked.

"There are two barrels in the back of the UAZ. I estimate about a thousand pounds' worth."

"For curiosity's sake how much was at the mine depot?"

"Tons of it. We loaded sixty-eight barrels onto the train before Mercer showed."

A wistful look crossed the ambassador's face as he considered what could be done with such a deadly cache.

Even for a stone killer like Poli Feines the look was disquieting. "That fishing boat out there," he said just to cut the eerie silence, "is that the one they are going to use?"

"Yes. It was stolen a week ago in Albania. Her name's been changed of course so she's completely untraceable."

"And your crew?"

"Are ready to travel to Turkey and are most eager to martyr themselves."

After the fire had died down some Mercer

and Cali checked the wreckage for survivors, first tying strips of cloth over their noses and mouths in case any of the barrels had ruptured. Neither was surprised that no one had survived the crash and subsequent explosion, but both were relieved that the barrels they could see in the twisted pile of railcars remained intact.

They set out for the long walk up the tracks back to the mine, Mercer using a stout branch as a crutch. At dusk they built a fire and slept in its rosy glow, Cali cradled in Mercer's arm, her silky hair caressing his face. They reached the mine two hours after sunrise. The Russians were camped near the remains of the helicopter. Ludmilla, the heavyset scientist, was cooking rations scavenged from the chopper, while the other scientist and the pilot, who'd run from the gunfight because he had no weapons, tended an injured man. When they got close they could see it was Sasha Federov.

Mercer hobbled up and knelt next to the soldier, grinning. "I was certain that RPG had your number on it."

"Bah," Federov dismissed with a pained smile. "Nothing more than a little shrapnel in my shoulder and one hell of a headache. Did you stop the train?"

"Derailed it about twenty miles down the

valley. No one got off at their last stop."

"I'm afraid someone didn't get on it at this one."

Mercer's relief that Federov had survived turned to instant concern. "What are you saying?"

"Yesterday I sent Yuri, the pilot, down to the tracks. One of the UAZs was there, its engine destroyed by gunfire, so we couldn't use it. The other was gone."

"Son of a bitch," Mercer shouted and got to his feet. "Fucking Poli. He took off in the truck knowing I was going after the train."

"Do you think he had any of the barrels?"

"Yes, goddamn it. There wasn't enough time to load the last two. I had assumed Poli would have cut his losses and left them behind."

"What are we going to do?" Cali asked.

"Sasha, how long before your superiors send someone out here when they don't hear from us?"

"Do not worry, my friend. The real train should arrive sometime today."

"Thank God."

"That still gives him a day's head start," Cali pointed out. "Those barrels could be anywhere in the world by then."

Her remark soured Mercer's mood even further. She was right and he began to understand the stress of her job. Being right ninety-nine percent of the time when dealing with nuclear materials wasn't good enough. He'd stopped Poli from carrying off tons of the plutonium ore but failed to prevent a couple of barrels from slipping away. How many people would die because he screwed up? In theory that was enough plutonium to irradiate dozens of square miles or the water supply of an entire city.

What would happen when elevated radiation levels were detected in the aquifer feeding Manhattan? Thousands would die just from the rioting and looting that would break out. How many more would perish during the evacuation? And then how many would suffer the devastating effects of ingesting the plutonium dust? It was conceivable that cancer would claim tens or even hundreds of thousands more.

And what would become of New York City with every pipe and conduit potentially contaminated? It would be uninhabitable for years, a ghost town of skyscrapers.

Mercer had been so proud of himself for blowing the train off the tracks, and now he'd never felt worse in his life. It was his fault. All of it. He would feel as responsible for those deaths as if he was the one who released the plutonium.

"We'll get him," Cali said, reading the anguish in his eyes.

"And if we don't?"

"At NEST failure is simply not an option."

"Cali, that looks good on the letterhead but it's just not realistic." He didn't want to sound so harsh but his emotions were running at the breaking point. "There is a lunatic out there with a thousand pounds of plutonium and we're stuck here. By the time Sasha's train arrives, Paris or London or Rome could be a radioactive wasteland."

A voice came from the other side of the helicopter. "Or New York or Chicago or Washington, D.C."

Mercer recognized it immediately.

The Janissary who'd rescued Cali and him in Africa and had warned them off at Mercer's brownstone stepped from around the helo's scorched wreckage. He wore the same black suit he had in Washington and with him was the same assistant. "However, I believe Ankara, Istanbul, and Baku are more likely targets."

Mercer had his pistol out and trained on the Janissary's head. "Tell me why I shouldn't kill you now."

He smiled. "For a man who's been calling me for a week, you don't seem too interested in what I have to tell you."

It took Mercer a moment to understand. "You're Professor Ibriham Ahmad. Of the University of Istanbul."

He made a gracious half bow. "At your service. I am also General Ibriham Ahmad of the Most Exulted Sultan's Janissary Corps, tasked with being the last guardians of the Alembic of Skenderbeg."

Mercer lowered his pistol.

"This is Devrin Egemen." Ahmad introduced the young man next to him. "One of my star pupils and a trusted lieutenant."

Egemen bobbed his head.

Ahmad looked around the deserted mine, noting the bodies covered in tarps. "We knew the Russians returned to Africa to mine Alexander's adamantine ore but we believed they used it all up building their early bombs. How much was here and how much did they get away with?"

"I don't know for sure. We stopped the train. Cali and I could see dozens of barrels in the wreckage but there's probably more. Poli Feines escaped with two barrels, probably a thousand pounds' worth, in a truck."

"More than enough for their plans," Ahmad said thoughtfully. He moved away, forcing Cali and Mercer to follow, so they could have some privacy. Then in one graceful movement he sat on the ground with his legs crossed. He patted the earth. "Please sit. This story will take some time."

Mercer had seen his capacity for violence but he sensed that Ahmad's true strength came from his intellect. It was in the way he spoke, confident and assured and eager to teach. Mercer thankfully lowered himself and set aside his makeshift crutch.

"Like all Janissaries Gjergi Kastrioti was trained in Istanbul at the finest military college of his day. He was an excellent student who intuitively grasped strategy and tactics. So when he decided that the sultanate had become corrupt and revolted against Murad II, it was little wonder his men followed him."

"He went to Albania and held off the sultan's army for twenty-five years," Mercer said.

Ahmad cocked an eyebrow. "You've done some research. Very good."

"It was rumored he had a talisman that once belonged to Alexander the Great," Mercer went on. "I assume it's the alembic."

"Correct. The last credible report concerning the alembic came from a Syrian scribe who said that the generals who took over Alexander's army following his death

407

were squabbling over who should carry it. Because there was no consensus, they decided to return it to Egypt, where it would be buried with Alexander. Along the way a contingent of soldiers decided to steal the alembic for themselves and escaped with it into the desert.

"I can only speculate what happened from then. Suffice it to say the alembic was worth a fortune in the right hands and it must have passed from potentate to sheik to king over the next several hundred years. It eventually ended up in the hands of the most powerful rulers in the region, the Byzantines, and then when their civilization collapsed and the Ottoman Empire flourished, the Alembic of Skenderbeg was in their treasury. By then, however, no one knew what it was because it had sat forgotten for more than a millennia."

"But Skenderbeg figured it out?"

"That he did. The story is that as punishment for staying out past curfew, at the bedroom of a nobleman's daughter if the tale is true, he was sent to one of the army's massive storehouses and ordered to catalogue every item inside. The story says it took a month but during that time he became fascinated with a large bronze urn and the strange writing on its side. He found someone who could translate it for him and that's when he learned that it was Alexander's secret weapon. It must have seemed like fate to him, for already some of his men were calling him Skenderbeg, or Alexander the Great.

"When he planned his revolt against Murad II, he made certain he took the alembic with him."

Cali summed up, saying, "And having the alembic allowed him to hold off Murad's army for so long?"

"I don't get something," Mercer interrupted. "If Alexander used it for so long and Skenderbeg used it too, how much plutonium ore can there still be in it? It might be big but it isn't bottomless."

"There is very little," Ahmad said, "but it doesn't matter. The alembic isn't used to disperse the radioactive dust."

"Then how does it work?"

"There are two chambers within the alembic. When the mechanism is turned on, the shield separating them is moved and the two samples of ore are allowed to interact. Unlike the raw plutonium found in Africa and the barrels of it here, Alexander's alchemists had refined it somehow, changed it in such a way that rather than emit weak gamma particles that are unable to penetrate human skin, the alembic belches deadly swarms of alpha and beta particles that sicken in seconds and kill in minutes.

"It was an insidious weapon that Skender-beg employed only when absolutely necessary but Alexander used to wipe out entire armies. There are accounts of fifty thousand enemy soldiers killed in a single night when his spies activated the alembic in their encampment. When the siege of an ancient city called Qumfar wasn't going as planned, Alexander opened the alembic outside the city walls and left it there for a week. When he returned, every man, woman, child, and animal within the walls was dead. A scribe wrote that their skin had blackened and peeled off their bodies, that some were so covered in blisters that they weren't recognizable as human. He said many mothers had slit their own children's throats to ease their suffering before turning the blades on themselves."

Cali said, "When something is so heavily irradiated it would remain radioactive for weeks, months even."

Ahmad shook his head. "I am an historian, not a nuclear engineer. I can only tell you what I know of the alembic. Perhaps Alexander's scientists did something else to the ore so that the effects were short-lived. I do not know."

"Or perhaps the town was severely nuked," Mercer said. "And that is why today there is no such place as Qumfar."

"Could also explain why Alexander died so young," Cali added.

"All I know for certain," Ahmad said, "is that in the wrong hands the alembic is much more dangerous than the ore Feines made off with today."

"What happened to the alembic?"

"Upon his death Skenderbeg's generals knew that they would eventually lose to Murad's army. Even with the device, the driving force of their revolt was dead and it was only a matter of time before the soldiers lost their will to fight. Rather than risk the alembic falling into Ottoman hands they decided to honor both their leader and his namesake and do what Alexander's men had wanted. That is, return the alembic to his tomb."

"And did they?"

Ludmilla approached with plates of powdered egg and coffee from what little supplies survived the helicopter crash. It was the first food Mercer had seen since the flight from Germany to Samara, and while surplus Russian rations were far from

Cordon Bleu, he and Cali attacked it with relish.

"So did they return the alembic to Alexander's tomb?" Cali asked around a mouthful of egg.

Ahmad turned to her and said brightly, "Oh, most certainly."

"Do you know where it is?"

Ahmad didn't reply to Mercer's question for several seconds. "You would have died in Africa if we hadn't shown up. In Atlantic City too. You managed to find Chester Bowie's crates and make certain that Poli Feines didn't get them, but it was a close thing, no?" Mercer nodded. "And just now you came here to secure the last of the ore mined by the Soviets and yet Feines escaped with two barrels and there are many dead. Dr. Mercer, even if I knew where Alexander's tomb was hidden I would not tell you."

"You don't know where it is?"

"No, Miss Stowe. I do not. Every schoolchild learns it's someplace in Egypt, supposedly, but we have kept its location secret by not knowing it ourselves. The Janissaries thwart anyone interested in finding it long before they get close."

"How do you know when they're close?" Mercer asked, irritation in his voice.

"There are certain signs along the way. How do you think I knew about Feines?"

"How?"

"He made the same mistake you did, Doctor, only he made it earlier. I am the world expert on Skenderbeg. Anyone interested in him must first come to me. And just as I took over from my mentor, in time young Devrin here will become the gatekeeper of Skenderbeg's secrets, and anyone interested in following the lore of his alembic will have no choice but to contact him."

"So Poli called you?"

"We even met," Ibriham Ahmad admitted.

Mercer was outraged. "What were you thinking giving him enough information to lead him to the mine in Africa?"

"Alas, he was already in possession of that information, though I wasn't aware of it at the time. No, I tried to send him off in the wrong direction but he was more resourceful than I anticipated. That was why when we learned he had hired a local rebel leader to get him to the Central African Republic we made sure we were there to stop him. Of course he escaped and so he began to track the two of you."

"How did he already know about the mine?"

"Because my mentor made a mistake." There was a trace of bitterness in his voice, but also a touch of understanding. "He divulged secrets to a student, a beautiful and fiercely independent woman whom he met while on an archaeological dig in Palestine in the 1920s. She was the daughter of an enlightened businessman who indulged her passion for learning. She was to be the love of my mentor's life and he wanted her to know all his secrets so that their son could continue on in his role. He told her all about Alexander and how when he returned from the deserts of Egypt he carried a devastating weapon that gave him the power to pronounce himself God. He told her how Alexander believed the weapon was made of adamantine, the mythical metal used to forge Prometheus's chains. He even told her that after Alexander's death that one of his most loyal generals returned to the African village to erect a stele commemorating the great victories he won because of the alembic."

Mercer suppressed a smile. While he wasn't sure what made him think the stele he'd seen was important, he was glad that he'd asked Booker Sykes to photograph it. If it was put in place after Alexander's death there was a chance, albeit a slim one he admitted, that it might contain information on Alexander's fabled tomb. He said casually, "Cali and I recalled seeing the stele just before the attack."

"Beautiful, wasn't it?"

"Old oblique obelisks aren't my thing." Ahmad smiled at Mercer's wordplay, not knowing that Mercer was trying to distract him away from the subject. "Besides, we didn't take a close look."

"Oh, too bad, it was in marvelous condition. I had never seen it before. The hieroglyphics were barely weathered and were quite easy to make out, though I confess I don't know how to read any of them."

Mercer's heart sank. "Was?"

Ahmad gave him a look usually reserved for recalcitrant students who thought they could pull one over on him. "My dear doctor, do you think I would leave it behind for the next Poli Feines to discover? I had no choice but to destroy it. I do feel bad about desecrating such an important antiquity if that makes you feel any better."

"No," Mercer said miserably. "It doesn't."

CENTRAL AFRICAN REPUBLIC

"So what do you think, Book?" Sergeant Paul Rivers asked out of the corner of his mouth.

Booker Sykes didn't take the low-light binoculars from his eyes as he surveyed the ruined town of Kivu. "That I'm pretty lucky one of my ancestors wasn't the fastest runner in his village. I'd hate to have been born in a shit hole like this."

The two of them had come ahead, leaving Sergeant Bernie Cieplicki to guard their truck a few miles shy of Kivu. Although Caribe Dayce had been the greatest threat to the region, his death had done little to quell the unrest. Small bands of armed teens roamed Kivu and the surrounding villages, drunk off their asses or so stoned they could barely see. And that had made it easy for Sykes and his small team to arm themselves.

On the road up from Rafai they had been

stopped at an impromptu checkpoint by four kids looking to shake down anyone foolish enough to be traveling in the strife-ridden area. The checkpoint was at a spot where the trees crowded close to the road, so vehicles couldn't turn around. They'd forced the Americans out of the truck, and while one of them covered them with his AK-47 the others began to rifle the four-wheel drive Sykes had bought in the capital, Bangui, with cash Mercer had given them for the mission.

Sykes had prepared for this, actually he'd hoped for it, because he wanted weapons for when they got deep into the bush.

The kid watching the Delta Force commandos was probably sixteen or seventeen, with deep-set bloodshot eyes and an insolent mouth. He held his assault rifle with casual indifference. While the three men he was covering were big, it was his experience that bullets trumped size every time. He was more interested in the cartons of cigarettes and other items Sykes had loaded into the truck for just such an ambush. Everything he'd brought was chosen deliberately to make the gunmen want to probe deep into the back of the battered Cherokee.

"Hey, hey," one of the kids rummaging in the cargo compartment called excitedly. He emerged with a brand-new soccer ball and as Sykes had predicted he bounced it on his knee for a second and gently kicked it toward the kid guarding them.

Sykes watched the teen's eyes, and the instant they flickered from the captives to the approaching ball, he and his men went into motion. Sykes lunged forward, grabbing the AK by the barrel and thrusting the weapon skyward. Bernie Cieplicki had been folding a tightly rolled magazine. Inside it was a six-inch-long nail that had been ground down so one end was as sharp as a needle. He whipped the magazine forward, sending the nail through the air like a dart. It hit the gunman who'd found the soccer ball in the shoulder, embedding half its length in his flesh. Had Cieplicki felt the situation warranted it, he could have sent the nail through the kid's eye and into his brain. As it was, the teen cried out, startled by the sudden agony.

Paul Rivers, who at six four was the biggest of the commandos, shot past the wounded African and used all his weight to slam the Jeep's rear door. The two teens inside hadn't even begun to react to the attack. The impact of the heavy door, plus Rivers's weight, broke three of the four legs dangling over the bumper.

With the gun pointed harmlessly in the air, Sykes struck the teen in the jaw with his elbow. His eyes fluttered and he dropped unconscious. Bernie leveled the gunman with the dart in his arm with a roundhouse kick to the side of his head.

The counterattack had taken four seconds.

Before continuing on, Cieplicki, who was the team's medic, pulled the nail from the African's shoulder, swabbed the wound with antibacterial ointment, and bandaged the puncture. There wasn't much he could do for the broken legs except fashion some splints and give the two kids morphine injections to knock them out for a couple of hours. The teen Book had decked wouldn't need drugs to remain unconscious.

Booker Sykes checked over the weapons with ill-disguised contempt. The assault rifles were serviceable, if dirty. What he hated was the gun itself. Liberal groups back in the States loved to point out how the United States was the biggest arms exporter in the world. And in absolute dollars that was true, but what they failed to mention was that the billions of dollars' worth of arms were generally aircraft like AWACs and F-16s or warships past their prime, weapon systems that invariably were never used beyond training and coastal interdiction missions.

Meanwhile here was the ubiquitous AK-47. There were more than a hundred million of them scattered around the globe, and nowadays you could buy one in bazaars and souks in most third world countries for as little as fifty bucks. They had considered buying arms in Bangui but knew it would take too long to establish contacts with dealers.

Booker had faced the AK on four continents and believed it had caused more death and more misery than just about any single weapon since cavemen started bashing one another with clubs. Nuclear bombs had killed a hundred and sixty thousand people at Nagasaki and Hiroshima. Men with AKs had caused the deaths of ten times that number in Africa alone.

So where were the protesters decrying how Russia and her old satellite states had flooded the world market with AKs with no regard as to who used them? But let the American government try to sell a couple of KC-135 aerial refueling planes to Taiwan and everyone screams warmonger.

It pissed him off.

They left the inept highwaymen loosely bound, and with a couple of cartons of cigarettes and enough food to see them through a few days, and continued on toward Kivu. Dusk was settling as they approached and rather than risk driving into an unknown situation, Booker ordered Cieplicki to stay with the truck while he and Rivers reconnoitered the town.

"About the town, smart-ass," Rivers said to his captain. In Delta, rank had little meaning.

"Looks quiet enough," Book rumbled.

The hotel where Cali had stayed was deserted, its Lebanese owner having fled with his family. A couple of youths lounged on the veranda. All the liquor from the bar and the food from the restaurant had long since been stolen, so they simply sat at a table and watched the sluggish river roll by, showing interest only when part of the bank fell into the waters from the constant erosion. A pair of men were working on Cali's abandoned Land Rover. From what she'd told Book back at Mercer's house, all it had needed were tires and he was surprised it was still here. He dialed up the binoculars' resolution and noted the dark patch under the truck's high chassis. Someone had either drained the oil or more likely put a few rounds into the engine block. He spotted a few families trying to put their lives back together, and an old woman sat at the entrance of her mud hut with a squealing infant in her arms. Book imagined the child's mother had probably been raped to death.

God, he hated Africa, because the cycle would never be broken.

"So how do you want to play it, Capt'n? Drive right on through now or wait?"

"Mercer said the village we're looking for is another two hours up the road. I don't see any cars or trucks down there that look like they can follow us, but I'd rather pass through when it's oh-dark-thirty so they don't even know we're in the area."

"Roger that."

Booker had wanted to bypass Kivu all together but the only road cut right through the town center. He did a comm check of their tactical radios and sent Rivers back to the truck with orders to approach the town at three A.M. He'd make sure nothing changed in the desolate village, then meet them before they entered.

Booker Sykes couldn't remember how many nights he'd spent watching over villages such as Kivu. Places in Iraq, Afghanistan, Pakistan, Somalia, Sudan, and a dozen other countries he'd just as soon forget. But somehow knowing that this mission was connected to Philip Mercer made it all the more important.

He didn't know what to make of Mercer. Without a doubt he was the smartest, shrewdest man Book had ever met. He handled himself well in any kind of fight despite the fact he'd never been in the military. At heart he was a loner but people seemed to gravitate toward him, finding in him a calm strength that few knew existed. And Booker was well aware of the way Cali Stowe looked at him even if Mercer himself was blithely ignorant. He knew Mercer was still grieving over Tisa Nguyen, but the boy was going to miss out on someone pretty special if he wasn't careful.

Mercer was a close friend of the deputy national security advisor yet hung around blue collar guys like Harry White. He had a ton of money but didn't possess an ounce of ego or pretension. Booker hadn't figured out what made Mercer tick, what drove him to get involved when other people ran. He suspected Mercer himself didn't really know, and that was just as well. Sykes didn't delve too deeply into why he joined the military then volunteered for its most dangerous missions, because if he found the truth he probably couldn't do his job anymore.

Without electricity Kivu shut down as the

sun sank lower to the west. The rebels on the hotel veranda grabbed up their weapons and climbed to the room they'd commandeered. The woman with the baby entered her little hut. She lit a lantern but only let it burn long enough to feed the child and tuck it into a makeshift crib. The single street through town and the small square were deserted by nine o'clock.

Yet Booker stayed with his plan, and as insects fought their way past his barrier of DEET repellent and feasted on his blood he sat motionless on a small bluff along the road and watched Kivu sleep.

He called Rivers at a quarter to three to tell him everything was set, and retreated a hundred yards up the road. The instant he heard the Jeep's engine over the din of insects and nocturnal animals, he radioed Rivers to kill the engine. He loped another hundred yards away from Kivu to where the Jeep Cherokee sat silently.

Wordlessly Booker and Paul Rivers moved to the back of the four-wheeler while Bernie Cieplicki stood at the open driver's door. Together they began to push the two-ton truck along the dirt road. True to his role as the team prankster, Bernie Cieplicki made Sykes and Rivers provide the bulk of the horsepower while he merely steered.

They passed through Kivu as silently as wraiths and continued down the road for another two hundred yards. Sykes and Rivers were lathered in sweat and blowing like draft horses.

"You guys look a little spent," Cieplicki quipped. "I guess I shouldn't have left my foot on the brake."

"You're an asshole, Bern," Paul wheezed.

"That's what people keep telling me," Cieplicki replied with a grin cocky enough to make Rivers want to swipe it off his face.

"Let's mount up," Sykes ordered.

With the lights off and using night vision goggles, Cieplicki drove them away from Kivu, at a crawl at first, to keep the engine noise down, but within a mile he had them up to forty. The wind whipping through the open windows was hot and stank of the nearby river but they needed the windows down because Book and Paul watched the surrounding jungle with their weapons ready to engage.

It took them two and a half hours to reach the Scilla River where it flowed into the Chinko. Someone had destroyed the makeshift ferryboat Mercer had mentioned, the barrels lay scattered along the riverbank, and there was no sign of its corrugated metal deck.

"From here it's all on foot," Sykes said, unlimbering his big frame from the Jeep. "Let's hide the truck and wait until dawn. I don't want to go stumbling around the jungle without knowing who's out there."

"You mean what," Bernie said.

"That too."

In the predawn hour, they made their approach to the village where Mercer had seen the stele. The nocturnal animals had already found their dens for the day and the diurnals had yet to emerge. There was no evidence that anyone was in the area, but they took no chances. They crossed the ancient mine, noting the breach in the levee where Mercer said he and Cali had been sluiced down to the river. Farther on they came to the village. Covered by Cieplicki and Rivers, who stayed at the tree line, Sykes entered the clearing. Nothing remained of the village but the burned husks of the huts, blackened piles of grass and mud that had once been home to the innocent. The air reeked of putrid flesh.

The utter futility and waste of it all sickened him.

He cast around for the stele. Mercer said it was about seven feet tall and impossible to miss, but Sykes didn't see it. Unable to shake the feeling that he was being watched, and not only by his own men, he methodically crisscrossed the jungle clearing. The grass was littered with hundreds of spent cartridges. He picked up one to sniff it. It still smelled of gunpowder. He passed a pile of loose rocks and was about to ignore it when he stopped and went back. In the tricky dawn light he had to squint to make out the odd writing that remained on the larger pieces.

"Oh, Mercer ain't gonna be happy 'bout this."

He jogged back to the tree line where Rivers and Cieplicki waited.

"What's the word, Boss Man?"

"The stele thing's all smashed up. Can't be more than a few pieces the size of a brick."

"Explosives?" Cieplicki asked.

"No. I'd say they broke it with hammers or rifle butts. Also I've got the feeling we aren't the only people in the area."

"Could be villagers returning."

"Not at five o'clock in the morning." Sykes went quiet, thinking through his options. He had gotten a few hours of sleep on the flight to Africa but that had been thirty-six hours earlier. He was exhausted. His eyelids felt like they had an inner liner of sandpaper. But he'd been trained to ignore such distractions. He came up with his plan and issued his orders. Cieplicki and Rivers took off at a run while he remained in the jungle watching over the clearing. He heard no movement, no coughs or the scrape of cloth over vegetation, but he was certain he wasn't alone.

Moving as carefully as a stalking leopard he made a wide half circle around the village, careful not to step out on the exposed bluff overlooking the river. He found nothing.

Rivers and Cieplicki were back in eleven minutes, and had Sykes not been so uneasy he would have reproached them for how long it had taken to run the mile to the truck and back. They brought back three military-issue backpacks, heavy nylon bags that could support more than a hundred and fifty pounds. Leaving Cieplicki to cover the woods, Sykes and Rivers took the bags to the ruined stele and carefully started filling them with pieces of the ancient marker. They were careful about weight distribution, for while Bernie could more than handle a load, Sykes and Rivers were much bigger and stronger men.

When they had one filled, Rivers heaved it off the ground.

"What do you think?" Book asked.

"Hundred and sixty, hundred and seventy."

"Thank God it's only a mile," Sykes said and looked up sharply when a bird suddenly launched itself from a tree. He waited a beat but nothing more happened.

They had secured all the larger pieces and were down to fragments the size of acorns half-buried in the ground when Cieplicki opened fire. His single shot was answered by at least eight guns ripping on automatic. Sykes and Rivers dove flat, shoving the bags into a row for cover, their guns resting on the priceless relic.

Cieplicki came out of the woods a moment later, laying down a wall of fire to keep the rebels in the woods. He reached his teammates, leaping over the bags and rolling around so his AK was pointed back at the woods.

The jungle fell silent again.

"This isn't good."

The Delta operators only had two spare magazines each; that's all the kids they'd taken the guns from had carried. It wasn't nearly enough for a protracted fight with more than a half dozen rebels.

"Discretion and all that," Sykes said. He fired a quick spray into the woods and slid his pack's straps over his shoulders, using the power of his legs to deadlift the heavy burden. Cieplicki and Rivers did likewise. As a team, they started running back toward the Jeep at the confluence of the Chinko and Scilla rivers.

The packs were too heavy to slap against their backs as they jogged along the embankment, and before he'd gone a hundred yards Sykes felt the tendons and ligaments in his lower back popping. Then the muscle pulled. It was a merciless knife-edged pain that exploded against the top of his skull, and every step served to deepen the agony. Yet he did not slow. He gritted his teeth against the torment, the thought of dropping the pack never entering his mind.

The gunmen kept to the woods as they pursued the team, taking poorly aimed potshots that forced the team to zigzag as they ran, adding tremendous pressures to knees and spines as they returned fire to keep the rebels at bay.

Grimacing with each footfall, Sykes kept telling himself to ignore the pain, but the agony was beyond belief. Searing waves of pain radiated from his lower back, and when he jinked, the added strain sent a bolt of fire to his brain. He could barely twist to return fire, so he held the AK one-handed and popped off covering shots.

He'd carried an injured man in Afghanistan, a local fighter who'd taken shrapnel to the gut, but it was nothing like this. The deadweight in his pack ground him down, made him question everything he'd ever done in his life to bring him to this torture. He glanced at his men. They knew the pain too. It was etched in their faces and in the sweat that poured from their skins. Even Paul Rivers, a towering ox of a man, was feeling it.

And still they ran on.

They reached the mine, plunged down into the section of blown-away levee without pause, and gutted their way up the other side, legs moving like pistons. Sykes faltered near the top and felt Bernie ram his shoulder into the pack to see him up those last couple of feet.

Unbelievably they were outpacing the rebels thrashing their way through the thick jungle. One of the rebels realized their quarry was getting away and dashed out from the bush. As rear guard it was Rivers's job to cover their backs. Every few moments he'd look over his shoulder. He saw the skinny African leap out of the jungle and start sprinting. Without breaking his pace, Rivers fired a quick burst. The rebel went down as if he'd been jerked by a string.

"Last one . . . ," Cieplicki panted, pausing to swallow the pre-vomit saliva that flooded his mouth. "Last one to the Jeep is a rotten egg."

He retched and a trickle of bile dribbled down his chin onto his khaki bush shirt.

More of the rebels emerged from the jungle behind them, a phalanx of them coming on hard.

"Cap't," Rivers called out.

Unable to stop running because they knew they'd never start again, the three men slowed enough so they could lay down a blistering wall of autofire. The range was pretty extreme for firing from the hip, but one rebel spun to the ground when his shoulder was shattered by one of the 7.62-millimeter bullets and the others dove for cover.

The last part of the run was down a slight grade and the men let gravity work for them, their boots slapping the hard African ground with each rubbery step. Sykes had tears coursing down his cheeks as he ran those last couple hundred yards. It was the first time he'd cried since his grandmother died when he was twelve.

The Jeep was well hidden off the main road. Rivers didn't bother pulling away the branches they'd used to camouflage the vehicle. He popped the rear door and turned to lower the backpack into the cargo hold. The shoulders of his T-shirt were sodden with blood from where the straps had chafed his skin.

Despite the agony, or maybe because of it, Sykes let Cieplicki unload his pack next. Rivers was already moving to the driver's door. Cieplicki dumped his pack and just shoved Booker into the back of the four-wheel drive. He climbed in after his team leader and slammed the door.

As soon as everyone was in, Rivers gunned the Jeep's engine, reversing out of the jungle just as three of the rebels reached the mud flats around the convergence of the swift Scilla and sluggish Chinko. They opened fire as soon as they saw the Cherokee emerge from the jungle. The rear window exploded, raining gem-sized chips of glass on Cieplicki and Sykes. Cieplicki was working on a large bundle in the cargo area, opening it flat and maneuvering the three packs onto its rubbery surface, while Sykes returned fire through the shattered window.

A bullet found a rear tire, blowing it flat. Rivers fought the steering wheel, not daring to slow but knowing that the tire would slough off the rim if he didn't. "Talk to me back there."

"I need a minute," Bernie replied without pausing from his work.

"Shit!" Three more gunmen raced out of the jungle in front of the Jeep just as they started back down the road to Kivu. "You don't have a minute."

More automatic gunfire ravaged the Jeep, punching holes through the windshield, blowing off the passenger-side mirror, and puncturing the radiator, so steam billowed up from under the hood.

"We gotta do it now," Rivers shouted. The steering wheel shook so hard he felt like he was holding an electric fence.

"Don't wait for me!" Bernie cried.

"I'm not. Hold on!"

He cranked the wheel to the left, aiming for the broad river cutting through the jungle. The banks were about five feet above the level of the water, so he pressed the accelerator to the floor. The tired engine responded as if knowing it was going out in a blaze of glory.

The Jeep hit the bank, reared up, and shot over the water. It hit like a charging hippopotamus, a frothing swell of water surging over the windshield and a bow wave curving out to crash against the far bank. The SUV was caught in the slow current almost immediately, pirouetting in unseen eddies so it soon faced backward. It also started sinking.

"How's it coming back there?" Paul asked as the water quickly filled the foot well.

"You could help by bailing," Bernie said as he struggled to re-adjust the packs that had lurched forward when the Jeep slapped the water. Sykes helped him as best he could, but his back had so stiffened, now that he'd stopped running, that he could barely move.

Paul Rivers climbed over his seat and knelt on the rear bench, helping Cieplicki with the packs. The water was only an inch or so below the blown-out rear window. Once it found that inlet, the Jeep would sink like a stone.

"Any piranhas in these waters?" Bernie asked without looking up.

"That's South America, dipshit. But they got crocodiles here the size of speedboats."

A wave washed over the rear sill and in seconds the cargo space was flooded. The men braced themselves as Bernie lunged to open the rear door. Then the Jeep slid below the surface, leaving just a small ripple on the water.

The rebels on shore watched it vanish, and after a minute they began to cheer when none of the men surfaced. They'd been denied any spoils but were just as satisfied with the kill.

Thirty yards from where the Jeep disappeared, the water heaved upward unexpectedly and a huge set of jaws emerged from the river, a gaping red maw surrounded by daggerlike white teeth. The rebels pointed and shrank back as the rest of the flat, oval monster erupted from the depths. Then it seemed to spit out bodies. Three heads emerged next to the creature. First one, then another jumped onto the animal's back. One of the men helped the third one mount the beast while the first man did something near its broad rump.

"Hurry," Bernie said as he helped drag Sykes out of the water.

The three-man inflatable boat had been Mercer's idea. He'd reasoned that since they were going to be along a river it might not be a bad idea if the roads were impassable. Sykes had bought it at an outfitters in Virginia, liking the model with the shark's mouth painted on the bow, and paid extra to have it flown to Africa with them. They'd shoved it out the rear of the Jeep moments after it began to plummet to the bottom of the river. Cieplicki had waited as long as he dared to pull the lanyard that filled the rubber raft's hull with compressed air, something they'd neglected to tell the airline about.

As Sykes rolled over the soft rail Paul Rivers wrestled with the five-horse outboard motor. He didn't bother mounting it to the transom. As soon as he pulled the starter, he greased the throttle and held the whirling prop underwater. The overloaded inflatable didn't exactly roar down the river but they picked up speed quick enough. The rebels on shore merely watched them vanish from view, not sure exactly what they saw.

"All together now," Bernie called out merrily. "Row, row, row your boat . . ."

Despite the pain, Booker couldn't help but laugh at Cieplicki's antics.

Samarsskaya Mine, Southern Russia

The sun had burned away the morning mist that had filled the valley like a blanket of snow. A few birds fluttered around the tops of the nearby pine trees, and the cloudless sky seemed to arch forever.

Ludmilla and the other Russian scientist, whose name Mercer didn't know, had salvaged a pair of radiation suits and some radiation detection gear from a crate that had survived the chopper crash, and using a handcart found on a small siding under the ore-loading hoppers, they had headed down the tracks to make certain none of the barrels had been breached by the train derailment.

Sasha Federov was resting while the pilot, Yuri, was inventorying their meager supplies.

As soon as Professor Ahmad had told Mercer the stele had been destroyed, he had gotten to his feet and begun to pace with his head bowed. He'd sent Booker and his team on a fool's errand into one of the most dangerous places in the world. Book knew how to take care of himself, and Mercer wasn't too worried about him, but the thought was heavy on his mind. What bothered him more, or at least in a different way, was the dead end he now faced.

He was convinced that the stele would have told him the location of Alexander's tomb, especially since one of the conqueror's generals had erected the marker well after his death. Archaeologists had been searching for the tomb for centuries, so without some new clue Mercer was stymied.

The worst of it was he was sure Ahmad hadn't been lying about not knowing the tomb's location. The Janissaries' system of protecting the location eliminated temptation among their members. It was truly brilliant.

Mercer returned to where Cali and Ahmad sat on the ground, but he said nothing as Cali and Ahmad continued to talk.

"What became of the woman?" Cali asked. "The one that your mentor fell in love with."

"Montague and Capulet I'm afraid," Ahmad said, lighting a cigarette. "Her father would never allow her to marry a Turk and he made her return home as soon as he learned of the affair. He was enlightened only to a point, you see, and the girl had already been promised to another, a member of a royal household."

"That's so sad."

"They were different times, although I'm sure if it happened today the results would probably be the same. Marrying outside one's tribe is a modern idea that has really only taken root in the West."

"Outside your tribe?"

"For lack of a better word. What I mean is it isn't uncommon for an American to marry someone from France, or Germany, or a white to marry a black, for that matter. In the Middle East you would never see a Shi'a marry a Sunni or a Turk marry a Kurd. It just isn't done. And ever since 1980 any chance there could be a melding of the various sects and ethnic groups has been further eroded."

"Why is that?" Cali asked. "What happened in 1980?"

"Iraq invaded Iran," Ahmad told her. "That conflict is largely a footnote to you but it was a watershed moment in the Middle East. The Iranians were totally unprepared for the invasion and were nearly defeated early on. In order to inspire his people Ayatollah Khomeini delved back into history, resurrecting the story of the Battle of Karbala, when in 860 Husayn ibn 'Alī, grandson of the Prophet Mohammad, was defeated by the Umayyad caliph, Yazid. The date is still a holiday for Shi'a Muslims. Khomeini cynically turned what was a sectarian grab for land and oil resources into a holy war."

"How is that?" Mercer asked, drawn back into the conversation despite his foul mood.

"Husayn and his army were slaughtered to a man. They became Islam's first martyrs. What Khomeini did was tell his people that Saddam Hussein, a Sunni, was the modern reincarnation of Yazid and that in order to defeat him it would be necessary for every Iranian to sacrifice themselves, as did Husayn. He went on to decree that anyone who martyred themselves was guaranteed a place in heaven. In one move he negated the Koran's pronouncement that suicide was a sin against God and created the Middle East's first suicide bombers.

"Even as he was battling the Iraqis, Khomeini sent cadres of trained men into Lebanon during their civil war and occupation by Israel, to spread the word that suicide bombing is not a sin, but a glorious sacrifice to Allah. Remember this is something expressly forbidden by the Koran, yet he managed to convince desperate people that his word superseded the very words God uttered to Mohammad.

"Of course word of his pronouncement spread from there to the West Bank and Gaza, where again Muslims were fighting a superior force. Thus we had young men convinced by a madman that taking your own life by blowing up a bus or a restaurant serves God's purpose."

"And then on to 9/11," Cali said.

"And Madrid and London and Indonesia and Pakistan and Iraq and the list goes on and on." Ahmad ground out his cigarette bitterly. "While Shi'a and Sunni have always had a difficult relationship, it wasn't always like it is today. Now it has become acceptable for a Sunni carrying thirty pounds of plastic explosives to walk into a Shi'a mosque and blow himself up. Khomeini unleashed the savagery of the bloody war that first divided Islam, just to defeat his neighbor."

"Can it be stopped?"

"Not until there is a cleric powerful enough to rescind Khomeini's declaration and make suicide a sin once again. I cannot emphasize enough the importance of his actions and how it has damaged our faith. And I'm afraid your country's invasion of Iraq hasn't helped matters." He held up a hand when he saw a blaze of anger flash in Cali's eyes. "I'm not saying Hussein wasn't a tyrant or that he should have remained in power. At the time of the invasion, France and Russia wanted to end the embargo and I am certain that the Iraqis would have gotten the nuclear weapons they so desperately wanted. No, the invasion was a necessary step in the larger scope of world events, but that doesn't mean it hasn't, ah, stirred a hornet's nest."

Mercer suddenly remembered Ahmad's first words when he entered the camp. "You said Istanbul, Ankara, or Baku are more likely targets for Feines and the plutonium. Why?"

"You've been paying attention. Very good," Ahmad said as if now praising the unruly student he'd chided earlier. "I believe you've been operating under the misconceived notion that Al Qaida is bankrolling Poli Feines and that they want to contaminate an American city using the plutonium, thus spreading more fear around the world. That is not the case. There is no such thing as terrorism for terrorism's sake. Each act has a specific goal."

Cali interrupted. "Like getting the U.S. out of Iraq or Israel out of the West Bank."

"Not entirely," Ahmad said. "Those are the stated goals, yes, but what the organizers behind the suicide bombers ultimately want is power after those withdrawals. The poor soul who blows himself up next to a police checkpoint thinks he's fighting for the liberation of his people. The men who gave him the bomb are merely using him as a tool to further their political ambitions. They want to rule over that man's family.

"This is true in all cases. The men who carried out the London and Madrid bombings want to force the United States and Western interests out of Iraq, even though the bombers weren't even Iraqi. It was the men behind them who wanted these things. The men who blew themselves up just wanted to obtain paradise. Unfortunately your media focuses on the soldiers and pays scant attention to the generals."

Mercer saw a flaw in Ahmad's logic. "If that were true, who does Osama bin Laden want to rule, since he was the one who masterminded 9/11?"

"Masterminded," Ahmad agreed. "But did he pay for it?"

"The guy's worth a couple hundred million. Sure he paid for it."

"Ah, but where did he get his money?"

"I think his father was a rich contractor or

444

something in Saudi Arabia?"

Professor Ahmad said nothing, waiting Mercer out, knowing he'd make the connection.

"Are you saying the Saudis paid for the attacks? There's no evidence they were involved other than that most of the bombers were Saudi citizens."

"Isn't that enough?" Ahmad said archly.

"By your way of thinking, the U.S. government was behind Oklahoma City because Timothy McVeigh was an American. I don't buy it."

"Perhaps I overstated," Ahmad conceded. "However, there are factions within the Saudi government who would like nothing more than see the United States off balance. And now they have selected someone new to help them carry out their plans. Before it was bin Laden. Now they are paying Poli Feines to do their dirty work. The man most directly involved is the Saudi representative to OPEC currently working with the United Nations in New York, Mohammad bin Al-Salibi."

In the silence that followed, Mercer and Cali exchanged a look. This wasn't what Mercer expected at all. Apart from exporting Wahhabi fanatics to the four corners of the globe, Saudi Arabia had never threatened her neighbors. Ibriham Ahmad was saying that the Saudis were responsible for the greatest terrorist attack in history and now wanted to use a dirty bomb against their neighbors.

"And just so you understand our culpabilities as Janissaries in what has transpired recently," Ahmad added, "Salibi's great-grandmother was the woman who stole my mentor's heart. I can only assume she told Salibi about the alembic and its fearsome potential."

Mercer couldn't care less about that. He was still grappling with the reason why anyone in Saudi Arabia would perpetrate such an act. "I don't get it," he said after a moment. "Why?"

"Think like Khomeini thought," Ahmad said, wanting Mercer to come to the right conclusion on his own. "This is war, Dr. Mercer, and all war is about power. Be more cynical than you usually are."

"Oil," Cali said. "Caspian oil."

"Sorry, Mercer, but Miss Stowe gets to move to the head of the class."

She turned to Mercer. "What we were talking about back at your house. About how the only way to defeat fundamentalism is to make oil obsolete. Well, the only way for the Saudi government to maintain their house of cards is if they continue to be our principle source of oil. If we start getting crude from the Caspian Sea, they become marginalized."

"Two major pipelines are already running, one to the Russian Black Sea port of Novorossiysk, and another will transport a million barrels a year to the Turkish city of Ceyhan on the Mediterranean," Ahmad said.

"Poli's orders are to take out the Caspian oil infrastructure?" Mercer asked, then went on to answer his own question. "Won't work even if he got his hands on a lot more plutonium. Nothing short of nuclear bombs or a full-scale invasion could take out all the refineries, tanker ports, pipelines, and terminals surrounding the Caspian. I'm no petroleum geologist but I've seen pictures of Baku. The infrastructure in just that city alone is enormous."

"You're not being cynical enough. You don't need to destroy those things you mentioned. All that need happen is to introduce suicide bombings at a few key locations and have clerics and imams in place to rile the faithful. In short order there will be dozens, or hundreds, of 'martyrs' ready to kill themselves, believing they are fighting a holy war against Christianity when in fact they are preserving Saudi oil interests. In a few months oil from the Caspian will slow to a trickle and Saudi Arabia and the rest of OPEC will be secure."

"Do they have such clerics in place?"

"I've heard them in the mosques of Baku and Istanbul, Ankara and Groznyy, where Chechens are already employing suicide bombers for their own aims."

"What the hell is wrong with the world?" Mercer said rhetorically, hating that he saw the logic behind the plot.

"The question I often ask myself," Ahmad replied sadly, "and one that is more difficult to answer is, What remains right with the world?"

Mercer would never let himself fall into that trap. He'd spent a lifetime searching for the good amid the chaos. The image that would be with him longest from his most recent time in Africa wasn't the misery and bloodshed. It was the refugee giving him the tomato for saving his family, an intimate act of friendship that he would cherish forever.

It was too easy to give in to the hate and ugliness. He'd been numbed by Tisa's death, struck hollow by his own loss, but he realized just now that he was allowing that pain to turn him away from who he'd always been. Yes, he would mourn her for the rest of his life, but that wasn't the same as allowing her passing to poison him.

Harry White had been trying to tell him that all along. Mourning wasn't about how a person's death made you feel. It was about what that person's life did and how you carry forward with those memories. The choice is yours.

"We're going to stop them." There was a flinty edge to Mercer's voice, honed by a new sense of confidence he hadn't realized he'd lost.

Cali noted the difference and gave him a long sideways glance. She smoothed the goose bumps that pricked the skin of her arms.

"My duties as a Janissary are to protect the Alembic of Skenderbeg," Ahmad said rather pompously. "Beyond that we have no responsibilities. If Feines attempts to locate it directly we will act. However, the plutonium ore and what he does with it isn't our concern."

"What about your responsibilities as a human being, for Christ's sake?"

"It is not for his sake I do anything, Miss Stowe. I have devoted my life to protecting the people of this planet from a devastating weapon, as have all the men who have come before me. I think that is enough to ask."

"Bullshit!" Mercer was nearly shouting.

Again Ahmad arched his eyebrow, a half smirk canting his dense mustache.

Mercer went on, hotly. "You've been feeding us just enough clues to whet our appetites and keep us going. You wanted us involved because you needed our help. You couldn't have pulled off the salvage job in New York, but you practically led us to it by planting that canteen in Africa."

Ahmad's jaw loosened and his dark eyes widened. "How did you know?"

"Two reasons." Mercer was on a roll and checked off fingers as he spoke. "First of all the woman who gave it to me seemed unsure of it. It even slipped from her hands. A canteen like that would have been very familiar to her since it was probably her job to fetch water, but she acted like she'd never seen it before. Secondly there's no way in hell the canvas would have survived seventy years in the jungle. You gave it to that woman a couple of days before we entered the village because you knew we were coming."

Cali was as stunned by Mercer's deductions as Ahmad. "Wait, Mercer, how did he know we were going to be in that village?"

"Remember when I told you I was there on behalf of the United Nations looking for a mineral deposit I knew wouldn't be there? It was a setup from the beginning. What's his name, Adam Burke, the UN representative who requested I go, wanted me to find the plutonium mine instead." He turned to Professor Ahmad. "I assume you know him."

"You're mangling his name," Ahmad said. "It's not Adam Burke. It's Ah-dham Berk with a silent r. He was a student of mine fifteen years ago."

Mercer had never met the man, only spoken to him on the phone a couple of times, and he hadn't detected an accent. He would have never guessed that Berk, with a silent r, was Turkish. He sounded more American than Mercer did.

"So yes I did set you up." Ahmad suddenly sounded very tired, but also relieved to get the truth out. "You have rather unique talents and contacts that no one within the Janissary Corps possesses. And you, Miss Stowe, I hate to admit, are as much a victim of my machinations as Dr. Mercer."

"What?" she cried.

"Who do you think made available the information about the elevated cancer rates in that village? You haven't had time to speak to him much but perhaps you will

451

recognize my pupil, Devrin's, voice when he returns with our vehicle. He was the one who called posing as an archivist from the Centers for Disease Control."

"What would have happened if Cali and I hadn't met?" Mercer asked.

"It was inevitable," Ibriham said dismissively.

"No it wasn't," Cali shot back. "I would have gone on alone if some stupid kid hadn't used my truck for target practice." Ahmad gave her a patient, long-suffering look. "That was you?"

He nodded.

"What if I had refused to help her?"

"My dear doctor, you weren't chosen at random, I assure you. Neither of you were. Did you seriously question whether to help her or not? Of course you didn't. You would have no more refused her than you would push an old lady into a crosswalk. Your dependability is one of your greatest assets."

"Jesus," Mercer muttered, raking his fingers through his thick hair. He'd been played for a sucker the entire time, blithely following the trail of crumbs Ahmad had doled out. He'd called it dependability. Mercer saw it as predictability. "So what the hell happened at the village?" His tone was accusatory. "You let Dayce and Feines slaughter those poor people."

A shadow of guilt and remorse crossed Ahmad's face. "After all the planning we put into this, would you believe something as stupid as a flat tire? We were delayed on the road up from Kivu when we were following you, and only arrived after it was all over."

"And what about poor Serena Ballard," Cali said. "Have a flat in New Jersey too?"

"Miss Ballard spent a frightened day being watched over at a hotel in Philadelphia so Poli could get no information out of her. The scene at her house was staged using blood drawn from my men. She's back home now, more than a little confused I'm sure, but I needed some way to warn you Poli Feines was aware you had gone to Atlantic City. I didn't realize he'd get to your hotel so quickly."

Mercer and Cali shared a relieved glance. Both had liked Serena and had taken her senseless death especially hard because they'd believed her last moments on earth being tortured by Feines had been excruciating.

A truck raced up the mine's access road, a newer model of the UAZ four-wheel drives Poli Feines had brought to loot the old weapons depot. Young Devrin was behind the wheel. No sooner had he braked next to where Mercer and Cali had been talking with Ibriham, than he threw open the door and spoke quickly to his teacher in Turkish. He brandished a satellite phone, and judging by his ashen pallor and the restrained anger in his voice the news wasn't good.

"What? What is it?" Mercer asked, his guts suddenly tight.

"We're too late."

NOVOROSSIYSK, RUSSIA

Originally founded as a colony of the Italian city-state Genoa in the thirteenth century, Novorossiysk was later an Ottoman fortress town, until its capture by Russia in 1808. Since the disintegration of the Soviet Union, when many Black Sea ports were handed over to Ukraine and Georgia, Novorossiysk had become Russia's largest warm-water export center, with visits by more than a thousand tankers, container ships, and freighters each year. Half of Russia's grain exports left through Novorossiysk and one third of her oil. Surrounded on three sides by the Caucasus Mountains, the city of a quarter million sat nestled on the northern part of a deep-water bay that bore its name.

Ships weighing more than two thousand tons were required to report to the harbor master several days before entering the port, and a pilot was compulsory. With tankers of up to three hundred thousand dwt regularly visiting the oil terminal on the eastern side of the city, ocean-borne traffic was tightly monitored. This was why the eighty-foot commercial fisherman easing into the inner harbor just after dawn went unmolested by the maritime authorities. Only a few gulls paid it any attention at all, wheeling and diving above her stern deck, drawn to the smell of fish oil and scale but unable to find a meal.

The three men aboard the stolen fishing boat had trained on it for only as long as it took to get the vessel from Albania, through the Bosporus, and across the Black Sea, where the professional hijackers had taken their money and returned to their native country. The oldest of the three was a twenty-three-year-old Saudi, and while he headed the mission, a Syrian teen named Hasan was more adept at the controls.

They would have been incapable of taking the ship back out the Bosporus and around Turkey to the port of Ceyhan as Al-Salibi had told Grigori Popov to convince him to help secure the plutonium. As it was they had a hard enough time covering the thirty miles across the sheltered bay of Novorossiysk.

Hasan's thin, almost feminine, hands

looked too delicate on the rough wheel, and he peered out on the world from behind long, curling lashes. His two comrades stood behind him in the cramped wheelhouse. One clutched a small Koran while the other's fingers danced with the set of worry beads he'd been given by the leader of the madras religious school in Pakistan where he'd been recruited for this mission.

They'd been told that their martyrdom today would guarantee their place in heaven, where a *har'em* of virgins awaited them. Hasan had been especially teased about that because of his girlish good looks. They were also told they were striking such a blow against the crusaders that their names would be remembered forever and all the Muslim world would unite in a brotherhood of jihad against America.

Hasan had never met an American but he'd been taught to hate them with a consuming passion he could barely understand. His teachers and friends and the imams at the mosques all said that America wanted to destroy Islam, that they had caused the tsunami in Indonesia that killed hundreds of thousands of his brothers and sisters, that they had tried to spread diseases in Muslim countries in Africa, that they themselves had destroyed the World Trade Center as an excuse to attack the Arab world.

He was a bright boy, had done well in school, and yet he never questioned anything he'd been told about the United States, because none of his friends did and he didn't want to be ridiculed. In fact they would often boast among themselves, creating ever grander lies in an attempt to show off how much they hated America. Most of what they said was puerile and ribald — Americans have sex with animals or they eat their own excrement — but it served to fuel their ardor until Hasan volunteered to help put a stop to America's offenses against God. In a sense, he had been peer-pressured into blowing himself up.

As they sailed deeper into the harbor, they could see the massive oil tankers at their moorings. Some were more than a thousand feet long, more resembling steel islands than vessels meant to cross the oceans. Next to them was a container port with a spidery gantry crane for unloading the ships. In the yard behind it, the brightly colored boxes resembled a child's set of building blocks stacked in neat ranks. Even at this early hour workers were loading containers onto the vessel from flatbed trucks that were lined along the quay.

Their orders had been specific. They were

to bring the fishing boat as close as they could to the tanker terminal before detonating the five hundred tons of fuel oil and fertilizer crammed in her holds. The special barrels brought to them the night before by the one-eyed man were sitting on the deck.

Hasan tried to clear his mind as they approached the tanker facility's outer buoy. When that failed he tried to picture paradise, but all he kept seeing was the tears on his little sister's face when he left Damascus to join the Pakistani madrassa where he'd been recruited by the great Saudi caliph, Mohammad bin Al-Salidi. He recalled his father staring at him stonily, not understanding why his son would rather die than take over the family hardware store. His mother had wailed inconsolably that morning and locked herself in her bedroom.

The cell's leader, the acne-scarred Saudi named Abdullah, spotted the trouble first and hit Hasan's shoulder. A sleek harbor patrol craft had rounded the tall bow of a tanker awaiting its turn to be filled with crude piped to the facility from Kazakhstan.

So wrapped in his own memories and feeling the weight of dread in his stomach, Hasan was startled as soon as he saw the patrol boat. Its lights weren't on and they had yet to cross the boundary reserved for the supertankers, but he panicked nevertheless. He rammed the throttles to their stops and spun the wheel to its starboard lock so fast the spindles blurred.

While the hull and upper works of the fishing boat were weather-worn and used, she had a new Volvo marine diesel in her engine room. Black exhaust jetted from the twin stacks as the engine responded to Hasan's inexperienced command.

The boat heeled over as it accelerated, the angle increasing as Hasan kept the rudder buried. In moments her port rail was awash. The netting hanging from her stern derrick was caught by a swell and wrenched off the vessel.

"Hasan! The barrels!"

The two barrels sitting on the foredeck had fallen over and were rolling toward the rail.

Behind them the harbor patrol had noted the fishing boat's erratic behavior. The security forces at the new facility were well trained and responded immediately. Red and blue lights mounted on a horizontal bar above the open cockpit snapped on. The siren started to scream as the swift vessel began chasing after the fishing boat.

Hasan saw that they were about to lose

the precious barrels, though he didn't know what made them so important. He spun the wheel to the opposite lock without easing back on the throttles. The big fishing boat leaned over to starboard, stopping the barrels' headlong plunge. But then they started rolling the other way. For a giddy moment it reminded Hasan of a handheld plastic game he had as a boy where you had to maneuver tiny metal balls into little cups and keep them from falling from their slots until you had them all in.

Only this game he lost. He was too slow reacting to the barrels' inexorable slide. The first five-hundred-pound drum smashed into the salt-weakened railing. The metal sagged, but held. Then the second barrel caromed into the first. The rail tore away and both steel casks rolled over the side and vanished under the black waters of the bay.

Hasan looked to Abdullah, his beautiful face a mask of confusion and shame. "What do we do?" he cried.

The patrol boat was a half mile away and closing fast. There were three uniformed men aboard, one cradling a shotgun. While another steered the speedboat, the third was shouting into a walkie-talkie.

Abdullah cursed. This wasn't how he envisioned meeting Allah, running from a

461

little Russian boat. "Turn us back," he snarled.

Hasan spun the wheel once more, cutting across their own wake and driving the boat closer to the tanker terminal.

When the patrol boat was fifty yards from the fishing boat, one of the sailors called across with a megaphone, and when his hails were ignored the man with the shotgun fired a blast across the bigger boat's bows.

"They're shooting at us," Hasan screamed. "We must stop. We are not close enough. We can surrender."

"No." Abdullah held the detonator that would blow a small charge of plastic explosives set amid the barrels of ammonia nitrate and fuel oil.

The fishing boat was still a mile from the nearest tanker when it erupted. The explosion blew a hole in the sea a half mile wide and eighty feet deep. The fisherman and the patrol craft were atomized instantly while the shock wave that raced from the epicenter at supersonic speeds blew out every pane of glass in the harbor. Flimsier structures along the quay were blown flat. The container crane withstood the blast but the containers behind it were strewn in haphazard heaps, many of them broken open, their contents littering the ground.

The explosion sent a tidal wave rearing up in all directions. Part of it went harmlessly out into the open sea, while massive walls of water pounded the port facility. Because the tanker was waiting to be loaded, she carried no ballast and rode high in the water. The wave smashed into its thousand-foot flank, rolling the ponderous vessel on its side. The titanic forces acting on it split the hull at the keel and she started to sink. The sub-sea pipelines that fed the floating terminal structure were sheared off and crude began to erupt through the surface of the bay in great reeking clots.

The fireball rising in the middle of the harbor seemed to rival the sun climbing over the Caucasus. It topped out at four thousand feet, a roiling column of fire and smoke that resembled a nuclear detonation. As the explosive force dissipated, the ocean surged back into the void the blast had gouged in the water. The torrent created by the backflow ripped floating docks from their moorings, swamping pleasure craft and small fishing smacks in the process. A bulk carrier leaving the port was dragged back a hundred yards by the surge and slammed into another big freighter entering the harbor. Both vessels were holed and started taking on water.

The echoing roar of the explosion faded, leaving in its wake the angry shriek of thousands of car alarms.

And under the surface of the churned waters of the bay two containers that had fallen from the deck of the fishing boat lay silent, their tough metal hides dented, as they'd been tossed like leaves in a maelstrom, but they had not been breached. They had come to rest close enough for the plutonium in one container to begin calling to the material in the other like a separated lover. It would take time, but the increasing exchange of charged particles would go critical and their bond would be consummated in a blast more deadly than the one that had just destroyed the harbor.

"What happened?" Mercer asked as Devrin and Ahmad continued to speak in rapid-fire Turkish.

"An explosion in Novorossiysk."

"That's the oil port you just mentioned," Cali said.

"How bad?"

"Reports are just coming in now. They say the harbor was leveled. There are ships on fire and many buildings too. The media estimates the death toll in the thousands. Some eyewitnesses claim it was a small nuclear blast."

"Poli couldn't have refined the plutonium to make a bomb that quickly. If anything it's a dirty bomb."

"Which is just as bad," Cali remarked. "And spreading plutonium dust over the sea will make cleanup virtually impossible. It will be decades before the area could be rendered safe, if it's possible at all."

"We have to tell the authorities about the plutonium," Mercer said, thinking through the logical steps the Russians would be taking. The harbor would be jammed with rescue personnel, firefighters, and medical teams. They'd be running into an invisible cloud of highly charged plutonium atoms. Inhaling just a tiny amount of the radioactive dust would cause cancers of unspeakable intensity. "They have to evacuate the city as soon as possible."

Ahmad said something to Devrin and the college student handed Mercer his satellite phone. "I do not know who to talk with to get the Russians to evacuate a city," Ahmad added.

Mercer checked the phone, waiting a second for it to make a link with an orbiting satellite. He dialed Ira Lasko's direct office number. Ira's secretary answered.

"Carol, its Philip Mercer. I need to speak

with Ira right away."

"I'm sorry, he's in a meeting with the President and the national security team. I assume you've heard what happened in Russia. Can I take a message?"

"I have some critical information about the explosion. You've got to get Ira for me."

"They should be done in an hour or so. I can have him call you."

"I'm on a satellite phone and I may lose the connection any second," he said, keeping a tight rein on his exasperation. "I know you're used to dealing with crises but unless you get him for me, thousands of people are going to die a horrible death."

A few seconds passed, the phone buzzing in Mercer's ear. "Give me a minute to transfer you to the situation room."

She transferred Mercer to a Marine colonel stationed outside the situation room buried deep under the White House. Mercer had only to say the words "dirty bomb" for the colonel to step into the inner sanctum and bring Ira Lasko to the phone.

"What's this, Mercer?" he asked gruffly.

"We're too late. I stopped Feines from getting the bulk of the plutonium but he managed to make off with two barrels; I estimate about a thousand pounds' worth of the ore. I believe it was in Novorossiysk."

"Any proof?"

"Not a shred, but Feines steals two barrels of plutonium and twenty-four hours later a city within driving distance gets leveled. I don't believe in coincidences."

"We've already been in touch with the Russkies. My buddy Greg Popov is apoplectic that extremists would pull something like this but he says they've already swept the harbor with Geiger counters and gamma ray detectors. The site's clean."

That wasn't what Mercer had expected. "It has to be there. Maybe the drums didn't rupture or maybe their equipment's bad but I know it was there." He thought for a second. "How did they do it? The explosion I mean."

"Greg tells me it was a fishing boat loaded with explosives, amfo most likely. Ammonium nitrate and fuel oil. They were approaching the tanker side of the harbor when they were spotted by harbor patrol. Last transmission from the patrol guys said the boat was turning away and throwing away contraband. A minute later it went up and leveled about two square miles."

"Ira, the contraband was the barrels. I bet they rolled off the deck when they turned the boat. Go over Popov's head if you have to."

"I almost had to when I talked to him about the plutonium in the first place. I told you he's a cagey operator."

Something in the way he said it gave Mercer an idea. What was it Ahmad had suggested earlier, "Be more cynical than you usually are." That cynicism had been borne of grief but Mercer could use it. He spoke even as the idea coalesced in his mind. "The explosion happened this morning, right? It takes hours to begin any kind of relief operation and your guy Popov says they've already scanned for nuclear materials so fast. Is that standard operating procedure?"

"I really don't know," Ira replied warily. "What are you getting at?"

"You told me that the Russians didn't even know they still had this plutonium until you called them on it. Then two days later Feines shows up just before we arrive. He's got RPGs capable of bringing down a chopper and enough firepower to hold off an army. What if Popov tipped him?"

"And let Feines nuke one of Russia's most important ports? The guy's cagey, not insane."

"Ira, I have it on good authority that a faction inside Saudi Arabia's behind the whole thing in a bid to prevent Caspian oil from cutting into their bottom line. What if

Popov was told they were going to hit the other big oil terminal in Turkey? He wouldn't have cared less. It would actually help Russia by eliminating competition."

"Only he was double-crossed?"

"I just remembered he was supposed to be coming to the mine today. What was he doing in Novorossiysk anyway?"

"He did mention he'd been there since yesterday."

"Hold on a second." Mercer strode across the camp to where Sasha Federov was chatting with the pilot. "Sasha, can you think of any reason Grigori Popov could have gone to Novorossiysk last night?"

The soldier looked confused by the question. "Novo? I don't know why he would be there. He was supposed to land in Samara last night so he could follow the train. Which is late, by the way."

Mercer thanked him and spoke to Ira once again. "Popov should have been in Samara, not on the Black Sea. Ask yourself, do you think he's capable of helping Feines if he thought the plutonium would be used outside Russia?" Ira didn't answer for a long moment, which told Mercer everything he needed to know. "Go over his head, Ira. He's stalling so he can recover the drums, get them back up here, and sweep this whole thing under the rug."

"I hate to say it, but it's possible."

"Remember Ibriham Ahmad, the Turkish professor I've been trying to reach. He's here with me right now. Turns out he also heads the Janissaries, but the important thing is that we stop fundamentalists from taking credit for the blast and inspiring others in the region from taking up the fight. This shit feeds on itself. If we stop it now, it's going to save us a whole lot of problems in the future."

"What do you think we should do?"

"You have to convince the Russians not to disclose this was a terrorist act. Have them report it as an industrial accident, gas buildup in a tanker's hull or something." Ahmad mouthed something to Mercer. He clamped his hand over the phone and asked him to repeat himself.

"Some extremist group will claim the attack on the Internet. The authorities must be ready to discredit any such statement."

"Good idea."

Ahmad bobbed his head in acknowledgment. "I do this for a living."

"Ira, you've also got to monitor Web sites and shut down anything having to do with terrorists taking credit for the blast."

"What else?" Lasko asked, sounding like

he was writing notes to himself.

"I don't know. You're the spinmeister not me. Hey, any word from Booker?"

"Nothing yet. Give me a phone number and I'll call as soon as I have anything on either Book or the Russkies. And Mercer, don't beat yourself up about this. You've done a hell of a job."

Ira clicked off. Mercer's friend's last words were meant to cheer him. If anything, they made him feel worse.

Mercer handed the satellite phone to Federov. "Contact your superiors. The train's not coming. They need to send another chopper because I think Grigori Popov has betrayed us."

"What?"

"I think he tipped off Poli about the cache of plutonium here. At first I thought there might have been a security leak on my side, but it makes more sense that Popov betrayed my boss and his own country. What do you know about him?"

"Not much," Sasha admitted. "He is a deputy minister, a former admiral. I have heard he favors Western sports cars and is how you say, a maverick, a cowboy. I would not be surprised if he's had dealings with criminal elements because in Russia these days that is the only way to gain power."

"Do you think he would sell black market nuclear material?"

Sasha's eyes turned sad as he considered such a betrayal. "I do not know. In this world anything is possible."

Ludmilla and her colleague trudged up the switchback road from the railhead. While she seemed as fresh and imperturbable as ever, the male scientist looked on the verge of a massive coronary. She spoke to Sasha for five minutes, answering a few questions before heading off to eat.

"What did she say?" Mercer asked. Cali joined them while Ibriham Ahmad and Devrin Egemen confided privately.

"It appears none of the containers split open."

"Thank Christ."

"They were loaded into two of the box-cars. The rest were empty. She says there were sixty-eight barrels, bringing the total to seventy accounting for the two Feines stole. So far there is little heat buildup but she says we must get the barrels isolated from each other soon to prevent the plutonium from obtaining critical mass and exploding."

"She's right," Mercer said, "but there's not much the group of us can do for now." He paused. "Maybe there is. Is there any kind of record of what was in the depot?"

"Not that I'm aware of."

Mercer looked to Cali. She spoke first. "I guess we're going to play grocery clerk and take inventory."

The rubberized contamination suit smelled of stale sweat and halitosis and what he was pretty sure was urine, a nauseating combination that churned the tinned borscht lying in Mercer's stomach.

"How you doing?" he asked Cali as she sealed the hood over her head.

"Ugh. Smells like a locker room of a girls' volleyball team."

"I've got bad breath and pee in mine. Want to switch?"

"Pass."

They were standing outside the entrance of the old mine with Ahmad, Devrin, and Ludmilla. The Russian scientist checked over their suits, using a role of duct tape to seal their gloves and boots. She ran her hands over the suits to make sure there were no rips or tears from when she had examined the train wreckage. Mercer wasn't sure who's backside she lingered over more, his or Cali's, but the examination in that region had been more than thorough.

"Perhaps you should leave this for the

Russians," Professor Ahmad suggested for the second or third time. "Devrin and I plan to leave here before the helicopter that Captain Federov requested arrives. We can take you and Cali with us to the airport in Samara."

"I told you, Ibriham." Mercer had to raise his voice to be heard outside the yellow suit. "The man partially responsible for the theft will want to hide his culpability. He's in Novorossiysk right now looking for those two missing barrels. When he finds them he's going to return them to the train wreck and act like nothing happened."

"It will be your word against his."

"Trust me this won't be going to any court of law." Mercer checked his flashlight and the spare in the bag slung over his shoulder. He had no intention of being in the mine long enough to drain even one, but he'd spent half his lifetime underground and knew you could never be too prepared. "Ms. Stowe," he said with a gallant sweep of his arms toward the small forklift Poli had brought and abandoned. "Our chariot awaits."

They climbed onto the little machine, each sharing part of the single seat, their hips pressed tight though there was no feeling through the thick rubber. Mercer keyed the electric motor, which hummed to life. A foot pedal controlled the motor speed and a small wheel directed the agile rear wheels. He noted that there was plenty of juice left in the batteries when he flicked on the lights.

Mercer tossed the Turks and Ludmilla a wave over his shoulder and guided the forklift into the mine. As soon as they'd traveled just a dozen yards down the dark tunnel, he felt the temperature begin to drop, as if the stone was leaching the heat from his body. The shaft was at least forty feet wide and fifteen tall, much bigger than Mercer had expected, so the lift's puny lights cast a feeble ring along the ceiling, walls, and floor that retreated just a few yards ahead of them as they drove downward. The triple set of tracks for hauling ore and waste rock from the mine were dulled from exposure and the mine's constant dank humidity.

The main shaft shot arrow straight into the earth for nearly a mile before they came to their first cross tunnel. Mercer cut the power to the lift to conserve its batteries and jumped to the ground. Cali followed him as he entered the secondary tunnel. She carried a gamma detector and watched its readings intently.

After fifty yards they came to a chamber

where the miners had employed what was called room-and-pillar mining. In essence they had excavated a broad cavern, but left thick columns of rock undisturbed to support the weight of the mountain above.

Mercer played his flashlight around some of the columns and whistled when something reflected the beam back at him. He felt like he'd stepped into a military museum. He recognized the sharklike snout of an ME-262, the extraordinary jet fighter the Germans introduced in the latter stages of the war. The aircraft's wings had been removed and leaned against a pillar next to the deadly plane. A little farther on he came to another and another. Then he saw planes he didn't recognize. They were advanced even for today. They were small and sleek one-man attack aircraft that looked capable of incredible speeds.

He said, "These must have been prototypes of planes the Nazis ran out of time developing."

"Good thing too. Our prop jobs wouldn't have stood a chance."

"Anything on the gamma reader?"

"Background's a tad high but nothing like what we found on the *Wetherby*."

They spent another fifteen minutes exploring the cavity just to be sure. There were at least fifteen aircraft stored here, all in remarkable condition. They also found early rockets. Some were mounted on trailers to be launched as the world's first surface-to-air missiles. Others were small enough to be carried aloft for direct aerial combat. All of them were far more advanced than anything the allies had at the time.

"Clever, weren't they," Mercer said, examining a multiple rocket pod intended to fire a deadly swarm of small unguided missiles.

"Just think what the world would be like if they'd turned their genius to helping humanity rather than destroying it."

Satisfied that the plutonium had been stored deeper in the mine, they retreated back to the forklift and continued their descent down the gently sloping floor. The next cross tunnel revealed another chamber of captured German arms. On benches were man-portable weapons — machine-guns of a type Mercer didn't know, a bazooka-like weapon that unspooled thin wires for guidance, a table littered with rifles with curved barrels, for shooting around corners presumably. Dominating the entrance to the chamber was the biggest battle tank Mercer had ever seen. It had to be three times the size of a modern M-1 Abrams. The tracks were three feet wide and instead of a single cannon mounted in the boxy turret, this behemoth sported two side by side.

"It's a *Maus*," Mercer said, awed. "My grandfather was a military modeler. He built one from scratch using a couple of old pictures. Hitler ordered the prototypes when someone suggested their tanks were vulnerable to attack from railroad guns. Never entered his mind the Allies didn't have any railroad guns, of course. I didn't know any of these survived the war."

Cali looked at him askance. "Ever thought of going on *Jeopardy!*?"

"Hey, don't blame me. A photographic memory is both a blessing and a curse. Want me to tell you the tank's specifications?" He tapped his helmet. "They're in here too."

"Another time, maybe. I got something."

"Where?"

"That way." She pointed deeper into the chamber.

Despite the mine's chill Mercer was sweating in his suit, adding his own unwashed body to the stench permeating the rubber. Guided by the readings on the gamma ray detector they carefully made their way into a subchamber of the main excavation.

"Look." Mercer shot a finger toward the stone floor. They could make out tracks cut through the dust by the forklift's solid rubber tires.

"Great job of tracking there, Cochise," Cali teased. "We could have just followed the trail."

Mercer shrugged. As he stepped forward he felt something snag his ankle and for a microsecond he wished he could take back that fateful stride. He should have known Poli would have left behind a surprise. He threw himself onto Cali, knocking them both to the ground, his body shielding hers as best he could.

The booby trap was a simple trip wire attached to a couple of grenades with their pins already partially pulled. The wire ran around the room, where the grenades were hidden behind a massive timber balk supporting the entrance back to the main tunnel.

The suit prevented Mercer from hearing the pins pull free and the spoons flip up to activate the grenades, but he knew it was happening. "Open your mouth," he shouted in the seconds before the bombs went off.

The trio of grenades exploded almost simultaneously. Confined by the surrounding stone, the overpressure wave shot across the room and slammed into Mercer and Cali, causing their suits to squeeze in on them painfully. Had Cali not heeded Mercer's timely warning her eardrums would have ruptured.

He rolled off her as soon as the wave of compressed air had rolled over them. The cavern was filled with so much dust his light could not penetrate more than a couple of feet. He got to his knees, then shakily to his feet. He was dazed by the explosion, his head ringing and his balance shot by the brutal assault on his inner ears. He glanced down at Cali and ignored all the priorities of mine rescue he'd ever learned or taught.

Hobbling because he'd smashed his bad knee again, he approached the exit to the main shaft. He played his light over the portal. The grenades had blown the timber support from where it had stood for a half century, and the wooden lintel, as thick as a railroad tie, had fallen too. The stone above the opening had been fractured by the blast, and with nothing to support it, cracks appeared and widened as he watched. A chunk the size of an anvil crashed to the ground. Mercer took one last look to where he knew Cali lay stunned, perhaps injured or worse, and raced through to the main shaft, abandoning her behind an avalanche of rubble that buried her alive.

THE WHITE HOUSE, WASHINGTON, D.C.

"You have to believe me, Vladimir, it's in both our countries' best interest that this doesn't appear to be a terrorist attack," the President of the United States said, his smooth voice covering his irritation. He listened to the Russian president's reply. "Would you rather call it a mishap and look incompetent or admit it was a terrorist act and embolden more fanatics?"

Ira Lasko and John Kleinschmidt, his immediate boss, listened to the President's side of the conversation from the laager of sofas in the middle of the Oval Office. As national security advisor, Kleinschmidt had immediate access to the President day or night and had presented Mercer's findings to the chief executive an hour before. The administration had been saved more than once by Philip Mercer, so when he asked for the President to intervene, the former senior Senator from Ohio generally listened.

"Apples and oranges," the President said in response to the Russian. "One plane flying into a skyscraper can be an accident. Three on the same day while another goes down over Pennsylvania all on live television isn't something you can pretend didn't happen. You have a different opportunity with the situation in Novorossiysk.

"We've talked about this before. This is a war, Vlad, and every time they score a victory a couple more fighters join their ranks. A blow like this is going to incite hundreds, maybe thousands, to carry on the fight against us. . . . What? No it doesn't matter. If they feel that Caspian oil is a threat, they're going to take it out. What better way than to exploit a bunch of brainwashed kids who think they're buying their way into heaven, while sitting back and saying how awful it is that a tiny fraction of their population hates the West so much. Yeah, you're the West now too whether you like it or not."

The President made a rude masturbatory gesture with his hand as the Russian leader spoke for several minutes.

"That's right, Grigori Popov." The President chuckled for the first time since the conversation began. "I've got a couple hundred deputy this and assistant thats. I don't know half of them and I don't expect you to know all of yours either. But I have it from a good source that he was responsible for getting the plutonium into the hands of the bombers. I don't know why it wasn't released but we know Popov is there now when he should be meeting a member of my staff five hundred miles to the north.

"I'm asking that you send someone you trust to Novorossiysk to find out what this Popov is doing. If it's a coincidence, fine, I owe you a personal apology, but if I'm right and he's scouring the harbor for those missing barrels while everyone else is trying to coordinate relief efforts, then you'll know I'm right." The President's voice deepened and took on a familiar companionate timbre that connected immediately with any listener. Pollsters had shown that this tone alone garnered him ten points in the election.

"Vladimir, you're facing a national tragedy that could help fuel a global war if it isn't handled properly. You've got the full resources of the United States behind you on this but you have to make the right call. Don't give the bastards the satisfaction of claiming a victory here. Take it away and spare both our nations a much tougher fight in the future. This is about hearts and minds as much as it is about oil and power." He paused again, his handsome face showing nothing. "Thank you, Mr. President."

As soon as he hung up the phone John Kleinschmidt asked, "Well?"

"He said he'd think about it."

"He doesn't have the luxury," Ira said. "It's going to be all over the Internet in an hour or two that terrorists destroyed that tanker terminal and stopped the flow of oil from Kazakhstan."

The President met Lasko's gaze. "We've put him in a tough spot, asking him to lie to his people about the most significant act of terrorism since 9/11, while at the same time telling him that one of his own top advisors might be involved."

"What would you do, Mr. President?"

"I'd like to think I'd come clean and let the chips fall where they will, but our esteemed Russian colleague is a hell of a lot more pragmatic than I am. My gut tells me he'll follow our script, but he's going to ask for quid pro quo when the time comes."

Mercer wanted to tear the suit from his body and attack the pile of debris with his bare hands, knowing that on the other side Cali must assume he'd left her for dead. He calmed his breathing because the suit's filters couldn't keep up with his pumping lungs and he felt he was going to start hyperventilating. The helmet's plastic eyepiece was also fogged, though with the dust choking the mine's main shaft it was impossible to see more than a yard or two.

He groped his way along the shaft like a blind man, his flashlight turned off since it was worthless anyway.

One of the first rules about mine rescue he'd learned, going back to stories his own father had told, was that during a cave-in you never leave your buddies. You are going to live or die, that was up to fate, but you were always supposed to do it together. That way you could rely on each other as you waited for rescue. That's the reason Mercer disregarded his training and instinct to leap through the collapsing mine entrance. There would be no rescue.

The blast hadn't been big enough to be felt on the surface, and even if Sasha, Ludmilla, and the others became worried after an hour or two, Mercer and Cali had the only three flashlights. If the soldiers on the rescue chopper tried to dig through the avalanche they would probably make matters worse and entomb themselves. And if they were prudent and called in mine rescue specialists it would take days to assemble them here, days Mercer couldn't afford.

His heavily gloved fingers brushed against something smooth. He'd found the forklift. He hoisted himself onto the seat and flicked on the motor. He felt its reassuring vibration through the suit. It took just a moment to reach the rubble that lay strewn halfway across the main shaft where it had collapsed. Rather than attack the pile closest to the entrance, Mercer began moving larger stones away from the area to give himself working room. He lifted them with the forklift's tines and then manhandled them off farther down the drive.

By the time he'd finished clearing a wide swath of debris, the dust had settled enough for him to examine the rockfall. He tapped a few stones with the butt of his flashlight, and while his ears continued to ring, he could feel the rocks' stability or looseness through his hands, reading the stones like a blind man reads Braille. In his mind he mapped out every boulder he wanted to remove, calculating its effect on the rest of the pile in the same fashion a chess master plans out entire games before making the first move, because he knows how his challenger will react. Mercer knew this opponent all too well, had faced it a dozen times for real and a thousand times in his nightmares. He shut out the distraction of knowing Cali was on the other side of the barrier, scared that she would die alone in the cold womb of the earth.

For twenty minutes Mercer studied the pile, and when he finally reached out, he plucked a little chip of stone no bigger than his fist and watched as it created a cascade of pulverized rock. He got down on his hands and knees to examine how the pebbles had settled on the floor. Satisfied that the effects of his action were within the parameters he'd established, he removed a larger stone and again analyzed the results.

Noting that they weren't exactly what he'd anticipated, he adjusted his attack plan slightly and got to work. In a way he was like a master jeweler facing the most important diamond cut of his career. Only it wasn't one swift motion that determined success or failure, it was dozens as he slowly whittled the pile away, ever careful that the stones didn't become unbalanced, shifting weight loads from stone to stone as he bored a hole through the debris.

When he'd cleared enough away from his hole, he used the forklift to remove the detritus. It took him an hour to worm his way through half the mound and that's where he encountered a slab of stone he couldn't move. The jigsaw of rock was locked tight.

He tried shouting for Cali, but with the bulky contamination suit muffling his voice the gesture was futile. At that point Mercer should have left her, and returned when rescue personnel arrived, but he'd spent enough time with the stone to know how far he could push it. He returned to the forklift and smiled to himself tightly when he saw that the tines were held on by knobs welded to the lift chassis with thick carbon steel pins. He jerked one of the pins free and wrestled the hundred pound lance from the machine, then slid the cupped end onto the other tine, doubling its length.

Careful not to disturb the edges of the hole he'd created, he eased the single elongated tine into the burrow, hopping off the lift several times to ensure he was positioning it correctly. The tip scraped against the slab of rock and he lowered the metal bar slightly to wedge its leading edge under the stone. Again he inched his way into the hollow to check the position.

He weighed odds, cursed, then tore the soft rubber helmet from his head. "Cali, can you hear me? If you can, don't take off your helmet. Bang something metal against the rocks." He then realized his precarious situation and added, "But not too hard."

A second passed, then five. Then ten and Mercer began to worry. She had been injured in the blast, maybe hit by a piece of shrapnel. She could be bleeding to death just a few feet away.

Tap. Tap. Tap.

Mercer sagged with relief. "Hold on. I'm going to get you out."

He slithered back to the forklift and slowly drove the elongated tine under the rock. He could sense by the way the motor's vibrations changed how much of the load the machine was taking, judging the weight and balance of the rubble with his instinct and experience.

Something in the pile shifted suddenly. Mercer eased off the accelerator and safed the chain drive that lifted and lowered the fork. He peered into the hole, the beam of the flashlight casting bizarre patterns on the fractured stone. There was a foot-high gap under the big slab, but he could tell it lay at an angle; the side closest to Cali was still on the ground. By hand he moved a few other rocks, his earlier plan all but abandoned. This was no longer a chess match, but a frantic game of checkers.

He got back onto the seat and tried to ram the fork deeper under the stone. It wouldn't budge. The slick wheels began to spin uselessly against the stone floor. He wasn't going to get Cali out anytime soon.

Enraged, he was about to give up when the plucky little forklift lurched forward another foot. He raised the tine as high as it would go and leapt off the machine, diving headfirst into the hole. A brilliant light nearly blinded him. Behind it he could see the bright yellow of Cali's contamination suit. She slipped her lithe body through the tight aperture, and when their fingers locked Mercer wanted to give a shout of triumph. Slithering backward he guided her out of the hole.

As soon as they were clear Cali ripped off her helmet. Mercer opened his mouth to warn her that the mine could be contaminated, but he never got the words out because her incredible lips were pressed to his in a kiss that squeezed his heart.

"I'm so sorry," he breathed into her. "I had to do it."

"Shut up," she panted and kissed him more fiercely.

They held each other in the dim light of the forklift for all eternity, it seemed, or a blink of an eye. When they parted there was laughter in Cali's eyes. "Professor Ahmad is right, you know. You *are* predictable. I knew you wouldn't leave me."

"If I hadn't jumped out we would have both been trapped."

"That's what I figured when I realized you were gone."

"It must have been terrifying."

"Not really. I said I knew you'd come get me. While I waited I checked the rest of the chamber."

Mercer couldn't believe it. When they realized they were trapped most people would have thrown themselves at the pile of rock or sat in the dark and cried themselves insane. But not Cali. She went exploring.

"I found the rooms where they stored the plutonium. Just as we calculated they had seventy barrels left. The rooms were pretty big; I think to keep the barrels segregated so the plutonium wasn't allowed to reach critical mass. The walls had absorbed some radiation, but nothing too bad. I'll avoid dental X rays for a year or two and I'll be fine."

"You are amazing," Mercer said, pride catching in his throat.

She smirked at him and he could imagine her freckles glowing pink on her cheeks. "Sometimes I am." She kissed him again, a brief yet promissory caress of her lips. "No sense taking any more chances, let's make like a tree and blow."

"I thought that was make like the wind and leave."

She laughed. "We could make like a Japanese board game and go."

"Make like a left-wing Web site and move on."

This time she groaned. "That's enough."

"Right."

The forklift died before reaching the mine's entrance, forcing them to walk the last half mile, Cali helping Mercer because his knee still bothered him. Ludmilla was the only person waiting for them when they emerged from the stygian realm. She gave a little snort when she saw them but her bovine expression didn't change.

"Great to see you too, Milly old girl," Mercer said to get a reaction. He didn't.

She accompanied them down to the remains of the helicopter. Sasha was sitting up against a tree stump; the pilot and the other scientist were dozing near the chopper.

"It looks like it went well," Sasha said to greet them.

"Hit a little snag," Cali said airily, "no big deal."

"Where are Professor Ahmad and Devrin Egemen?"

"When the helicopter reported they were

lifting off from Samara, they got in their vehicle and left." Sasha handed Mercer a piece of paper. "He asked me to give you this."

Mercer unfolded the note.

Dear Doctor,

I want to apologize for how I manipulated you and Miss Stowe into helping us. My Janissaries have defended the alembic for generations and if not for a conversation among lovers decades ago we would not have faced the crisis we have. It is almost contained now thanks in part to you. The rest is our responsibility. I pray you will heed my advice and return to your lives, satisfied with the knowledge you have contributed a noble cause.

It was unsigned.

"What do you think?" Cali asked after she read it.

He crushed the piece of paper. "Without the stele there isn't much we can do this side of digging up half of Egypt. The Russians will handle the plutonium and Popov too if I'm right about him." He felt the heat of their kiss once again and looked into her eyes. "I guess we go back and resume our lives like he says."

"Exactly like it was before?" she said teasingly.

He took her hand. "I foresee a change or two."

ARLINGTON, VIRGINIA

By the time their connecting flight from Frankfurt touched down at Dulles Airport, thirty-six hectic hours had passed since Cali and Mercer were picked up at the mine by the Russian military. With no luggage except the bag of duty-free Jack Daniel's Mercer had bought for his depleted bar, they were through Customs quickly. Ira had sent a government car to take them home. They'd agreed earlier they would drop Cali at her condo first. It had been a grueling couple of days and the promise of a budding relationship couldn't overcome two exhausted, worn-out bodies.

Mercer saw her to her door, and together they checked out her cozy two-bedroom to ensure no one had been there in her absence. He felt like a teenager on a first date as they kissed under the porch light. It was their first since the mine. Without the bulky contamination suit, her long-limbed body was all bone and hard angles but fit perfectly in his arms. Their eyes were at almost the same level and neither closed them.

"I'll see you tomorrow?" Cali asked.

"And the day after that," Mercer promised.

"I have to report in to NEST in the morning, then I'm taking a couple of days off."

"And I don't have any contracts lined up for two weeks."

"I'll see you at noon."

The twenty-minute drive to Mercer's brownstone passed in a contented blur.

The lights were on when he opened the door and he heard a voice. He tensed momentarily before recognizing Harry White's jackhammer laugh. He climbed the spiral stairs up to the bar, his knee feeling better but still noticeable. As he passed through the alcove library and the French doors he heard another voice and laughed aloud, calling, "Booker Sykes, don't you get in the habit of drinking my booze too."

Book and Harry were sitting at the bar with a couple of drinks and a nearly depleted bowl of pretzels. A baseball game playing on the big television held Drag's rapt attention, like he was almost following the action.

Mercer slapped Booker on the shoulder.

"I already know your trip was a bust. Sorry about that. Are you and your men okay? When'd you get back?"

"Couple hours ago," Sykes said. "And there isn't anything wrong with us that some ice and a chiropractor can't fix. What the hell do you mean bust?"

"I talked to the guy who blew up the stele."

"Shit, man, you are a pessimist." He waved his beer bottle. "Check it out."

Mercer turned to see what he was talking about. On the floor behind one of the couches were three large backpacks. Mercer flipped open the biggest one. Inside was a bunch of gray stones. So exhausted by the past days, he couldn't comprehend what he was seeing. He lifted one of the rocks from the bag. It was a lump of unremarkable granite about the size of a blackboard eraser. One side of it had been poorly smoothed. He looked closer at the tool marks. His eyes widened. He'd never be able to decipher it without expert help but he clearly recognized an Egyptian cartouche and hieroglyphic writing.

"It wasn't blown up," Booker explained. "Looks like they broke it apart with hammers or rifle butts. Rivers, Cieplicki, and I humped out every piece bigger than a marble."

Mercer was grinning like an idiot. "Booker, you have my permission to drink as much of my booze as you want." He tried to lift the bag. "Jesus, this thing must weigh a hundred pounds."

"The lightest was a hundred and seventy-five according to the airline, which charged an extra four hundred bucks for the weight. That's the reason I look like a question mark when I stand up."

Mercer reached into the bag for another smaller piece, his smile fading when he realized he was actually holding two chunks of a seven-foot-long, six-hundred-pound, three-dimensional jigsaw puzzle. It would take months to put the stele back together, if it was possible at all.

"Hey, Mercer, check out behind the bar," Harry said from his stool.

"Huh?" Mercer grunted distractedly.

He carefully set the pieces of stone back in the knapsack and stepped behind the mahogany-topped bar. Nothing seemed out of place. "What is it?"

"Nothing. Just wanted you to make me another drink."

"Bastard." Mercer scowled as he freshened Harry's Jack and ginger and made a gimlet for himself. "How the hell are we going to put the stele back together?"

"That thing is in more pieces than Humpty Dumpty," Harry commented. "You guys ever wonder what made them think the king's horses could fix him?"

"No," Booker and Mercer said in unison.

"Seriously," Harry went on, "there must be five or six hundred pieces, most of them are freakin' tiny, and the ones I examined at all look pretty much the same."

Mercer said, "I'll call Ira in the morning; he might have an idea who can reassemble it. There must be some forensic guys out there who have experience reconstructing bones. Maybe they can do something." He didn't sound optimistic.

"Should we tell him?" Booker asked Harry.

"He called me a bastard. I say let him twist awhile longer."

"Tell me what?"

Booker kept looking to Harry, until the octogenarian threw up his arms. "I give up. Go ahead and tell him, only you're no fun."

"I spoke with Admiral Lasko as soon as we landed. We've got a meeting at the Goddard Space Flight Center over in Greenbelt, Maryland, tomorrow morning at nine."

"What's there?"

"From what Ira tells me, magic."

Greenbelt, Maryland, was on the opposite side of the nation's capital from Arlington, and it took them two hours battling a nearly gridlocked Beltway to reach the exit. Fortunately, the Goddard Center was two miles from the I-95 and Mercer eased his Jaguar convertible to the main gate with five minutes to spare. Next to the gate was the public visitor's center where a couple examples of NASA's earliest rockets were on display in an outdoor garden.

"Nice lawn ornaments," Booker remarked.

"Beats pink flamingos."

After checking their identification and making sure they were on the day's visitors list, a guard handed over two passes and directed them to a new building at the end of Explorers Road on the far side of the sprawling government research campus. Mercer parked in a large lot next to a storm runoff pond. A trio of ducks was lazing in the early morning sunshine.

The building was an unremarkable brick affair with only a few windows high on its façade. Mercer and Booker were met in the reception area by a twentysomething man in a white lab coat. Below it he wore black pants and a black T-shirt. Mercer assumed it was his black Miata among all the minivans and SUVs in the parking lot. He had slicked back dark hair and stylish glasses, not the image of a government scientist Mercer had pictured.

"Dr. Jacobi?"

"Alan Jacobi. You must be Dr. Mercer."

"Call me Mercer." They shook hands. "This is Booker Sykes."

"Hi. Call me Alan." He looked behind them. "Do you have the samples?"

"They're in the car. Do you have a trolley or anything?'

"Oh sure."

Ten minutes later they had the three bags in Jacobi's lab. The room was at least fifty feet square, packed with workstations, computers, and sleek, humming boxes whose function Mercer could only guess.

"I have to say when I got the call from the White House yesterday I was pretty blown away. I mean we don't do anything high-priority here."

"What do you do?"

"As you know the Goddard Center is one of the leading research laboratories in the country for earth and space sciences. We run expeditions all over the world, and beyond for that matter. My lab here deals with three-dimensional holography and materials analyses. We're adapting it for medical research and possibly archaeology."

"And you think you can help."

"Oh no doubt. Let's see what you've got."

Mercer opened one of the backpacks and started removing fragments of the stele and setting them on a table. Jacobi picked up one of the bigger pieces, a twenty-pound misshapen chunk of stone that resembled a head of broccoli.

"This should work nicely for a demonstration." He took the stone to a piece of equipment that looked like a microwave oven and set it inside. He closed the door and turned to a nearby computer. He spoke as he tapped at the keys. "What this machine does is scans a three-dimensional object into the computer, creating an exact digital reproduction down to one micrometer or one millionth of a meter."

"Wow," Mercer said.

"That's nothing. They use machines like this in Hollywood all the time to turn clay models of monsters and spaceships and stuff into digital effects. My machine is just a lot more precise."

He swiveled the screen to show them what the computer had created. It looked exactly like the chunk of stone, only the computer had rendered it in green. Jacobi made a few adjustments and the digital rock turned gray. "There."

"So now what?" Booker asked.

"Now I scan every piece of stone into the computer. When I'm done I will tell it the approximate shape of the object and it will digitally put it all back together." He waited for a reaction. "Ah, now's the time you say 'Wow.' The fuzzy logic algorithms alone took me the better part of three years to perfect. I'm asking the computer to make tens of millions of decisions by itself as to how to reassemble the digital pieces. This is cutting edge stuff." Jacobi laughed. "What did you think, I was going to glue this mess back together or something?"

"No, not at all," Mercer said to hide the fact that that's exactly what he thought would happen. "A digital image is perfect. How long will it take?"

"I'll get a couple of post docs in here to do the scutt work of imaging the fragments. That'll take some time because the imagers are slow and we have to number each piece if you want to reassemble the real thing." His voice rose in pitch as he finished his sentence, as if asking if his team could avoid the tedium of cataloguing every fragment.

"No, I think you should number them. We might need the actual artifact." Mercer just wanted the rebuilt stele. He thought it would look great in the bar.

"You got it then." Jacobi shrugged, knowing he wouldn't be doing the work anyway. "You passed a cafeteria on your way to this building. Why don't you give us a couple of hours and we'll see what we come up with."

Mercer and Book Sykes returned to Jacobi's lab at eleven thirty.

"Perfect timing," the young scientist said to greet them. "We're just about finished with the last small pieces." The bits of the stele were lying on workbenches and atop equipment. All of them were in individual numbered glassine envelopes like the police use for collecting evidence.

"Well done." Mercer smiled.

"I forgot to ask what this thing looked like originally. I was told it was a stele but I have no idea what that is."

"A small obelisk. It was about seven feet tall."

"The computer *can* do the digital reassembly without knowing the parameters since there's only one way the bits and pieces fit exactly, but knowing its size and shape will save a whole lot of computing power and time."

"I'm finished with the last one," a post doc said, removing a chip of stone from the digital imager and slipping it into a clear envelope numbered eight hundred and sixty-three.

Mercer decided he'd hire someone to rebuild the stele for him.

"Okay then," Jacobi said from his desk. He drew an obelisk using a wireless pen. "Like that?"

"A bit skinnier."

"Got it." He typed in the size. "Seven feet. And here we go."

Mercer blinked and a realistic representation of the stele was on the screen in front of him. He could plainly see the hieroglyphs covering all four sides as the image rotated in space. "Holy shit. How long would it have taken if you didn't know what it looked like?"

"Oh, God, at least a minute," Jacobi replied smugly.

As Jacobi zoomed in on the stele's surface, Mercer could see where Ahmad and his men had smashed it. There were a few chips missing that either Book didn't find or that had been powdered by the blows. Still there was more than enough to work with from what Jacobi had been able to reconstruct.

Mercer shook his hand. "Thank you. You did an amazing job. I can see how this could help doctors map out how to rebuild broken bones and archaeologists to put ancient pottery back together. Truly remarkable."

"I wish I could tell you why the government wanted something like this in the first place, but it's classified."

Booker Sykes smirked. "Only reason is to put blast zones back together after an explosion, to determine what type of bomb was used."

Jacobi went pale. "How did you, I mean that's, you couldn't . . ."

Sykes clamped a big hand on the scientist's shoulder. "Don't sweat it, man. It's the only thing that makes sense."

Mercer and Booker drove straight to the Smithsonian. Mercer had called while Jacobi's people were imaging the stele, and used his White House credentials to arrange for one of their top Egyptologists to be waiting. He'd also left a voice mail for Cali at NEST, telling her the hunt was on again.

A small woman in her sixties wearing a threadbare cardigan despite the rising heat was pacing the steps outside the Museum of Natural History, where she'd said she'd meet them.

She saw them mounting the steps and descended toward them with quick birdlike movements. "Do you have it?" she asked breathlessly. "You're sure it was placed by Alexander the Great. Do you know what a find this is? I must study the actual stele." She said all this in a rush, her words blending together in her excitement. "You are Dr. Mercer and Mr. Sykes, right?"

Mercer smiled. "That's right. You're Emily French?'

"Yes. I've already accosted two sets of tourists coming into the museum, hoping they were you. I just can't believe this. There are so few new discoveries in Ptolemaic Egyptology anymore, at least that the Egyptians don't publish themselves first."

"Ptolemaic?"

"Yes, the time when Egypt was ruled by the Greeks, 331 to 30 B.C. It ended with Cleopatra, who was actually Cleopatra VII but no one would make movies about the first six. Oh, listen to me I'm babbling. Let's go to my office and take a look, shall we?"

"How can this possibly be a matter of national security?" she asked as she led them through the public part of the museum and into a warren of offices on the third floor. "This is an ancient artifact, not the plans for a nuclear bomb or something."

Mercer almost gasped at how closely she'd guessed.

"We're not at liberty to discuss that, ma'am," Book replied in his deepest baritone.

"Oh, my." She led them into her cramped and cluttered office, making an apology for the mess as if it wasn't always so chock-full of books, stacks of papers, and knickknacks.

"And, Mrs. French," Mercer added, "you are not allowed to discuss this matter with anyone. What I believe is written on the stele could change history and lead to one of the greatest archaeological discoveries since Tutankhamen. If I am correct and these findings are made public you will receive all due credit, I assure you."

Her enthusiasm waned until Mercer slipped the computer disc into her laptop and the stele appeared on the screen. She plucked a pair of large glasses from her desk and settled them on her tiny nose. Mercer showed her how to use the mouse as Jacobi had taught him, to manipulate the image and zoom in on specific spots.

"It's magnificent," she breathed. "Look there, that's the sign for battle. Here's something about a burial, a king perhaps." She kept changing her point of view, peering at the computer with her face only inches from the screen. "Some of this is in ancient Greek but here's a cartouche. Let me see. It *is* about a king's burial. That's . . . Oh my Lord!" She looked across her desk at Mercer and Book, her eyes wide and owlish behind her glasses.

"Alexander the Great," Booker said. "We know."

"We believe the stele reveals the location of his tomb. It was placed near an old mine in Central Africa after Alexander's death."

"His tomb?" Her enthusiasm peaked again. "His actual tomb? Do you know how many people have searched for it over the years?"

"Yes, ma'am."

"Can you do a full translation of the stele?" Mercer asked.

"Of course. It will take me some time, hieroglyphs are open to interpretation. They tell a story more than lay out words like a sentence."

Mercer handed her a business card from a gold-and-onyx case he'd gotten as a gift years earlier from a petroleum heiress he'd dated for a short time. The number on the card was an answering service, so he scribbled his cell and home numbers on the back. "You can call me day or night."

For dinner Cali cooked Mercer, Book, and Harry pasta carbonara, which she claimed was her best recipe and which made the men fear her worst. Her disappointment that she couldn't be alone with Mercer had given way to excitement when he explained what they'd done that day and showed her a copy of Jacobi's disc.

After the meal they settled in the bar with brandies, still talking and speculating about the possibilities. Beyond the alembic, Alexander's tomb was rumored to be the richest, most magnificent in history. His crystal-and-gold sarcophagus was said to be the greatest work of art ever produced in the ancient world.

Mercer was on his second snifter when his phone rang. The conversation died with words still poised on lips. "Hello."

"I have good news and bad news," Emily French said without preamble.

"Okay," Mercer said, drawing out the word, hoping but trying not to.

It took her five minutes to explain her findings. She summed up by telling him she'd e-mail the entire translation. He gave her the address, set the cordless back on the coffee table, and roared with laughter. The others stared at him, but soon his laughter caught on and they started to chuckle and laugh along with him, until Harry finally said, "Are you going to let us in on the joke?"

Mercer actually had to wipe tears from his eyes and take several deep breaths, and still the laughter was in his voice. "It was there all right."

"The tomb's location."

"Yup. He wasn't buried in Alexandria or the Sawi Oasis as some scholars speculate. They took his body north along the Nile and buried him in a cave at the very head of a valley they called Shu'ta."

"So we go find this valley, grab the alembic, and put an end to this nightmare," Cali said.

"Not so fast." Mercer chuckled again. "Emily French did some research on our behalf and discovered the exact location of the Shu'ta Valley. In the process she learned that in 1970 it was submerged under about a hundred feet of water when they built the Aswân High Dam. I still want to go see it for myself but she says the area is totally inaccessible." The irony of it all made Mercer break out in laughter all over again.

Aswân, Egypt

Mercer couldn't help but recall the last time he was in Egypt. It had been a couple years earlier and he had spent two weeks cruising the Nile with an Eritrean diplomat named Salome. He hadn't seen or heard from her since, making her memory just an enigmatic smile.

"Penny for your thoughts," Cali said. They were seated by the pool of a luxury hotel on Elephantine Island right in the middle of the sluggish Nile. Between them and the town of Aswân, tourist boats and lateen-rigged feluccas plied the waters.

"I was here once with somebody," Mercer replied, refusing to cover the truth with a white lie no matter the consequences.

"Lucky girl," Cali said. "She comes here for a romantic getaway and I'm stuck chasing old tombs and dirty bombs."

He should have known Cali didn't have a jealous bone in her body.

Booker approached their table. In a black tank top and khaki cargo pants cut off at the knee, he made an imposing figure. He eased himself into a seat, mindful of his still-tender back. "We got us a boat."

"Terrific."

When Mercer had told Ira Lasko about the tomb's location, the admiral had reported the findings to the President. Two hours later Ira phoned Mercer back, telling him that they didn't want to involve the Egyptian government just yet. In truth they didn't want to involve them at all if they could help it. By the terms of international law the tomb and everything within it belonged to Egypt. No one in the administration wanted to see another Middle Eastern nation with nuclear capabilities. Relations with Cairo were good but that didn't mean they couldn't deteriorate in the future. Like so many other Arab nations they had a minority population of fundamentalists eager to turn their country into a theocracy.

It was decided that Mercer, Cali, and Booker would travel to Egypt as tourists and reconnoiter the sunken valley first. If possible the President wanted them to snatch the alembic. A guided missile cruiser was being diverted from a courtesy call to Cyprus and would transit the Suez Canal. If they could get the alembic, they could meet the vessel on the deserted coast of the Red Sea. At that point the location of Alexander's tomb could be revealed in such a way to politically benefit the United States. If they couldn't retrieve the alembic covertly then it would be up to the diplomats to figure out the best solution.

Although the head of the Shu'ta Valley was only a half mile from the shoreline of Lake Nasser, Mercer decided to use a boat rather than an aircraft to reach the sunken tomb. They needed to bring a lot of equipment and he didn't trust any of the charter flight companies to keep their activities secret.

Booker had gone out first thing this morning to find them a suitable vessel.

"What is it?" Mercer asked.

Booker smiled broadly. "Hope you're keeping a running tab on what the government owes you 'cause the only thing that would work for us is a Riva."

Mercer was familiar with the Italian luxury boat builder and could just imagine the rental price. "How bad?"

"She's a sixty-foot Mercurius. Sleeps four and has a compressor for refilling scuba tanks, provided extra, of course. According to the lease agent she has a top speed of forty knots and was only available because the German couple who had rented it this week ran into a little difficulty when the husband found the wife in bed with his business partner. And because we don't want to use the owner's crew, the price is a paltry two grand a day."

Cali winced. "Admiral Lasko will need to be awfully creative explaining this during his next budget hearing."

Mercer slipped on his sunglasses. "When can we leave?"

"They're topping the tanks right now."

They checked out of the hotel, putting the three rooms on Mercer's Amex, and took the ferry to Aswân's riverfront corniche, where hawkers immediately tried selling them statues, postcards, T-shirts, and assorted tourist geegaws. There was a taxi stand near the main post office. Ten minutes later they were passing the Aswân High Dam, a two-mile-long concrete behemoth that held back the waters of the Nile.

Built at a cost of a billion dollars in the 1960s, it was financed partly by the Soviet Union in a political ploy to curry favor in the region and partly from revenue generated by the Egyptians' seizure of the Suez Canal. To make way for the fifteen-hundred-square-mile lake it would create, nearly a hundred thousand Nubians in northern

Sudan and southern Egypt were relocated, often to unsustainable lands. Twenty ancient temples and shrines were disassembled and rebuilt above the flood mark, the most famous being Abu Simbel far to the south and the Temple of Philae near Aswân. Countless more ancient sites were left for the inundation, and an unknown number more would remain undiscovered because of the project.

While the dam did its job of preventing the Nile from flooding its banks and wiping out villages all along its length, it had also prevented nutrient-rich sediment from reaching farms, necessitating the import of a million tons of fertilizer per year. The fragile Nile Delta was being slowly eroded away without the replenishment of dirt from the interior of Africa, and salt contamination from the Mediterranean had reached as far south as Cairo.

Ten miles south of the dam they came to a marina. Mercer paid off the driver while Booker hauled their luggage from the trunk. The waters of Lake Nasser were deep blue and still, hemmed in by desert hills sprinkled with the occasional palm. It reminded Mercer of Lake Powell in Utah where the Columbia River had been penned behind the Glen Canyon Dam. It wasn't yet

ten in the morning but the sun was a sizzling torture baking the dry earth.

The Egyptian leasing agent greeted
Booker like a long lost brother and ordered
two marina workers to lug their bags to the
jetty. Amid the houseboats, water-ski run-
abouts, and hundred-foot tourist cruise
ships, the Riva looked like a thoroughbred
in a herd of Shetland ponies.

She was beamy but her long, rakish lines
made her look like a javelin. She had a small
dive platform at her transom, a white inflatable, and an open cockpit over the main
salon. Her hull was a deep black while her
upperworks and radar arch over the cockpit
were snowy white. With a pair of MAN
1300 horsepower engines under her deck
Mercer didn't doubt her speed. She looked
like she was already on plane just sitting
tied to the dock. Her name, *Isis,* was painted
in gold at her bows.

Cali pecked Booker on the cheek and
threw Mercer a look. "Now, you know how
to treat a lady. Mercer would have gone for
that rowboat over there."

"Yeah, and made me row," Book laughed.

"I won't tolerate a mutiny until we're at
least on the boat."

The slick leasing agent led them aboard
and showed them the highlights. He demon-

strated how to remove the little inflatable from its concealed garage, as well as the compressor and all the dive equipment. The interior of the motor yacht was as elegant as the outside, with sleek leather furniture, marble in the two baths, and silk sheets on the beds. The galley was small but functional and the refrigerator was packed. They were shown where extra stores were hidden in secret compartments throughout the salon. Mercer said he was satisfied when he found an assortment of liquor in one of the cabinets.

The agent had a wireless point-of-sale device and happily swiped Mercer's card. If he had any questions about two men and a single woman going out for a week alone on a floating bordello he kept them to himself.

"Just think of all the airline miles you're racking up," Booker said.

"When this is all said and done I'll have enough for a flight on the space shuttle."

The master's cabin in the bow had a queen-sized bed and private bath. Cali staked it for herself. Book had already tossed his bag into the other large cabin, leaving Mercer with a single bed tucked into a tiny room in a corner. Booker laughed at him and nodded at the closed master suite door. "Damn, man, just go in there and do it already."

He grinned ruefully. "I've got the feeling if your sorry ass wasn't here I'd be invited."

Booker shook his head and went for the stairs leading to the main deck, muttering, "Crazy white people."

Mercer threw his duffel onto his bed and changed into shorts and a Penn State T-shirt. Cali emerged from her stateroom as he was about to join Booker. She wore sandals, a brief pair of shorts, and a bikini top. Her red hair fell over her shoulders in a shimmering cascade. It was the most revealing Mercer had ever seen her and his imagination hadn't done her body justice. Though her breasts were small, they were perfectly shaped and proportional to her lean torso, and her legs seemed to stretch forever. Her skin was flawlessly smooth and freckled.

"I'm sorry about the sleeping arrangements," she said shyly. "It's just with Booker here . . . you know I wouldn't feel comfortable."

"That's okay," Mercer said, stepping close enough to smell the tropical sunscreen she'd already applied. "If I didn't bring you to a screaming orgasm in the first five seconds he'd never let me hear the end of it."

She slapped him playfully. "Pig."

The leasing agent was still on the dock, and without ever taking his eyes off Cali he managed to cast off the lines when Mercer fired the Riva's engines.

After the engines had come up to temperature Mercer bumped the throttles and eased the motor yacht from her berth. There was a lot of boat traffic around the marina, fishing boats mostly and a little cruise ship coming back from its regular six-day excursion to Abu Simbel. Mercer kept his speed to ten knots, working the wheel to get used to how the boat responded. It came as no surprise she was as nimble as a JetSki.

A few tourists waved as they passed, while fishermen either ignored them all together or eyed them with ill-disguised contempt. When the boat traffic thinned as they reached the broad lake, Mercer began to edge the throttles. The big boat reacted instantly as vessel and master tested each other, and the more Mercer asked for the more the Riva wanted to give, until they were planing across the water at thirty-eight knots.

He could hear Cali's laughter chiming over the bellow of the engines and the wind whipping past them. "I love boats," she screamed. Her upper chest and throat were

flushed, her lips had plumped and reddened, and her eyes had gone startlingly
wide. The adrenaline rush of speed had
obviously aroused her. Mercer felt it too
and once again he cursed Booker's presence. He looked over his shoulder. Booker
had also noticed and he shot Mercer a
cocky wink.

They stayed well out of the regular shipping lanes used by the tourist boats, so it
seemed they had the lake to themselves.
Mercer took lunch at the helm, enjoying the
chunks of flatbread smeared with hummus
Cali fed him. And while beer had first been
perfected in Egypt thousands of years ago,
there were no modern breweries in the
Muslim country so he settled for an Italian
Peroni from the fridge to wash it down.

Booker and Cali took turns spelling Mercer at the wheel as the day wore on. She'd
put on loose cotton pants and a top to
protect herself from the sun, a baseball cap
taming her wind-tossed hair.

At six thirty they turned westward as if
chasing after the sun as it sank toward the
barren horizon. It painted the desert surrounding the large bay they were entering,
in a hundred hues of red and purple. Mercer
thought Cali looked especially beautiful in
its scarlet glow.

According to the boat's GPS the Sha'ta valley was at the end of a long bay that cut into the Nubian Desert like a dagger. The coastline was mostly sandstone bluffs that fell into the lake. There were no inhabitants in this region, no sign that anyone had ever lived here, and the sparse vegetation clinging to the hills, sage and camel thorn, could only survive by absorbing evaporation off the lake. They were entering an area as desolate as the moon and one even less well studied.

With five miles to go Mercer inexplicably throttled back the engines.

"Why are you slowing?" Cali asked.

He pointed ahead. Coming out of the sun, another boat was cutting across the water toward them. At this range it was impossible to tell what type of boat, but Mercer doubted the occupants were fishermen or tourists.

"You know that scene in horror movies where someone always says they've got a bad feeling about this?"

"Yeah."

"I've got a bad feeling about this."

Booker came up from the galley where he was throwing together their dinner. "We there?"

"We've got company."

"Poli?"

"Possibly. He had time to take pictures of the stele when Dayce's men were tearing that village apart. And this is the last place on earth he can get his hands on natural plutonium."

"How do you want to play this?" Book asked.

Mercer ducked below the dash so the men approaching wouldn't see him. "Poli doesn't know about you so maybe seeing a black face will throw them. You two are tourists just cruising the lake on your honeymoon. I'm going to hide." He crawled to the stairs at the stern of the Riva and vanished.

Booker put his arm around Cali when the other boat was a hundred yards off. It was a twenty-five-foot speedboat painted a military gray. There were two men in uniforms aboard, and from his high vantage Booker could see they had pistol belts strapped around their waists.

One said something that was carried away by the wind, and made a gesture for Booker to cut the power. He idled the big engines to a low gurgle.

"S'up, man?" Sykes called down, sounding like a hip-hop artist.

The helmsman spoke in Arabic again.

"I ain't diggin' your rap, man. Speak English."

"There is military training in area. You must leave."

Booker looked around the deserted shoreline and said, "I don't see no trainin', man."

"How many are aboard your vessel?"

"Just me and my ho."

The two boats had drifted close enough for one of the uniformed Egyptians to leap onto the dive platform.

"What the fu' you think you're doin'?" Booker shouted.

The man still on the patrol boat pulled the automatic from his holster and pointed it up at Book's head. Booker raised his hands, smiling now. "It's cool, man. It's cool. No need to draw down on me. You want to have a look at the boat, you take your sweet time."

The soldier who'd jumped aboard looked through the salon, peering into closets and under beds. He checked the two shower stalls and any storage bin large enough to hide a man. And while the Riva was a large boat, its open floor plan meant his search only took a minute. He emerged once again, climbed up to the flybridge, glaring at Booker and Cali, then descended and leapt back to the patrol boat. He spoke briefly with the helmsman, shaking his head. The helmsman brought a radio to his lips and spoke for a moment.

When he was finished he shouted back up to Booker. "You will leave now."

Booker flashed another wide smile. "You got it, bro."

He rammed the throttles almost to their stops and spun the wheel. The powerful wake rocked the smaller Egyptian boat, forcing the two men aboard to clutch the railing to keep from being tossed overboard. Booker eased back on the power and kept his attention straight ahead while Cali surreptitiously studied the patrol craft. It lingered for a couple of minutes where they had met, presumably to make sure someone hadn't jumped from the Riva to elude detection. It then took off in the opposite direction, to wherever they maintained their picket line.

Mercer reappeared well after they were out of range of the patrol craft. "We're still alive, so it went okay, huh?"

"Where were you hiding?" Cali asked. "I heard the soldier check everywhere down there."

"The garage for the inflatable on the stern. He walked right over me, didn't even know it could open. What do you make of them?"

"They claimed they were conducting military maneuvers in the area, but they weren't regular army."

Cali shot him a look. "Really? Could have fooled me."

"The Egyptian Army patterns their uniforms on the British. These guys were wearing U.S. issue BDUs and neither of them had any rank insignia and their gun belts didn't match. Also their boat was a civilian craft painted gray. I could still see the white of her hull along the water line."

Mercer went quiet for a moment. Their plan to sneak in and out was blown. Once again Poli had beaten him to the prize. For all he knew the one-eyed mercenary had had a team working in the desert since right after he saw the stele. They could be moments away from finding Alexander's tomb and the deadly alembic.

"We need to see what's going on up there."

"Say again," Poli repeated into his handheld radio.

"There were two people on the boat," the patrol leader said over the crackling communications link. "A man and woman."

"What was their nationality?"

"American."

"Mercer," Poli hissed under his breath. "Was the man about six feet tall, muscular but not big, with dark hair and gray eyes?"

"No. He was much bigger. Almost two meters. Very muscled. And he had black skin, a kaffir."

Feines wasn't sure how he felt. In a way, he was disappointed it wasn't Mercer. Surely he had realized the significance of the stele and gone back to photograph it and have the writing translated. That would lead him straight here. Could it be the American had given up?

"You're sure no one else was aboard?" he

asked the guard out on the lake.

"Yes, Tawfiq searched very careful."

"Okay, let them go and tell them not to return."

"Yes, sir."

Poli clipped the radio back onto his belt. Around him was a small tent city, housing for the fifty workers and guards Mohammad bin Al-Salibi had arranged. Most were Saudis or Iraqis who'd been trained at Al Qaida camps in Pakistan and Syria. Poli had gained their fear if not their respect his first day here when one of the guards spat at his feet when he was given an order. Feines had summarily shot the man on the spot, telling the others through his translator that the guard hadn't been a martyr, just an insolent fool who should have seen Poli as an ally, not the enemy.

When it became clear that the attack on Novorossiysk had failed to produce the desired results, Salibi had practically begged for Poli to find the Alembic of Skenderbeg for him. The Saudi's pleas did nothing to move him, but with the promise of an additional twenty million dollars Feines had agreed, telling Salibi that there were no guarantees.

He'd made his way to Odessa, where he caught a flight to Cairo. Salibi had given him the name of an Al Qaida operative who could put together everything they would need, including finding a translator to decipher the photographs he'd taken of the stele. Of course the academic had to be killed to ensure his silence. The biggest delay had been finding men with scuba experience once they realized the tomb was under Lake Nasser.

Now that they were here they found that diving wouldn't be necessary. Sometime in the five centuries since Skenderbeg's men had returned the alembic to Alexander's tomb, an earthquake had cracked the sandstone hills that once towered over the flooded Shu'ta Valley. Many of these fractures were mere cracks in the earth, but there was a long gouge that extended up from the lake. The feature was too straight to be a natural phenomenon. Poli recognized immediately that there was a tunnel rising up from the bottom of the valley and the quake had collapsed part of its roof. He set teams of men to begin digging at the top of the depression where he believed the tunnel's ceiling had remained intact. Already they had dug down six feet.

Just offshore, the boat he'd planned to use as a dive platform, a forty-foot houseboat they'd bought in Aswân, sat quiet. They'd also bought two outboard boats to act as pickets to keep fishermen and others from the area.

Poli saw Mohammad bin Al-Salibi emerge from one of the tents. With his darkly handsome features and traditional white robes, he cut a dashing figure. The men all stopped as he passed, greeting him with deference or touching the hem of his robe. They might all be fanatics, but they knew who the money man was.

"Who was that on the radio?" Salibi asked.

"Picketboat stopped a yacht about five miles from here. Just some tourists."

"Ah." Salibi looked around the encampment. They'd accomplished an amazing amount of work in just a short time. All the tents were up, the kitchen was putting out meals, and the men had already settled into their routines. "So how long do you think this will take?"

"I do not know. The tunnel may be under another inch of sand or another fifty feet. It is possible I am wrong all together which means I will have to dive and look for the cave's entrance. You have to be prepared for the likelihood that it has been buried by the earthquake and may never be found."

"Allah will bless us, I know it." Salibi gazed out across the bay and continued in a dreamy voice, "We failed in Novorossiysk because the plan displeased Him. It wasn't a blow worthy of our abilities. When you find the alembic we will strike at the very heart of our problem."

"Yeah, and what's that?" Poli asked, curious at the depths of depravity Salibi was capable of. He fully understood that the Saudi was doing this for political gain and economic advantage and not for some religious cause, but how he could warp his motivations to convince himself he was doing God's bidding was fascinating.

"Turkey is the key. Their leaders are all godless secularists who care nothing for *Sharia,* the blessed laws of Islam. If we can make the people see that their government will not protect them they will rise up, throw off the yoke of Western influence, and embrace their faith."

Poli thought to himself, thereby giving you the ability to cut off the million barrels a day that flows across the country in pipelines and use the Bosporus as a choke point to prevent tankers from entering the Black Sea.

"This is about saving the souls of the Turks because they believe women should have rights and that the church and state should be separate.

"This is about freeing a people and letting them know God's love. I wish I could join the martyrs who will die in Istanbul for their glorious deaths will lead to a revolution that will see Islam elevated to its rightful place."

"You plan to use the plutonium against Istanbul?"

"Yes. It will be like in Russia, only this time we will not fail."

Feines gave a little thought to the fourteen million people who lived in the city straddling the Bosporus and shrugged. "Whatever makes you happy."

In a secluded bay twenty miles from where they'd been stopped Mercer killed the Riva's engine and dropped the anchor. The silence seemed to rush in on them after so many hours on the loud boat. They'd already made their plans and used a satellite phone to appraise Ira Lasko of the situation. He agreed they should reconnoiter the head of the bay before bringing anything to the President.

Dinner was subdued as they ate in the cozy dining nook. After the meal they changed into dark clothes. Mercer wondered if subconsciously they'd all known this could happen, because each of them had brought clothing suitable for a night operation. They waited another hour for the last rays of the sun to be snuffed out before hauling the small inflatable raft from the stern garage.

With the three of them plus one set of diving gear it was a snug fit and the little rubber boat sank almost to the gunwales. Their only weapons were a four-inch dive knife and a two-pound hammer Booker had found in the Riva's tool box.

Using a handheld GPS they motored to within two miles of where they'd been stopped by the guards. Book was at the controls. He slowed the little dinghy to an idle and they crept forward another mile.

"This is good," Mercer whispered. Book drove the inflatable onto a beach and he and Mercer dragged it out of the water.

"Bring the tanks or leave them?"

There was sixty pounds of equipment to lug another couple of miles over the rough desert but with three of them they could spread the load. "Leave 'em for now. We can always come back later."

They walked single file and widely spaced. With his years of military experience Booker took point, and Mercer had the drag slot. Book took them inland about a half mile in case Poli had men watching the shore. With the GPS there was no chance they could get lost. The ground was mostly sand and small rocks, easy enough in the daylight, but a misplaced step could turn an ankle and it wasn't until the landscape was bathed in the milky glow of the half-moon that they started to making time.

There were no sounds except the gentle wind and their own careful footfalls.

An hour into the march Book raised his hand and lowered himself to the ground. Such was his skill that it was as if he'd vanished. Mercer had seen the spot where he had been standing a second earlier but now there was no sign of his friend. He and Cali paced forward in a crouch until they came to a shallow wadi that hadn't seen a flood in a century. Peering over the far bank of the old streambed, Mercer saw the moon's reflection on the lake, a dancing white line that stretched to the horizon. Nearer, he saw lights and quickly made out an encampment. He counted a dozen tents. Anchored near the shore was a speedboat identical to the one Book said the guards had used, and a larger boat farther out in the bay. It looked like there was a guard aboard it manning a heavy machine gun.

The sounds of men talking wafted above the rumble of a generator.

Book handed Mercer the binoculars he'd

been carrying.

Looking closer, he spotted armed men on patrol walking the perimeter of the compound and another guard stationed near the speedboat. A few men sat in a loose circle listening to another. By the listeners' expressions Mercer could see the speaker held them spellbound.

"Nothing short of an air strike is going to take them all out," Booker whispered, his mouth so close to Mercer's ear he could feel his breath.

Mercer just nodded. He was looking at a spot where Poli's men were digging into the side of the hill that rose at the head of the bay. The excavation was lit by floodlights and the men worked in teams hauling buckets of sand and loose dirt from the hole. Mercer saw that their work was at the apex of a straight trench that ran down to the water's edge. By mentally extending the line, Mercer realized it went directly to the bottom of the valley, exactly where the stele said they'd find the entrance to Alexander's tomb. He thought back to his visit to Egypt years earlier. He'd toured the Valley of the Kings with Salome and he recalled that the ancient Egyptians had dug long tunnels into the mountains in order to bury their pharaohs. He imagined what the Shu'ta Valley would have looked like before the Aswân Dam had filled it with water. It would have mildly resembled the fabled burial place of Egypt's kings, so was it possible that Alexander's men had ordered the excavation of a tunnel, only instead of descending into the mountains, his had risen from the valley floor.

"They're going to have the alembic by tomorrow or the next day," he said softly and explained his suspicions. "For a tunnel collapse to show on the surface like that it can't be more than ten or fifteen feet deep."

"What are we going to do?"

"That'll be up to Ira. There's nothing the three of us can do against that army down there."

"What if there were more than three?"

The voice had come from behind them. Mercer whirled around, bringing up the knife in a lightning move. Ibriham Ahmad had approached so silently that even Booker hadn't heard him. He wore his trademark black suit even in the desert, though he prudently wore a dark shirt and tie. Behind him were five more men. They wore dark camouflage and combat harnesses loaded with ammunition pouches. All carried several high-tech automatic weapons. Mercer recognized Ahmad's protégé, Devrin

Egemen. The young man bobbed his head shyly in greeting when he met Mercer's gaze. Even bedecked with an arsenal of weaponry, Mercer couldn't see the young scholar as a fighter.

"I should have known you'd find a way," Ahmad told Mercer. His admiration was clear even though he whispered.

"And I should have known you lied to me about not knowing the location of Alexander's tomb." Somehow Mercer wasn't surprised Ahmad was here. "How long have you been here?"

"I've had two men camped above the tomb's entrance since Feines first approached me months ago. I myself arrived this afternoon."

"You know he's going to find the tomb quickly."

Ahmad looked shamefaced. "I never realized the significance of that trench until Poli started digging. I had hoped to bring more men but we are attacking tonight."

"Are you out of your mind?" Cali hissed. "There are fifty or sixty of them and only six of you."

"Caribe Dayce had more than a hundred," Ahmad replied.

Mercer remembered the savagery of that counterattack as he and Cali awaited execution. And he estimated Dayce had at least a hundred and fifty fighters. Ahmad's team had killed them to a man in minutes. "That was just the six of you?" He couldn't believe it.

"Actually Devrin was in Istanbul. We were only five. Dr. Mercer, the Janissaries are a military order. We've trained for warfare our entire lives."

"Mercer told me about what you did in Africa," Booker said. "Taking out a bunch of drunk and drugged up teenagers isn't the same as going up against fifty battle-hardened terrorists."

"We don't have a choice," Ahmad said simply. "This ends now."

"It's suicide," Cali said. "You know what these fanatics are capable of. They'll blow themselves up if they think they can get just one of you."

"He's right, Cali," Mercer said. "There's no other option." He couldn't believe what he was about to say when he turned back to Ahmad. "I'm in. What's your plan?"

Before Ahmad could outline his strategy there was a loud cry from Poli's camp. Everyone in the wadi looked to where the workers were digging into the hillside. Several of them were dancing in tight circles, cheering and raising their shovels over their heads in triumph. When nearby guards realized the diggers had succeeded in burrowing down to the tunnel, they fired triumphant bursts of gunfire into the air. One of them ran off toward the tents. Mercer followed him with his eyes. Even before he arrived at one set a little apart from the others, Poli emerged. He was wearing just pants and desert boots. His chest was very pale in the dim light but the breadth of it defied imagination. His arms looked as thick as tree trunks and hung from shoulders as broad as a hangman's gallows. He started jogging up the hill to the excavation.

The man who had been giving a lecture to some of the terrorists stood in a swirl of robes and crossed the desert in Poli's wake.

"Shit. They've broken through."

Ahmad wasn't watching the workers celebrating their success. He studied the man in the robes, his mouth set in a grim line, fiery anger behind his dark eyes. "Al-Salibi."

"That's the guy funding the operation?" Cali asked. "The one who works for OPEC?"

"He is using Islam as a tool to increase his wealth and power," Devrin said with as much hatred as his master.

■ ■ ■ ■

Poli waded into the cheering throng, shouldering aside Qaida fighters until he was at the top of the hole. Al-Salibi joined him a moment later, slapping the big mercenary on the shoulder, a broad smile on his face. Even Feines looked pleased with himself for coming up with this plan to gain easy entrance to the tomb.

"You did it, my friend," Salibi said to congratulate him.

Salibi would never be his friend but Poli let the comment pass.

The hole was four feet square and sand poured over the sides into the darkness. The sides of the tunnel below were dressed with stone laid in neat blocks. Playing the beam of a flashlight over their surfaces Poli could see they were covered in hieroglyphs. He couldn't see the floor of the tunnel because it was flooded, water that must have seeped through the rock over the eons and become trapped. He called for a rope. Once an end had been tied around a nearby boulder, Poli tossed the other end into the fissure. He climbed down using just the strength of his arms. As he reached the still surface, he tentatively lowered himself into the cool water, feeling for the floor with his foot. When he touched bottom the water was as high as his upper chest. The tunnel had to be fifteen feet tall and at least as wide. Aiming his beam downslope he could see the loose rubble of where the roof had partially collapsed. There were gaps in it where the ceiling slabs had only crashed partway to the floor. Pointing the flashlight up the gentle grade the beam of light was swallowed by darkness. The tunnel could climb another two hundred feet before reaching the top of the hill.

He ordered that the construction lights ringing the pit be lowered into the tunnel and for more wire to be readied. He also ordered someone back to his tent for a shirt, his Geiger counter, and a set of scuba tanks in case they needed them. It took ten minutes to get everything in place. Al-Salibi had changed into more practical clothes and joined him in the ancient tunnel along with two of his most trusted fighters.

Every square inch of the walls and the ceiling where it hadn't collapsed were covered in two-thousand-year-old glyphs depicting the Egyptian creation stories and commemorating Alexander's journey through death. The natural pigments were as fresh and vibrant today as the day the master artisans had applied them. One of the fighters nudged his comrade to show him how he could scratch out the faces of the gods with his trench knife. They shared a laugh at the senseless desecration.

Poli tied the scuba tanks to the rope and started up the tunnel carrying one of the halogen lights high over his head. In his wake the shorter Saudis were forced to half walk and half swim to stay with him.

"We have to act now," Ibriham said. "They will load the alembic onto a boat as soon as they bring it to the surface."

"We have a boat of our own."

"You do? Excellent. How long will it take to get it?"

Mercer thought through the timing, added a thirty-minute cushion, and glanced at his watch. "By two A.M."

"The boat might be necessary," Ibriham mused.

Mercer shifted his gaze to Cali. "Can you do it?"

She looked defensive. "Trying to protect me again?"

Mercer was. He didn't want her anywhere near the fighting. They'd been lucky so far but this went beyond anything they'd faced since meeting in Africa. Having her with them when they took on Poli's men wouldn't make a dent in the odds so there was no sense putting her in danger. Then he asked himself if he was doing it for her or him. He remembered Tisa lying bloody in his arms as they were lifted off a sinking ship by a rescue helicopter. She never heard him say he loved her. "Do you really want to be here if our attack fails?"

"Do you?"

"No, but I feel a responsibility here."

"And you don't think I feel it too," Cali shot back.

"Cali, this isn't about protecting you. I lost someone I cared very deeply for. I can't go through that again."

She touched his cheek tenderly. "I'll do it, but Mercer, I'm not her and you can't always be there as my knight in shining armor. Okay?"

"Thank you," was all he could say.

"I'll come charging in at exactly two o'clock."

Ibriham said to her, "If you see one of their boats attempting to escape, stop them." With a whispered order from him, one of his men gave her an automatic pistol while others handed over some of their weapons and ammunition to Mercer and Booker Sykes.

Cali gave Mercer one last look but didn't kiss him. "Good luck."

"You too."

"Man, you've got yourself a handful," Booker remarked quietly after she faded into the darkness with Book's GPS. "She is one fiery redhead."

Mercer said nothing, trying to put the awkward exchange out of his mind and focus on what lay ahead. He didn't care that they were standing feet away from perhaps the greatest treasure in human history, the value of which was incalculable in the monetary sense. Even more important was the insight the tomb would give on perhaps the greatest military mind who ever lived. Alexander the Great had single-handedly drawn the map of the ancient world, establishing boundaries that were still in effect today. All Mercer thought about at that moment was preventing Poli Feines and his sponsor from getting their hands on the Alembic of Skenderbeg. Let the archaeologists have their day when it was over. Tonight was about preventing genocide.

"What's your plan?" he asked Ibriham again.

"Ten minutes before Miss Stowe is to return, we attack the compound."

"What, just a frontal assault?"

Ibriham nodded. Mercer and Book exchanged a look and shook their heads.

Booker said, "We can do better than that."

By one thirty the revelry infecting the camp had yet to die down. Men still talked animatedly as they peered into the hole, no doubt excited by the promise of so much death. Only a few had drifted back to the tents, where they were kept awake by celebratory gunfire. Mercer and Devrin were in position fifty yards from the kitchen while Booker had made his way around the encampment toward the lake's edge. His job was to take out the houseboat. If he failed, the guard on board could turn the camp into a slaughtering ground with the machine gun they'd mounted on the boat's rail.

For the first time in his life Mercer found he was eager for a fight. He wanted revenge on Poli, on Al-Salibi and on the men who thought wholesale destruction was their god's greatest desire. The adrenaline pumping through his body was as familiar and rousing as an addict's drug of choice. Even with the darkness he felt he could see perfectly. He could feel the barest whisper of the breeze against his skin and hear the muted lapping of wavelets on the shore. He could smell the spices from the kitchen as though he were standing at the stove.

The gun Ibriham had given him was a Heckler and Koch HK416, a compact 5.56-millimeter assault carbine with a detachable 40-millimeter grenade launcher. In the pockets of his cargo pants he carried four extra twenty-round magazines and two additional grenades. Although unfamiliar with this particular weapon, he was more than confident of his abilities with it.

He checked his watch for the fifth time in five minutes, more anxious than nervous. Booker would be slipping into the water about now. He looked toward the lake but couldn't see his friend, whose skin blended with the night.

Keeping low so only his eyes appeared above the surface, Booker Sykes moved easily through the water. The houseboat was only fifty yards from shore, and while the gunner was still awake, he wasn't looking around the craft, only at the celebration he was certainly disappointed to miss.

Book cut a wide circle around the boat to come at it from the seaward side. Light spilled from a window on this side of the boxy vessel and he could hear Arab music being played on a cassette deck. He edged closer to the stern, away from the guard. The boat was wooden-hulled and slimy. He reached for the railing that circled the low deck, moving slowly so water didn't drip from his clothes. Rather than heave himself up, he slipped a leg through the railing's stanchions and slowly rolled onto the deck. He made no sound and his motions had been so smooth that his added weight didn't rock the flat-bottomed houseboat.

The square superstructure took up most of the deck space, leaving a narrow catwalk ringing three sides of the boat. Only the back deck, where the machine gunner stood vigil, was open space. Booker padded aft, ducking when he reached the lighted window. Moving a millimeter at a time he positioned himself so he could see through the grimy glass. Two Arabs were at the dining table reading their Korans while a third was asleep on a threadbare sofa.

Booker eased himself down again. He'd expected there would be more than one man on the houseboat, but he hadn't expected four and he didn't know if anyone was asleep in the cabins. During a combat mission Booker was able to keep a precise clock ticking in his head so he knew the time almost to the second. He had two minutes before Ahmad's men broke cover and started their assault.

He didn't know how many men he'd killed in his military career. In just one night in

Mogadishu he estimated a hundred rebels had fallen under his guns, but the ones he remembered, eleven of them, were the ones he'd taken with a blade. His nightmares were filled with every detail of their deaths, from the smell of their last meals to the heat of their blood. He could still feel the stubble on his palm from the sentry he'd taken at a drug lord's hacienda. He could still hear the wheeze of air when he severed the throat of a North Korean sailor guarding a mini-sub packed with explosives. And their eyes. The eyes were always with him, asleep or awake.

Slowly, so it made no more sound than an infant's sigh, he withdrew the knife given to him by one of the Janissaries.

Mercer slithered under the side of the kitchen tent. He'd heard only one man snoring inside. With the moon nearly set, the tent was pitch black. He waited a moment for his eyes to adjust. There was a gentle glow from the stove's pilot light that allowed him to discern the layout of the tent. There were actually two stoves, several large plastic drums of water, and serving tables. A cot was against one wall, a single figure sprawled under the sheet. The cook's clothes lay in a pile next to a small prayer rug. An AK-47 hung from the tent pole.

Moving silently Mercer approached the bed. He found the man's kaffiyeh. He had no idea how to properly wear the traditional headscarf so he just draped it over his head and wrapped the tails to hide his face. He checked his watch. One minute.

Though the man was part of a terrorist cell, he was just a cook. Mercer imagined he'd been given these duties because he wasn't a capable fighter. And no matter how Mercer tried to rationalize it in his head, he simply couldn't kill him in cold blood. So when he smashed the butt of his HK into the man's skull, he checked his swing just enough to render him unconscious. He bound the cook's wrists behind his back with the Kalashnikov's sling and was just about to stuff a greasy rag into his mouth when he sensed motion. He whirled, bringing up his assault rifle, but it was only Devrin.

"You are taking too long." He saw what Mercer had done and quickly strode over to the side of the bed. He looked down at the unconscious cook then glanced at Mercer. "This is why you will never defeat them," he said and unceremoniously plunged a knife into the cook's chest. "They ask for no quarter so you shouldn't give it."

He wiped the blade on the sheet, resheathed the knife, and together they exited the back of the tent.

Booker came to the edge of the superstructure. There was about eight feet of open deck between him and the machine gunner. He had twenty seconds. He crept forward, lifting his feet no more than a fraction of an inch from the Astroturfed deck. Book came to within a foot of the guard and he still hadn't felt his presence. He kept leaning against the rail and watching the celebration on shore. Sykes was grateful he'd never see the Arab's eyes.

He moved no slower or faster in those final seconds, simply took another practiced step and prepared to reach around the guard's head with one hand while the knife in the other was poised to open his throat.

A casual voice called from the open door to the cabin. The guard turned to answer. He saw Booker no more than a foot away. With reflexes honed through decades of training, Booker lashed out even before the guard realized what he was seeing. Sykes drove the blade into the Arab's neck and ripped outward, tearing through muscle and blood vessels so nearly half his throat was slashed open. Blood fountained from the ragged wound, splashing across the deck and into the water.

The man inside called again. Booker let the body fall and tried to swivel the Russian-made fifty-caliber so it pointed at the cabin door, but the gimbal only moved through thirty degrees.

Another guard appeared at the doorway. Booker threw his knife in a desperation toss because the weapon wasn't balanced for throwing. The butt end hit the bridge of the man's nose, breaking the delicate bones. As he reeled back roaring in pain, Booker kicked at the machine gun and grunted when it swung freely. To get the proper angle he had to jump over the rail and hang off the side of the boat. His finger found the trigger as a third guard appeared at the door. Booker was ahead of schedule by eleven seconds but there was no help for that now. He pulled the trigger and the big gun came alive in his hands, empty brass casings arcing into the night. The heavy slugs blew the guard back through the doorway, ripped the door off its hinges, and shredded the cheap wood superstructure.

Unable to see where the other gunman was inside the houseboat, Booker let go of the railing and dangled by his grip on the machine gun. Even with the superior firepower, he knew he was too exposed to counterfire from inside the boat or an astute sniper on shore. He cross-drew the Beretta pistol Ahmad had given him and aimed at the fifty-caliber's ratcheting bolt. Before he pulled the trigger a pair of guns opened up from inside the cabin. There had been more men than Booker had seen. With bullets whizzing by, Book fired five rapid shots. The machine gun fell silent as the bolt jammed in the ruined receiver. The plan had been to use the weapon to cover Ahmad's assault but he had to settle for denying Poli's men from using it themselves. He took a deep breath as he dropped off the boat and began swimming away from the craft a good five feet under the surface so he would create no wake.

As soon as he heard the machine gun out on the houseboat bellowing its deadly tattoo, Mercer started running boldly across the camp. He wasn't dressed exactly like the Arab fighters but he hoped the kaffiyeh would give him anonymity. The men had instantly ended their reverie and reached for their weapons, their gaze directed at the dark houseboat.

Mercer was halfway to the sheltered hole they'd dug down to the tunnel when Ibriham Ahmad's Janissaries engaged. Two of them appeared on the hill above the encampment as if defying the Qaida terrorists. They took down several of the confused men before anyone even saw they were there.

In seconds thirty AK-47s roared as one and the crest of the hill disappeared in a hail of gunfire and kicked up dirt. Mercer could only trust Ahmad's men as they caught the Arab fighters in a withering crossfire. The ground exploded at his feet as bullets flew in every direction. He had another thirty yards to go when the officers began to organize their men behind natural cover positions. Their return fire became more disciplined and Mercer could only detect three of Ahmad's men still in the fight. So far no one had paid him any attention but there were two men guarding the excavation who hadn't left their posts. They stiffened as Mercer came closer.

He tried to shield his face but the wary men started to raise their weapons. Mercer kept on running, gesturing wildly and shouting gibberish. His ruse worked to a point. Neither man fired, but neither did they lower their assault rifles. Mercer was five feet away from them when he staggered. As he pretended to trip he swung the barrel of his HK just enough to put a round through one of the guard's chest. The other man reacted a fraction slow and Mercer rammed into him with all his strength.

The two of them crashed to the ground just at the edge of the pit, with their guns sandwiched between them. Their faces were inches apart. Mercer could see the mad fanaticism in the other man's eyes, like the glassy stare of a fever patient. The terrorist shouted something about Allah and fired his AK.

The heat as the gun discharging seared the flesh of Mercer's stomach and the blood that pooled between them was as viscous as oil. The guard's mouth split into a filthy smile but then his expression changed. Mercer nimbly pushed himself off the terrorist. His clothing was sodden with blood but apart from the burned skin he was unharmed. The guard looked down the length of his body and saw the barrel of his assault rifle pointing up into his own chest. In seconds the murderous light faded from his eyes. In an attempt to kill them both he'd only managed to commit suicide.

"You can't be a martyr if you don't kill your enemy," Mercer said and heaved himself over the precipice into the tunnel.

He'd been prepared to hit the water

because he'd seen Poli bring dive equipment, but he nearly impaled himself on the scuba gear dangling from the rope. The sound of the raging gun battle was muted by the stonework. Even when he heard a grenade explode, it was little more than the sound of distant thunder.

With no light to guide him, Mercer started up the long tunnel, keeping the HK over his head. After twenty feet he couldn't hear the fighting at all, which meant Poli and Salibi didn't know about the assault, preserving his element of surprise.

He'd gone fifty yards when he tripped over a set of steps hidden under the water. As he climbed, he became aware of light ahead, a ghost's glow as feeble as a guttering candle. His hands unconsciously tightened on his rifle.

He left the water completely at the top of the stairs and saw that the tunnel turned ninety degrees. Mercer approached cautiously, peering around the corner with his cheek almost touching the floor.

This had to have been as much wire as Poli had brought, because the powerful flood lamp sat in the middle of a vast chamber. The ceiling lofted thirty feet over Mercer's head, supported by tight ranks of sandstone columns fashioned in the shape of palm trees. It was typical Ancient Egyptian architecture. They knew they didn't need that many supports for the ceiling, but the design was to depict a dense and bountiful forest. The sides of the room were hidden in shadow but the parts close enough for Mercer to see were covered in hieroglyphs.

Straining to hear anything, Mercer almost laughed aloud when he thought the immense space was as silent as a tomb.

He slid into the chamber, keeping close to the walls. He had passed twenty columns when he spotted something glinting in the darkness. Mercer forgot himself for a moment as he stared at the object. It was a marble statue of a man holding a short sword in his right hand. In the other was a ball of rope that had been sliced in two. Mercer realized this was Alexander the Great after he had cut the impossible to untie Gordian Knot, fulfilling the prophesy that he would one day rule Asia.

He continued on. On the opposite wall from where he'd entered was another open portal. Wavering light spilled from the next room of the tomb complex.

The room was smaller than the first, the ceiling a bit lower, and there weren't as many columns. Flames danced atop several low bronze braziers. The oil that Poli had poured from the earthen amphorae could still burn after twenty centuries. As stunned as Mercer had been by the statue, this room revealed something even more remarkable. He immediately thought of Chester Bowie and his crazy ideas.

There were eight dioramas set up in the room, each one depicting a different monster from mythology. A towering, man-shaped giant had a rib cage made of some large animal, a horse or cow, but its head Mercer realized was the pelvic bone of a creature he wasn't familiar with, a prehistoric cave bear or maybe some kind of giant sloth. He recognized the skeleton of a griffin, a fabled creature with the body of a lion and the head of an eagle. The body was that of a large extinct cat, but its eagle head was the armored frill of a triceratops. Beyond it Alexander's artisans had created a three-headed snake. The heads were from some kind of dinosaur, like a raptor or another flesh eater. The teeth were four inches long.

Everything was held together with bronze braces and wire, as expertly assembled as anything in a natural history museum today.

Bowie had been right that the creatures out of mythology were the ancients' way of making sense of the bones they'd discovered of animals that had long ago gone extinct. They didn't know what parts fit with what so they made it up as they went along, producing fantastical creations and the stories to go along with them.

Mercer wasn't sure what impressed him more — the imagination it took to put together such marvelous creatures or the fact that an obscure professor from New Jersey had figured out the truth.

There came a sudden jolt and bits of sand rained from the ceiling. Mercer shook his head to bring himself back to reality. Something massive had exploded on the surface and for a moment he was sure Cali had arrived, only to have the Riva blown out of the water by an RPG. But the explosion had been much closer, and for it to shake the ground it couldn't have occurred on the water. He heard voices from the next chamber. He moved behind one of the dioramas, a massive skeleton with elephant tusks for ribs.

Seconds later a terrorist with a thick beard hurried past carrying a flashlight, heading for the exit tunnel. Mercer waited in the shadows for him to return. He came back a minute later, sprinting through the gallery and into the next room, shouting incoherent Arabic as he ran.

"In English!" Mercer heard Poli roar.

Mercer could barely hear the words. "Someone has collapsed the tunnel. We are trapped."

On shore about two hundred yards from the Al Qaida camp, Booker had cached the machine pistol given to him by a Janissary. He climbed out of the lake and found the weapon hidden in a tangle of dried grasses just as a searchlight on the houseboat snapped on. The beam turned the darkened shore into daylight just a few feet from him. A second gunman kept his weapon trained on the ground illuminated by the light.

There was nothing Book could do about the wet trail he'd left on the beach, so he waited, more exposed than he'd have liked. The beam brushed past the wet sand, paused, and returned. The two men on the bow of the houseboat jabbered excitedly, pointing. A third man emerged from a door that led to the pilothouse. All three raised their weapons.

Book fired first. The range was long for the stubby machine pistol and rounds just sprayed the boat randomly. Their return fire was much more accurate. He dove to his right to get away from where his fire had at-tracted their aim. Bullets peppered the ground all around him as he combat rolled a dozen times, never losing his bearings. His movements kept giving away his location on the open beach, and the firing intensified.

Sykes knew he didn't have a prayer.

A streak of light shot from the hill above the camp, followed by a sharp whistle. The rocket-propelled grenade fell a little short of the houseboat, hitting the lake at its side in an eruption of water that doused the three fighters. Book used the distraction to lunge to his feet and start running.

The terrorist he'd seen manning the light saw him dash into the darkness and opened fire again, walking his bullets up Booker's trail. He felt a bullet pass between his legs, knew the next one was coming for his spine, and threw himself to the left. He hit the rocky earth, rolled once, and was back on his feet in an instant, but the torn muscles in his back sent searing lances of pain radiating in all directions. His attempt to sprint away from the lake was little more than a drunken hobble and he came under fire almost immediately.

A second RPG slashed through the night, flying in a flat trajectory that sent it into the houseboat just aft of the bridge. It exploded and the houseboat disintegrated. The superstructure was peeled apart like an orange, fire erupting from the jagged seams as chunks of wood and metal rained down across the lake. Two of the gunmen were killed instantly, their backs flayed open by shrapnel. The third was blown off the boat and could have survived had there not been thirty pounds of rusted chain lodged in his abdomen. He hit the water and sank like a stone.

Booker turned and started limping back toward the compound. The battle was the most intense he'd ever seen. The two sides were exchanging fire at a staggering pace. He ultimately knew it was unsustainable. The Janissaries had only brought what they could carry — at most a couple hundred rounds each. Poli's men had arrived with a near limitless supply. The simple truth was the Janissaries would be out of ammunition long before the Qaida forces.

He paused behind some cover to study the killing field. There were still twenty men firing up into the hills and he could see an officer organizing a patrol of another ten men to try to outflank the Janissaries. Of Ahmad's troop of six he was only sure that three were still in the fight. Then he spotted a fourth. It was Ibriham himself. Somehow he'd found a gap in the Qaida perimeter and was crawling toward the excavated section of tunnel. From the Turk's perspective he couldn't see that there were two new men guarding the hole. He'd stumble right into them blindly.

Behind Booker was a twenty-foot sandstone cliff. He slung the machine pistol over his shoulder, reached for a handhold, and hauled himself off the beach. The agony in his back was like a hot coal lodged in his spine. He gritted his teeth against it, lifting himself another eighteen inches on stubbornness alone. Sheets of sweat bathed his body and he could feel tears rolling down his cheeks.

He found another toehold, braced himself for the pain, and lifted himself higher up the sandstone face. Nauseous saliva flooded his mouth and a whimper escaped his lips. Fearing he was doing permanent damage to his body, Booker thrust aside concerns for himself and fought on. It took him five minutes to scale the cliff and when he rolled over the top he wanted to lie there and let the pain wash over him.

Instead he got to his feet and surveyed the battle from his elevated perch. A pile of dirt was all that separated Ahmad from the men guarding the pit and still he hadn't seen them. The range was nearly three hundred and fifty yards. Booker's massive chest heaved and his heart was racing. He raised the machine pistol but his hands shook so badly he couldn't get a sight picture.

One of the guards spotted Ibriham. He pointed and was going for his weapon.

"Dear Jesus, don't fail me now." Book tensed every muscle in his body for a second, drew down again, and opened fire, letting instinct guide his aim.

The first two rounds went wide. The third drilled the guard through the thigh, spinning him in place and dropping him. The fourth and fifth hit the second guard center mass, the bullets slowed enough that they ricocheted through his body, shredding his internal organs. Book put the sixth through the wounded guard's head just as Ahmad rolled over the pile of excavated earth.

He didn't acknowledge his guardian angel. He fumbled with a knapsack he'd carried to the pit and disappeared down the hole, leaving the bag behind.

Booker knew that Cali should be arriving any second, and even as he thought it he looked up the dark bay and could see the white of the Riva's upper hull. She had idled the boat far enough out so she could react to a speedboat coming from the encampment, but not too close to draw attention.

As much as he knew she wanted to be in the fight, she knew how to take orders and do her job.

He had turned back to study the battle and see where he needed to help the attack, when the knapsack Ahmad had left near the tunnel entrance exploded. The bag had to have contained thirty pounds of plastic explosives because the blast was massive. The fireball lit the head of the bay like a second sun as it climbed into the night. Fighters within fifty feet of the explosion were killed by the concussion scrambling their insides. Others a little farther were scythed down by debris, their bodies lying as limp as rag dolls.

In the fading light of the diminishing fireball Booker could see that the tunnel entrance had been obliterated. Ahmad had sealed the tomb to prevent Poli's escape.

Poli and Salibi emerged from the farthest reaches of the tomb complex to see for themselves. The two guards followed in their wake. Mercer couldn't guarantee taking them all so he let them go. As soon as they retreated to the first room, he dashed into the space where they'd been.

The oil lamps burning all around the chamber revealed it to be smaller still. And unlike the others, there were just a few columns. Instead the room was filled with the possessions Alexander would need in the afterlife. There were boats made of wood and reeds, tents, and furniture. There were several chariots and countless chests that would contain such household items as bowls and utensils. Unlike Tutankhamen's tomb, there was very little gold, for Alexander hadn't been a man bent on material wealth. Instead his tomb was filled with all manner of weapons — swords by the hundreds, javelins and lances, shields and helmets as well as bows and slings. Alexander's generals had provided him everything he would require to outfit the army he would need for his military conquest of heaven.

Mercer wouldn't let his attention focus on the golden sarcophagus sitting on a raised dais at the front of the room, with its panels of rock crystal shaved so fine they were as transparent as glass, or the mummified body within. Instead he looked at the large bronze drum that had been taken down from a niche in the wall. Its surface was dented and pitted from having been dragged all over the ancient world and later used in battles in Europe.

The Alembic of Skenderbeg was about six

feet tall and four wide and was covered in Ancient Greek script. The two chambers were separated by a complicated mechanism that prevented the active plutonium from coalescing. There was something ominous about the device that went beyond Mercer's knowledge of what it did. He sensed the alembic as a presence in the room with him, not alive exactly but aware. He could tell that it wanted to be found, that it wanted to be taken from this place so it could unleash its deadly radiation on a new world. The hairs on Mercer's arms stood erect when he realized he was in the presence of pure evil.

The sound of gunfire echoed through the tomb. Mercer whirled as one of the guards burst into the burial chamber. Mercer was a fraction of a second slow reaching for his assault carbine. The guard fired a snap burst from his AK-47. The rounds stitched Alexander's sarcophagus, shattering the delicate panes of crystal and powdering the mummified remains.

Mercer dove as the string of bullets cut through the air toward him, and came up hard against the wheels of a chariot. He slithered under the ornate vehicle as the terrorist started taking better aim. The filigreed wood splintered as it was savaged by the assault. Mercer got to his knees and fired through the spoked wheel, catching the gunman in the legs. The guard kept his finger on the trigger as he fell. The wild spray tore apart more of the chariot and sparked off the stone floor where Mercer knelt. His HK virtually exploded in his hands when a lucky bullet slammed into the receiver. The AK-47 fell silent when the bolt came down on an empty chamber. The terrorist had fired through the entire magazine.

Mercer jumped to his feet before the guard could reload. He snatched a short sword from the pile nearby and vaulted over the chariot. For a moment he didn't understand what the wounded guard was doing. The object in his hands wasn't the distinctive curve of a Kalashnikov magazine. It was round. Then he saw the beatific smile. The guard yanked the pin of the grenade and held it to his chest.

Mercer had five seconds and knew it wouldn't be enough to get clear of the blast radius. He rushed forward and without pause swung the sword down onto the prone figure. The ancient weapon held a keen edge and the terrorist's head jumped free in an eruption of blood and escaping air.

Mercer scooped the grenade from his lifeless fingers and with an underhanded toss flipped it over the sarcophagus. The explosion destroyed the rest of the priceless casket and sent Alexander's remains into the air like so much dust, but the blast wave passed harmlessly over Mercer where he lay with his head cradled in his arms.

He got up and blinked, the gunfire in the next room sounding distant to his tortured hearing. He shot a concerned look at the alembic and breathed a sigh when he saw it hadn't been hit by the fragmentation grenade. He grabbed the fallen Kalashnikov and searched the corpse for more magazines, cursing when he realized the man hadn't been carrying any.

Alexander's burial chamber was a storehouse of state-of-the-art weapons for their day but they were worthless against automatic rifles. Mercer could only hope that however many Janissaries followed him into the tunnel could take care of the remaining three killers. Then he saw the bows.

One in particular caught his eye; the wood was glossy smooth and it had a handle of inlaid ivory. It was a magnificent weapon, surely Alexander's own. Hanging from its tip was a bowstring of tightly wound wire. Mercer took up the ancient weapon, reversed it, and tried to bend it to hook the string on the top notch. He could barely cause it to flex. He repositioned himself and pressed with all his strength, throwing his weight on the bow and digging in with his feet. The tough wood dug into his chest as it bent ever so slightly. Mercer ignored the pain and redoubled his efforts.

Slowly the weapon bent, curling downward so the loop on the string was tantalizingly close to the notch, but Mercer couldn't get it that last half inch. He felt his body weakening and the half inch gap grew to an inch, then two. He wasn't up to the challenge. Only Alexander himself had ever managed to string the mighty bow. What made him think he could handle the weapon of a god? Yet Mercer refused to give up. He pressed all the harder, closing the gap once again. He drew a deep breath, strained with everything he had, and the loop touched the top of the bow and then slid over the notch. Mercer relaxed and the wire held.

He marveled at the weapon's balance and how the handle fit perfectly in his hand. The quiver for the arrows was a bronze tube. Its strap had rotted away eons ago so he improvised one with the sling of the AK.

He nocked an arrow and tried to draw the string back, the muscles in his chest and shoulders taking the strain. No matter how hard he pulled he could only get the bow to about half cock.

Not wanting to become trapped in the dead end burial chamber, Mercer made his way to the exit. In the diorama room he could see tongues of flame shooting out from the darkness as Poli and his men fired at the unseen Janissaries.

He padded silently around the perimeter of the chamber, keeping to the shadows away from the burning braziers as he sought a target. A long burst of autofire to his left caught his attention. He could just make out a man on the other side of three of the skeleton tableaus, firing at someone farther down the arcade of columns. Mercer drew the bow and paused, not sure of who he was aiming at. It could be Booker or one of Ahmad's men.

The gunman moved just enough for light to flit across his face for a second. Mercer recognized Mohammad bin Al-Salibi and his hatred flared.

Between Mercer and Al-Salibi the three rearing monsters out of mythology made the shot next to impossible. Mercer would have to thread the arrow through the gaps in their skeletons if he wanted to hit the terrorist leader, and he hadn't fired a bow since summer camp when he was thirteen.

He drew back on the wire, pulling it past

what he'd managed before, until the downy feathers at the end of the arrow touched his cheek. Salibi had shifted position, hiding behind a towering thighbone of what the ancients believed was a cyclops. Mercer could just make out a sliver of his face through the forest of interwoven bones.

Shifting his aim a fraction of an inch, Mercer let fly. The ninety pounds of pull he'd maintained on the ancient weapon sent the arrow singing through the air. It shot through the gap between the hips and tail of the hydra, passed the length of its rib cage and out a hole in its shoulder before streaking to the next skeleton. Here too Mercer's aim held true. The arrow barely brushed the tooth of the snake-like creature as it arced through its open jaw. And then it passed through the bones of another monster.

Salibi must have heard the sound of the bow because he turned at the last second. The arrow sliced though his cheek, breaking when it hit the bone but still carrying enough speed for the tip to pierce his skull. He was dead before he hit the ground.

Mercer readied another arrow and continued the hunt. The firing suddenly stopped and he lowered himself behind a column, waiting to see what would happen next. He detected shadowy movement heading in the direction of Alexander's tomb, but he wasn't quick enough with the bow. He continued around the perimeter of the chamber, his eyes straining to see in the uneven light of the braziers while making sure whoever had entered the third room didn't reemerge.

A hand reached out and grabbed his ankle. He jerked it free and heaved on the bow, letting off the tension when he saw Ibriham Ahmad lying on the stone floor. His customary black suit was shiny at the shoulder and along his side. The sheen was fresh blood.

Mercer knelt at his side. "How bad are you hit?"

"I am dead, Dr. Mercer." His voice was a hoarse croak. "Yet I go to my grave knowing the alembic will not leave this place."

"You dynamited the entrance to seal us in."

He nodded stiffly. "When I blew up the tunnel only Devrin and one other were left. I could not risk losing the fight."

Had the Turk not already been dying, Mercer would have killed him with his bare hands. "You could have fucking warned me you were going to pull something like this, for God's sake."

"It is for God's sake I did it. There was no

other way. Our sacrifice will save millions."

That was the difference between them. Mercer was willing to risk his life on even the slimmest odds, but willingly knowing there was absolutely no chance was something he couldn't comprehend.

"I only managed to get one of them," Ibriham slurred. He was going fast.

"Poli?"

"No, an Arab."

"I got Salibi."

"May Allah's blessing be upon you, and may he rot for all eternity in the most foul hell."

Trapped in this subterranean nightmare he might be, but as long as Mercer was alive there was always hope. He'd take care of Poli first and then try to figure a way to get himself and Ahmad out of here. That must have been the one-eyed assassin he'd seen skulking back into the burial chamber.

"Where's your gun?" Mercer asked the Janissary.

"I am out of ammunition. I think we all are. That is why Poli stopped shooting."

"Haven't any of you heard of fire discipline?" Mercer spat. "Well, if I could take Salibi with a bow I can do the same to Poli. Are you going to be okay for a couple of minutes?"

"No, Doctor. I will be dead." He said it with calm resignation.

Mercer didn't know what to say. He laid a hand gently on Ahmad's good shoulder. *"Via con Dios."*

"What does that mean?"

"It's Spanish. It means go with God."

"You could give me no better blessing," Ibriham said with a faint smile and then he simply didn't take another breath.

Mercer gently closed his eyes. "Enjoy your virgins, my friend. You've earned them."

He stood and quickly made his way down the columned promenade, an arrow at the ready. At the entrance to the burial chamber he paused and scanned the space, unable to see anyone hiding amid the clutter of funerary artifacts. He took a cautious step into the room.

The bronze sword swung in a tight arc and sliced into the tough wooden bow, which saved Mercer's life. Poli had been hiding just inside the entrance ready to ambush him.

The blow sent Mercer staggering back, and with the sword lodged in the bow it was ripped from Poli's hand. Stunned by the attack, Mercer tried to dislodge the blade but it was stuck fast. Poli reared from around the corner, his single eye glinting in the firelight. Mercer backpedaled to give himself room. When he drew the bow the weakened wood broke where it had been sliced and the weapon just sagged in his hands.

Poli was only a couple feet away, his massive arms outstretched as he towered over Mercer. Mercer threw the bow at him. Poli caught it, contemptuously tossed it aside, and came on like a machine.

"You are a dead man."

"Funny," Mercer said. "I was about to tell you the same thing."

Poli lunged at him. Mercer dashed to his left to avoid the attack and almost got free, but one of Poli's big hands clamped down on his wrist. He turned on the inside and punched the Bulgarian under the arm. It was like hitting a truck tire.

Poli bent his wrist back, forcing Mercer to his knees. The mercenary fired a fist into Mercer's face using all his weight. Mercer felt his nose break and the blood jet from his nostrils before he lost consciousness for a second. Poli yanked on his arm to rouse him and punched him again, even harder.

Mercer felt like he was being worked over with a sledgehammer. Poli heaved him to his feet and shoved him back against a wall. He tried to knee Mercer in the groin but Mercer shifted just enough to take the blow on the thigh. The leg went numb to his toes.

"I have never particularly enjoyed killing people," Poli said. He wasn't even breathing hard. "It is something I happened to learn I was good at doing."

"So maybe now's a good time to quit," Mercer said and spat a glob of blood on the ground.

"But I am going to enjoy killing you. It will be hours before they dig us out so I am going to take my time." He casually cuffed Mercer on the side of the head.

When he let go, Mercer couldn't stay on his feet and he collapsed. Poli grabbed him by the hair and started dragging him back into the burial chamber. Mercer grabbed Poli's wrist to lessen the pain as his scalp was nearly ripped off.

Poli dragged him upright again and, using one hand to hold him and one hand to punch him, fired a rapid series of shots into Mercer's already bloody face. There was nothing Mercer could do but take the beating. He'd fought, and even defeated, men who were bigger than himself, but nobody with Poli's size or immeasurable strength. He felt as powerless as a child at the hands of an abuser.

When Poli stopped, Mercer collapsed again. The big assassin went to a pile of swords leaning against a stack of sandal-wood boxes. He came back, testing the edge and showed Mercer the bloody line it left on his thumb.

"How do you think you'll look without skin?"

Mercer could just lie there and stare up at him. Poli set the weapon down and forced him onto his feet again, saying, "I thought you were tough. The least you could do is make this interesting." Holding one of Mercer's arms Poli spun in place like a discus thrower and tossed him across the room. Mercer smashed into one of the chariots, almost flipping over its side. He couldn't straighten himself by the time Poli grabbed him and threw him again. This time he crashed into the long wooden skiff Alexander was to use on the rivers of the underworld.

Poli reached for him again and just as his hands clamped on the back of Mercer's neck, Mercer turned and rammed the butt end of a skinny oar into the giant's eye.

Poli Feines roared in pain as blood and clear ocular fluid sprayed from the wound. Mercer took a painful step forward and rammed the oar deeper into the eye socket. Poli's screams turned shrill.

Mercer reached out and yanked the oar

from Poli's eye and the merciless killer fell to the ground, clutching at his ruined face. "You've blinded me."

Mercer grabbed a nearby lance to help keep him on his feet. "Not exactly an eye for an eye, you sadistic son of a bitch, but I think you get the point."

Dawn was just brushing the eastern horizon and when Cali Stowe brought the big Riva close to shore, where Booker Sykes and Devrin Egemen were waving her in. Behind them the camp was still, littered with the corpses of fifty terrorists. The Janissaries had won but at what cost? She scanned the beach for Mercer but there was no sign of him.

"He's not dead," she whispered as tears formed in her eyes. "He's only a little wounded. He's okay."

As soon as she was in earshot she shouted, "Where's Mercer? He's not dead. He can't be."

Booker and Devin looked at her stonily. She dropped the anchor and raced for the stern dive platform. She didn't even kick off her shoes before jumping into the cool lake and stroking for the shore.

She scrambled to her feet as soon as it was shallow enough and charged out of the water, practically colliding with Booker. "Where's Mercer?" she screamed.

There was blood on Booker's uniform and his eyes were glassy with exhaustion. He could barely stay on his feet. Devrin was in even worse shape. His pants leg was sodden where he'd taken a bullet.

"He was underground when Professor Ahmad blew up the entrance to the tomb," the young Turk said.

Cali fell to the ground and started to sob. "Was there anybody else down there?" When no one answered her Cali knew the worst. "How many?"

"Four, including Poli Feines," Booker said.

"He might already be dead." Her sobs turned into choking gasps as the enormity hit her. Mercer was dead. "Oh God, oh God."

Booker hunkered down next to her. "We don't know that for sure. He's one tough piece of work. We'll dig him out. We just need to get people here with heavy equipment."

"That will take days. What if he's injured? He could be bleeding to death right now."

"Honey, there's nothing we can do," Booker soothed. "The quicker we get going the quicker we can come back. We'll call

Admiral Lasko and he'll get the ball rolling. We have to go. Devrin needs to show that leg to a sawbones."

"But . . ." Her voice trailed off.

"Cali, I know you think you should stay but sitting here watching a pile of dirt isn't going to help him. We can be back here first thing tomorrow with a chopper and enough people to get him out."

"I just can't. I mean he's . . ."

"I can't believe it either but this is the only thing we can do. Come on."

Cali let Booker draw her to her feet. They used the terrorists' speedboat to motor out to the Riva. Booker and Cali had to carry the injured Janissary onto the luxury yacht. The scholar was going into shock from exhaustion and loss of blood. They set him in Cali's cabin and they tucked blankets around his shivering body after Booker had redressed his wound. Booker asked Cali to stay with Devrin until he fell asleep, and then climbed up to the cockpit. Cali stroked Devrin's feverish forehead, carefully brushing back his hair, her emotions in such turmoil that she could focus on nothing but the simple gesture.

The big engines rumbled to life and the Riva started to pull away from shore. Cali left Devrin and made her way to the stern window. The camp was quickly receding behind them as Booker brought the boat onto plane, a fat white wake forming a V that spread across the whole width of this narrow part of the bay.

She was about to turn away when she spotted something else marring the flat surface of the water. She almost dismissed it as a rogue wave but something piqued her curiosity, a vague sense of something she knew was caused by grief. Still, she ran out into the open dive platform. Unable to make out what had caught her interest she launched herself up the stairs to the top deck for a better vantage.

"Book," she screamed, and when he didn't hear her over the rumbling diesels, she ran up and smacked him on the shoulder. "Go back. Go back. There's someone in the water."

"What?"

"There's someone in the water. Turn around."

Booker shot her a dubious look but cranked the wheel over anyway. They backtracked fifty yards, keeping the engines at low RPMs, both of them scanning the water but unable to see anything except their own wake.

"You sure you saw something?"

Doubt crept into Cali's eyes. "I thought I did."

"Come on, we've got to get Devrin to a hospital." He had cranked the wheel again and eased up the throttles when Cali shouted and pointed. On the crest of their fading wake a man was lying facedown in the water. Booker changed direction and gunned the engines. In seconds they were gliding by the pitiable figure.

"I don't believe it."

Cali grabbed a life ring and jumped over the side of the boat. The ring was torn from her hands when she hit the water and was driven deep but she found it when she resurfaced. She began to paddle wildly, pushing the ring ahead of her. It hit the man and turned him over. One arm came out of the water and draped over the flotation device. Mercer lifted his head from the water with a rakish grin on his battered but still handsome face. "I never figured Booker would try to steal my girl."

Cali kissed him hungrily but Mercer had to push her back. His mouth was a bloody mess. "How?" she asked as they bobbed in the water.

"The tunnel was only partially collapsed," Mercer panted. "I used Poli's scuba gear to swim down until I found a place where the earthquake had opened up the ceiling enough for me to fit through. I let buoyancy do the rest."

"Hi, Harry. I'm home," Mercer called as he stepped through the doorway, feeling like a suburban husband from a fifties TV show.

Harry must have gotten the same feeling because he growled down from the upstairs bar, "I'm not getting your pipe and slippers."

"What about mine?" Cali asked with a smile.

"Pipes are unladylike and I've got a foot fetish so I'd rather see you without slippers." Harry's tone then darkened. "Can you guys come up here? There's something you have to listen to."

Mercer was on crutches because of his bad knee and it took him a few moments to negotiate the curving staircase. Harry got up from his bar stool when they entered. He looked at the crutches and scoffed. "I lost my leg fifty odd years ago and only just started using a cane, while you get a little boo-boo on your knee and you're on crutches."

"Painkillers too," Mercer said a little dreamily. "Lots and lots of painkillers, which I plan to mix with a drink and promptly pass out."

Harry kissed Cali's cheek. "With his face all banged up like that no one would blame you for dumping him and going out with me."

"I don't think I could keep up with you," she teased back.

"I'd go easy on you." He smiled lecherously. "Seriously, when Mercer called from Egypt I was very relieved you were okay. And Booker too. I like him."

"What about me?" Mercer asked sarcastically.

"I've seen your will. I get the house if you buy the farm so I was rooting for the terrorists."

"You're all heart." Mercer settled onto one of the couches, laying the crutches on the floor. Drag sprawled on the opposite couch with his legs raised stiffly in the air. If not for his snoring Mercer would have thought he was dead. "You've got something we need to hear."

Harry went behind the bar. He fixed drinks for everyone then set the answering machine on the polished mahogany. Cali handed Mercer his gimlet and sat next to him. "Couple of things actually. First off, Ira called with a report out of Russia. Seems they recovered seventy barrels of plutonium from that train. They're on their way to a permanent storage facility"

"We counted sixty-eight," Cali said.

Harry held up a finger for her to be patient. "They did a check of them and discovered two had recently been submerged in sea water."

"We were right about Popov then," Mercer said. "He was in Novorossiysk to find those last two drums and cover his ass."

"Ira said that his arrest, trial, and execution took place yesterday."

"Gotta love Russian justice," Mercer said. "What's the second thing?"

"A guy called yesterday when I was doing the crossword. I let the machine pick it up but when I figured out what I was listening to I grabbed the phone. Listen for yourself." He pressed the play button.

"Ah yes, Dr. Mercer, I apologize for not calling sooner, however I was on an archaeological dig near Ephesus." Mercer didn't recognize the voice but the accent sounded Turkish. The speaker also sounded elderly. "This is Professor Ibriham Ahmad of the

University of Istanbul. I understand you wanted to discuss the legend of the Alembic of Skenderbeg. There's really nothing to it but I will be happy to talk to you. Feel free to —" The answering machine beeped.

"That's when I picked up," Harry said.

The warm glow of the Percocets coursing through Mercer's veins turned into a cold chill. When he found his voice he said stupidly, "And you talked to him."

"For about twenty minutes. And I can tell you right now that he's not the guy who kidnapped Cali or saved our butts in Atlantic City or died in Alexander's tomb four days ago like you told me."

Mercer and Cali just stared at each other.

"He is the professor you originally called about Skenderbeg," Harry went on. "He's an expert on him, knew everything down to his hat size but he said that the legend of him using a weapon belonging to Alexander the Great is just that, a myth. It never happened."

"Well he's wrong. I saw the damned thing."

"I'm just repeating what he told me. He also said that he's never heard of any new Janissary order."

It took Mercer a second to grasp what Harry was telling him. "Then the guy in

Egypt and Russia?"

"Isn't Ibriham Ahmad, Skenderbeg guru and professor at the University of Istanbul," Harry finished for him.

"Who was he?" Cali asked.

Harry shrugged. "Couldn't tell you. It's not like any of us asked him for ID."

"Toss me the phone will you, Harry?" Mercer rifled through his wallet for a slip of paper. He held it up. "This is the phone number of the nurses' station in the Aswân hospital." Mercer dialed and let it ring for a minute before someone picked up. It took a few moments to find someone who spoke English. Harry smoked through a cigarette. Cali went to the kitchen to get some ice for Mercer's knee. "I'd like to speak with Devrin Egemen," Mercer said when an English-speaking doctor came on the line. "He's a young Turkish man brought in with a gunshot to the leg a couple of days ago." Mercer shook his head as he listened. He thanked the doctor and hung up. "Devrin left the hospital yesterday without permission. They don't know where he went."

After a pause Cali asked, "What does this mean?"

"Other than the fact he sacrificed himself to stop Poli and Al-Salibi," Mercer replied, "we'll never know who he was."

"Consider this," Harry said. "They guarded their secret so closely that the world expert didn't know about them. Now they've gone back to ground."

"Our government is negotiating the location of Alexander's tomb with the Egyptians so we get the alembic, so hopefully they'll never need to emerge again."

"Well I do have something else," Harry said in a brighter tone. "After I transcribed Chester Bowie's notes about adamantine I finished the rest of his letter. As we all know he was partially right about the mythological ore and was dead bang on about how the ancient Greeks created mythological monsters out of fossil bones. He has another theory that might be worth checking out."

"What's that?" Mercer asked warily.

"He believed that the story of Jason and the Argonauts is true, sort of. He believed that the *Golden Fleece* Jason sought was actually a treasure barge used to pay for the protection for a queen of Thessaly's children when she sent them to live in the kingdom of Colchis. He thinks the barge sank in a storm on the Black Sea off the coast of present-day Turkey."

Mercer and Cali broke out in laughter.

"What?" Harry said looking from one to the other.

"No more adventures, my friend. Chester Bowie's got his place in the history books. If someone else wants to prove the rest of his ideas they're welcome to it. I'm done."

"That goes double for me," Cali agreed. "I want nothing more to do with Bowie, ancient legends, or myths."

"Hey, come on," Harry wheedled. "There could be a fortune out there for us. Think about it, a treasure barge loaded with loot. We'd be rich."

"I've got everything I want right here." Mercer put his arm around Cali as he spoke. She nestled into his embrace.

"Oh great." Harry threw up his hands. "You end up with the girl and I've got nothing."

"You've got the satisfaction of knowing you helped mankind," Cali said sweetly.

"That don't pay the bar tabs," he groused.

"And I'll pay you back the twenty grand I borrowed in New Jersey," Mercer added.

Harry suddenly looked like he wanted to be anywhere but in this room. "Ah, you, ah, don't have to bother."

Trepidation crept into Mercer's voice. "Why? What did you do?"

"You know I was on a roll right, at the craps table, I mean, and if you're on a streak you keep going, right? Well, Tiny knows a guy who floats a game. It was a sure thing. I couldn't lose so I sort of borrowed something of yours for collateral."

"You didn't?"

"I did."

"Did what?" Cali asked, switching attention between the two men.

Harry looked at her with an expression more pitiable than anything Drag was capable of. "I used Mercer's Jag to cover my marker." He turned to Mercer. "If it makes you feel any better I lost the rest of my thirty grand, too. Besides, Ira promised to cover all your expenses. We can get your car back no problem, or better yet buy a new one. And I swear on my soul Tiny and I will never borrow it, either."

Mercer's head was cradled in his hands. "Harry, when the vodka and Percocets wear off, you and I are going to have a very long talk about boundaries — like how I need to set some. Drinking twenty grand worth of my booze over the years isn't the same as hawking my car." He looked at his old friend with a rueful smile. "And you don't have a soul."

Knowing he'd be forgiven Harry's old face scrunched up in a matching grin. He lofted his highball in a salute. "You're a prince and I don't care what anyone else says about you."

"I'll drink to that," Cali said. They both downed their cocktails and as Cali went behind the bar to recharge their glasses she said, "There's something I don't understand."

"What's that?" Mercer asked.

"We're pretty sure the Janissaries sank the *Wetherby* on the Niagara River but we discounted them being behind the destruction of the *Hindenburg*. Was it the Russians who blew it up or the Nazis themselves who sabotaged it?"

"I'm afraid that's one more mystery piled up on all the rest. Hell, it really could have been an accident after all."

"You don't really believe that."

"Not really. I've never liked coincidences. Someone wanted to stop Chester Bowie from telling the world about the plutonium. We'll just never know who."

POSTSCRIPT
MAY 6, 1937
PRINCETON,
NEW JERSEY

The rain continued to fall as evening turned to night. It wasn't a fresh spring storm but something darker and uglier that kept people indoors and huddled under blankets. The residential street on Princeton's campus was deserted. The only motion was the swaying of naked branches and the flutter of sodden leaves stripped from the trees by the wind.

A shadow detached itself from where it had cowered behind a parked car, and approached a white two-story house. Its street number, 112, was affixed to the steps leading up to the broad front porch. The home was an unassuming Greek revival with black shutters and just a tiny patch of front lawn. The man who approached had never been there but had corresponded with its occupant numerous times.

He knocked on the door. His suit was soaked through and because he wore no hat his longish hair hung past his collar in greasy strings.

A woman opened the door. She was in her fifties and slender, with dark hair just turning to gray and a pinched, severe expression. She had the look of a guard dog and said nothing when she eyed the unkempt stranger with the thick mustache and crazed eyes.

"Is he here? I must speak to him." The stranger spoke in a heavy accent that was more guttural than the woman's native German.

"He is not seeing anyone tonight. Go away." She made to close the door and the stranger blocked her by slamming his hand against the wood and sending the door crashing back to its stops. Glass rattled in the windowpanes.

"You cannot come in," she said forcefully.

The stranger ignored her protests and stepped into the entryway, his shoes squelching on the floor. He looked around, his eyes narrowing. "Are you here?" he called.

A gentle voice called from further in the house, *"Wo ist, Helen?"*

"A man, Herr Doctor," Helen Dukas said in German. "I do not know who he is and I don't like the look of him."

594

The most celebrated scientist of his day emerged from the kitchen wearing baggy trousers and a cardigan. His hair was a wild tangle atop his head and he smelled of pipe tobacco. While he was normally an affable man, there was concern and sorrow etched around his eyes and mouth.

He studied the stranger dripping rainwater on his carpet but didn't seem to recognize him. Then his eyes went wide as he realized who the man was.

"How could you do it, Nikola?" Albert Einstein thundered in an accusatory tone.

Nikola Tesla met his piercing gaze. "I had to stop you, Albert. I couldn't let you unleash that horror on the world."

"As soon as I heard the news on the radio I knew you had done it."

"I know an anarchist, a Croatian immigrant who was more than willing to help me," Tesla said defiantly. "You left me no choice. Writing to you about natural transuranic elements was just an intellectual exercise. You were never supposed to try to find them."

"Are you mad?" Even as he said it Einstein knew the Serb inventor was. "Do you think blowing up an airship full of innocent people will stop others from seeking out such elements? My God, man, in a few years we will be able to create them in a laboratory."

"To what end?" Tesla shot back. "We both know there can be only one outcome of such research. You and I are the only two people in the world who can foretell the death and destruction. We can not spread that knowledge."

"Nikola, you must understand that a war is coming, a war for the very soul of humanity. We have to be ready. It is only a matter of time before Hitler grabs more territory Germany lost after the Great War, and a clash between America and Japan over the Pacific is inevitable. Teller and Fermi and Szilard and I have seen this coming and have been working on a plan so we have a weapon before the Nazis. We could stop such a world war from even starting with a single demonstration of its power but we needed that plutonium. Otherwise it might take us a decade to create a bomb. We were planning on telling the President as soon as we verified the sample Bowie was bringing us from Africa. If we started work right away Teller thinks that with a couple pounds of plutonium we could have a working weapon by 1939. Now we must wait and pray that somehow Bowie managed to ship some ore separately. If he didn't then all is lost because only he knew the mine's location.

"Without an atomic deterrent there is nothing to stop that Austrian paper hanger from taking over all of Europe or the militarists in Japan from continuing their expansion. You not only killed the passengers of the *Hindenburg*, you've sentenced millions more to die needlessly."

Already close to the breaking point because others had profited from his genius while he languished in a Manhattan cold-water flat, Tesla said nothing, his lips working like a fish gulping air.

A string of saliva dripped unnoticed from the corner of his mouth as the enormity of what he'd done echoed in his fractured mind and the last vestiges of sanity slipped quietly away. He started to sob.

"Come inside and warm up," Einstein said softly. "Let us get you some dry clothes."

He placed a hand on Tesla's shoulder. Tesla shoved him away, his expression feral. He said nothing as he raced from the house and back into the storm.

"Who was that?" Einstein's longtime secretary asked.

"The man who has prevented me from averting a second world war."

AUTHOR'S NOTE

Since reading it in the ninth grade I've believed Homer's *Odyssey* is the archetype of today's action thrillers, the one that set the standard for everything we have out there today. It was a hero who has to overcome staggering odds. It has exotic locals, fantastic chases, epic battles, and yes, even sex. While I chose not to copy Homer's formula of a man trying to get home to his family (Would you really believe Mercer fighting to get back to his brownstone knowing only Harry and Drag were waiting to welcome him?), I wanted to pay homage to this masterpiece in my novel. I think once you know I slid in some references, and you've recently brushed up on your Homer, they're fairly easy to spot.

A one-eyed giant of a man named Poli Feines is of course the Cyclops, Polyphemus. In *The Odyssey,* Odysseus escapes the monster using a bunch of sheep as cover, like the flock Mercer saved in Africa, and in the end does leave the Cyclops blinded. Calypso in *The Odyssey* becomes enamored of the hero, and at one point saves his life by supplying him with a girdle that buoyed him above the waves just before he drowned — a little like how Cali Stowe saved Mercer at the end of the book.

Others are certainly more obscure. One of Odysseus's adventures found him caught between the Scilla and the Charybdis, which were a whirlpool and a sea monster. In my book it's Mercer who's caught between the Scilla River and a rebel general named Caribe Dayce. There are a few other references sprinkled throughout the novel and you might have fun finding them, or you might be like my wife and think I have too much time on my hands.

Speaking of time, the cipher Chester Bowie used to hide his message to Einstein based on Lewis Carroll's doublets is a real word game, one I wasted too many hours playing. It's actually a lot of fun when you can get them to work. Some of them include turning head into tail, ape into man, or four into five, or you can make up your own.

And on the subject of Chester Bowie, if you liked his theory about the monsters of Greek mythology being the bones of extinct animals, I highly recommend the book *The First Fossil Hunters* by Adrienne Mayor, which lays out a pretty good case for how some of these mythical creatures could have been devised.

I'd also like to clarify an intentional inaccuracy. Herb Morrison's famed eyewitness account of the *Hindenburg* tragedy wasn't broadcast over the radio — it was actually recorded to be the voice-over for a movie news company — but I wanted to include those immortal words in my prologue. Most everything else about the crash is true however. It was most likely water-repelling dope used to coat the airship that first caught fire from an engine spark and caused the catastrophe. Skenderbeg is a real person out of Albanian history who revolted against his former Ottoman masters. And scientists are still studying the natural nuclear reactors at Oklo, Gabon, only it is geologically impossible for any highly radioactive deposits to have survived to this day as they do in the book. Of course a natural reactor was geologically impossible until one was discovered in 1972.

And what of Alexander's tomb? It still hasn't been discovered. So who's to say there isn't something inside to explain how he managed to conquer so much of the ancient world?

Truth is always stranger than fiction.

ABOUT THE AUTHOR

Jack Du Brul is the author of numerous thrillers, and he has also collaborated with Clive Cussler on the *New York Times* bestseller *Dark Watch* and the upcoming *Skeleton Coast.* Du Brul was educated at the Westminster School and holds a degree in international relations from George Washington University. He lives in Vermont with his wife, Debbie.

www.jackdubrulbooks.com